MOUNTAINROOT

BOOK ONE

IN THE SAGA OF THE LAYMONK

Library of Congress Control Number: 2023900962

United States Copyright Office Registration Number: TXu 2-340-060

First Edition Printing, 2023

Front Cover and Map by Casey Gerber
Book Design by Lorna Reid
Copy Editing by Elaine Friedberg
Development Editing by Ayla Batton Wyman

ISBN: 979-8-9876216-0-8 (Paperback)
ISBN: 979-8-9876216-2-2 (Hardback)
ISBN: 979-8-9876216-1-5 (ebook)

Printed by Small Circle, LLC.
Three Oaks, MI
www.mabwyman.com
malkam@mabwyman.com

For my joyful light,
for my oak lance in the trees,
for my noble guide.

Crossing into death,
there is a path through the Wreath,
into the next life.

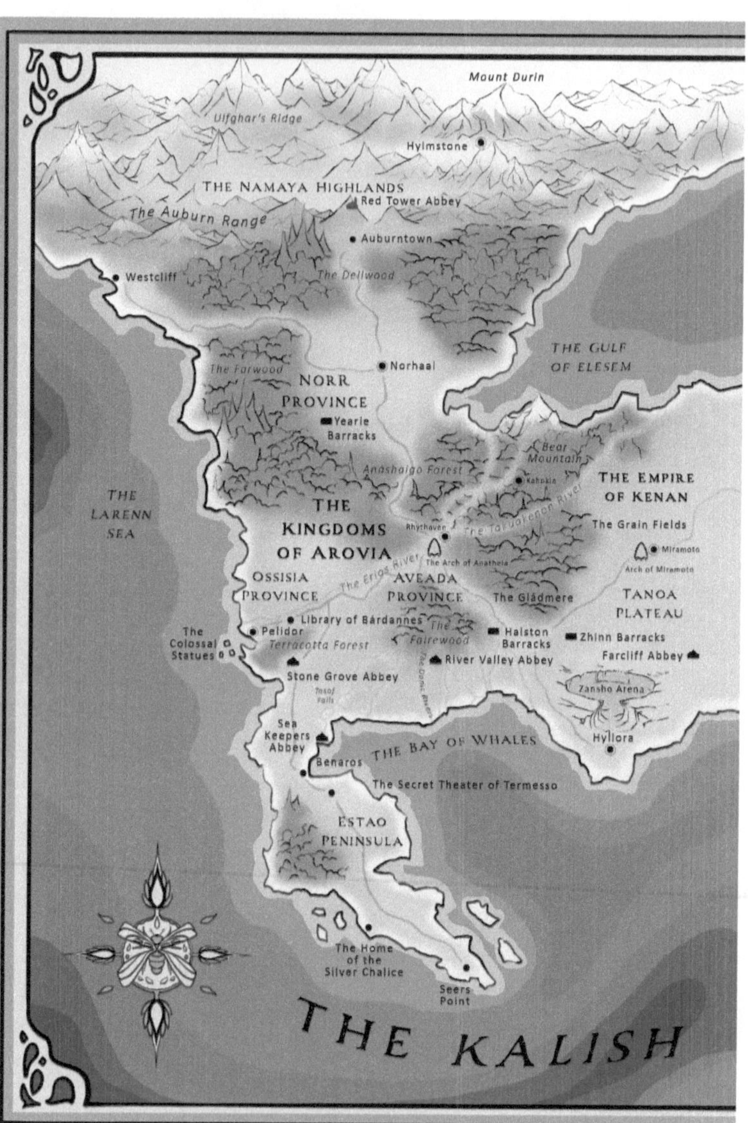

Mount Durin
Ulfghar's Ridge
Hylmstone
THE NAMAYA HIGHLANDS
The Auburn Range
Red Tower Abbey
Auburntown
Westcliff
The Dellwood
THE GULF OF ELESEM
The Farwood
Norhaal
NORR PROVINCE
Yearie Barracks
Bear Mountain
Anashaigo Forest
Kahokia
THE EMPIRE OF KENAN
THE LARENN SEA
THE KINGDOMS OF AROVIA
Rhythaven
The Arch of Anatheia
The Talvakenan River
The Grain Fields
Miramoto
Arch of Miramoto
OSSISIA PROVINCE
The Erios River
AVEADA PROVINCE
The Gládmere
TANOA PLATEAU
Library of Bárdannes
The Fairewood
Halston Barracks
Zhinn Barracks
The Colossal Statues
Pelidor
Terracotta Forest
River Valley Abbey
Farcliff Abbey
Stone Grove Abbey
Tasof Falls
The Danic River
Zansho Arena
Sea Keepers Abbey
Hyllora
Benaros
THE BAY OF WHALES
The Secret Theater of Termesso
ESTAO PENINSULA
The Home of the Silver Chalice
Seers Point
THE KALISH

The Arctic Wastes
THE KNOWN LANDS OF KUEI
The Eight Islands of Johan
The Alps of Hanshu
THE MYSTIN SEA
Mount Kenan
Moskóvra
The Steppes of Thrail
Gaansa Ot
Bati Talari
Igura River
Eastgate
Neftya Doru
Shijing
Ugdi Vadisi
Böyuk Ot
Muhtesem
The Canyons Of Quay
Ankhan
Zakariya
The Firefields
Tesuradad
KEY
Abbey
Barracks
Arch
Capitol City
City
Hashaan
The Archipelago
The Lost Island of Amphassa
OCEAN

MOUNTAINROOT

BOOK ONE
IN THE SAGA OF THE LAYMONK

M.A.B. WYMAN

Small Circle, LLC
Three Oaks, Michigan
Published 2023, First Edition

CONTENTS

PROLOGUE

The war drum rises in the sky; two tigers run south, then a
shadow's gambit.

BATTLE AT TWO CREEKS

Panting breathlessly, Garrat ran through the cool summer night. A spare wind pushed to the east over the grasslands and he looked upward at the stars to keep himself oriented to the south as he went. He saw one or two trees in the distance but otherwise there was only the gradual rising and falling of small valleys. Even as a few clouds drifted overhead, the sky was wide open for a hundred miles in every direction and the tall grasses were pale and unending in the starlight.

Garrat knew he needed to move quickly if he wanted to escape. Already he had been forced to stop at the edge of the army encampment where two sentries watched the hillside. After hiding in the brush for several minutes, Garrat could see no way to get past them without being seen and soon he was forced to decide, *Do I want to escape or not? Do I want to warn them, or not?*

With the longspear he carried at all times, Garrat thrust until the sharp tip pierced one sentry through the back of the neck and the other hardly had a chance to speak before he was also impaled through the throat. As quickly as he could, Garrat dragged the bodies into the darkness knowing they would probably be discovered at the next guard change.

The attack only took a few minutes but he still tried to make up time by sprinting over the small rise of the hill and then lying down to conceal himself in the grass, gripping his spear in one hand. Garrat looked back briefly where nearly five hundred men slept in the low valley under canvas tents. Several dozen campfires were beginning to smolder out, and on the far side were rough pens that held the horses at night, which he knew would have been faster, but he would certainly be seen if he tried to steal his usual mount.

So he ran, ready to betray them all. He betrayed the kingdom he had sworn to protect and the comrades he had come to know over the last several weeks. Yet he was not an enlisted man in the Sovereign's Army, but rather a paladin sent by Queen Zayan to bear the faith of the gods into battle. Garrat had sworn a different vow; the Oath of Service to the Queen who blessed his spear, the smooth red oak shaft inscribed with the name of the silver god, Amaritabhe the Wise. Even now as he paced over the grasslands he saw the symbols there, blazing silver in the moonlight, visible past the yellow tassel that dangled from the tip, which was tapered and made of folded steel.

As he hiked for an hour in one direction he thought deeply on the circumstances that brought them to this distant land. There were no shadows to run through or trees to hide under for a respite. Anyone with keen eyes would see his figure crossing the grasslands under the light of the crescent moon and the swath of stars, so he had no choice but to move quickly across the sloping lands and the waving grasses where he had little advantage.

From what he had seen the Thrailans were a pastoralist people that lived in yurt camps, following the wild herds to new pastures at the change of the seasons. They were mostly family clans of shepherds and their wives, with only a few horsemen that hardly posed a threat to the Third Company, but recently there were reports of raiders that attacked the trade caravans setting out from Zakariya. The army had been sent by the Sovereign to secure the trade route to the Free Cities and to put an end to banditry on the Oil Road, which was not really much more than a wagon path that cut through the grass.

Since their departure from the capital Garrat had been counted among the Third Marshal's closest advisors, along with Commander Toro Li and the scout Kevor, both of whom had been enlisted with Zukov for many years. They were all loyal soldiers, but Garrat thought things had gone seriously awry when they began to follow the commands of an enraged madman, shuddering with tears at the thought of that first massacre in the north hills.

After weeks of marching through the Canyons of Quay they had arrived to the edge of the Steppes of Thrail. The Marshal knew the Thrailans would not put their camps on the road itself, and sent scouts in three directions, which soon returned after sighting three clans, one of them being north by a day with a horde of at least thirty riders. Zukov contemplated the information, though it had not taken long for him to decide as he ordered his commander, "Gather a hundred marchers," and waited impatiently for Toro Li to declare their readiness before leading them away from the rest of the army at the Oil Road.

The hundred men had sprinted over the hard hills until they came upon a Thrailan camp by the end of the day. They waited, crouched at the crest of the dune until nightfall with only the gray light from the moon to see by. The yurt tents flapped in the wind and their campfire licked the haunches of the game elk on the spit. Zukov silently gestured and Toro Li broke off with thirty men that followed him through the dunes until they were out of sight.

They appeared to have brought two men for every one person. Garrat had only seen a few Thrailans actually wearing hard leather vests while most of them wore plain wool tunics as they readied themselves to sleep for the night, and it did not seem like a camp of raiders to him. Before he could say anything, Zukov had released a war shout that resounded over the grass hills and led the army with weapons drawn, descending like marauders to slay any person there. Several people tried to run only to be flanked by Toro Li and his men as he approached from the south.

In the chaos of the attack Garrat carried his spear, running into melee. He had come upon a Thrailan man that fought wildly with a saber and wore only a long woolen sleeping robe. It was a simple maneuver for Garrat to plunge the spear tip into his abdomen and leave him bleeding in the grass. Amid the sounds of fighting, Zukov could be heard cackling as he raised his massive broadsword to mercilessly cut down a man and his young son who had dared to draw their knives on him.

Then Garrat turned a corner between tents and suddenly encountered a white haired grandfather that stood in his way. He thrust by instinct. Blood shone brightly in the pale moonlight as the paladin pulled his weapon away. The old man wore a striped, many-colored robe that pooled heavily around the wound. He fell to his knees, the devastation of his people reflected in his eyes. Soon afterward the elder was dragged into a line along with thirty-four other Thrailan bodies in the camp and Garrat looked upon him with miserable guilt, knowing he had been defenseless.

In a rush after the battle the men searched every tent. They slaughtered anyone they found hiding, until they had added more than twenty women and children to the line of the dead. Before long they had taken the horses, several sacks of rice, bolts of wool and silk, leather boots off their feet, and several flasks of pitch oil. They were small rewards, yet Marshal Zukov had still grinned with satisfaction, his curved blade gleaming with blood in the moonlight from every prisoner he had executed, from every throat he had cut.

Without sleep they returned to the main company of men. Horrified, Garrat choked in the dust of their march, realizing, *I've broken my Oath,* as he imagined every Thrailan as candles in a sanctuary that had been snuffed out within those grisly few minutes. Rejoining the supply wagons, the strict Marshal Zukov had uncharacteristically allowed them to celebrate their first successful engagement with the savages. He said, "Kill the damn twillies!" as they poured out cups from the stolen casks of sour ale, and the men howled into the darkhour of the night, threatening the grasses themselves.

Everyday after that Kevor and the other scouts found other encampments for them to attack. Some were groups of no more than ten or twelve, while others were as much as fifty people. They were clearly family clans, but the Third Marshal focused only on which could be conquered next, moving boldly ahead of their supply wagons under the cover of night. The jasper talisman around his neck glinted with new shades of red, and Marshal Zukov had begun to possess a crazed look as he drew the horsecutter from its sheath before every attack.

Garrat decided to remain in the rearguard when the army swarmed over a clan while they were asleep in their tents. He tried to shut his eyes to the clash of steel and the anguished screams of women and children, but it was impossible to avoid because Zukov always ordered that all prisoners were to be slain. The Third Company left behind the corpses of entire families, violating them, maiming them, and butchering them. Several of the men laughed as they claimed scalps and pointed ears as keepsakes, desecrating the bodies long after their souls had departed.

Garrat rode in an aggrieved, confused fog, and when they settled at a small running creek in a low valley to water their newly acquired horses, Zukov saw Garrat's forlorn expression and sneered, "Maybe now you can pray to the gods? If they answer, then we'll know we've avenged our people," before he bellowed with laughter and clapped him roughly on the shoulder and sauntered away.

For the next day the men reclined there. They caught several young bison that had strayed from the herd, drank from the casks, and smoked their pipes. It was not normal for Zukov to discard military protocol, but nevertheless he had allowed the men to relax as he waited for the scouts to return from another expedition. By then it had been ten days since they had entered the steppes and Garrat came to the uneasy realization that the Marshal would only end the campaign when he no longer had the numbers to conquer the indigenous clans, and he wondered, *How many more hundreds of people will die before we go home?*

Garrat walked miserably through the encampment between aisles of canvas tents where the soldiers played with tiles or sharpened their weapons. They laughed with each other while they took respite from the march, but Garrat saw guilty visions of the innocent families they had slaughtered. He saw the old man he had murdered. He heard the screams of women and children as the Third Company butchered camp after camp, ashamed that he could not lift his spear to stop them; pale from sleepless nights of despair, the flames of anger rising in his heart.

This is not right! he concluded, knowing that Queen Zayan would never endorse the murder of defenseless people.

When the scouts returned to the camp, Kevor brought word of the largest Thrailan camp they had encountered. He said, "It was quite easy to find them," and explained that he followed signs of the wild herd all the way to their yurts, which were thirty miles south of the Oil Road, nestled against two creeks.

"There are at least twenty families," Kevor said.

"How many twillies?" Zukov demanded.

"Perhaps three hundred," Kevor responded. "They have a hundred horses, some boys learning how to ride and shoot, the rest are women and children."

Zukov was pleased as he made the decision to march south, and ordered Toro Li, "Have the men ready before dawn."

The paladin's anger had finally bolstered his resolve. The symbols of wisdom blazed silver on the shaft of the holy longspear as he stood to confront Zukov in the command tent, knowing he was acting as the voice of the Queen. The three of them stared over a map of the Oil Road, only looking up when Garrat had said, "This has gone on long enough."

Zukov narrowed his thick black eyebrows as he replied, "I seem to remember that you have no command here, queensknight." He wore full lamellar armor and carried a huge curved broadsword in its sheath, quickly scanning the distance between them. The jasper talisman hung on a chain around his neck and was a muted red color with black flecks, like blood and oil set within a gold ring.

"I can say for certain the Sovereign never intended for this slaughter," the paladin insisted.

Commander Toro Li carried a steel helmet under his arm, and

exchanged glances with Kevor the scout, who leaned back in his chair and flipped a dagger in his hands, smirking as if he were enjoying the show.

Zukov had pretended to take offense. "How can you say slaughter? We're liberating the grasslands from thieves. You said yourself we must find everyone responsible and put a stop to banditry on the Oil Road."

"Not like this," Garrat said. "You're waging war on these people!"

"That's enough!" Zukov snapped impatiently. "I have orders from the Sovereign and you will obey my commands."

"Your commands betray the gods," Garrat said as he gripped his blessed longspear tightly around the shaft; both men were ready for battle, fully armored and carrying their weapons just as the soldiers of the Third Company had done for weeks. The young knight accused, "You're not a Marshal. You're a butcher!"

Zukov sneered and drew his sword as easily against the paladin as he would against an enemy. Without a second thought the Marshal cleaved at Garrat, who responded by parrying with the tip of his spear, he stepped back toward the entrance of the tent and gave up an opportunity to slash the Marshal's front knee. Each of the advisors nearby glanced significantly at each other, not knowing exactly how to respond to their leader's sudden assault on the paladin.

Marshal Zukov grinned with all his teeth and leaned the dull edge of his huge broadsword against his shoulder, "Should we duel to settle our differences then, or are you afraid I'll break your Zansho record?" and his cruel laughter echoed through the encampment as Garrat walked away, glowering and humiliated.

Somehow Garrat had known that Zukov would be irrational, and even cruel about the paladin's misgivings, yet it had never occurred to him that the Marshal would draw his weapon and attack so deliberately.

I knew something wasn't right! Garrat said to himself as he ran, thinking that at their departure from the capital twelve weeks ago

Zukov had been austere and grim, holding his soldiers to an impossible standard. He was reserved and rarely broke a smile, yet as soon as they entered the grass fields and began to slaughter innocent people, Zukov was seen with blood in his mouth, grinning from ear to ear, laughing with the soldiers, and celebrating their victories. Garrat couldn't help but sense that the man who attacked him was not the same Marshal Zukov that had set out from the riverlands. There was a new intelligence behind those brown eyes, tremendously horrid in his delights, hungry for death at the end of his sword.

So that night he had decided that he had no choice but to warn the clan that Kevor had scouted. He waited until most of the men were asleep, and after he managed to get beyond the low valley Garrat hustled for a mile before he dropped into a steady pace for the next two hours. The grassy hills rose over him like low mounds easily surmounted to give a wider perspective of the land. To the north was a long flat pasture; directly south were the high grass savannahs and going east were undulating fields, all with very few trees.

I'm sure Zukov can't wait to personally hunt me down, Garrat thought wryly as he remembered how their last meeting had occurred at sunset that evening in the command tent.

The starry sky was wide open and after a while Garrat distracted himself with the idea that each of the infinite pinpricks of light was a spirit in the Wreath. He thought of the people he knew from home, which seemed to be thousands of miles and hundreds of years away, even though it had only been three months or so since they had departed from the capital. He thought desperately of his home on the riverfront, a delightful villa granted to him by the Queen with a winding front path and an arbor of grape vines. There, his wife waited for him in their down featherbed in the quivering candlelight, and Garrat longed for his luxurious home filled with the pleasantries of beauty and comfort.

Memories of Magritte ran through his mind. He remembered her drowsy smile in the mornings when they would sleep late with the dogs in their bed, enjoying the sounds of the river and the shafts of sunlight through the window. She had big curly reddish and brown hair, and a pointed chin with a bold lower lip that he feared he would never kiss again. They had known each other for years, but Garrat was merely the third son to Oathlord Merras, learning how to carry a sword and spear but with no real chance of inheriting the family lands. Magritte, however, was the youngest daughter of the Oathlord Orvyn, who managed the lands of the Fairewood and the royal hunting lodge. She had many brideprice inquiries but none that intrigued her father enough to arrange a meeting.

So, when Garrat had turned eighteen he went south to compete in the Zansho tournaments to earn his own title, winning forty-three matches, desperately fighting some men to the death. Only those that remained undefeated continued to fight, and Garrat had a long scar over his left ear from his last match when he was struck with the flat of his enemy's sword against his temple, leaving him unconscious. Clerics of the shrines, Wardens, Oathlords, or even the royal family would often invite a favored Zansho fighter to join their paladin guard, and when Queen Zayan anointed him as a knight he could finally afford to make a generous offer to Lord Orvyn for his daughter's hand in marriage.

The Queen conducted the ceremony and bound their wrists at the altar of the Raegods in the cathedral, and his thoughts lingered on the memory of their first night together after years of secret love. Then he grieved for Magritte's spontaneous laughter, and their lovely estate that overlooked the cherry orchards on the riverfront, knowing that he would never return home until he had atoned for the crimes he had committed.

He thought about the other knights he had served with, and how each of them had sworn the same Oath of Service he had sworn. Nine men bonded to one woman, the Queen. They were all brothers in arms protecting Queen Zayan, as their oath demanded. Each of their weapons carried the inscription of her blessing, which were holy marks of wisdom to guide them on their journey. For the last five years there had been so many skirmishes on the road, and tournaments to win, and ten times as many days standing guard in the Royal Forum while Queen Zayan spoke to councilors and magistrates on behalf of the people. Garrat had witnessed the subtleties of politics in court, and many times he had been crowded shoulder to shoulder in the Royal Forum to hear the Sovereign's decree.

She was often called the Healer Queen, but her name was Lakshmi Meidiwar Prishna al'Zayan, the Queen of the Kingdoms of Arovia and a Matriarch of the Raegods, Chosen by Amaritabhe the Wise himself.

Garrat didn't know if it was a dream or a memory, having a vivid vision of when his wife invited the entire Royal Forum to the villa for his birthday. The ladies drank wine and plum mead on the terrace while the lords and knights milled around the casks of lager in the courtyard and their squires fenced with blunt swords for entertainment. Even the Sovereign and the Queen had attended last year, stepping confidently from their carriage and strolling with Garrat across the ten shady acres that surrounded his home on the riverfront.

He knew in his heart he did not deserve even a piece of the life he once took for granted. Even as the men of the army laughed about the scalps they had brought back, and the women and children they had cut down, Garrat could not escape the bitter sorrow of betraying his vow to uphold truth, honor, and especially justice. He knew that if he did nothing he would be haunted for the rest of his life by the dead eyes of the old man he had murdered.

Suddenly, he heard the pounding of horses from behind, glancing back to see two riders at the crest of the last hill. Hardly stopping, he scanned the area for anything he might be able to use for cover, finding nothing except a wide field of switchgrass nearly as high as his shoulders. Commander Toro Li's steel helm glinted in the starlight as the two riders charged down the hillside, and he assumed the leather-clad man was the scout Kevor.

Garrat gripped his spear in both hands, staring down the riders as they came galloping alongside each other. At the last moment, he dropped to his belly just as their swords came slicing for his head, lucky that the hooves went over him. He leapt up and sprinted laterally while the riders were forced to turn, losing sight of him. A wall of spearmen would be difficult against any mounted cavalry, but Garrat knew from experience that against two horsemen he would be overrun within minutes unless he could beguile them.

Dropping into the switchgrass, he was hidden as they turned. Kneeling, he could see them just over the fronds that waved in the wind, and the white gleam of their curved broadswords were held high and ready as they came through for another pass. They searched for him in frenzied paces, Toro Li shouting, "Where is he?" while Garrat remained hidden until they were directly beside him.

Suddenly he rose out of the grass and thrust upward until the spear plunged into Toro Li's abdomen from the left side. The soldier groaned terribly as he was lifted out of the saddle and sent crashing to the ground with Garrat tumbling on top of him, the horse careening into the darkness. They stared face to face, and Garrat withdrew the spear that had invaded the Commander's abdomen, rending him open. Spitting blood, Toro Li's eyes broadened with some new realization as he shuddered and died.

Standing upright, Garrat barely dodged the curved blade as it swept over him. The scout galloped past and made a wide turn. Garrat hustled away, keeping his spear tip low as he sprinted through the grass. Then, unable to help himself, he shouted, "Kevor!" drawing the scout's attention toward him as he went up the hill out of the long grasses. Within moments the horse came over the ridge and they could both see each other in the starlight.

Kevor's face contorted into pleading scowl. "Garrat! Stop this. Come back to the camp and we can talk."

Garrat demanded, "Can't you see that Zukov has gone mad?"

Kevor pulled harshly on the reins of the horse, coming to a stop several feet away. For a moment he looked as if he understood the paladin's words, until he barked out, "Stand down, Garrat, or you'll regret this," gripping his broadsword in his right hand.

"You know I'll never stand down," Garrat replied, holding his spear ready in both hands, the inscription shining with the endorsement of the gods.

Kevor charged. At the last possible moment Garrat leapt to the right and tilted the spear tip directly into the eye of the horse, sending it reeling sideways, bucking Kevor to the ground in a rolling heap. The horse ran in widening circles around them, braying painfully until it faded into the darkness.

Garrat had sought the advantage but the scout expertly tumbled to his feet and immediately drew his short arming sword in its reverse grip, with the blade pointed down in the classic military form against a pole arm.

Rather than thrust and give Kevor an opportunity to deflect and advance, Garrat waved the tip of the spear from ten feet away in unpredictable sweeps, shouting hoarsely, "Kevor! Can't you see that Zukov is not who he says he is?"

In an angry rush the scout tried to raise his sword and come through. Garrat gripped the end of the shaft and maneuvered the spear tip against Kevor with a slash through his kneecap. Instantly the scout's leg ceased to support him in mid-stride and he collapsed to the ground. Garrat rushed over to Kevor who lay on his back cursing and yelling, sweeping the air with his sword until the paladin caught his arm and wrenched the blade away from him.

"Don't fight," Garrat told him as he leaned over the fallen comrade, who squirmed to escape.

"Get away from me!" Kevor hooked a fist into Garrat's eye and sent him reeling back.

Garrat clutched his brow but he was otherwise unharmed. The paladin saw that blood flowed thickly from a gash across Kevor's knee that was at least two inches deep or more, and his leg was shaking uncontrollably. It was a familiar wound since he had used this technique often to win several Zansho matches, and while in defense of the Queen, often disabling the enemy with a similar attack.

Kevor chuckled haggardly, "Well, I always wondered which of us was better."

Garrat shrugged, "I'm a tournament champion."

"No," Kevor said, his voice quavering, "I think you're a holy warrior."

Breaking his composure, Garrat asked, "Kevor, what happened?"

The pain seemed to clear his mind from the strange curse he was under and Kevor shook his head as if there was no explanation, moaning instead, "We should've listened to you."

Looking around Garrat noticed it was the forehour of dawn when the moon and stars dimmed into total darkness and he could hardly see. He knew he wouldn't have much more time, staring down at Kevor who was trying to sit up to look at his wound even as blood was streaming from his leg.

"How much farther?" Garrat asked the scout.

"Not far," he grunted. "Six miles, maybe less."

Garrat began to cut long strands of switchgrass and gathered up several bundles from all around him.

Kevor exclaimed, "What are you doing? You need to hurry. As soon as Zukov found out you escaped he raised the whole company. They're less than two hours behind you by now."

"I think I know what I'm doing," Garrat said as he knotted some of the grass, twisting it tightly until it made a long cord that he tied off at the other end. He took several minutes to chop down more grass until he made ten or so cords of similar length. Eventually Garrat set aside his weapon and kneeled beside Kevor to wrap his wound in an improvised tourniquet, knowing that the scout would be dead in less than half an hour if he did nothing.

"You were sent ahead to stop me?" Garrat asked, presuming to know the answer.

"We figured two of us would be enough," Kevor chuckled dryly. "Remind me not to underestimate you Zansho fighters anymore."

Soon the leg was tightly cinched above the wound and the bleeding had begun to slow. Garrat stood up and wiped his red-stained hands on tufts of grass, saying, "There, that might give you a chance until they find you."

"Zukov doesn't care about me," Kevor said, as he lay back and stared upward, beginning to fade from consciousness.

Unable to do more, the paladin turned and went quickly over the next three hills, until the endless grasslands concealed all that had happened. He found Kevor's horse rearing and shaking its head from the wound the spear had inflicted to its left eye, punctured and glistening with blood. Coming along its blind side, Garrat managed to grab the reins and calm the horse until it stood trembling beside him. He stepped into the stirrup and swung his leg over, fitting somewhat awkwardly into another man's saddle. Garrat clutched his longspear in one hand and the reins in another as he kicked the horse into a heavy gallop over the steppes.

They ran with the expeditious wind, hooves pounding the ground as they crossed the green slopes until they came to a stop on the lee side of a high mound that overlooked an encampment settled along two creeks that forked to the south. There were several dozen yurts made of animal skins in circles that surrounded a central yurt, spreading outward like a ripple in water. Horses seemed to move idly, or graze and water themselves at the first creek, and most of them were sprawled across the grasses, loose from any hitching rail or post.

A single pink line traced the flat horizon in the east. Garrat knew he was running out of time. Without hesitation he came down from the mound and dismounted, urging his horse between a few yurts adjacent to each other until they were into the camp. He saw two old ladies that looked at him suspiciously as they readied a cauldron of water over a fire, and there were three or four men rising sleepily to relieve themselves outside of camp before returning to their furs and blankets.

He came to a fire pit where an old woman simmered rice, and suddenly a young man charged forward from around the yurt, demanding, "Shiend yüu khiij baijaa yun?" and Garrat guessed that he was asking what he was doing there in their Thrailan language. With only the gray light of dawn to see by, Garrat thought the young man was not much older than nineteen, carrying just a knife at his hip and wearing a wool-lined jacket and warm leather hat with fur flaps over his cheeks.

The paladin realized the two of them looked cautiously at his weapon. He lifted the spear tip to the sky and held up one hand as he said urgently, "I need to talk to your leader."

They glanced at each other and spoke in their own language.

"Your chief?" Garrat asked desperately, knowing that it was unlikely that anyone would understand him. He looked to the mound where the Third Company would come and pointed urgently in that direction as he said, "Your people need to run! Now!" which startled the boy into going back into the yurt, reappearing within seconds with an older man that might have been his father.

Soon the commotion brought several others out from their tents. Garrat continued by gesturing to himself and then pointing to the west, "People like me are coming. You need to run, now!" before realization dawned on several of them at once and they began panicking and running all around.

The older man grabbed Garrat's wrist and demanded, "Ansaro!"

"Yes, lead the way," Garrat nodded, following the stranger through the rings of the camp to the central yurt. Some women were shouting, drawing the attention of the chief of their clan as he emerged from under the flap of his tent. He was a sharp-eyed man not much older than Garrat, who kept his long black hair tied and upraised behind his head like the tail of a horse. Already he was wearing a thick leather tunic with fur fringes, although it wouldn't be much protection against the steel swords of the Sovereign's Army.

"Khanar Usaka Kato," the man called out and shoved Garrat forward, declaring, "Khoid nortin!"

Several men that were similarly dressed in leathers and furs, wearing curved swords, quivers and bows, came from between the yurts to surround him. They looked expectantly at their leader. A few of them talked quickly, exchanging rapid sentences, although when Usaka Kato said, "Onördae bid baruun tedniio sünai wessai," and pointed to the hill, Garrat knew they were planning to stay and fight.

"No," Garrat said in outrage, gesturing to himself and then sweeping broadly with his hands, "There are too many. You won't survive."

Kato seemed to curl his lip at Garrat, showing his disdain for the soldiers from the west. He pulled the hilt of his saber three inches from the scabbard and flashed the steel at his hip as if it were a threatening gesture. This move seemed to embolden the other riders and soon they all ran quickly to get their horses amidst the shouting of women and the scurrying of people.

In the disarray, Garrat found his horse and mounted with his spear in hand. The curve of the sun had broken the horizon and he could see movement high on the mound where he knew the first line of infantrymen were kneeling just out of sight. The entire camp was too disorganized, the riders were too scattered. Garrat searched again for Khanar Kato, spotting him at the far side of the camp with two young boys that he picked up and set astride the saddle of a young tan stallion with a white mane.

The two boys' brown faces were wet with tears, and he comforted them both in gentle tones, "Usho, usho, odori yah, kol yav."

Garrat galloped around the encampment and shouted, "Kato!" pointing toward the mound where the chief turned to see the helms of the invaders kindled by the rising light of the sun.

"Temuje!" the chieftain called out.

Two riders approached, though one replied, "Bid belen bäina, Khanar?"

Kato issued a loud command, "Khövgüddgee dakhij, keshik teniiga ayuulgüi bailgaarai."

The two riders stiffened, glancing around at the upheaval of the clan. The one called Temuje tried to argue, as if he wanted to stay, but Usaka Kato insisted until they both nodded their agreement, affirming, "Tiim darga," steering themselves ahead of the boys' horse and guiding them away from the encampment. The two sons of

Kato were nearly identical to each other, perhaps six years old, having the same crop of dark brown hair, high and flat cheekbones, and wide set eyes. They looked back just as their guardians urged the horses into a gallop and they crossed the two creeks to disappear into the south.

Suddenly Khanar Kato was mounted on a warhorse, holding his saber overhead as he announced, "Onördae türem bulaan ezleg ükhech!"

Garrat joined the Thrailan riders, their horses edging against each other. He imagined that Khanar Kato declared today would be the day the invaders would die — today would be the day the western devils were sent back to the underworld they came from. Riding into the plains, Garrat galloped alongside them with his spear gripped tightly in his right hand. To the south dozens of people crossed the shimmering waters of the two creeks and Garrat realized the men were lining up to give their families any kind of chance to escape.

Zukov's riders galloped fiercely from the north as the sun rose ten degrees above the horizon. Both cavalries spread over the steppes and Garrat leveled his spear forward, offering a war shout to the thunderous collision of their armies. The steel tip pierced the throat of a riding swordsman like it was tearing through paper. Garrat turned as if he were in the lists and charged. He rode the horse with both hands on the spear and gripped the saddle with his knees, thrusting through the gaps in their armor, or into their eyes, against men he had served with for months.

Yet the riders of Kato took heavy casualties on the first assault. They rode instinctively, not knowing how to maneuver against longswords until they were hacked out of their saddles into the dust beneath their hooves. A cheer erupted from the Third Company when Zukov lopped Khanar Kato's head right from his shoulders. After that the men surged past the line of defense, littering the ground with bodies as they descended across the field.

"No!" Garrat screamed helplessly as he watched dozens of soldiers gallop around the encampment, fording the creek and rounding up the slowest women and children for a brutal slaughter. Within seconds the marchers came over the mound from where the attack had begun. A hundred men combed the grasses for survivors of the first assault, and they murdered any Thrailan riders they found alive. Brutal sounds filled the air. Men choked on blood, or they screamed toward a sudden silence as they were scalped to death.

Beyond grief, beyond fear, Garrat urged the wounded horse back toward the camp, searching for Zukov. Once again he was at the edge of a massacre as they harassed the women and the elderly, trampling children under their steeds for sport. There he was horrified to come behind Marshal Zukov as he brought down his sword to slice a woman in half at the waist as easily as a butcher dropped a cleaver through a piece of meat.

Releasing a war shout, Garrat charged his horse into the camp with his spear tucked under his arm and gripped firmly by two hands. With an expectant sneer Zukov walked calmly to meet him, wielding the wicked horsecutter weapon, a massive saber that was nearly as long as he was. Raising the blade over his head, the Third Marshal stepped widely and cleaved the leg off the galloping horse in one deft sweep. Garrat was flung from the saddle as the steed crashed to the ground, landing flat on his chest and knocking the air out of his lungs.

Shocked and gasping, Garrat scrambled away just as the madman's sword came ringing through the air as he growled, "Queensknight!"

Unable to find his spear, Garrat ran frantically as three or four men hounded him through the camp.

"Where are the gods now, Queensknight?" Zukov bellowed, his eyes bulging, his teeth coated in blood, the red jasper talisman glinting around his neck.

Garrat was cornered as more soldiers approached, each of them crazed and spattered in filth after less than an hour of butchery. Turning around in circles, it was impossible to watch them all and eventually someone thrust from behind and buried three inches of his sword just above Garrat's hip. Blood poured across his scalemail and down his legs as the weapon withdrew from the wound.

"Not the face," Zukov commanded sharply from behind as the soldiers began to hack at Garrat, slashing his legs, stabbing him through the chest, plunging daggers into his side, until he staggered several steps away where he collapsed into the wreckage of the camp. Screams came from the yurts nearby as the soldiers terrorized the last women and children that tried to hide. Blood soaked through Garrat's gambeson under his armor and he took short panicky breaths, realizing he had utterly failed to keep his Oath.

In the last ebb of his heart the paladin had visions of his wife's embrace. For so long he had been dreaming of their villa in the riverlands. For so long he had wanted desperately to hold his wife in bed, to smell her curly auburn hair, to whisper her name, "Magritte," in the tones of his love.

It did not take long to ransack the entire encampment, finding very few useful items beyond provisions and casks of sour ales. The men saw that Marshal Zukov was extremely pleased, encouraging them to continue their sadistic games of cutting scalps and ears, until they came upon the traitor and he ordered them to keep that corpse for him, laughing, "I'm going to put his head on a spear for all the gods in heaven to see."

Yet, behind his spellguise, Semarin had other plans. The vile sorcerer deceived them all as he looked and sounded and even smelled like the man whose face he wore, playing the role of Marshal Zukov as he barked orders to pillage thoroughly and gather as many new horses as possible so that they could return to the supply wagons they had left twenty-five miles away.

Semarin thought irritably, *Commanding the army is such tedious work!* until he eventually snatched up a soldier he knew from the journey, saying contemptuously, "You, Wei Lin. Field promotion! You're officially the Commander now," leaving the startled man to step into the role.

To any onlookers it appeared that Marshal Zukov was walking

alone through the devastation, kicking over wreckage, kneeling down to examine bodies. It was an illusion that Semarin created, being quite thrilled by his success at impersonating the Marshal these last few weeks. He wore the mask at all times, even taking up the massive and unwieldy broadsword – the horsecutter that Zukov carried – after he had eaten several ounces of the gray and pink folds of his brain to absorb the skill to use it convincingly.

Semarin, however, had no patience for military structure, unable to conceal his desire for wanton chaos. He had used whispers of abyssal speech to fill the men with an insatiable war lust. He drew out their worst impulses and released them onto the innocents like ravenous wolves in a cruel and morbid theater of his own design. Once he departed from their presence, their minds and hearts would likely clear from the spell and the men would wonder how it had all gone so wrong. They might spend years feeling the trauma of those last few days, the moral injuries they had committed, the everlasting guilt and shame – or, he hoped, it might fuel their prejudices and convince them to teach their hatred to their children.

I love this world! These people are so easy to manipulate against each other, Semarin laughed to himself.

Of course the Red Seer would be happy to know the bloodstone he wore around his neck had worked better than she could have ever hoped. It was a rare item that could only be created from jasper bathed in the light of the red sickle moon in autumn, the consecrated time of the Fallen One that only came every few years. Semarin knew most of the slain would rejoin the Wreath and possibly be reborn, but any person he killed himself made the bloodstone glow brighter until it was red like a ruby, filled with all the essence it had collected by his hands.

She had better appreciate all this work I've gone to or we'll have to change our arrangement, Semarin thought crossly, wanting to see the face from beneath her veil just to cut it from her head if she displeased him.

Yet, so far it served his goals to work with the Red Seer. She obviously knew the Forbidden Lore and had predicted his arrival after the long, hard climb from the Nether when he emerged at the threshold of a mausoleum, falling into her arms like a lost child. Semarin had no way of knowing what she looked like beneath her red hood and silk veil, except that her brow appeared level and her voice was sonorous and strong as she said, "Welcome to the lands of Kuei."

Within the first night the Red Seer entered his chambers and whispered, "My goddess has sent me a reward," as she undressed in the darkness and climbed over him, biting him through the silk of the red veil, becoming his lover. She painted her body in black glyphs; her skin glistened with oil, her face and eyes were covered. Afterwards she squatted onto a cloth to recover his emissions, saying that he was the Netherchild, the son of the jade goddess, and it would add power to the forbidden rituals.

The Red Seer took him into the hidden catacombs of the capital city where the old shrine was sealed under rubble, showing him a deep cistern where the lower passages had been conjoined to the sewer system and flooded. In the corridors other people wore black silk veils and the priestess called them the Order of the Shroud, a secretive cult that hid their faces so as not to compromise their work to each other as spies and thieves and assassins in the outside world. Semarin discovered they were all that was left of a once-great cult reduced to hiding, carrying on the blood rituals in secret.

"Tell me what you know about the book," he demanded.

She crossed her arms and flatly refused to tell him anything, insisting, "Become my acolyte. Obey my commands. Act as an agent of the Shroud," all of which greatly amused his twisted mind, since he knew that he had already sworn the oath in blood from the moment he was conceived.

He gave the appearance of reluctantly agreeing to her request, but stipulated, "Tell me everything you know about the grimoire," not wanting the Red Seer to think he was easy to satisfy, but Semarin thought, *I'll swear any oath she wants if it makes her think*

I'm loyal to her, but as soon as I find the book I'll do as I please!

In spite of being a small cult, the Shroud had a network of spies all over the world, and the sorcerer realized that if there was anyone who knew where to begin searching for the Mal Goetia Grimoire it was the Red Seer. Of course the high priestess was a double agent herself, embroiled in politics, knowing all the intricacies of the Kingdoms of Arovia and the Empire of Kenan, moving her pieces into play for purposes known only to her.

One day she revealed, "There are rumors of an abyssal page in Zakariya," knowing his obsession would take him there one way or the other and she wanted to at least send him alongside the Third Company as an agent for the Shroud. The king was reacting to news that raiders had ransacked several caravans on the Oil Road, and by sending the Third Marshal Zukov he hoped to establish checkpoints and regular patrols that would stabilize the trade route through the Steppes. Semarin was thrilled to set out from the catacombs, released into the world to wreak his favorite kind of mayhem – devious intrigue that built into days and days of bloodshed.

He wore a heavy gray and black cloak like it was a shroud and concealed himself under the hood so that very few people saw his flashing green eyes or the several deep scars that passed across his face. Still he was unwilling to travel through the riverlands with everyone gaping at his strange looks, so Semarin used his darkwood staff to find the head of a shadowtrail that went alongside the Third Company as they departed from the capital. He remained hidden as long as he carried the staff, which was a charred brand with a rough piece of coal embedded in the top. Among other things it allowed him to see glimmering silver trails that went for miles and miles in a world of endless darkness. He had quite enjoyed the peaceful silence as he followed the army through the countryside, hearing only the whine of huge bats overhead and hellhounds screaming in the distance.

From the outset he was infatuated with Garrat, a handsome and upstanding young knight from a rich family, yet bold and self-assured in the way that only a man could be after earning his own title. He was famous among the enlisted soldiers and Semarin rolled his eyes jealously anytime somebody mentioned Garrat was undefeated in forty-three Zansho duels, or that the Healer Queen herself blessed his holy spear. The Netherchild quickly came to hate Garrat for his good looks, for his idyllic life, for his virtue, for everything that made him a paladin to the queen.

For weeks the soldiers of the Third Company marched across the Canyons of Quay and Semarin gradually wove a net of abyssal speech between them, infiltrating their minds until the whispers were all they could hear. Then, the first night they slept in the steppes, Semarin filled the Marshal's tent with an impenetrable darkness, reaching out with a dagger until the blade plunged into Zukov's throat like a needle into thread. Exalting in the murder, Semarin drank the blood that gushed from the wound and when the body was drained he set to work for the rest of the night, making good use of the pieces he needed, getting everything ready to fool Garrat, Toro Li, and Kevor into thinking he was the actual Marshal Zukov.

It's a shame about the other parts, Semarin lamented, having only the mask and the huge broadsword as mementos of his first victim. With a cudgel he had managed to crack open the skull for the brain, absorbing fragments of what Zukov knew with each raw bite. Unfortunately without time and a place to work in secret there was no way to harvest everything from the body that he wanted; like the heart, or the liver, and even the intestines, which would all be useless once they began to decompose, so he took what he needed and abandoned the corpse in the darklands for the hellhounds to enjoy.

The next day he wore the dried and lacquered mask, looking through Zukov's brown eyes for the first time. Kevor greeted him and went past, and later when Semarin ordered Toro Li to change the guard rotation the commander obeyed without hesitation. As long as he wore the leather skin mask none of them would ever know the truth, and soon the abyssal speech that tied them all together was like an endless echo that called them to destruction.

Semarin wanted to push Garrat into a torrent of madness. He

wanted Garrat to renounce his vows; to feel just one day of the misery that he had felt his entire life – to feel just one day of the utter shock and horror he had witnessed since the day he was born. But as long as the paladin carried the blessed longspear he resisted the spell, being unwilling to participate in the massacre of the native clans, and the Netherchild didn't care so long as Garrat was a witness and he could watch him grieve. He had not expected Garrat to betray them all. Otherwise his plan had gone perfectly, especially the part when he chopped off the chieftain's head with Zukov's huge sword and in a matter of minutes the Third Company had run through the camp, creating fields of butchery.

The paladin gave them no choice. He was put to death for treason by a dozen cuts, and Semarin was absolutely delighted by everyone's performance. In the ruins he gazed upon Garrat's lifeless body, rigid in the dirt, open with wounds in several places. The sorcerer thought, *It's a shame*, wondering what the courageous heart of a paladin might taste like, but he was virtually in parts already and most of the organs had been punctured so many times they weren't recoverable.

Instead, he knelt over and set to work recovering Garrat's head, planning to make another mask – planning to make more mischief.

CHAPTER ONE

THE TWENTY-FOURTH DAY OF VILIKAI, 1019 EC

*The classics say, "Season Trees are the / crossroads for
wandering souls / between the two worlds."*

THE LAYMONK

From the moment the boy awoke, the day felt immeasurably
bright to his eyes. The sunlight glanced through the leaves
that stirred in the wind along the roadside, shining in the
grove at dawn. The boy sat upright. He felt a throbbing headache
and dimmed his brow with a hand until he could make out the
objects of their campsite. Sore and stiff, he moved slowly, gradually
becoming accustomed to the light. At a distance he saw his old
teacher already seated in contemplation under a broad Season Tree
where the bower cast shadows across his face.

The boy groaned as he thought, *It's too early for meditation, and
besides I have a concussion,* finding the perfect excuse to avoid
disturbing the laymonk, not that he thought he could achieve the
Still Mind right now anyway.

Instead he gathered some kindling from around the camp
where there was barely an ember smoldering in the firepit from last
night. A few dry twigs snapped and the leaves crinkled as the flames
rose up, encouraged by his breath. Soon there was a small fire and he
set a kettle down to heat some water for morning tea, rummaging
around in his pack for the pouch of dried leaves given to them by the

herbalist monk before they had departed Red Tower Abbey just a few days ago.

Like most travelers through the Dellwood they spent their nights in the grove, or at a ranger's trailhead, and the boy had wondered miserably, *This is the life of a laymonk?* with only a thin bedroll to lie on to break the hard ground. The straw mattress and the wooden bunk he slept on at the abbey weren't much better, but Genshai still lamented that they were already on the road again after spending so many weeks abroad in the highlands. Occasionally they would find a comfortable hayloft, or cots in front of a warm hearth, to sleep at night, since by now Genshai had discovered that his teacher had made numerous friends over the years that had come to expect his irregularly timed visits; although if he were still at home at least he would have had a pillow to ease his aching head, like when he was a novice growing up in the Iron Style after a day of sparring with his brothers in the abbey.

After several minutes the water was hot and Genshai steeped a pinch of dried tea leaves, wondering about breakfast. They didn't have much, and in fact they had eaten the last of their potatoes last night, with the butt of a parsnip and a skinny carrot, a few foraged morel mushrooms, and three pungent ramp stalks, which the old laymonk plucked from the ground after noticing their broad green leaves, waving like flags in late springtime.

Their lack of food made Genshai anxious but luckily they were within a day's hike from Norhaal, the capital of the province, where Taisan said they would find more provisions, and gain answers to the cryptic words the Warden had written in his letter, "There are rumors of a haunting in Westcliff," which stirred eerie memories of what happened to them at the full moon just under a month ago at Ulfghar's Ridge, the last crest in the north.

They had originally set out in the last days of winter when the afternoons were humid and the nights were still cold. To his surprise, Taisan took him northward, deeper and deeper into the valleys of the Namaya Highlands. Quite often they were alone for miles and Genshai came to realize that his teacher was very accustomed to that solitary life on the road. He moved easily. He shouldered his pack like it was part of him; he rationed their food, and was always foraging as they hiked, teaching Genshai which herbs, wild berries, tubers, and mushrooms were edible and which were poisonous; and in the evenings Taisan showed the boy how to dig a proper firepit to avoid sparking a blaze in the forest, and how to be wary of wild animals that lurked at night.

Those days on the Hylmrodes were the first time the boy had ever been beyond Red Tower, and the hikes began to strengthen his legs. They usually practiced the Eight Simple Sets each morning, just as they had done in the abbey, before they grabbed their smooth hickory staves and kept a steady pace for several hours. During the break at midday the old laymonk taught Genshai several other deep-stretching drills to avoid tightness in the legs, even though it was inevitable that by the fourth night of traveling the boy's calves were as taut as a drum, and he felt his hamstrings were like thick cords pulling him down, becoming painful for days.

The boy sipped his hot tea as he considered all his travels so far. They had already journeyed more than five hundred miles that spring; on stone roads all the way from Red Tower Abbey to Ulfghar's Ridge and back again in only a few short months, walking ten to twelve hours a day, depending on the weather. According to the histories that Genshai had read in the abbey library, the ancient Dweroh tribes had settled in the highlands during the Age of a Thousand Swords, laying the Hylmrodes favorably from east to west while the Hebra warlords fought each other for all the arable countryside and eventually united their banners under the Son of the Bear. In spite of their complicated history the Dweroh wanted to trade down from their stronghold, and formed a Covenant with the Hebra people of Norr Province eight hundred years ago, allowing caravans to use the roads ever since.

Upon their return the boy could tell they were back into the Auburn Range by the sight of the thick forests and the sloping brown earth. He even spotted Red Tower in the distance when they were still a few days away, standing stalwart on the peak amidst evergreen trees, and thick clusters of maples, oaks, cedars, and so many others. Seeing the abbey there Genshai realized that he would never view his childhood home the same way again, knowing there was once a time, not long ago, that he was willing to swear an Oath to sequester himself there in pursuit of Illumination.

It's no wonder so many monks leave once they get older, Genshai had thought, as he felt the wanderlust now more than he had ever felt it before. He had never expected to become the laymonk, feeling completely inexperienced, and now especially with his aching head he knew that there was still much for him to learn, yet when he had stood in the highlands looking southward past Red Tower he had thought that the world was so vast; *but maybe one day I'll walk across the entire province, or even all the way to the southlands to see the Kalish Ocean!* and those thoughts were more exciting than anything.

They had hardly returned home from their journey when the abbot gave them a handwritten letter stamped with the Warden's bear sigil, summoning the laymonk to the great lodge at Norhaal. They left the next day at the forehour of dawn. Even though it was sudden, and he would have liked to stay home a bit longer, Genshai did have to admit he was excited, and a bit impatient, to finally descend the five-mile trail from Red Tower and leave Auburntown to go across the province the way it was said the laymonks were meant to do.

The boy noticed his old teacher approach the campsite. Taisan was a rangy man with a purposeful stride, which he had used to go back and forth across the province after his thirty long years of service to Red Tower Abbey. From his cloth satchel Taisan brought out a handful of melona fruit, which were the spring bounty of the Season Tree. They had rich garnet skins and pale yellow flesh that was juicy and tart when slightly overripe, perfect after falling from the branches into the lush grass.

The kettle was still hot by the edge of the fire. Taisan poured himself a mug of tea and sipped slowly, contemplating something after his Still Mind meditations. His eyes were hazelbrown, framed by heavy gray brows, and he had a short graying beard around his narrow chin. Genshai grimaced, still slightly sensitive to the light, and his teacher's attention shifted toward the boy, breaking his silence, "How's your head?"

"Just what you'd expect," the boy responded, with a slight edge in his voice.

Taisan reprimanded his student, "Well you're lucky you aren't dead. That might've been a knife in his hand instead."

"I fought one of them off, didn't I?" Genshai responded indignantly, despite his slight dizziness and flushed cheeks.

"The results speak for themselves, don't they," Taisan gestured, and Genshai could hardly argue with that. He was embarrassed about being taken by surprise since he had trained his entire life in the warrior methods of the Iron Style of Red Tower, and two days ago when he finally had a chance to show off his skills he was knocked unconscious by a small club to the back of the head.

They had come upon a wagoner who was overpowered by a robber on the road through the Dellwood. Not thinking, Genshai had rushed forward without hearing his teacher's words of caution, successfully fighting off the villain and knocking a rusty machete out of his hand. He drew back with the Iron Fist and hesitated, unsure if he wanted to strike to kill the man when he was suddenly hit from behind by a second person. Genshai went down to one knee. He braced himself against the wagon. His vision blurred to nothing as he collapsed in a heap.

Later, Taisan shook him awake. He was so stunned that his vision was somewhat fuzzy and he could hardly move without inciting nausea. Taisan examined his eyes until Genshai focused his pupils to his satisfaction, as the wagoner asked, "Is he going to be alright?" and offered to let the two monks stay the night in his hut in Loweshire.

Genshai sat in the wagon and held his aching head, desperate for details as he asked, "What happened after I...?"

"After you got sapped!" the wagoner teased in spite of the boy's efforts to help him. Eventually he told Genshai that the old monk had jumped around the wagon to fight the two bandits, using his warrior staff with the iron cap to swat their hands out of the air like they were flies. Genshai looked ahead of the mule where Taisan browsed the roadside for herbs, realizing this travel-worn, penniless old monk could really fight, and that he actually might know the secrets to achieving the Ascendant Powers.

The wagoner cackled. "I guarantee they ran off with a broken wrist and a concussion of their own," he said as he snapped the reins to catch up to Taisan.

Yesterday they embarked earlier than Genshai would have liked, and when he complained the old man had shrugged and said, "We should make up for the time we lost yesterday," even though Genshai struggled to keep pace with Taisan for most of the day. They hiked only a few hours, taking frequent breaks, and he was relieved to come upon where Taisan decided to make camp in the grove near the Season Tree that was blooming with its wide green leaves and flowers that had white petals and purple stamens. They spoke infrequently and Taisan disappeared to meditate at eventide, returning later when the fire had died down to glowing coals and there was very little starlight to see by.

Genshai fell asleep on the hard ground with a cold wet cloth on his head, as Taisan said, "Don't worry kid, I'll watch over you."

So far that morning the bruise at the back of his head was painful to the touch. He still had a throbbing ache that disrupted his focus, and the light flared brightly through the trees in his eyes. Only time would heal his concussion, but Genshai desperately wanted willowbark, or vervain, from the abbey, but they didn't even have hit medicine, which was the strong liniment the monks used after their daily Iron Palm conditioning. It was one of numerous secret recipes the herbalist monks used to aid them in recovering from bruises, sprains, and broken bones, and it was said the hit medicine had over a hundred ingredients.

"Eat the melona fruit," Taisan said, "We're going to resume your training today."

Genshai braced himself by taking a deep breath. "I don't think

I should train today. Master Thornwood always said not to push ourselves if we're injured," referring to the old healer in the abbey.

"Thornwood's not here, is he?" Taisan said flatly.

Genshai was at a loss. He felt miserable, and Taisan had never been so dismissive before, even though the old man displayed no emotion whatsoever. Instead he casually put away their campsite, rolled up his sleeping mat, and folded a heavy quilt that a Dweroh woman had given to him when they visited her cottage outside Hylmstone earlier that spring. The old man packed everything into their designated places in his bag as he sucked on a length of lemongrass between his teeth.

"Come on," Taisan eventually said, forcing Genshai to begin practicing.

The movements of each routine were very familiar, and to his surprise Genshai felt his mind clearing with each step. He had trained everyday at the forehour of dawn ever since he was a five-year-old boy under the watchful eye of the teacher Heavy Earth, who was a tall, barrel-chested monk who moved as lightly as a feather in all the stepping patterns of the Eight Simple Sets. Feeling his joints loosening, Genshai recited to himself, "Begin reaching down / your legs straight, touching your feet / slowly raise your spine," which were ancient instructions.

Yet Taisan's movements were different. He made deep stretches that benefited the legs and hips. Even though he was in his fifties, he was lean and muscular. Taisan clearly looked as if he had been sculpted from the Iron Style, but his interpretation of the Eight Simple Sets was divergent from the masters of the abbey. At first Genshai had wondered how many monks practiced the forms this way, eventually not caring since he came to rely on the new calisthenics for relief in his legs at the beginning and the end of every day.

The old teacher said, "To raise the spirit / begin to align yourself / in thirteen places," quoting the verses of Being from the classics of Sibudat.

They practiced in the grove by the roadside all morning. They heated more water from the nearby spring until the flavor had faded from the tea. After stretching and warming up, Taisan demonstrated the Mountain Form. He explained the breathing exercises necessary, and said, "Once this skill is unlocked you will be completely immoveable, and you'll know all the ways to take someone off their feet!"

Genshai desperately wanted to understand. His entire life he had seen monks at home that could shatter granite slabs with a single punch, or break staffs and clubs against their ribs like they were wearing plate armor. Even the old abbot Horn of Ram could step through the trees like a fluttering bird and break rough stone with a single crack of his knuckle. He taught that the Iron Fist was hidden within them, but to the boy all of the Ascendant Powers of Sibudat seemed supernatural and impossible to achieve. The Iron Body! The Running Deer! And especially the Seat-of-the-Mountain – the form of his namesake, which claimed to make the monk rooted to the earth.

"Do you want to be like the mountain or not? Sit deeper!" Taisan demanded. The boy shuffled his feet and tried to adjust his hips somewhat, but the old teacher looked at his student's stance disapprovingly and shook his head, saying, "No. No. No."

"What do you want from me?" Genshai howled, his legs shaking.

"Hands up," Taisan barked and the young boy instantly switched positions, ready to fight with his fists up to his cheeks. Following his teacher's signal he delivered a firm left jab, but in a single step the old laymonk had somehow absorbed the boy's stance and snapped him to the ground. Taisan declared, "Your body must have a counterbalance. Sit forward and backward at the same time. You will never be rooted any other way."

Genshai began to understand in only the way that hard throws to the ground could teach. They practiced the Mountain Form all morning and Taisan articulated every sweep and cut and twist until Genshai had been tossed on the ground more in one morning than he'd ever been after the sound of the training bell in the courtyard of the abbey.

"Mountainroot? Really?" the old laymonk taunted, "More like a landslide."

"Well, throw me when…"

"When what?" He interrupted harshly, "When you don't have a concussion? Give me a break! You're a warrior of Red Tower. We don't lose fights with small villains on the road. We don't get concussions that keep us from training for two days. You need to be ready at all times!"

The boy panted heavily, his head pounding, the back of his neck tender from Taisan's hard grip in all the throws. Suddenly Genshai released a wild flurry, to which the laymonk deflected every one until the boy delivered a firm heel to the man's chest, sending him backward. In spite of the hard kick Taisan released a grin, finally betraying some of the enjoyment he felt by training the boy he had selected to bear his legacy to the abbey.

"Come on!" Taisan demanded, "You want to fight, but you won't follow through."

"I will follow through!" Genshai shouted, like a boy upset.

"No," Taisan said. He turned away as if he didn't care that Genshai was posted there and ready to fight. "I know you won't."

The boy released a shout. He stepped roughly, punched widely. The old teacher easily avoided every movement. He swatted every punch out of the air and pulled the boy harshly; he struck with the forearm across the collar and tripped him by one firm leg that was like a pillar of stone itself. Genshai went straight down into the grass, not springing back up as he had done, and they both knew that was the end of practice for the day.

They walked in a circle taking deep breaths. Taisan said pointedly, "I can see that you're not afraid, but when you were a boy all the fighting drills were placed on the outside of the body. After all, we can't have the novices hurting each other too seriously," even though Genshai remembered plenty of bruised ribs and swollen knuckles growing up in the abbey.

"You need to hit for real," Taisan continued. "It's not just punching and kicking the air. To become immoveable you must understand how deep the mountain actually goes."

The Seat-of-the-Mountain skill had fascinated Genshai since he was about twelve when he came upon a secret meeting of the elder monks in a ruined temple where the laymonk was demonstrating the form. He was called the Enduring Mountain for a reason, since once Taisan settled his root in his legs no monk could throw him, or even succeed in pushing him. The boy had continued to practice what he had spied upon that night, imagining what it might feel like to be unshakable the way the old man claimed he could become. Perhaps his efforts had impressed the abbot Horn of Ram who assigned him to become the laymonk's apprentice, which meant he would learn the Mountain Form until he unlocked the skill – or not.

"Out here, it's a matter of life and death," Taisan said. "You need to follow through or you might not be here to try again next time," expressing the purpose of the hard lesson that day.

They were covered in a sheen of sweat after their vigorous practice all morning. Genshai was breathing heavily while the old man was hardly winded at all. There were new bruises blooming on his arms and legs from being gripped hard, and he wished again that they had hit medicine from the abbey, or even the body rub, which was a hemp oil blended with many herbs, steeped in camphor bark and turmeric that made their skin glisten like gold when it was applied.

Finally they went to a nearby spring outside the grove to wash and Genshai could feel that his head was already bristling with hair after the clean shave he had received at the abbey last week. Most of the monks of Red Tower kept the orthodox tradition of shaving their head even though it was not unusual for the Dweroh among them to grow a beard or occasionally keep a short haircut. In the meantime Taisan had thick curls of gray and white hair that blew in the wind like puffs of cotton.

The laymonk was different from his brothers in the abbey. He lived both inside and outside the traditions. He was allowed to grow his hair, and to have fine clothes, and jewelry, or any other personal possessions. Genshai was intrigued to learn he was also permitted to handle money and flying cash, or even to eat meat, drink alcohol, or smoke tobacco; raising an eyebrow when he learned the laymonk could even have a family, keeping their abbey names as long as all their deeds in life were for Red Tower. Any of the brothers that learned what the laymonks did quickly realized that they were essential to the survival of the abbey since they were the ones that brokered with merchants and spread the holy Scripts of Sibudat far and wide.

He wondered, *What do my brothers think of me now?* since they were all raised under the shadow of Red Tower, learning the legacy of that place, and a few months ago they had all been named, just as he had been, when they swore the Oath to become monks. As orphans and children of the abbey they didn't know their exact birthdates, so when it was assumed the boys had come of age they were summoned to the abbot's courtyard in the first month of the year. At fifteen they were hardly men but no longer boys, and it was fairly common for novices to take the Oath and then later leave the abbey in their twenties to seek a family or find their own fortunes.

By breakfast that day there were already rumors that the abbot was planning to name someone as an apprentice for the Enduring Mountain. Many of the novices expected it to be Jakk, who was still thought to be a year too young to swear the Oath, even though he was acrobatic and proud, lightly jumping and flipping without ever touching his hands to the ground. Instead the boys were shocked to learn even before he had returned from the abbot's courtyard that it was Genshai who would be the laymonk's apprentice.

It was a cold winter afterfade when he was summoned to take the Oath and all the masters looked on him expectantly as he crossed under the square arch into the abbot's snowy courtyard. They were an impressive group of warriors, and when he said, "My body, my mind, and my spirit are given to Red Tower," he embraced his future in the abbey as a monk.

Then the abbot said his new name, "Mountainroot, you will be the laymonk of Red Tower," and the boy raised his head in shock, looking at the old man in his eighties seated at a stone bench as he said, "Now you carry the honor of us all," with an expressionless stare.

Genshai held those words in his mind as they gathered their packs onto their shoulders and Taisan led them across the gully between the grove and the road until they were heading southward again. He was sore and hungry and a fog of drowsiness was already settling in his thoughts as they walked, and he found himself leaning on his hickory staff for every step, wearier after dawn practice than he had ever been before.

By midday they emerged into a vast field of buckwheat flowers on a farmroad that led toward the walls of Norhaal far in the distance.

———

Their feet led them quickly over the hills of the meadow until they reached the Norshire. It was one of three wattle and daub villages surrounding the city, filled with farmers, a few craftsmen, clothiers, and weavers at work on their looms. They passed several wooden pens where the shepherds brought in their flocks at eventide and Taisan nodded politely to the women and children who came to their doors to see what kind of travelers were on the road. A farmer even stopped them to talk for a few minutes and the boy was still surprised whenever his old teacher knew people by name, even though by now it seemed like Taisan had friends everywhere.

Soon they came to a rise on the hill where they took a break in the shade of a tall Season Tree, which were considered sacred since it was believed that Sibudat had Illuminated while meditating below the wide bowers of that kind of tree, and they could flower and bear fruit all year. Anytime they came across one it always reminded Genshai of the Season Tree that grew in the abbey courtyard, under which he had meditated and trained and gathered baskets of fallen fruit, soft white petals, and nuts every season.

They each took long warm draughts from the waterskins at their hips. Looking out, Genshai saw they had come through the Dellwood from the northern road, while many furrows of farmland stretched ahead to the east and south. Pointing with his finger he said, "Look at the mills!" thrilled at the sight of half a dozen windmills slowly spinning far off in the distance.

Taisan looked at his apprentice with a bare smile, as he thought, *He's still not ready,* knowing that he was just a boy in the trappings of a man.

"Let's eat," the laymonk said, looking around for overripe melona that had fallen from the generous Season Tree. When they sat down in the shade, Taisan asked, "Which road did we come from?" since he frequently asked his student to recite all the places they had traveled, forcing the boy to create a map of their journeys in his mind.

"The third quarry road," Genshai replied, knowing that there were six such roads leading north through the Dellwood toward the foothills of the Auburn Range, which were rich in granite, slate, and soapstone, that all had their uses – but only Auburntown produced the brick of rare red hue that made Red Tower so distinguishable. Between bites Genshai explained that they had taken the quarry road south through the Dellwood for six days, and before that they had come down through Oathlord Brayden's lands, past long furrows of winter barley that waved on the stalk in late spring.

Genshai threw the pit of a melona fruit into the distant gully by the roadside, thinking that a few plums in his belly were hardly satisfying after a long day of training and hiking with the old man.

"Then what?" Taisan asked.

"Then we were in Red Tower," Genshai replied impatiently, remembering they had only been home for a single night before they descended the five-mile trail right into another journey. They passed through Auburntown where the greathouses and manors of the city were built from bricks the colors of dark amber and rust, cherries, and ruby flowers. He had gazed up at the enormous bell tower at the peak of the Auburn Range, and witnessed the full height of the abbey, always within its shadow until they crossed the Redshire.

Genshai noticed that Taisan was distracted, watching the flocks in the meadow like puffs of cloud drifting in the distance. Hungry and tired the boy finally asked, "What are we going to do now?" as he observed that the sun was thirty degrees from the west horizon.

Taisan gathered up his pack and stood with his staff readily in hand as he said, "I know an Alderman in the village. We might be in luck tonight."

"Shouldn't we visit the Warden?" Genshai looked at the laymonk with just enough energy to still be curious about the great lodge inside the walls, and the man they called 'Son of the Bear,' just as his father and all his ancestors had been called before him.

"We'll go soon enough. Tomorrow," Taisan said, leading the way down the road.

They went by timber farmhouses and one or two manors in the field, and for the first time the boy had a clear view of the Hall of the North. The Warden's lodge had three towers that flew the banners of Norr: two bears that faced away from each other, which folks said were like brothers departing into the wild. A stonewall rose up around the hillock where the lodge was built and they could see guildhalls and greathouses, brick buildings and artisan shops, behind the gates. Defenders patrolled the ramparts, watching traders that moved through the streets of the city, heading home after a long day of work.

Just as he was telling his student, "This place is a sort of crossroads between quarters of the north..." they turned at the sound of his name when a few folks passing by recognized him and called, "Hey Taisan." Genshai was introduced to Myrssa, a weaver, and her husband Brannagh who was a plowman, and a few other traders who he couldn't remember; also a taverner named Desi, who was there to place his order for two barrels of abbey ale, which Genshai knew they would occasionally do for merchants, taverners, and even Oathlords.

"Mattos, good tidings," Taisan reached past a few folks to

shake hands with the defender that had walked up while out for a stroll with his wife and two boys who were running around the laymonk's feet shouting, "Uncle Tai, uncle Tai!" as if they knew him well.

Genshai gathered that Mattos was an abbey brother who had come down from the mountain to seek a family instead of swearing the Oath. He was a darkhaired man with a brown complexion, in his mid-thirties wearing the blue guard's tunic with the patch of the Shield of Shao Daan embroidered in white and yellow over his heart. He kept an arming sword at his hip and a wooden shield on his back, a leather coinpurse and a skirmish dagger on the opposite side, and he was accompanied by his wife Aida, who wore the yellow and green cloth of the Ladies of the Patient Field, indicating that she was a cleric of the shrine.

"Now Brondon, just slow down," Taisan laughed, stepping away from the excited boys as if he were avoiding a kick in a fight.

Smoke rose up from the chimney of the local tavern and Genshai could smell meat pies baking in the oven somewhere down the road. His head was spinning with fatigue and he clutched his rumbling stomach, hoping there would be more than just melona fruit to eat at the end of their travels that evening. Meanwhile, the old laymonk inquired after the health of the children, checked in to be sure that folks were well, and caught up on stories from abbey friends.

After more than thirty years visiting Norhaal, Taisan had come to know many residents in the city and surrounding shires. Everywhere he went he forged relationships with the laity of the abbey, and it wasn't long before nearly a dozen folks had gathered around wanting to hear something from the laymonk until young Genshai felt absorbed into the crowd. They were in the street adjacent to the well where Taisan set down his staff and began to pull up water for folks that intended to fill their buckets to carry home to pour into their ceramic cisterns.

"Let me help you, madam," Taisan offered pleasantly to an elderly woman.

"Thank you, teacher," she said, setting a copper coin on the edge of the well.

"Okay, okay, that's fine. Now who's next?" Taisan looked at them all.

"You're a great man if you want to pull everyone's water tonight," Mattos laughed.

"It's no trouble," the laymonk said as he pulled up the rope. "Sibudat talks about the Noble Actions, 'As hawk, deer, and crane / live beside the lonely wolf / should man live with man. Like trees of the wood / in harmony with nature / we stand together.'"

"How do you mean, teacher?" the old woman asked politely.

Taisan gave a slight smile, "The classics say, 'Avoid deception / abusive speech, lies, gossip / and idle chatter. Act with pure kindness / offer a generous hand / and live with honor. Always speak the truth / abstain from theft and murder / and move with virtue.'"

They were simple verses to live by and the monks of the Aegin Tradition had taught them for centuries. Genshai appreciated how easily Taisan incorporated the syllable structure of the classics into his speech as if they ran together, and the people nodded along in agreement; however, he knew that if any of them began to study the successive chapters of the Scripts of Sibudat they would be challenged by the innate paradox held within those ancient words.

At first it was a small crowd that gathered until word went through the streets that the laymonk was giving a sermon outside the Alderman's house. Some women with their children stopped to listen standing with a few masons, a carpenter, and an old cobbler who smoked his pipe on the stoop of his shop. Nearby at the guardpost the defenders listened as well as they could while folks passed through the gates into the village to go home for the day. The evening sun granted its light. It hung above the west horizon and brightened the faces of the northerners, who were darkhaired, golden and yellow like honeycomb, or the color of wheat on the stalk.

"We must consider that Noble Actions lead to Lumier in the next life, bringing us closer to Illumination," Taisan explained and the people listened intently to a lesson that Genshai had learned all his life.

The old laymonk continued, "We are all spirits from the Wreath, reborn in a cycle that never ends. None of us wishes to die, but the great Sibudat says, 'The ebb of the Wreath / is like the flow of the sea / and the ceaseless winds. All moments of life / lead to pure death, and the Wreath / beyond – then rebirth!' These are the words from the writings of his disciples who taught his wisdom through the ages."

"Teacher," a man called. "Is it true that monks have the knowledge of their past lives?"

He answered, "All beings, man or woman, beast or bird, has the wisdom of their spirit, but you must live by the Scripts and practice the Simple Sets like the monks of Red-Tower to touch back on those lives. Understand! Your bodies are a home for a Great Spirit on a long journey, that's why Sibudat says, 'Past the starry Veil, / beyond the seasons of life, / beyond what is seen. A vast Wreath abounds / and spirits follow a path, / elegant and bright. We are made of light / traveling in a cycle / of different lives. Knowledge is revealed / and clouds do not drift idly / as they seem to do.'"

"Then why do we suffer?" called a young woman wearing the holy cloth.

"We are brought to where we are through the will of the spirit," Taisan answered readily. "Suffering is the lesson of life. No person is exempt, and we are measured by what we learn."

"But then what's the point of being reborn?" she asked from along the side of the crowd, with arms crossed. "If the Wreath is a prison of suffering?"

"It's not a prison!" Taisan exclaimed. "The Wreath is a place of awakenings, a place of opportunities. We have no choice but to be reborn, but 'Crossing into death, / there is a path through the Wreath / toward the next life,' for all of us, and the Scripts say we need only to follow the journey to the end. 'Illumination / by shedding identity / and releasing form!'"

Eventually the crowd was shuffling in the street, eager to get home, and Taisan waved, "Be well, my good friends, thank you," and most folks walked off in the orange glow of the sun that descended at eventide.

"Thank you, teacher," someone called, while another said, "May the Mother bless you, sir."

Those that were moved by his sermon came forward to shake his wrist, or to ask for clarification on the Scripts. People gave whatever alms they could; whether they were just square copper Lirros, or the occasional silver dragon, or even a gold crown. One magistrate even donated some crimson coins, which were hammered hundreds of years ago but still had their worth in copper, four times more valuable than the average penny. Other folks gave whatever goods they could spare. The chandler offered a bar of soap and four candles, and the taverner from across the street brought him a heavy flagon of ale. A few housewives also donated a handful of potatoes, some carrots, a parsnip, and a huge turnip, just as Genshai was handed two loaves of wheat bread, a wheel of hard sheep's cheese, and a length of cured sausages. Somehow he also ended up with a huge sack of honeyed oats mixed with nuts and dried fruit, immediately devouring three handfuls, munching furiously without caring if anyone saw him.

Soon the last of the common folk dispersed until only a few close abbey friends were left. Mattos and his wife took up their boys, getting ready to say goodbye for the night until little Brondon wailed, "No, Uncle Tai, I want to go with you! I want to be a monk, I want to see the world too!" as his mother Aida shushed him and Mattos just rolled his eyes.

"Well, it's a hard life and none of us are born to it," Taisan tousled the child's silken brown hair. "Don't worry, you'll see the world soon enough, boy."

The young family moved off down the streets while the monks stood in the new darkness of the evening. Genshai drew one more bucket from the well for his own thirst, finding that his old teacher had gone around to greet one of the last guests in the audience; a man wearing a tailored linen tunic and the Alderman's amulet around his neck, with relaxed flaxen skin, neatly trimmed gray hair, and a beard streaked with the black of his youth.

They greeted each other in a warm embrace and the Alderman whispered, "That was a good speech," to which the old monk replied quickly, "Let me introduce you."

"Genshai," Taisan called to his student, "This is Dannol," gripping the man fondly around the shoulders. "He's an Alderman for the people here."

"A pleasure to meet you, Genshai," the Alderman said with an easy smile. "Come on, you must be hungry and tired if you've been walking all day."

"Can you tell that easily?" Genshai moaned, much to their amusement.

Dannol led them past the crowded steps of a raucous tavern. Houses lined the street and most of the windows were alive with candlelight at eventide, their shutters open to the night air. Voices rose up at dinnertime and some people blessed their meals by invoking the goddesses, saying, "We thank the Three Sisters for hearth, harvest, and flock," while others were busy chattering about the day, their knives and forks scraping the plates as they ate.

The air was humid in late spring and the waning moon hung low over the Warden's lodge behind them as Dannol led the group up the front walkway of a greathouse made of heavy timber and brick. The smooth woodpaneled door was already unlocked and he whispered, "Mama is probably asleep," as he entered, knowing that his old and widowed mother was in bed upstairs.

"How has she been?" Taisan asked with concern in his voice.

Dannol whispered that she had just turned ninety so he recently hired a young nurse from the local shrine who visited several such clients during the day. The laymonks waited quietly as Dannol went up the polished wooden stairwell to visit his mother in her bedroom. Genshai glanced around at the Alderman's fine furniture and the darkened study adjacent to the front sitting room where the windows were shuttered to the street at night. It was easily the finest house Genshai had ever stepped foot within, although he knew nothing would ever capture the size of the opening cavern at Hylmstone in the Namaya Highlands.

"She's sleeping," Dannol whispered when he returned, and the three men moved silently through the house to the back kitchen where they found a cold meat pie on the countertop beside a note from the maid. She was another local woman who Dannol had hired to take care of things around the house while he worked late in the village hall. With a certain kind of familiarity, Taisan lit a candle with a tindertwig and assisted Dannol in serving them each a slice of pie and a draught of cool water from the cistern in the corner.

The older men chuckled as Genshai swallowed his portion in four huge mouthfuls until Dannol said, "You aren't feeding this boy enough."

"What? Melona fruit doesn't count?" Taisan asked gruffly.

The Alderman set down a second hearty slice for the boy to eat. The pie was cool, and made of sweet pork and onions, with potatoes, scallions, and leeks, topped in a buttery biscuit crust. Genshai had never eaten anything quite like it, having grown up on temple food, which was vegetarian, and was now eating whatever they were given or had foraged on the roadside.

"We ran out of food last night," the boy declared, wolfing down the pie. The men laughed at his abundant appetite and Genshai couldn't help but to laugh also.

Soon Taisan pulled the cork out of the flagon of ale and Dannol said, "Well, you know what this old man has had his eye on," followed by another round of laughter before he poured them both a hearty mug of smoked blackbier.

"Not for you, kid," Taisan said to his student, who gave him a sad look until the old man said as if it were obvious, "You have a concussion."

Dannol, however, did not hesitate to light his wooden pipe with a matchstick, filling the room with thick layers of smoke, putting a thumb of heady sweetleaf on top once the ember was lit.

The experience was new to Genshai, having never even been into a tavern or a smoking parlor. Just sitting nearby he felt a dull fog creep over his thoughts, relaxing in his chair as the two older men smoked the pipe and traded news of the province and talked about politics.

From what Genshai could remember from his classes the Aldermen were the people's voice to the local Oathlords. Once elected they served a term of six years and would be eligible for re-election so long as the people continued to enjoy their service. An Alderman presided over meetings of public interest and organized community events during the holidays. They also collected taxes for the Oathlord that would then be moved to the Warden's treasury. If they had enough influence they could even compel magistrates, and sometimes even the lords themselves, to pass new legislation.

While serving as a politician, Dannol had been quite busy over the last few years. In the seat of the northlands he advised the Warden directly and his proposals resulted in better market prices for fleece, a more favorable tax for the millers, and four fresh water wells dug in the local shires. Each one was inscribed with the ox of Maitreija, and Dannol said that it was, "The purest water for thirty miles. Just blessed by the Lady Vaness," whom they knew was the Warden's wife after the young couple had married last summer.

Dannol seemed to anticipate for the future and had an interest in partnering with the High Cleric Vaness on founding a new shrine in Norshire dedicated to the Three Sisters. Of course there was already a shrine in the center of Norhaal ordained for Maitreija, the goddess of the harvest and the Ladies of the Patient Field, but Dannol argued that a beautiful shrine, such as the ones found in the riverlands, would be seen as a great tribute to the Raegods. Most of the judges and court officials also agreed that if there was a school near Norshire the girls could be educated and in ten or fifteen years there would be a significant increase in brideprice gold in the marketplaces.

"But really, I think it's just such a long distance for them to walk from Norshire to the marketplace to go to school every day."

Dannol shook his head. "There should be something closer for them."

Taisan told Genshai, somewhat proudly, that Dannol was the son of a former monk who had left the abbey. Most men were illiterate, but his father had taught Dannol how to read and write as well as the principles of Red Tower, and it was this upbringing that had granted him the knowledge to run for office. His father's abbey name was Clearstone, though it was a long time before either of them were born that he had been a monk of Red Tower.

"He was a wise man," Taisan said as he looked at Dannol with sincere eyes and gripped his hand until their fingers were like knots, as if he were talking of a beloved father who they had both known years ago.

"Well, he's been reborn by now," Dannol exhaled deeply, shaking off the memories.

Genshai suddenly realized, *By the gods, it's so obvious – they're in love!* as they exchanged soft glances, or shared stories from over a decade ago, and Taisan clearly possessed more than a passing familiarity with the Alderman's house. They said nothing about being discrete, but Genshai knew there was stigma against those sorts of couples. Two men in a union were unable to receive a marriage license since there were no brideprice negotiations, or taxes paid to the shrine. Probably most folks would not be too bothered by it, but Genshai imagined they wanted to avoid appearing as if they had a conflict of interest in their duties to the people.

And now that he saw his teacher was in a relationship, Genshai secretly wondered, *Will I ever love someone?* as he realized that all this time he had never considered a future in which he was not alone. He knew that sometimes monks fell in love. Every so often there was a story of a young monk that lusted after a girl in Auburntown, leading him to abandon the abbey. Or other times two men who had kept their affection a secret from the other monks would go off together in pursuit of their own happiness.

Genshai nodded off in his chair at the table until Taisan shook him awake and said, "Better get to bed," and drowsily the boy went to lay out his bedroll in the front sitting room, grabbing up a stuffed cushion for his head. It was much later than he normally went to sleep and he felt the haze of exhaustion as he collapsed into his blankets, to dream about distant Season Trees, rolling green hills, yellow ribbons, and then nothing.

CHAPTER TWO

*Three scholars browsing the market find loose stories, and
pinch two pennies.*

NORHAAL

Genshai awoke with a start at the sound of wagons colliding and men shouting, jumping to his feet and clenching his fists until he remembered where he was, in the Alderman's front sitting room. He shook off the frightful images of his nightmare, and the ravenous growl of the dire wolf faded from his ears as the morning light peered through the crack in the shutters. He lay back on his fleece bedroll and tried to suppress the memories of the last full moon at Ulfghar's Ridge, which came unbidden to his thoughts.

I still can't believe what we saw, Genshai thought as he shut his eyes so tight that they began to water, as if that would drive the ghosts away – but instead he remembered when they had come upon a place where three Hylmrodes converged and found a dozen Dweroh men led by an Yldhamer who said in a heavy northern accent, "There are strange tales of ghosts haunting the ridge," which intrigued the old laymonk enough to change their plans and accompany the group all the way to the edge of the highlands where a derelict watchtower stood on the last ridge before the arctic tundra.

The trees twisted and groaned with the wind at eventide and

the doorframe was darkened by evening shadows. Taisan had warned, "Don't go near it," even though it was like a gaping pit their eyes could fall into. The old laymonk meditated on the Still Mind, keeping his thoughts clear and ready – but Genshai was taut with dread and the young Dweroh soldier Bolmak only made things worse by pacing back and forth in front of the doorway as he muttered, "Let me fight an enemy I can see and touch," getting angry to avoid becoming afraid, creeping up to the door, until Genshai finally yanked him back and threw him down, demanding, "What do you think you're doing?"

All through the night the men had clutched their weapons with trembling hands and listened to the vicious growls of a phantom wolf that thrashed just inside the door of the derelict tower. The shades flashed in the dark woods, their distorted shouts echoing like nails on slate. "Don't touch them," Taisan warned, but it was too late. Half the troop was already crawling on the ground in terror. Some of them ran in opposite directions and Genshai wanted to go after them until the Yldhamer called, "What happened to Bolmak?" and they all realized the young soldier had rushed inside the watchtower.

I don't understand! Why was he so obsessed with going inside the door? Genshai shuddered, not wanting to think anymore about Ulfghar's Ridge as he said to himself, *Well, I guess this is why we learn the Still Mind,* and remembered that his teacher had used meditation to endure against the evil ruins of the tower. So Genshai crossed his legs and closed his eyes, drawing his breath down into his Navel Gate the way he was taught to do in the abbey.

He focused on the sound of folks that passed in the street. He tried to imagine the source of all the noises he heard – hooves trotted on the road, two or three wagons trundled by, several Ladies of the Patient Field sang out a hymn of the Raegods from down the block – eventually the sounds were overwhelmed by a line of heavy footsteps that matched with the clinking of steel, which he guessed might have been a troop of defenders on dawn patrol.

From a very young age he had meditated with the other novices in the abbey, learning the Still Mind mantra, "Still as floating clouds / still as the place between thought / still as steady rain," repeating the only phrase that mattered to him, "Be as still as a floating cloud," again and again until he arrived to a neutral place – aware and unaware.

That stillness lasted for just an instant before all the dreams and curiosities and anxieties of his journey came crashing back into his mind. Meditation was always a challenge when his mind scrambled like a squirrel from tree to tree. He groaned and collapsed onto his bedroll, wondering, *When will I be able to handle this?*

Soon enough, Genshai heard voices and the sound of pans clattering together. He went to the back kitchen and emerged into the light of the morning sun as it fell through the open door. Taisan poured mugs of tea from the kettle and Dannol was frying up a mess of eggs with lard and salt in a cast iron skillet on a tall trivet in the hearth. The coals blazed red and filled the room with warmth and the two men moved in familiar ways, murmuring softly to each other.

"Well, good morning, sleepy," Dannol teased when he noticed the young boy standing in the doorframe.

"How're you feeling?" Taisan asked.

"Better," Genshai nodded, the scenes of his dream beginning to fade. There was still a dull throbbing in his head but his neck felt slightly less tender beneath his fingers, which Genshai counted as an improvement from yesterday.

"I hope you're ready for breakfast," Dannol declared as he set the skillet of fried eggs on the table before turning back to the hearth to pull out a few scorched and blistered red sausages that squealed when he dropped them out of the skillet. With a knife he cut thick slices of wheat bread as he said, "Help yourselves," assembling a plate with one egg, half a sausage, and some bread, before he disappeared into the house.

"This smells delicious!" Genshai exclaimed.

Taisan laughed, "Yes, usually Dannol's larder is well stocked."

"We should stay with Aldermen more often," Genshai said as

he shoved a whole fried egg in his mouth, his cheeks already stuffed with sausage.

It was clear that Dannol had done well for himself, being wealthier than anyone Genshai had ever met. Yet Taisan knew that Dannol made a modest living compared to the Oathlords of the province, and even across the entire kingdom, some of whom lived in palaces and castles with a hundred servants. The young boy had yet to see that level of wealth and the kind of people who wielded it, but Taisan liked the boy's excitement and wisely reminded him, "Remember, we accept generosity but we never expect it."

"I know, but still, let's at least ask him if we can keep one of those pillows."

Taisan laughed good-heartedly and soon Dannol returned from tending to his elderly mother. The two men chatted about their plans for the day. The Alderman said he was going to visit the marketplace within the city walls and that he had a scheduled interview with the High Cleric Vaness that afternoon. They made plans like their lives had been intertwined for years, and sometimes Taisan touched Dannol fondly on the shoulders, or they gripped hands across the table.

They haven't seen each other in months, Genshai suddenly realized. He knew he had been training and traveling with Taisan since the beginning of the year, but it made him wonder how long they stayed apart from each other, and what other kinds of relationships his teacher had with people that he didn't know about.

After breakfast Genshai followed Taisan out the backdoor where the Alderman's house had a stable that was not in use and a broad flagstone courtyard covered in the fallen pink and white starflowers of the neighborhood magnolia trees. Without any explanation the old laymonk walked over to the stable where he rang a bronze bell, giving out several long tones that echoed through the streets of the village. Then he returned with a broom in his hand and said to the boy, "Sweep up all these leaves," before he went to ring the bell again, loudly and clearly.

Genshai knew they were going to train. There were several

bells used in the abbey to summon the monks, and it was a regular chore for the novices to sweep the courtyard and clear the branches where they practiced martial arts every day. In fact abbey life was full of chores and schoolwork, lots of warrior training, meditation twice a day, and many different bell tones to call them up to the temple. Rarely did they ring Haegearth's Bell, which was the great bronze bell of Red Tower itself that was only used to mark the New Year, or when a monk died, or during the festivals, since it could be heard across the entire countryside.

Soon the courtyard was swept and voices came down the shady lane around the greathome where folks arrived for dawn exercise. Genshai realized there were more than two-dozen guests who had heard the sound of the bell from the Alderman's house: some older folks, several men and women on their way to work, and even Mattos the guardsmen and his two young sons, were there to learn the Simple Sets. Dannol greeted everyone like they were old friends, but they all took their places behind Taisan as the leader of the class.

At first Genshai was surprised there was such a big following of students, and he mused that the old laymonk taught the more conventional motions of each set instead of his own unique version. The eight movements were stretching exercises set down in the classics by Sibudat that aligned the meridians of their bodies in a way that promoted the flow from the Great Spirit within them. Genshai followed along, remembering the lessons that his very first teacher Heavy Earth had taught him as a novice in dawn classes when he was a child.

Afterwards, one student asked about the fourth set, which was arguably among the more difficult. Receiving the signal from his teacher, Genshai jumped forward and quickly demonstrated the correct movement on both sides of the body. The old laymonk repeated the lines from the Scripts of Being, "Hands trace the body, / the Wise Owl Gazes Behind, / twisting back the spine."

More than half the group followed Genshai's movement while Taisan looked on them flatly, betraying no emotion, just as the masters of Red Tower would do, until he raised a finger and pointed to where Genshai had twisted to his left side like an owl looking at its own tail, and said, "This exercise will benefit the lung meridian, but you can also receive adjustments to your spine and hips as well."

By the end of the hour most folks moved on with their day, and a few even left coins for the laymonk until he had received twenty-two more copper squares and four silver dragons. Taisan nodded graciously to each student that said, "Goodbye teacher," and he replied, "Okay, see you next time," usually knowing their names.

Genshai wondered if they would continue to train. He felt warmed up from the Eight Simple Sets and wanted to practice the Mountain Form, doing a few moves nearby while Taisan said farewell to people. But instead a few old weavers remained in the courtyard to chat with the laymonk, who looked completely at ease without having broken a sweat at all. Dannol disappeared from the courtyard and reappeared after a bit of time with a new robe and sash, wearing the amulet of his office, looking refreshed after the vigorous practice.

Taisan eventually turned to Genshai and said, "Go get cleaned up. We're paying a visit to the Warden today."

In the washroom Genshai used the cistern of warm water and a block of soap to clean his face, feeling the rough bristles of hair growing on his head. He wore the traditional Aeigi from the abbey, which was a thick gray woolen jacket that crossed in front and was held in place by a triple-stitched black belt tied in a knot. His jacket was a little too loose around his shoulders but it was still a durable grappling uniform that also kept him warm, and when he returned to the courtyard his teacher passed him the smooth hickory staff he had carried for the last few months.

In the second hour after dawn the three men moved around the Alderman's house, going down the street until they were in the center road that led toward the north gates of the city. At first, Genshai thought, *Why is everyone staring at us?* Until he realized they each carried long staves, which hardly anyone did, and their clothes were frayed and their boots travelworn. He figured that standing beside the distinguished Alderman most folks saw them and thought they were vagrants, although Genshai had learned there was not much difference sometimes between a beggar and a monk. He did feel, however, that monks carried themselves well as he tried to mimic Taisan's purposeful stride, holding the crown of his head upright and his eyes straight ahead.

They went toward the gates of the keep where Dannol greeted the defenders readily. Some of them even knew Taisan by name, or said, "This way, teacher," leading them under the massive iron grate locked in place by two winches. Genshai looked up at the height of the ramparts, where the sun was just below midday, and he could see the flags of Norr flying in the wind: displaying two brown bears that faced away from each other, departing for the wilderness.

"Much obliged," Taisan said, bowing appreciatively to the guards as they went under the gate into the city that bustled with wagons and travelers, and barkers that called from the corners, and vendors on the side of the street. There were several forges within the city, and a thriving industry of clothiers that processed and refined wool to be spun at the loom, and the harsh smell of their works filled entire city blocks. Many shops and guildhalls were tucked together around the hillside, most of them two or three stories tall, but Genshai couldn't help but to stare up at the Hall of the North ahead of them, made in the lodge style of the northlands with heavy timber beams that crossed each other at the peak.

"That's the Shrine of the Patient Field," Dannol pointed to the green banners that had yellow sheaves of grain encircling a wide horned ox, which the boy had learned were the symbols of Maitreija, goddess of the harvest. The shrine was a massive stone citadel with a domed roof and seven narrow minarets at specific points around the entire building, and there were medallions carved like delicate flowers down the length of each wall. A huge throng of people filled the gaps between eight decorative columns, waiting under the carved panels that depicted the story of the Raegods sowing the world with seeds for the first time.

"What's happening?" Genshai asked.

"The last day of the week is healing day," Dannol said, until he saw the young boy's confused expression and explained that clerics of the shrine offered free healing to the people four times a year during the holy festivals, and on the last workday before Sabat, the day of rest, and sometimes during festival seasons.

"They seem very busy," Genshai observed as the crowds lined up from the door all the way out to the market.

Dannol nodded, "Most people wait until healing day to get treatment, but sometimes emergencies happen," and he explained that he had been trying for years to negotiate with the elderly High Matriarch on the excessive cost of healing from the shrine. He had succeeded in convincing her to at least offer better services to the defenders or anyone with a guild seal, and their wives and children, which helped a good portion of the workers in Norhaal but still left out the serfs and fieldhands, shepherds, livery workers, weavers, and a handful of other professions.

"Then it's good there's a free healing day," Genshai realized.

Dannol shook his head, "That's not my doing. It was after the Healer Queen died the Sovereign set down the decree in the Royal Forum," he said, as he considered the time that had passed, "I'd say it was about six or seven years ago now."

"How did she die?" Genshai asked, although he thought he remembered hearing some stories of it as a boy in the abbey.

"The news was that she died in a fire," Dannol said. "Before that I heard she offered free healing in a chapel in the riverlands, so the king decided to pass the law in her honor."

"People have said that Queen Zayan was the greatest healer in all the five kingdoms and the treatylands," Taisan contributed. "She actually tried to abolish Servitude, but it never passed in the Royal Forum."

"Servitude?" Genshai asked.

"When folks can't pay for healing they become indentured to the shrine," Dannol frowned. "It happens less now than in the old days."

"It is still common enough," Taisan said pointedly.

"Indeed," Dannol nodded as they passed by the shrine of the Patient Field.

Heading into the lower marketplace they went by townswomen that gathered around wagonfuls of fleece, haggling for their bales; and in the corner some of the miller's boys hauled last year's harvest off a small cart to deliver sacks of malt to the local alehouse. Taisan briefly scanned the market, taking little notice of all the heavy materials stacked in the guildhalls where men sold planks of planed oak, or bricks of soapstone and granite, since they had no use for them. In fact, Genshai even spied a stack of red stone, which he would recognize anywhere, since every northerner swore on the tenure of red stone from Auburntown, claiming it could outlast any other castle stone by more than five hundred years.

As if there was an unspoken agreement between the two older men, they soon disappeared to browse at their own pace. The market was noisy and laughter rang out nearby while vendors bartered at their stalls, or under their canvas canopies where they sold all sorts of pewter cookware, oil lanterns, staples of wool dyed every color, ceramic pots, and countless other things. The young monk nervously entered the crowd, stepping lightly between folks like he was walking through heavy bramble in the forest.

The spring had been plentiful to the growers, and Genshai thought, *These tables are neverending!* as he walked by baskets of cucumber, radishes, piles of onions, bulbs of garlic, heads of lettuce, cabbage, and leafy bundles of spinach. There were baskets of every bean imaginable, sacks of fingerling potatoes, even early-ripened beets and carrots that were still coated in soft brown soil. Then he encountered the butcher's alley and his nose prickled with the wet mineral smell of freshly cut meat at the chopping tables where the cleaver dropped through the haunches of a slaughtered lamb, trimming and salting the meat for preservation.

He walked away quickly, wandering over to a stall of cheesemakers, a family of busty and round girls who scooped a bit of soft cheese onto flatbread for him, before one of them squeezed his arm and asked laughingly, "Are you really a monk?" making him blush, much to their amusement. Abashed, and a bit confused he couldn't help but to just steer himself away, as he thought, *What do I even say to a girl?* feeling very ill-prepared after growing up in the abbey surrounded by boys of all ages.

Naturally, Genshai was curious about girls and sometimes his friends Beryl and Tennan gossiped about the ladies of Auburntown who visited the abbey with their families. They imagined their lives and developed crushes without knowing anything about them. Genshai was even envious of Tennan, who had kissed a girl during the last midsummer festival, but then surprised everyone by taking the Oath to become a monk at the New Year.

Suddenly he saw girls everywhere. They walked through the marketplace and stood at every stall, women of all ages buying and selling, chattering with each other as they kept an eye on their children. They were the wives that ran the shops while the men labored in the field, and Genshai saw an entire row of girls just about his age in green school dresses with yellow hems as they ran away from the shrine and disappeared into the marketplace.

The boy exhaled sharply and rubbed his eyes; his cheeks flushed all the way to his ears as he turned away. He looked around for something familiar and saw over the heads of the crowd the sun glinting off the iron tip of his teacher's hickory warrior staff. He found Dannol and Taisan outside the lower markets browsing the back of the alchemist wagon filled with gourds of pungent potions, jars of salves and ointments, numerous books of all types, and scrolls tucked into every spare cranny.

The alchemist was a Dweroh fellow wearing a scholar's robe, talking casually with them as the Alderman purchased a new box of tindertwigs and a flagon of elderberry tonic for his mother. Like most Dweroh he was not much taller than Genshai's chest, with skin the color of brown and red clay, wearing a woven cap that did little to contain his tangles of gray and black hair. He had large hands and feet, round ears, and a long beard woven with brass rings that descended to his waist.

The boy examined a single arrow from a barrel of a hundred arrows until the alchemist said shrewdly, "Be careful with that, boy. It's coated in poison," and Genshai raised his eyebrows with alarm. He cautiously returned the arrow to the barrel with the tip down while all of the older men exchanged grins and Dannol couldn't help but to laugh and cough until Genshai realized they were pulling a prank on him and he tried to smile good-naturedly, feeling a bit embarrassed, but mostly nervous the alchemist would try to trick him again.

Genshai saw casks of distillate along one side of the wagon, baskets of unusual gems and crystals, and wooden crates with corked jars of every color. Nothing was labeled, but there were gray and white mineral powders, sprigs of ridge pine and boughs of rare hemlock, feathers of every type and even a collection from the wings of giant eagles from the Highlands; lumps of iron ore, or salt from inside the mountains, and many other things that Genshai, wide-eyed, had no explanation for.

They admired a table of delicate objects placed over several striped linens that fluttered slightly in the wind. There were glass goblets and chalices of various sizes, and quite a few handblown smoking pipes streaked with color; even a mirror encased in bronze where any person looking down would see their own reflection, which was a curiosity for Genshai who had rarely seen his own likeness except in pools of water, making him look closely. He saw that his eyes were so brown they looked black. His skin was amber brightened by gold, and he had a scar through one eyebrow and his nose was broad from being flattened half a dozen times in sparring with his brothers. His shorn head was dark with new growth after more than a week away from the abbey and Genshai even noticed a sparse black mustache above his lips.

With fluency, Taisan asked in Dwern, "Dá cloiche an táinag kom Hylmrode du vilken?"

The alchemist blinked and answered naturally, "Mit dhaoine ved bukten arkus síos kystvagen tial estvann."

"Estvann kan vaere slaveskopp kynnertaght tráilleagh fra Kenan."

The Dweroh shrugged and said in the king's speech, "There are dangers for travelers no matter where you go."

"Sant nokka," Taisan acknowledged in Dwern, looking down at the table of glasswork as he asked, "How much for the reading lenses?"

"Four crowns," the alchemist replied.

"Móran takk," Taisan thanked the man, peering through a strip of glass that promised anything within ten inches would be magnified, but after a while he set it down and selected a new box of tindertwigs.

"I'll pay for it," the Alderman quickly offered, palming several gold Aurants into the alchemist's hand. "And we'll take that reading glass as well."

"That's very kind, my friend, but that's not necessary," Taisan declined.

"I want too," Dannol insisted, "You should have it if you need it."

"Well, I suppose you have my thanks," the laymonk said, not wanting to make too much of the situation as he took the piece of glass wrapped in a cloth and carefully placed it in a small pocket of his pack.

Soon they stepped away from the wagon to ascend the road on the hill and when they were out of earshot Dannol asked, "What did he say?"

"His people are in the north cliffs, and he comes down the stone road by way of eastwater," Taisan replied easily. "I've always avoided that road since the region is treacherous with slave ships from the Empire of Kenan, but he seems willing to take the risk."

The Alderman's eyes glinted. "You're full of surprises, aren't you?"

Taisan looked quickly at his student beside him as he said, "Well, when you're in other lands, you may as well learn other languages," and by now Genshai was fairly accustomed to when his teacher spoke Dwern, since they had already traveled all the way to Hylmstone together where he spoke the local language to the merchants the entire time they were there.

The boy looked back over his shoulder, fascinated by the alchemist, wondering what strange skills the man could work until Taisan explained, "Alchemy takes a specialized knowledge like what the clerics teach at Seers Point, or the scholars learn from the Library of Bardánnes."

Genshai said with dismay, "But we only bought tinders from him?"

"We don't have a great need for their wares," the laymonk shrugged. "Maybe if we were glassworkers, or clerics, we might need a lot more. Even the chandler buys lye from the alchemist, and the brewers can get dried yeasts that are from other parts of the world, but monks have little use for their chemistries."

"The Fifth Marshal of the Sovereign's army keeps an alchemist at Yearie Barracks," Dannol interjected.

"For what?" Genshai wondered, thinking they might be brewing their own beer.

"For making warfire," Dannol replied as if it were obvious.

Genshai realized they hardly had time for more questions as they arrived to the high square wooden doors of the great lodge of Norr. He was distracted when he observed three girls wearing shrine school dresses running past the guards, their hair bouncing freely around their shoulders. The boy trailed behind, daydreaming, wondering if he should ask Taisan what to say to a girl just as the Alderman pronounced with a tone of deep respect in his voice, "Here we are, the Hall of Norr."

———

Passing the knights at the entrance they emerged into a long hall built of massive timbers that crossed toward a peaked ceiling. There was a line of several wooden tables in the center and chandeliers with unlit tallow candles hung overhead, and three large wrought iron braziers stood on either side of the room. Norhaal was an ancient homestead where the Warden had lived for longer than a thousand years, and at the head of the hall was a massive stone fireplace, above which hung a regal tapestry of a mammoth brown bear that approached from out of the wild – and even Genshai knew that it was the image of the legendary bear that once protected the northlands, and that it was his son, a man raised in his cave in the forest, that became the first king in the north.

There were a few servants bustling around the hall and they recognized a group of magistrates from their black robes with red thread and the official round headcaps that marked them as judges in the lower courts. "Excuse me," Dannol said politely to the laymonks, striding away to join another Alderman and three or four Oathlords who wore silk tunics and ornate sideswords on their hips.

A few people greeted Taisan warmly, and one maidservant asked, "Are you the laymonk of Red Tower?" as she explained that one of the monks in the abbey was her younger brother. He was called Kaelder and her parents had given him up some twenty years ago, but she said he wrote letters to her quite often and his abbey name was Oakheart. The laymonk listened politely as she told a story of her family visiting two years ago for the abbot's midsummer discourse, spending the day and evening with Kaelder so that he could at least meet his nieces.

"I know he's not supposed to have attachments, but I miss him," she said, putting a letter in Taisan's hands in the hope that it would get to her brother.

While the two of them talked, Genshai found himself walking down the length of the great hall in awe, standing on heavy flagstone tiles as he gazed upward at the highest ceilings he had ever seen. It was one of the last original strongholds that remained in the northlands from when the Hebra people began to unite around the Norr banner more than millennia ago in the Age of a Thousand Swords. Over the centuries the earthen walls were reinforced with stone, additional wings were built that crossed the hall, and now three towers rose up on the hill; but still it was all strangely so familiar that Genshai felt he had been there before.

Following an instinct, he wandered through an arched frame into an adjoining corridor until he found a heavy walnut door propped open by a bronze cast carving of a bear. The room was square with arched glass windows framed in black iron along the south side, and Genshai's eyes widened at the rows and rows of shelves filled with books of all kinds. *This has to be the biggest collection in the north!* he thought as he walked by hard leather tomes, or vellum-covered journals, stacks of Annuaries from Seers Point, and even slotted shelves that contained hundreds of scrolls.

Beside the arched windows was a long wooden table with shallow bins for sorting letters that arrived from the courier's office, some of which had yet to be read and were still sealed by wax. At the far side of the table there were several ledgers, a wood-handled sigil of two bears looking away from each other, and a silver-tipped quillpen and dry inkstone set out for writing, although Genshai was particularly drawn to a large map of the Norr Province spread between several heavy brass paperweights. Even though he had memorized the parts of the world in the abbey, he was newly fascinated by the illustration of the northlands now that he had become a traveler on the road.

He saw that the Auburn Range spread for six hundred miles across the northern ridge of Norr Province from the Gulf of Elesem to the saltcoasts of Westcliff, with Red Tower Abbey sitting nearly in the middle. The Warden's lands themselves were more than a thousand miles across from the last valleys of Anáshaigo all the way to the Auburn Range. On the map there were lines that split the northlands into many fiefdoms assigned to the Oathlords and his knights. Some were granted one acre of farmland or forest, while others with old ties to the Norr family controlled huge regions with hundreds of acres and multiple villages under their governorship.

Distracted, Genshai was looking down at the map when someone entered the room, pausing in the doorway, she demanded, "Who are you?"

Genshai glanced up, frozen in shock as he realized that he had been inadvertently creeping around the lodge uninvited. It was a girl around his age in the school dress of the shrine with wavy jet-black hair around her shoulders. She held her hands on her hips with an expectant look on her face as she said, "What are you doing in here? This is the Warden's study. You aren't supposed to be here."

"I'm sorry, I mean, my pardons," Genshai stammered awkwardly, stepping away from the table. "I'm here with my teacher, Taisan, I mean, the laymonk. We're from Red Tower. We were summoned by the Warden."

She looked him up and down suspiciously, "You're a monk?"

"Yes," he grimaced, not exactly confident in any answer he might give as long as this girl was staring at him.

"Wait here," she said abruptly, narrowing her black eyebrows, "Don't touch anything," before she vanished down the corridor.

Genshai considered that he could have easily escaped in the amount of time she was gone, but soon enough the girl returned followed by another woman whose voice rang into the room, "Well, you aren't the Enduring Mountain," nearly laughing in surprise at the sheepish boy in baggy clothes that stood in her husband's study holding a hickory staff.

He gawked at the sight of the cleric standing in the doorframe. She was about his height and athletic, and appeared to be in her early twenties, with brown eyes that looked at him amusedly, and long thick, dark hair that descended around her shoulders. It seemed that Maitreija, the goddess of the harvest, had a fondness for maidens of the northlands because this woman wore the green cambric dress like most Ladies of the Patient Field, but also the yellow flower vestments around her neck as if she had just come from attending services in the shrine.

"Eryn, go find Taisan," the Lady said to the girl, adding, almost as an afterthought, "and my husband."

They were left alone and Genshai stood motionless as the two of them observed each other. He had never met a woman of her status before. She had an oblong face with smooth cheeks like golden honey, and he thought she looked extremely poised and beautiful until he was uncomfortable with her calm stare.

She asked politely, "What's your name?"

"Genshai," he said, and without thinking he offered his abbey name, "Mountainroot."

She was bemused as she answered, "I'm Vaness, but I suppose they call me the Lady of Norr around here."

Genshai moved stiffly around the table, not sure what to say to the Lady Norr, while she watched him with a curious expression. He remembered Dannol had said that she and the Warden were recently married last year after she returned from studying at Seers Point, the lighthouse academy on the southernmost tip of Estato Peninsula more than six thousand miles away. The only thing he really knew about the clerics of Seers Point was that they compiled and published the Annuaries that were sent to the abbey every year; which were just soft covered almanacs for the wives of farmers and growers, travelers by land or sea, scholars, alchemists, and lords that wanted to know what to expect for the coming year.

He was grateful when Eryn reappeared outside the door, allowing Taisan to enter first, breaking the silence of the room when he said, "I see you found my apprentice."

"It would seem Genshai anticipated this meeting," Vaness replied, glancing surreptitiously at the boy.

"You're long past due, old man," said a voice with a gruff humor. A man walked briskly around the table, and instantly the room filled with the Warden's authority. Genshai could see why Headel was said to be the 'Son of the Bear' just as his father had been, since the Warden was tall and broad-shouldered, with hairy arms, and expressive brown eyes.

"Lord Warden," Taisan bowed politely at the waist, and Genshai felt compelled to do the same, just as they would do to honor the masters of the Iron Style in the abbey.

It was clear that Headel had been raised within the lodge, and perhaps had even been tutored in that library, since he went easily toward his seat at the end of the table beside the map of Norr. He wore a sword belt and a finely tailored blue and red wool tunic with the crest of the two headed bear on his shoulder, keeping a thick dark walnut beard and short-cropped hair. He only looked to be about twenty-two, not much older than the Lady Vaness, and Genshai thought he remembered hearing a tale that the young heir was thrust onto the seat of power in the northlands when his father died in an accident less than a decade ago.

"We haven't seen you since the wedding last summer," Headel began, and the old laymonk nodded as he recalled standing beside them in the shrine when the two swore their vows. He knew they had been in a marriage pact since childhood, and were finally in the Hall of the North together after many years of waiting.

"I've been training the new laymonk," Taisan gestured, introducing the boy. "This is my apprentice, Genshai."

Headel looked sidelong at Genshai, who tightened his grip on the staff and tried not to tremble at his gaze.

The Warden said bluntly, "Well, you have big shoes to fill."

"I'm constantly reminding him of that," Taisan winked.

"Headel," Vaness said his name with a hidden meaning, the tone of which he understood immediately.

The Warden nodded grimly, coming to the point of his summons as he produced a letter marked with the seal of a sailing ship on blue wax and asked, "Taisan, when were you last in Westcliff?"

"Not for several years, milord," Taisan took the letter in his hands.

Headel grumbled, "My father used to say only ill tidings come from Westcliff."

"This letter was sent by the Matriarch of the shrine there," Vaness said, as she observed that the hearth had burned down over the last hour and was mostly one smoldering log until her assistant Eryn came forward to stack a few dry splits of wood from around the mantle to build the fire.

"I didn't think Westcliff had any shrines," Taisan said, since he knew it was a remote fishing village in the northwest part of the province. Some merchants even believed the saltcoasts were cursed and that there were dire wolves and spiderfolk that lived on the roadside, or even trolls in the cliffs, which further dissuaded travelers from going that far west.

Glancing at her husband the cleric responded, "We sent Headel's cousin there, Lord Wynne, to take over the Oathlord's manor, and his wife to reopen the shrine."

Headel stroked his thick beard thoughtfully. "I never would have sent for you if I didn't know him to be an honest man."

The old laymonk opened the letter, his hazelbrown eyes scanning the page until he frowned, hiding his mouth in his gray beard. "She writes that six ghosts walk under the Lotus in Bloom," using the term the clerics preferred for the full moon.

"Ghosts!" Headel said scornfully. "It seems childish to speak of such things."

"Regardless of that, we need to know the truth," Vaness said earnestly.

The two laymonks glanced at each other significantly as they were reminded of their nights at Ulfghar's Ridge. Genshai's eyes were drawn to the new flames in the hearth as he remembered how the ghosts were raised out of the ground, silvery and translucent, wailing mournfully through the trees for hours. Anyone they touched with their ghastly finger crawled with terror, until young Bolmak sought refuge within the tower and was swallowed into the terrible throat of darkness the instant he entered the door.

Genshai snapped back to attention when Taisan declared, "Milord, by your leave we will go to parley with these angry ghosts."

"What?" the boy looked at his teacher.

"That is what I hoped you would say," the Warden nodded. He turned to his wife and asked, "Would that work?"

The High Cleric was thoughtful as she said, "I must consult the godmarks," moving around the stacks of shelves to a desk on the far side of the room. She returned with a bronze platter carrying eighteen round stones that were each engraved with a different symbol, tossing them at random into the rising flames of the hearth. She stacked on a few more pieces of dry wood until she was satisfied, eventually standing up to say, "I have a meeting with Dannol about the plans for the new shrine."

"Then we'll resume before suppertime," Headel decided.

Genshai was confused, not really understanding what they were all waiting for, although he was grateful to take a break from the discussion as he was now dwelling on the events of Ulfghar's Ridge. Taisan told the boy he was free to look around and instructed him to return to the library by eventide. The doors closed behind him as he left and Genshai realized the old laymonk was meeting with the Warden alone, which suited him since his curiosity for politics was content for now.

By then it was late in the afterfade and Genshai found himself wandering through the great hall gazing up at the crossed timbers until Eryn caught up to him, asking skeptically, "So you're really a monk then?"

"I took the Oath," Genshai affirmed shortly, until he explained, "The abbot said I'm going to be the laymonk."

Eryn appraised him. "You don't look like you're a warrior."

"Well, you don't look like much either," Genshai stumbled, unable to think of anything more clever to say, and she just snorted and laughed at him.

Changing the subject she suggested, "let's go outside," and he nodded a bit nervously, allowing her to lead him across the main hall and into the old servant's corridors, through a huge kitchen with three hearths and two brick ovens, bustling with cooks, before they ducked quickly out a small service door to where an enormous vegetable garden grew along the hillside. There were some old gardeners nearby wearing wide-brimmed straw hats to shade their faces, kneeling on the ground, hardly caring about two children walking in the late afterfade.

They went down the farthest rows on the west side of the lodge until Eryn said, "My mistress had all these planted," pointing to massive flowerbeds blooming with lavender, white elderflower and chamomile, violets, goldenrod and honeysuckle, and a dozen other types, explaining that Lady Norr wanted to attract insect pollinators into the area. Thousands of honeybees went between the flowers, nestling within their petals in search of nectar before returning to their hives on the north side of the keep.

"She seems very wise," Genshai commented.

"Oh she's wiser than any of the Matriarchs in the shrine I've ever met," Eryn nodded. Then she narrowed her dark eyebrows on the laymonk and said dubiously, "And your teacher, is he really a warrior?"

"I bet he's the greatest warrior in the north, except maybe some of the masters in Red Tower," Genshai boasted.

"Where's his sword? Don't you need a sword to be a warrior?" Eryn asked, to which Genshai gave her a sharp look. "Okay, sorry, I guess you don't need swords."

Soon they were on the north side walking past the shadow of the lodge but still on the rise of the hillock. Honeybees drifted through the air between the hives, and from where they stood he could see the Auburn Range in the distance, wreathed in forest and crossing the north horizon in blue and gray tipped peaks. It had to be three hundred miles away or more, and still he imagined that he could just make out the slender Red Tower, standing vigilant on the mountaintop.

She asked, "Is it true that monks know about ghosts and spirits?"

"My teacher does," Genshai said, considering all he had seen from Taisan over the last few months.

Actually there were some monks who spent their entire lives studying spirits and ghosts and monsters. Some had supposedly even entered the spirit country, although the most famous was Elosai the Sage, who had returned with the Lotusblade of Sibudat; the story was a well-known legend among the boys of the abbey, and he thought of his friends Beryl and Astel, who were appointed to become scholars when they took the Oath last winter, and how they loved to read about the spirits. He lamented that he had only spent a single night back at Red Tower; otherwise he might have had time to ask if they knew anything about angry ghosts, or if they even believed anything he had seen.

"Are you scared to go to Westcliff?" she asked pointedly.

"Of course not," Genshai shook his head and kept his misgivings to himself since he did feel a bit hollow and frightened when he remembered those three nights at Ulfghar's Ridge.

"Well, I'm jealous," Eryn said, which distracted him. "I never get to go anywhere. I was born here, and the farthest I've ever been is to the Gulf of Elesem for my sister's wedding."

"Won't you go to Seers Point one day?" Genshai asked.

"That's for highborn girls," Eryn frowned, and explained that she was the youngest of three daughters to a knight of the Warden, which was a position of some status even though her father did not have any major titles or lands except a greathome within the walls of the city. It would be expensive for her to travel all the way to Estao Peninsula, and to pay tuition to the academy would be more than her father could afford, and besides the matchmakers had already received marriage inquiries about her from several suitable boys in the northlands; although Eryn was clearly offended that her father had concealed from whom they came from, or whether or not he had responded, since he didn't want her consorting with boys at formal events in the great Hall of Norr.

"Is that how it works then?" Genshai asked. "In the shrines?"

"Sometimes," she shrugged. "There are all sorts of clerics. I guess I could keep learning at the Patient Field, but if I were taught in the lighthouse I would know the Schools of Lore and could command a higher brideprice! Or at least marry someone I might actually want to marry."

"Your sister is married, then?" he asked.

"My oldest sister is!" she exclaimed, before she grumbled, "I hate her husband. The magistrate of Fellview in the eastwaters, which is more than two hundred miles from here! Tell me, when will I ever see her again? I don't know! After all, she'll probably be pregnant soon."

Then she told him that her father was trying to settle the match with her middle sister, who was sixteen already and desperate to be married to a handsome young knight from Sawyertown. They were clearly in love, but the matchmakers said the position of the stars in comparison to their birthcharts were not favorable for marriage until the seventh month, Janien, in midsummer. Eryn talked animatedly while they sat on the north hillside, and Genshai found that talking to girls was easy if he could just listen, and he saw her eyes flash and her amber skin was bright in the fading rays of the sun.

"They had better let them get married already," Eryn giggled. "If they keep this up she'll definitely be pregnant before midsummer," and Genshai couldn't help but to laugh with her.

"What are birthcharts?" he asked carefully.

Her jaw dropped in surprise but she quickly recovered herself. "You know, a birthchart, it shows how all the stars were positioned when you were born."

"Oh," Genshai said as he considered this. Of course he knew nothing about his birthchart, nor had he ever had a real birthday, since as an orphan of the abbey he and his brothers rarely knew when or where they were born. Truthfully, his only real knowledge of the brideprice custom, or marriage inquiries, and matchmakers, came from the old stories of the early dynasties in the Age of Sovereigns, when kings would barter for queens, brokering alliances, extending their lineage, and even sometimes when they were desperate to marry for love. Now he was beginning to realize that the rules for love were more complicated than he thought, which made talking to girls that much more intimidating.

Eryn looked at him curiously, her black hair falling around her face in the wind as she asked, "So where else have you been?"

"Well, we just returned from the Namaya Highlands," Genshai said, describing the stone roads, which were long and at times narrowed to a single lane through the wilderness, occasionally crossing at the head of a valley before going on for miles in either direction. "My teacher says all Hylmrodes lead to Hylmstone," Genshai quoted.

"The laymonk is a funny kind of man," she commented, gauging his reaction.

"That's an understatement," Genshai rolled his eyes. "When we were hiking on the stone roads he only spoke Dwern to me for weeks."

She snorted and laughed, "Really?"

"Yeah, he wanted me to learn it for when we met the Dweroh at Hylmstone."

"You've really been to Hylmstone?" Eryn's eyes widened, gleaming a bit like the gems and jewels she imagined there. "Tell me about it!" she demanded just as a bell began to ring from one of the three towers on the hillside.

They looked to the east where the land was dark in the late eventide, and Eryn shouted, "Come on! We're late!" and they ran quickly together through the flower gardens, rounding the edge of the lodge and passing through the huge square double doors with frenzied laughter. The guards didn't even bother to stop them since they just seemed like two children running down the great hall, disappearing somewhere long before any grown man could catch up to them.

———

Eryn turned down an adjacent corridor that crossed the main hall, coming upon the closed study. They slowly pushed open the heavy wooden door and entered into the shadows cast by the bookshelves, broken by the red glow of embers in the stone hearth. Their older counterparts were already gathered there and they came up behind Taisan who stood with folded arms, his gray brows furrowed in concentration as smoke from the Warden's pipe drifted in lazy loops and Vaness held broad tongs to sift through the remains of the fire.

"Eryn, the zodiac tray," the Lady commanded, to which the young girl instantly appeared where she was needed. Vaness' face was tense, her brow beaded with sweat. By now she had changed into a simple green linen dress that was light and durable for when she was working in the forests, or on the open water, or under the stars, and also a creased and used leather apron that had followed her through classes in the alchemy shop at the academy. She was very careful since dropping a stone would mean an incredibly bad omen from the gods. The tongs simmered as the last of the eighteen godmarks settled at random on the circular bronze plate, which Eryn held in both hands, placing it directly onto a coarse green cloth spread across the middle of the table.

Everyone gathered to look over the stones. They hissed with heat, some of them red and emblazoned, others blackened with soot or whitened by ash. Each stone was about the size of a man's fist and carved with the symbols for the greatest Raegods of the heavenly island, though some appeared cracked from previous rituals. The circumference of the bronze plate was marked with the sign for each month of the year in the manner of the zodiac, with the six remaining stones placed inside the midseason, each one indicating where the gods had sent their auspices for her to interpret.

The Lady of Norr observed how each godmark was laid. She looked at their orientations with each other, taking mental notes as she analyzed the placements for several minutes in the fading light of the hearth. Eryn seemed to keep herself occupied by building up the fire, though Vaness had no doubt that her young handmaiden was curious about the secrets of the Runelore. Like most girls, she had learned in the shrines that the Golden Mother's right-hand advisor, Amaritabhe the Wise, set down the eighteen symbols that represented the gods and left them out on loose pages for mortals to find long ago in the Lost Age. Some scholars had even suggested the godmarks formed the basic symbols of the first common language known as High Arovian that was now comprised of more than five thousand characters.

Soon a lantern was lit and Vaness disappeared down a far aisle and plucked an old reference book from one of the shelves. After less than a year of marriage she had already taken over half the library with her own books, even if it was technically the Warden's study. She reviewed the symbols once again and compared their astrological placements on the zodiac tray to what was illustrated on the old hemp pages, wanting to confirm her conclusions. Vaness returned to the long table ahead of the windows and reached for the quill, dipping the tip into the well of the inkstone to compose a few notes of her own, leaving everyone in suspense as she wrote neat characters in columns down the blank page of a journal that was filled with hundreds of notes from previous readings.

The Warden moved a pewter tray toward himself on which he blended pinches of tobacco and sweetleaf into the bulb of his blue glass pipe. He struck a tindertwig, puffed four times, and filled the room with the noxious yet sweet smell of the smoke. He seemed to look once at the zodiac plate, taking in the signs at a glance before he turned away and waited in silent anticipation. Meanwhile Genshai was extremely curious, since the abbey hardly taught anything about the intricacies of the zodiac. He had only known the twelve months of the Eurysus Calendar and the regular festivals of the year, never fully realizing that they were named after the gods of heaven until now.

"The Raegods have spoken," the High Cleric finally said with a solemn gesture toward the zodiac tray that sat adjacent to the map of Norr Province. The stones were just beginning to cool even as the bronze tray remained warm to her touch. She took one last look at the placements, wanting to be certain before she pointed to the stone blazing red and marked with the crux, the key of life. "In the first place is the Golden Mother, Aurelai, who created the world," tracing her finger across the tray. "She is turned toward the sign of the harvest, which sits on the waning spring," as she indicated the stone marked with the oxen rune of Maitreija that rested upon the position of Vilikai, the fifth month of the year.

Vaness continued, "Today, I am the cleric of Maitreija that calls out, so the Mother speaks to me," and the group watched as she dipped her quill to carefully take down a note into her journal.

She soon resumed. "Some gods are quiet," referring to the stones turned down at angles that obscured the symbol, "but Adak-Purkah speaks." She pointed to the sign of the hammer that gleamed a pale red and sat in the eleventh place on the platter, facing outward. Even Genshai knew that it was the symbol for the god of the mountain, since the people in Hylmstone honored it everywhere.

Vaness explained, "The Forgemaster rests over his own month, suggesting the Dweroh people are readying their fortifications."

"Well, it's hardly unusual for them to guard the highlands," Headel commented, "Now that the gulf is thawed the slave ships will be…"

Vaness held up a hand. "Look, the Silver God Amaritabhe the Wise speaks," indicating the sign of a chalice in the seventh place, which was the month of Janien that belonged to Maitreija, the time when midsummer was celebrated every year.

"The Silver God looks toward Toru the Cat, the god of wanderers," Vaness gestured to the short distance from the seventh place and the inner circle where a stone was marked with the sign of roads and sat between the months of summer and autumn. "Which suggests it is wise for us to follow the counsel of the laymonk," she raised a palm toward Taisan.

Then she said with a hint of confusion, "The other Raegods turn their faces from me, except the Watcher," pointing to the sign of the eye.

"The Watcher?" Headel asked, also with a tone of uncertainty.

"Sayessqueaha usually keeps his eye on the Nether," Vaness replied as she inspected the godmark that landed on the second place, the final month of winter. "The Watcher is turned up, staring out for the gods."

"What does it mean?" Taisan asked.

"Something has drawn his eye," she explained, "Which may have happened in Henvidda, three months ago, or will happen in winter next year."

After a moment the Warden asked, "Anything of the harvest?"

Vaness nodded. "The Three Sisters are not aligned," she said of the goddesses of hearth, harvest, and flock, continuing, "but Alloraiha is at home in the zodiac, so I think we are bound for good fortune this autumn," as she pointed to the sign of the cauldron on the ninth place of Allora.

She ceased to speak and there was a long silence after the reading as they each contemplated what messages the godmarks had brought.

The Warden finally said, "It seems that by the will of the gods we are bid to trust your wisdom," leveling his chestnut brown eyes upon the old laymonk.

"So it is." Taisan gave a firm nod.

"You have our thanks," Vaness nodded. "And any provisions we can offer."

At that, there were a few last-minute plans to be made. The older laymonk said they would set out for Westcliff the following morning, figuring that it would be a three-week journey northward by the Second Quarry Road until they came to the crossings that would take them to the northwest coasts of the province. Mesmerized by the zodiac plate, Genshai didn't catch the entire exchange until the Warden said, "It'll save you time if you ride."

"We're going to be riding?" Genshai asked in surprise.

Ignoring the boy, the Warden said, "Here's a note for my livery in the city," and used his wife's quill to scrawl out a message in low-Arovian, stamped with his ink seal of two bears looking away from each other. He also pulled forth a finely bound ledger with notarized sheets of flying-cash, upon which he wrote a formal note for a hundred gold Aurants, once again stamping it with his ink seal before tearing it from the book and passing it to the old monk.

"Send a hawk as soon as you can," the Warden instructed.

With that, the plans were in motion. Everyone broke apart from the table and the laymonks left the room where the Warden and the Lady of Norr seemed to approach each other for more direct talks.

Already the first hour of the evening had whittled away. The tables in the great hall were being prepared for a meal with some of the Warden's closest councilors, and the servants moved briskly through the outer corridors while guests gathered in the main hall near the massive stone hearth. They found Alderman Dannol there with a group of officials under the old banner of Norr, filling his tankard from a cask of farmbier set on a table nearby that was tart and sour, aged with strawberries in the barrel since last summer's harvest.

"I see that you've been busy," Taisan said with a nod toward the tankard. "Committee meetings and drinking?" and Dannol laughed for appearances before he pulled away from the group, touching shoulders and talking in low tones, as if he were eager to speak to him without any listening ears.

Genshai would have followed behind them if it weren't for Eryn, whose eyes beamed with excitement as she came up to him. "That was amazing, I've never seen the godmarks like that!" before she grabbed his hand and said, "Let's get something to eat before it's all gone."

Savory aromas wafted from the kitchens nearby, and they sidled alongside the banquet tables laden with more food than he had ever seen. Folks gathered as much as they pleased onto their plates before they returned to the long table beneath the iron chandeliers, while the Warden and the Lady of Norr sat at the head of the room and received their meals from maidservants, talking with their councilors and laughing with their friends.

"There's so much cheese!" he exclaimed as they came across three cutting boards layered in wedges and cuts of all sorts, some salty and dry, and others smoked and covered in a hard rind. There was even a bowl of soft sheep's cheese mixed with dried cherries and wildflower honey to spread on sliced bread.

"Have you ever had ham?" Eryn asked with an impish grin as she used the tongs to give him several thin slices of pork thigh that had been cured in salt, smoked in hickory, and hung up to mature for three years.

The moist, buttery texture of marbled fat filled his cheeks, and he declared, "That's delicious!" picking up three more slices of ham, accompanied by a handful of cheese, pickled carrots, onions, and cucumbers. They helped themselves to bowls of creamy potatoes and softened parsnips coated in scallions, and then greens and red cabbage that had been cooked in grape vinegar with mushrooms, or blackened sweet carrots, which the boy excitedly piled as high as he could on his plate and ate to his heart's content.

"You think that's good, try this," Eryn said, pointing to the tray of seared lamb chops, golden and slightly charred, but perfectly pink and juicy. She said the chefs in the Hall of Norr would slaughter one or two yearlings every fortnight, biting through the lamb chop until the bone was bare within seconds. Genshai wondered if laymonks were permitted to eat red meat but soon he didn't care since the rich gamey aroma was too tantalizing for him to resist.

"Abbey food is nothing like this," he declared, belching deeply until they were both laughing.

Genshai and Eryn found two seats at the long table and talked for what seemed like hours while the lords and officials dined around them and the candlelight cast flickering shadows along the timber ceiling. "Will you finally tell me about Hylmstone, or do I have to fight you?" Eryn said as the gleam returned to her eyes, and her little fist glanced off his hard shoulder.

So he told her the story of when they came to the place where three Hylmrodes converged, gradually leading down into the valley nestled within the shoulders of a high peak called Mount Durin, capped in white snow and sheets of cloud. The Dweroh seemed to appear out of the ground itself to meet them, and Genshai had learned that most of their homes were indistinguishable from the surrounding forests, except for the old stone stairwells that led down to wooden doors and into earthen tunnels.

Most of the Dweroh stood no higher than a Hebra man's chest but they possessed nearly the same strength. Their skin was like clay, or brown soil, or granite, or any color of the earth, and some were fully bearded while others had proud mustaches with broad chins or neatly trimmed goatees, heavy brows, and wide noses. The women all appeared to be of similar build to the men, with curly black or auburn hair, kept long or in plaits, and usually woven with wooden beads, rings of copper or silver, or stone pendants etched with runes.

"I was so curious!" Genshai confessed to her. "I hiked for months in the highlands with just my teacher for company, and I really wanted to see the doors of Hylmstone I've read so much about."

"What about the eagle riders?" she interrupted. "Did you meet any of them?"

"I never did," he shook his head. "I guess there's only two or three of them every generation, and they're pretty reclusive. I think I did see one of the eagles though, but it was extremely high in the sky so it's hard to say."

Instead he told her about descending the valleyside where hundreds of Dweroh made their homes in terraces carved into the cliffs. The road was lined with twenty-four obelisks that cast their shadows toward the legendary steel-paneled doors of Hylmstone, which opened outward to reveal the immense cavern within where endless arches and pillars and tunnels had been carved by miners for centuries. The cavern itself was enormous, yet Taisan had advised him that sitting in a chair was the most comfortable way to talk to Dweroh, and the young laymonk could see why since every other passageway or household was so short in height that they were forced to crane their heads or duck under doorframes to pass through.

"How short was it?" she asked teasingly.

"About here," he said, gesturing to his collarbone height, and being just shy of six feet tall Genshai had decided to stay in the main cavern to browse the rock and mineral markets. The sound of hammers rang through the tunnels and there were wheelbarrows full of cut stone waiting to be loaded onto merchant wagons, and long sturdy pine tables holding crate after crate of ore veined with iron, or even silver, and gold. He saw boxes of polished agate and crystals, displays of jeweled amulets, glittering pendants, bracelets, and rings, all made by the finest smiths and gemcutters in the entire world. The Dweroh bought and traded with hammered coins, not that the laymonks carried more than a few pennies anyway, and eventually Genshai went away from Hylmstone without any kind of trinket, bearing only the memory of the place.

"It sounds amazing," Eryn shook her head. "You're so lucky you get to travel the world."

"I never went past Auburntown until this year," Genshai admitted. "The abbot told me to 'Cast aside the past, / the future is not yet here, / live in the moment.'"

Her eyes squinted and she laughed, "Is that some abbey wisdom, then?"

"I guess so," Genshai shrugged, embarrassed.

"Well then how do I know you're not going to just leave and never come back?" she taunted, and they laughed and inched closer, seeking opportunities to graze against one another's arms and legs. It was well past the darkhour of midnight and the candles had burned down when Taisan came along and said they were leaving for the Alderman's house. Reluctantly the boy said goodbye and the girl smiled, rubbing her palm across his bristly head. They wanted to remain together or extend their time without knowing what to say, or how to ask for it, so Genshai promised to search for her the next time he was in Norhaal, and Eryn gave him a light kiss, like a soft breath of wind on his cheek that sent him walking cheerfully into the night.

They descended the road through the city and soon Genshai went ahead to tell the defenders to open the gates for the esteemed Alderman, and after they rounded the corner of the street into the darkness below the magnolia trees Dannol looped his arm through Taisan's elbow as they walked. For so many years the two men had resisted displaying affection to each other, wanting to avoid the gossip of the townspeople, or the magistrates and other councilors, but Taisan knew that Dannol yearned for them to be together, even if they would never be able to get a marriage certificate from the shrine.

"I'll have to talk to the boy," Taisan said. "One day here and he's already found a girlfriend."

Dannol chuckled, "Well he's a handsome kid, and soon he'll be taller than us."

"And outweigh us both," Taisan nodded, seeing that his student would be formidable one day.

"I had hoped you would stay longer," Dannol said with a hint of regret.

"I know," the old laymonk patted his partner's hand, frowning in the darkness as they walked.

Taisan had come to expect this kind of thing from Dannol on his departures, even after they had been in love for many years. He thought somberly of his new possession, the reading glass. It was a good gift to be sure, but Taisan rarely carried trinkets or mementos, and already he was planning to drop off the lens to the abbey library next time he was home. It had always been the way he lived. Without attachments to places on the road or people within time – only filling his eyes and ears with what moments were unfolding before him.

"I've missed you," Dannol said and they were reminded of the last time they were together when he had demanded that Taisan make a choice and they had argued about what his commitments really were, then the laymonk disappeared for more than half a year and Dannol feared he had chased him away.

"I'm glad to see you take an apprentice. Maybe soon your labors will be over?" which was not a subtle question.

Yet Taisan's entire life was devoted to Red Tower, and he could not leave a task undone. Already his thoughts were gripped by news of the hauntings at Westcliff and the urgent mystery of six ghosts at midnight. He already felt the thrill of a new quest rising within him, growing into an impatient wanderlust that would always take him away from Dannol, whether for Red Tower or not.

Taisan had decided long ago that this life suited him, and he knew that what the Alderman desired most – a family and a partner – were just fanciful dreams for the laymonk. Tomorrow he would be gone and Dannol would be alone yet again, and it would always be like that. He never sought to hurt his closest friend, but he knew he would never cease to wander.

And besides things are different now, Taisan thought as he considered the joys and burdens of having Genshai in his care. The boy filled a void in his spirit, that much was true. When they practiced the Mountain Form together, Genshai's eyes were so brown and intent they were like coal, and Taisan felt a great desire to ensure the legacy of all that he had done for Red Tower and the people of the northlands. He knew the boy would carry pieces of him into the future, in a way that was still inconceivable.

CHAPTER THREE

SOME DAYS IN LATE VILIKAI, THE LAST MONTH OF SPRING, 1019 EC

In the Scripts of Identity, Sibudat says, "All myriad things / carry immortality / within their spirits."

RANGERS OF THE FARWOOD

By midmorning the next day they were heading quickly through the streets, accompanied by Alderman Dannol as they passed under the upraised iron gates and entered the lower markets of the city inside the wall. The guildhalls were closed along with most shops and stalls in the square, and the crowds in the streets were thinner than yesterday since most folks were at the shrine for Sabat, honoring the gods on their day of rest. People still greeted them politely, and one or two defenders saluted them the way brothers of the abbey would bow respectfully to their teachers, and the boy felt compelled to stand taller and hold his staff forward.

Actually, it was quite difficult for Genshai to maintain pretenses since he had been sick to his stomach most of the morning, wondering if something he had ate last night wasn't settling well with him. At dawn when he jumped up from breakfast to use the Alderman's washroom, Taisan had said, "I warned you not to eat so much rich food last night," since the boy had grown up on temple food, which was strictly vegetarian, and the hearty fare of the Warden's banquet was rich and delicious, but strangled his stomach.

He managed to keep himself distracted from his gurgling belly as they made their way along the main road around the hillock toward the west side of the lodge where they arrived to the Warden's livery to meet his manservant, who wore a green and blue cotton tunic with a patch of a two-headed bear sigil on his shoulder. Genshai looked cautiously around the corner at the horses in their stalls and noticed that a young stable boy was leading them by their tack, fastening the buckles of their saddles and clicking his tongue, completely at ease. Just as they had been promised they were given two horses outfitted with spare riding saddles, though Genshai looped the wrong foot in the stirrup and couldn't swing his leg over.

"Ain't you ever ridden a horse before?" the stable boy asked.

"Not yet anyway," Genshai grumbled.

The boy leapt up, scrambling easily onto the horse which was clearly too big for him. "This is Meora. She's two years old. She still has a little attitude, but she's usually good for a long ride when the weather is fair," he said as he wheeled the horse around the yard of the livery, acquainting Genshai with his new mount. Meora was a chestnut mare with an auburn mane that had been trimmed short and a swirl of white between her eyes, ready for a long journey. Eventually Genshai was able to swing his leg over and take a seat, and he began to learn the basic movements of the reins to direct the horse as the stable boy barked out directions from the ground.

Taisan took the opportunity to visit the courier's office nearby. The young runners carried letters in every direction through the city and the surrounding shires. There were a number of sorting shelves in the front room and the sounds of pigeons cooing could be heard from the aviary around the back. They used birds for urgent messages quite often, but usually letters or packages could be carried long distances by a rider on horseback, or a postal wagon, for a fee depending on the number of miles traveled. Sometimes the runners were robbed on the road, but these days that was the risk any traveler might take to find honest work.

He had two letters to send. One for Oakheart from his sister, and the other was addressed to Horn of Ram, the abbot of Red

Tower Abbey, which Taisan had written in the forehour of dawn. It was his duty to keep the abbot apprised of the events of their journeys, and he described their meeting with the Warden and the decision to send the laymonks to Westcliff in search of the angry ghosts, noting the progress of his apprentice Mountainroot. The letter was sealed in red wax, pressed with the sign of the tower from the laymonk's iron signet ring, enclosing most of the flying-cash from the Warden, which the abbot would set aside for him to redeem at the lending house in Auburntown when they returned next winter. At a bit per mile and three hundred miles to go, Taisan paid the courier one tarnished crimson coin that happened to be in his purse, six silver Yans, and seven Lirros to get the letters delivered.

Stepping outside the courier's house he rejoined Dannol and watched with amusement as the little stable boy led the mare around in a circle with Genshai in the saddle. The old laymonk was troubled, though he concealed it. He sought to touch Dannol, or to grip his hand and promise him they would be together one day, just as he yearned to be away from the city, free of society and the pressures of love, wandering aimlessly for weeks.

His feelings were complicated, but instead Taisan said, "Make sure to talk to Mattos in class next week, I noticed this morning his breathing is too heavy when he's Punching Heaven With Fire."

Dannol nodded, and said evenly, "I can mention it to him."

"He needs to slow down and only punch when the waist turns," Taisan indicated.

"Of course," the Alderman said, who was quite skilled at the Eight Simple Sets himself, but would never dream of questioning the laymonk's advice.

Taisan extended a wrist, but Dannol moved in for a firm embrace, simply to feel the warmth of his partner's arms around his shoulders one last time. Impassioned, the laymonk kissed him goodbye, and pressed his palm as lightly as a spring breeze on Dannol's bearded cheek. "I'll be back," Taisan whispered and Dannol nodded, withholding his own trembling words. If anyone was paying attention they would have seen the laymonk's tenderness, however brief, and would know instantly the two men were more than old friends.

Taisan went to mount a speckled gray and white destrier that was ready for him, an older horse named Snowcap. The stable boy gave him one or two instructions, and he swung his leg over easily, settling into the saddle. Within a few minutes, the two laymonks were going at a steady gait down the road, even though Genshai grimaced, bouncing uncomfortably in his seat as they went down the hillock and through the west village. Outside the city some farmers nodded politely as they passed, or waved and said, "Safe travels," and one cleric in the holy cloth blessed them with the sign of the crux and said, "May the Mother protect you," as they rode by her.

They went onward, holding their staves aloft until they were all alone on the west road toward the Farwood.

By the afterfade, they were crossing the bridge at the edge of the Springshire, a few miles outside of Norhaal, where they could see the lodge had shrunk on the hill behind them, but as they trotted further and further away, Genshai never felt comfortable in the saddle. At whatever pace they went the boy's stomach grumbled and clenched until he was finally forced to pull up the reins and dismount, running off into the woods while Taisan brought his horse around and chuckled, "I warned you," unsympathetic to the boy's urgency.

Genshai was thankful they were alone on the road since he figured anyone within half a mile would have heard him release his bowels into the ditch. Concealed by the brush, he was desperate for his discomfort to cease when he heard a hoarse cry break from the silence of the forest. A stick snapped and leaves rustled on the ground but Genshai could not see anything through the trees. Quickly cleaning himself with a wool cloth, the boy yanked up his pants, wondering, *Is it a boar?* from all the breathless snorting that came out of a low set of bushes.

There was a fraught squeal and Genshai shouted, "Taisan! Taisan!" just as a dirty bundle came tumbling out of the bushes into his arms.

"Don't tell me you need help," Taisan grumbled, dismounting just as Genshai appeared, awkwardly carrying a baby in his arms.

"Look," he presented the child and Taisan lifted him up like his hands were a gentle cloud. The child whimpered irregularly, covered in dirt and small scratches all over his body and face, barely able to kick his legs, drifting in and out of consciousness as if the last of his energy was spent crawling to the nearest human voice. The diaper wraps were clearly soiled and there was no sign of any swaddling cloth or other supplies, as if the baby was never meant to survive.

"Is there anybody here?" Genshai called several times into the woods, finally deciding they were indeed completely alone.

"I think he's been out here for two or three days." Taisan guessed, "Whoever left him is long gone by now."

"Who would do that?" Genshai demanded, able to see that the baby was on the edge of death, barely breathing, wan and pale, his eyes sealed shut.

"It's not so surprising," Taisan replied, "Nearly all our brothers are abandoned like this."

Genshai had always loosely understood that they were orphans, with no family ties – but not that they were unwanted; abandoned like this by the roadside with nothing to comfort them. Of course it was well known that since the days of Sibudat the monks took in boys orphaned by war or blight or draught, but more often they were the sons of brothels, or they were disabled, or they were the products of rape and incest, and Taisan said, "A trader on the road has every opportunity to leave their extra burden in the woods and never come back."

Rarely did anyone abandon a girl since they had value once they came of marrying age. If their daughter knew the family trade and was educated in the shrine school, then a matchmaker could find the best brideprice offer from all the available choices. Most boys, on the other hand, could hardly read more than their own names. Their only worth was as laborers or fieldworkers, unless they could earn a guild seal, or they joined the barracks to become a man of the Sovereign's army, or a squire for a knight, which was dangerous and expensive even though noblemen like the Oathlords and the Wardens still held much of the legal sway in the world.

More than once Taisan had turned around in a busy marketplace to find a swaddled bundle left at his feet; or occasionally after giving a lesson of the scripts, when the people had dispersed, there would be a child abandoned in the grass. He appreciated when parents asked him directly to take their boy, but mostly they preferred the anonymity and the secret of their humiliation. They were undoubtedly desperate, and hoped that their child could grow up in the abbey and learn to read and write and do arithmetic. Some people truly believed they were putting their sons on the path to Illumination – or at least by the age of fifteen they could pursue their own fortunes.

There would never be answers to the baby's appearance on the road, and Taisan was not in the business of passing judgment, so he wished good tidings to the unlucky parents and surrendered himself to the familiar burden of carrying a baby for many long miles. He was malnourished and a bit smaller than he ought to be, so the old man guessed he was half a year by the weight of him. As if it were a normal habit, Taisan set the baby in the grass to remove his soiled wraps and clean his bottom; then unpacking a few things from his bag he soon held a small pewter flask with a spout against the baby's lips, dribbling some cool water to soothe his little throat. After that Taisan smeared some raspberry jam onto the child's gums, noticing a few nubs where teeth were starting to sprout.

"How far away is Norhaal?" Genshai asked, "Maybe we can double back and find someone to look after him?"

Taisan shook his head, "Who would you give him too?"

"Well we can't just leave him here," Genshai said.

"He's coming with us," Taisan replied as if it were obvious. The old man tucked the child into one side of his Aeigi tunic as he gathered up his things and mounted his horse, and said, "There's a waypost just down the road that we can stop at for the night."

The infant clutched his lean chest with a dreamy expression, and the old laymonk looked onward through the waning light. The only sounds were the cool wind that rustled the trees and bent the long grass, and the hooves of their horses clomping against the ground as they went at a slow walk. The road led to a small river that flowed from the north, crossed by a wooden bridge that spanned fourteen feet with a brush torch on one side. There was an obvious campsite where they secured the horses before Genshai gathered firewood and kindling for the evening meal.

Distracted, there was no martial arts training that night. Taisan remained focused on the baby who started to open his eyes and breathe normally, the golden brown color returning to his big round cheeks. In the meantime Genshai glowered as he unpacked their bags and took care of the horses, thinking he'd rather do that than learn to change the baby's diapers. He slowly figured out how to unbuckle the tack, and Meora nudged him in the cheek and nickered for attention, which distracted his thoughts for a while as he brushed out their flanks.

Taisan set the baby down on his fleece bedroll and struck a tindertwig against the brush torch, tightly woven with dried sage and sweetgrass, dipped in pitch resin that would burn for several hours before it was extinguished. The torches were at every waypost on the northern trails, supplied by rangers who also cleaned the campsites, provided dry firewood, kept the roads clear of fallen trees, and inspected the bridge for damage. Without much need for talking, they heated water in a pot for a simple meal of boiled parsnip and carrots, and Taisan contributed wild garlic, spinach, and fresh laurel leaves he found in the woods, topped with thinly sliced hard cheese and walnuts from the boy's pack that he crushed between his palms.

When the shadows deepened at eventide Taisan stripped to his loinwraps and waded into the shallows of the cool river to bathe, the smooth round stones sliding beneath his toes. The child was naked in his arms and surprisingly calm as he glanced around at the trees in an exhausted daze. The old man cleaned all the child's wounds with soap and it wasn't long before they were dressed again, returning to the campsite to allow Genshai to visit the river alone.

He was more than a little disturbed by the discovery of the child abandoned on the side of the road. Genshai had always assumed that folks made the journey all the way to Red Tower to drop off their unwanted sons to the matron themselves, but now it seemed exceedingly obvious that they were more often abandoned for the laymonk to find. He certainly wasn't looking forward to babysitting, not wanting to get stuck feeding the baby, but gradually he realized that it was now part of his job as the laymonk.

I don't understand, he thought hopelessly. *How will we train? How will we travel, or do anything, if we have to take care of a baby the whole time?*

The stars winked under the shifting trees as they lay back on their bedrolls, the sound of the river coursing in their ears. Taisan cradled the infant under his arm like he was a proud grandfather, reciting a verse from the classics, "Sleep now, gentle child / dream, and bring forth your spirit / and its memories," until the two of them were fast asleep on their backs beside the fire.

Was he like this when he found me? Genshai wondered, feeling envious, but also bewildered as he realized that his teacher probably was the one that brought him home when he was a baby. All at once it became clear that he was also unwanted and that, like today, Genshai imagined the laymonk had come upon him abandoned in the woods, and he resolved that if he could never know his true parents he would at least like to know where in the northlands he was from.

His origin had never mattered much before since he had such fond memories of being raised by the old widow Joyce, who he called grandma since she was in her seventies and had cloudy white tufts of hair. She was the abbey matron and he still remembered just where she lived in Auburntown in a skinny brick townhouse two blocks from the market square. All his brothers were raised the same way and when they were old enough to memorize the Scripts and practice forms she turned them over to the abbey just as she had done with dozens and dozens of other boys over the years.

This was the way of things in the abbey and he had never questioned it. Genshai loved his brothers like they were truly family and until he came down from the mountain he had assumed his upbringing was normal. It was bittersweet as he wondered, *What would I have been if I was never in the abbey?* overcome with empathy for the baby they found under a tree on the roadside, as if by rescuing him Genshai was fulfilling a promise he never knew he had made.

Lying awake he listened to the buzzing and croaking sounds of the forest at night, reaching back into his mind as he remembered his grandma, since he had no real memories of anyone else.

The road meandered for the next three days through the west fields and hills, passing white clusters of yarrow, orange lilies, and purple azaleas blooming in spring. At times the forest pressed on both sides, though they were usually on long farmroads between fields of barley. What might have been a seven-day walk to the village of Faewoden became a four-day ride through the countryside, and Genshai soon began to feel comfortable in the saddle when going at all paces on the road.

The old man inexplicably produced a long silk sling to wrap the baby against his chest, wearing the Aeigi jacket around them both for warmth. Genshai thought he knew everything they were carrying, but Taisan also brought out a smooth wooden teething ring, and two or three linen diaper cloths, not to mention the pewter flask with a spout for the baby to drink from. Taisan sat upright in the saddle for hours. He kept his staff in one hand and the reins of his horse in the other and led Genshai further and further westward, letting the baby melt into his body until he knew all its moods.

They stopped often since the baby was restless, and Taisan

could tell the signs it was time for the child to relieve himself. Dismounting from the horse, the old man just held the baby over the grass with Genshai laughing, "You had better not be downwind of that," but it was easier than cleaning diapers all the time, so Taisan didn't mind. The two of them developed a language of their own and it wasn't long before the baby was staring after Taisan everywhere he went with huge eyes the color of acorns, yearning to be comforted by him.

Meanwhile, Genshai was glad to have the horses for company. He was still learning the commands to use with the reins, but it was largely Meora who taught him what she would respond too. She was young and adventurous; she enjoyed brisk trots in the afternoons and fresh grass in a new pasture, ripe melona fruit from beneath the Season Trees, and water from a spring more than water from a trough.

"We still outnumber him, Snowcap," Genshai joked as he brushed the old stallion's flank, saying, "Oh, stand still now," as the horse bucked his head, releasing an impatient grumble that meant he wanted to be left alone. Genshai imagined that he felt similarly whenever Taisan went off to meditate and he was forced to babysit, a bit resentful for how the baby had changed their routines while traveling.

Eventually Taisan decided, "It just won't do for you to go without a name," settling on Kyus – an old word in the ancient Norr dialect that meant 'rejoice' – which suited him since the baby was quick to smile anytime Taisan interacted with him, and his laughter bubbled up with the other sounds that filled the forest. Taisan swung the baby in his arms and then just as easily corrected his student's stances now that they had resumed practicing forms.

Genshai's entire body received a new kind of shock after several hours of sustained riding. His legs quivered weakly but that didn't mean he was excused from reviewing all the sequences he knew; including the first three Lion Forms, the Seat-of-the-Mountain, and even all Ten Staff Methods, some of which were new fighting techniques that Genshai had not yet learned from the masters of the abbey – his teacher's iron tip ringing out on the ground as he demonstrated every hit.

Nonetheless, all the traveling and martial arts training only seemed to focus Genshai's thoughts to a single point until one night he could not help but to ask, "So then where did you find me?" hoping to appear casual even though he yearned to know.

Taisan was surprised, "Why do you ask?"

"I'm just curious," Genshai shrugged.

The old laymonk was silent for a few moments as he considered the question, finally replying, "What would it change if you knew?"

"Well, what if I have family there?" Genshai insisted. "Maybe they would want to see me."

"The other monks never learn how they come to the abbey," Taisan said. "Why do you think boys like you have no attachments, like family?"

Genshai grumbled, "So there are no distractions."

"That's right, there's no need to burden your thoughts with those earthly tethers." Taisan took a deep, controlled breath, "The classics say we possess no true self. We are just a combination of lives, but it is possible for a monk to shed their ego and Illuminate. The Great Spirit…"

"But I want to know," Genshai interrupted.

"Why should you?"

"Because I'm the laymonk now," Genshai said it like it was obvious, although he didn't know if the question of his origin would have ever mattered if he had stayed at home with his brothers, but ever since they found Kyus it felt like it was burning through him.

"Perhaps." Taisan remained unconvinced and set the matter aside to be discussed another time, leaving Genshai distraught for the rest of the evening. He begrudgingly took care of Kyus, putting him to bed while Taisan meditated. The boy fell asleep early, cradling the baby under one arm while he waited for his teacher to return and woke up hours later in the wet gray forehour of dawn with the child still dozing beside him.

In the last day of the journey heavy white clouds mounted higher in the sky and the winds that blew through the fields and trees were brisk. They came upon a small stream that was barely ankle deep where they bathed in their loinwraps, and Taisan taught Genshai how to hold the razor so that he could shave his face without missing anything, "Not that I get many haircuts," Taisan said as he shook out his curly gray hair, which was fluffy and tangled until he pulled it back into a poofball above his head.

After that he demonstrated how to change the baby's diapers, giving Genshai his first clear look at the child's groin. The boy pointed, "What's that?"

"His penis," Taisan glanced at his student.

"No," Genshai shook his head. "That cover."

"The foreskin," Taisan explained. "Most abbey boys like you are circumcised."

The words glanced off his thoughts and Genshai furrowed his brows, "I don't understand? I thought that was normal."

"Well, it is a fairly common cut for boys," he nodded in agreement. "Especially for novices, so he'll be taken to the shrine for the procedure when we come home. It's one of the orthodox rules of the Aegin Tradition, since monks are celibate."

Genshai wrinkled his nose, a bit disturbed by the revelation. Of course he knew that every boy that grew up in the abbey was circumcised, but it was not really something the masters of the Iron Style had ever discussed with them, so he had not truly understood that a part of him was lost until now.

Taisan shrugged, "Be glad that it doesn't happen when you come of age to take the Oath, I suppose."

"Did it happen to you?" Genshai asked.

Taisan blinked once, holding his passive expression as he revealed, "No, I'm not circumcised, I was never a matron child."

Genshai swung his head around in disbelief. "Really? You weren't?"

Taisan sighed. "I left home to join the abbey when I was nineteen. The abbot made me train in the Iron Style for five years before I took the Oath."

They were silent for a long while during the evening as Genshai contemplated what he learned, but it was no secret that he was irritated. Taisan said nothing as the boy stomped around after dinner, huffing and sighing all night as they tried to sleep. He decided it was best to let Genshai sort out his own complicated feelings, since he figured his student would seek him out whenever he was ready. Taisan wondered, *Would the truth raise him up, or break him down?* in either case not wanting to chase the boy away from his appointed role in the abbey.

The evening was cool, so they built up the fire before they went down just to have some warmth at their backs through the night.

Standing on a hill of clover, they saw the onset of a huge forest that was said to spread for more than two hundred miles to the coastlands. The trees filled the horizon and dense white clouds loomed overhead. The city of Faewoden was just ahead and it was as if Taisan had memorized all the little communities and townships, as he said, "We're coming through the Elmshire, and yes, there's the Season Tree," pointing to where the canopy of the sacred tree spread from the center of the neighborhood.

They soon dismounted after a long day on horseback and while they passed under the shady lanes of the shire some people seemed to realize who they were, giving them friendly smiles, until a lady said, "Good day, teacher," to Taisan, and nodded respectfully to the young laymonk as she passed by.

"Are we staying in the village tonight?" Genshai asked, curious about Faewoden and whether they would ever stay in a tavern or even visit a shrine.

"We're going to the ranger's cabin," Taisan said, taking them to the end of a lane of loghouses where tall oaks and maples made up the border of the dense and trackless woods, and at the end of the row was the trailhead that passed between two broad evergreen trees. The cabin was made of square-hewn pine beams that interlocked in the corner joints with a chimney on one side. Even though it was at the end of the lane, it also appeared to be frequently visited since there was a sizeable stable with empty stalls ready to receive Snowcap and Meora for the night.

The sounds of laughter came through the gray light of eventide, and Taisan went knowingly around the cabin toward a bonfire in a ring of stones on the edge of a wide flat pasture where a few goats were grazing. There he saw the shadowed forms of two men sitting on upturned logs while a third man fed the fire, wearing a mirthful grin through his beard while the youngest of them complained loudly from his seat, "Don't laugh! I'm not joking! The lords do as they please, don't they? Count yourselves lucky, my good fellows, that none of us were born to such cruel sorts of parents as the rich and highborn of this world!"

Taisan called forth, "Hello there."

"Who's out there?" an older man answered, his voice harsh from tobacco smoke.

The younger one sitting beside him looked and said, "It's just that old monk," turning back disinterestedly.

"Don't be such a pismire," the third man snapped at his companion. He dropped the last dry split of wood on the fire and came forward eagerly, shaking wrists with both of them as he said in a low, booming voice, "Good tidings, teacher."

"How are you, Ekkard?" Taisan gripped the man's shoulder, happy to see him again.

"As well as any man can be that has no land, no title, no wife," Ekkard grinned through his thick beard. "Free as a bird."

"For truth," the younger one said. "You're better for it."

"Alright, these twines are ready," said the older man about the task they had to finish and Ekkard turned to join them. They were assembling torches woven with dried sage and sweetgrass, dipping them thoroughly into a bucket of pitch resin and then wrapping them in thick twine coated in sap.

Taisan explained that Ekkard was an abbey child. He grew up as a novice and took the Oath, but after a while he wanted to leave so more than ten years ago he went down from the mountain to seek out a different life. Taisan did not say in front of Ekkard or his young apprentice that he had thought the baby was perhaps eight months old when he found him abandoned outside the Dellwood. At the time Taisan was still a young man returning from his travels abroad, and he had carried the orphan in a sling across his chest for nearly ten days toward Red Tower, naming him Ekkard, which mean 'edge of the woods' in the old Norr dialect.

At first Genshai was sullen and quiet as they joined the rangers around the fire, but soon Taisan brought out the baby and told the boy to keep an eye on him, warning, "Don't let him swallow anything," since Kyus was on a mission to crawl through the grass, so they avoided the grazing pasture and the chopping block where dry splinters were strewn everywhere beside the inert maul on the ground. It seemed like every few minutes Genshai had to yank something out of the baby's mouth until he became so impatient that he just swept him up in his arms and carried him everywhere.

Genshai listened as they all talked, and the old ranger said that Oathlord Faewoden intended to have a stag hunt by the beginning of Janien, the seventh month, and they had been tasked to ready each waypost with supplies: dried trail rations, a cord of firewood, and plenty of brush torches. The trails and bridlepaths went for fifty miles through the south part of the woods and around the timber ridge where the loggers camped in ten-day shifts. "But beyond that the forest is untouched," the old man said gruffly, puffing tobacco in a clay pipe at all times. "It's as dense as a thicket, and the bears roam there."

"There ain't another person around for miles," the young fellow Steffen said with pleasure. He didn't look much older than Genshai, and was small and skinny with scraggly brown hair around his ears and chin. He lounged in his bedroll by the fire and barely helped with the brush torches, picking his teeth with a small knife.

"Here is the last of our supper, teacher." Ekkard brought two bowls of stew from a steaming cauldron beside the fire. He said they had shot six quail in the field earlier that week and stewed the small birds with whole potatoes and carrots on embers for half a day with crushed garlic, boughs of elderfir, sliced green leeks, dried pink peppercorns, and fresh laurel leaf, all foraged from the forest. Taisan fed the baby softened vegetables and broth, filling his flask with goatsmilk to wash it down. Afterwards they shared their trail rations, munching heartily on honey-baked oats, dried blueberries, and a variety of toasted nuts – even the keku nut, which came off the Season Tree in late autumn and offered a slight note of spice.

While they ate around the fire, Genshai realized that Ekkard had a deep respect for the old laymonk. He moved observantly around to hear his teacher's words, reminding Genshai of a few monks he knew back home at the abbey, which made the boy immediately feel a new kinship to Ekkard. The ranger tried to show his knowledge of the classics and that he still practiced the Still Mind meditation, by saying, "I want to keep my thoughts clear, so that when we're tracking I'm always mindful of what's around me."

"Oh yes, as mindful as a Sage this one is," young Steffen teased, puffing deeply on a sweetleaf pipe, and the old man chuckled to himself as he finished out the bundle of torches at his feet.

Ekkard's brown face burned in embarrassment and Genshai glowered at Steffen, turning his foul mood onto him, but Taisan hardly seemed to notice the teasing as he began a side conversation about the Iron Style. The boy bounced Kyus on his knee and listened as the old laymonk described the principles of drawing up force from the earth. Genshai saw that Ekkard's fists were like rough textured blocks. It was clear that he had mastered the Iron Palm technique before leaving the abbey and for that reason Taisan continued to teach him so long as he did not claim to teach it to anyone else.

"Continue practicing the Simple Sets," Taisan advised. "They will give you the breath control for all the Iron Body methods."

"How are you conditioning?" Genshai asked, looking around curiously. He didn't see any of the punching bags or stone blocks that they would strike their palms across for at least three hours every day at home. Many times during their journeys he had wanted to continue the Iron Palm training but they didn't have any of the supplies he needed, and Taisan had been preoccupied with teaching him the stances in the Mountain Form.

"I hit that tree stump," Ekkard pointed to a dead tree that had been left standing just taller than a man, which did indeed appear to have been struck until smooth by numerous fists and elbows.

"Do you have hit medicine?" Genshai asked curiously, since he knew that if someone practiced any of the Iron Body methods they would need the potent liniment to recover from the usual bruising, or even tiny fractures in the hand. Ekkard's face brightened into a smile and he showed Genshai a large pot buried in the field adjacent to the cabin, just as the herbalists would do in the abbey, to allow the alcohol liniment a cool place to infuse with the numerous ingredients.

He said, "I purchase it from the abbey since Taisan lets me train," even though it was clear such things were rarely done.

Later Ekkard came out of the cabin and said, "Take this, I don't use it anymore," and offered the boy an old hitting bag, which was a square of thick canvas, double stitched with heavy thread and filled with finely crushed gravel. In addition to that the ranger gave them a large portion of the hit medicine, passing Genshai a skin that could never be used for water again now that it had been filled with the harsh liniment. The boy received the impression that it was a generous gift since the buried pot was nearly half empty already, but nonetheless it made Ekkard happy to share it back to the laymonks of the abbey.

"Thank you!" Genshai said excitedly as he took the training bag, tossing it up and snatching it out of the air to get a feeling for the weight of it, which he guessed was about fifteen pounds and densely packed for hitting his hands.

"It's only proper that you have it," Ekkard said in his deep voice.

As they settled around the fire in the first hour of nighttime

Steffen, only a boy of seventeen suddenly produced a flask and took a deep swallow, before he offered it to them with a sly grin. "A warm nip for the abbey brothers?"

To their surprise the old laymonk reached out for the flask, took a swig of the dry whiskey, and said, "Oh yes, properly cask aged from the highlands," which made them all laugh unexpectedly.

Ekkard and Genshai were put at ease, and they each took two or three swallows from the flask. With his head buzzing, the young monk listened to Taisan coach Ekkard on the proper alignment of meridians through the body, to hit fully without using any force. In fact he advised them both to remain relaxed, to sit slightly with each strike, and to breathe naturally outward, which was confusing to Genshai since he had always heard the other masters of the abbey tell the boys to stiffen their fingers and hit their hands hard on the bag.

Taisan joked, "The Body Method is an elusive skill, maybe we should just not bother."

Ekkard's voice boomed, "But it's fun to hit stuff," and they all laughed.

Thick indigo clouds drifted over the crescent moon and the grazing pasture was oppressively dark from the overhanging trees at the border. The fire burned warmly and Genshai heard the discordant sounds of crickets and tree frogs, an owl call, and the voice of his new abbey brother, which filled his thoughts with notes of the past. Eventually the old ranger and then soon Steffen, Genshai, and Ekkard all went inside the cabin, taking their opportunity to sleep in a bunk with a straw mattress, which was softer than any bedroll on the ground. The boy was reminded of sleeping in the dormitory with forty other bunks, wondering about Beryl, and big Tennan, and his matron brothers Astel and Jakk and what they were doing at the abbey every day and what adventures he was missing with them.

Taisan fell asleep with Kyus under the bright sickle moon. The baby cuddled against his chest, breathing as light as a kitten and sucking his thumb, content for hours in that cool night. The next day the old man awoke in the gray forehour of dawn with the smell of ash and sage in the pit nearby, and he gradually built the fire back up with kindling and dry bunches of firewood, which they had in plenty.

Soon Genshai emerged from the cabin rubbing his eyes, and when Ekkard joined them the old laymonk said, "Let's stretch," before he led them through the Eight Simple Sets, in long routines of stepping, squatting, and twisting, until they were warm and sweating in the sunbeams that fell through gray clumps of slow drifting clouds. Before they could finish the seventh calisthenic, Sway Head and Shake Tail, it was obvious Kyus was getting bored, wanting to crawl until Taisan scooped him up in his arms. He had his own way of holding the baby up high and gradually dropping him down low in a Horse-Stance, and then making faces as if it were a game.

"He's not a monk, he's a nursemaid," Steffen taunted from where he had returned to his seat in front of the fire, packing his pipe with dried black flakes of tobacco and looking as if he had never left.

"Say that again..." Genshai blurted angrily, but was interrupted by Taisan who shook his head.

"It hardly matters what one boy says," the teacher said as he adjusted the baby in his arms. "Now show me your Iron Palm," pointing to where Ekkard had set up his own canvas hitting bag filled with crushed gravel on a flat overturned stump that reached to the height of his hips – slightly too high for Genshai, who was still growing. The boy began to hit in the three positions that he had learned in the abbey, swinging his arms and dropping through on the palm, the back, and the edge of his hand.

After just a few repetitions his skin turned red and stung with every hit. It had been nearly six months since he had been able to practice any of the Iron Palm methods, and besides, in the abbey the novices used bags filled with dry beans until they swore the Oath and began practicing with the heavier, denser gravel bags. During their travels, his teacher focused solely on the secret

Mountain Form, occasionally keeping up with the Lion Forms, and now Genshai worried some of the conditioning in his hands had regressed.

"No," Taisan shook his head. "You're hitting too hard."

Ekkard said helpfully, "Go slowly. Don't feel like you're hitting anything."

Kyus contributed to the lesson by raising a little clenched fist, babbling delightfully, followed by a bright laughter.

They practiced together for the better part of an hour. Genshai came to see that much of what he learned before he swore the Oath was the basic understanding of the Iron Palm and that his timing and power transfer needed refinement. He was shocked when he saw Ekkard simply pick up a round wedge of stone and set it upon the tree stump, cracking it straight through with one rap of his knuckles, almost as if he was hardly trying at all. The older man laughed at Genshai's gaping eyes and demonstrated one more time.

It was just like how the masters of the Iron Style punched through bricks or slabs of granite, reminding him of Red Tower. He had even been able to do it once or twice during their demonstrations in Auburntown on festival days. It was not an easy skill and often resulted in injury if there was any mistake, but there were all sorts of variations of breaking the stones, including with the flat of the palm, the back of the hand, the edge, and even with one or two fingers, which he had personally seen the abbot Horn of Ram do more than once.

Taisan grinned, "That's what it's supposed to look like."

"You would know, you're the tournament champion," Ekkard answered back.

"Champion?" Genshai asked, looking between them, but Taisan glanced away modestly and carried Kyus around the woodpiles, bouncing him up and down, until they were barely in earshot.

"You didn't know?" Ekkard was surprised. "It's written in the abbey histories, and all his letters to the abbot from those days are there in the library."

"What?"

Ekkard gestured with his thumb. "The laymonk was a Zansho fighter in the southlands. His Iron Fist is legendary in all the provinces. There are even songs about it."

"I had no idea," Genshai stared unabashedly at his teacher.

"He's the real thing," Ekkard nodded. "I think he fought more than forty matches before he was defeated."

"It's not important," Taisan returned to the conversation. "Now let's finish up. I have a feeling these clouds aren't going to stop moving west and we have a long way to go."

They practiced a bit longer and soon Ekkard appeared with a cloth that had been wet with hit medicine. It had a particularly pungent, acrid aroma that was quite familiar to them all after growing up in the abbey. Genshai wiped his hands entirely in the cloth. The liniment was tinted brown and red and already he felt the tingle of the alcohol on his skin and the relief in his wrists and hands. It was very common after training in the abbey for the old herbalist and his apprentices to apply the liniment with a wide brush, just to get ahead of any new bruises or sprains.

"Remember the Still Mind," Taisan said to Ekkard, reminding him of the Scripts of meditation. "Still as floating clouds / still as the place between thought / still as steady rain."

The abbey brothers joined the other rangers at the fire and Steffen teased, "Are you ladies all finished with your dance practice then?"

"You should show some more respect," Genshai declared. "This man can kill you with one punch."

Steffen looked at Ekkard, who simply crossed his huge arms and scrutinized him back. The weathered, old ranger glanced up from the skillet at the edge of the fire, but nobody said anything to rebuke Genshai. They all knew it was clearly true – one single punch to the side of the head, or to the abdomen, and Ekkard's Iron Fist would kill someone outright.

"By the gods, relax," Steffen rolled his eyes, yet after that he no longer made any quips about the monks.

It was midmorning and the old ranger had prepared them a breakfast of fried chicken eggs and salt pork in the skillet with huge buttery biscuits. They drank wild mint tea and Genshai felt flush and heady from the exercise, his hands reddened and stinging with hit medicine. Afterward Ekkard and Steffen took up their yew longbows and shouldered full quivers of white-fletched arrows. They carried light oilcloth packs and wore laced deerskin boots and bracers, with crenellated tunics that were two shades of green, and brown leather hoods that draped down their backs. They each grabbed a bundle of torches, sacks of rations, and their bedrolls, and soon were ready to set out for the trailhead.

In the meantime Genshai got the horses saddled and packed, and when they were all set to depart he thought they would leave by the road through the village, but instead Taisan walked the horses behind the rangers who led them past the threshold of the trailhead, entering the shaded canopy of the Farwood. Already the day was cloudy and gray, and soon their eyes adjusted to the dim light under the trees as the trail went neatly through the forest, coming over a slight rise that headed west.

They talked quietly as they walked and Ekkard explained, "The first waypost is seven miles down this trail where there's a crossing to the north."

"Lord Faewoden will be riding south on the stag hunt," Steffen said, "He enjoys the forest, but it hardly stops him from cutting into the timber ridge."

"The lords do as they please," Ekkard shrugged. "But years ago they would at least ask the rangers to select which trees to drop for milling."

"That's what the Effyra tribes do in the Ten Hills," Taisan said, following their example of speaking in a near whisper. He carried Kyus suspended in the sling, leading his horse with one hand and holding his staff with the other. The baby seemed to be in a relaxed daze, hypnotized by the flashing shadows and beams of light that passed overhead in the crowns of trees.

"Exactly," Ekkard nodded. "Now they cut out ten acres every season."

"But the Farwood is huge," Genshai said, looking around at the dense woods.

"It won't be huge forever," Taisan replied. "Be ready for change, / nothing endures beyond time / and all forms will end."

After nearly an hour of walking they came to the crest of the next valley where the rangers each knelt over a run of tracks that crossed at an angle on the path. Their voices were hushed as they spoke. "The buck was here," and Ekkard pointed to the cloven shapes pressed heavily into the dirt, and then indicated several other tracks as if a bunch of doe had also run through.

"Afoot barely an hour ago," Steffen said, peering southward into the deep green woods from the edge of the trail.

"We must take our leave now," Ekkard said to the laymonk. "We can track them to the glen where they graze."

"Good luck, brother," Taisan gripped the ranger's wrist.

"Take care, teacher," Ekkard said as he glanced upward. "Those are rainbearing clouds above us."

With predatory focus, each ranger notched an arrow in his bow and kept it loosely drawn as they left the trail. They scanned the dirt for tracks and crossed into the foliage until they disappeared. The rangers were keepers of the forests that ventured farther than any logger or woodsmen, living from what they carried, gathered, and hunted. *A lot like a laymonk,* Genshai realized.

CHAPTER FOUR

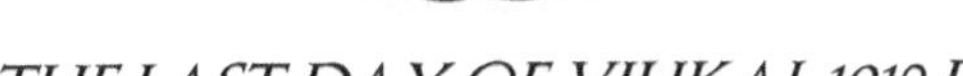

THE LAST DAY OF VILIKAI, 1019 EC

*The Epic of Elosai, "After the travails of Shenai, the great
Sage carried the Lotusblade, the holy sword of Sibudat, back
to the terracotta forest."*

THE CAVE

The two monks rode on horseback down the wooded trail that went west through the dense forest. Then Taisan found a narrow dirt bridlepath that forked from the path, heading north along a spring until the end of the day when they finally stopped at eventide. They were deep in the Farwood, at least twenty-two miles from the trailhead, far from any wayposts or cabins and completely surrounded by trees that all seemed to creak and whisper and twist in the heavy wind.

Genshai stood at the edge of the river that coursed over the rocks while Meora and Snowcap drank in the shallows. Kyus was fussy and restless from riding all day, and Taisan eventually said, "Take him," forcing Genshai to carry the baby in his stiff arms, unable to calm him down while Taisan rummaged through his pack to prepare some goatsmilk in the flask.

"I was planning to take this shortcut through the Farwood," Taisan grumbled, glancing upward at the heavy gray clouds that hung low over the trees, "but we'll see. If it rains, our journey will be delayed."

"I can go through the rain," Genshai shrugged. "Once you're wet, you're wet."

"No," Taisan shook his head. "Kyus can't stay out in the rain, besides if you spend two days in wet clothes you'll catch a cold and the journey will take longer."

The night began with a clap of thunder and the winds were hard. They decided to keep the horses saddled as the first shower came down and their fire flickered, eventually reduced to a smoky pit in the darkness. The travelers tucked themselves under the wide canopy of an elderfir tree, hoping the thick boughs would be good cover, but after they had only been resting for three hours the downpour was so thick that Taisan got them all back onto the bridlepath following the river, which had taken on the speed of the rain.

The baby cried inconsolably and Genshai tried to cover him with his Aeigi jacket to keep the storm from pelting his face. They each wrapped their blankets around their shoulders like hoods and walked the horses through the gale, weary and desperate after a day of heavy riding. "There," Taisan shouted over the storm, and pointed through the shivering trees to the granite arch of a cave high on the hillside, and when they crossed the stone threshold it was as though they entered an envelope of silence while the storm raged outside, battering the trees and raising the river.

Kyus howled like a frightened animal until Taisan said, "Let me have him," dropping his wet blanket to take the baby, he rocked him back and forth as he said, "It'll be okay, we're safe now," which quieted him down for just a moment until the booming thunder brought on another wrenching cry. The old man wrapped the baby in the sling close to his chest so he was able to move with his hands free to unpack some supplies from the horses.

Grateful to be out of the storm, Genshai dropped his backpack and found one of the brush torches that the rangers had given them, lighting it ablaze with a tindertwig that was thankfully still dry. They walked toward the rear of the cave and Taisan looked for any new tracks on the ground as he explained, "These forests are known to have bears and wolves, even mountain lions."

Yet the cave floor looked undisturbed, as if it had been vacant for years. In fact, as they went further back they noticed a gradual descent, a subtle winding of the passage until they heard the sounds of cascading water. Genshai led the way down, holding the torch overhead as they came upon the banks of an underground lake and a twenty-foot waterfall that surged from a crack in the riverbed above them.

"The path continues," Taisan pointed, and he walked alongside the shadowy blue lake, into a new tunnel that led promptly to a massive cavern with a high ceiling jagged with stalactites. The orb of their torchlight could hardly fill the room or reveal the full height of the ceiling, and the space was crowded with massive boulders and stones. The air was cool like the darkhour of the night, and Kyus seemed to sniffle and whimper in an exhausted daze.

"Let's go back," Genshai said fearfully, suddenly conscious of how deep they were within the earth, wondering what old powers might be hidden there.

Taisan looked around. Keeping an arm around the baby in the sling, he went away from his student and the torchlight and gazed at the high stones that were shining with water and streaked with minerals. He glanced into pits that seemed bottomless. He saw three paths that diverged into separate tunnels and knelt to inspect the soft untouched ground, taking deep breaths to smell the air until he was satisfied.

Finally, Genshai led them back up the winding tunnel. He held the torch firmly aloft, but on their return journey they discovered a passage they hadn't seen before and they couldn't remember which one they had come through until Taisan said, "Listen," and they heard the sound of their horses and the rain. He took the right fork and soon led them back to the mouth of the cave.

They looked out and saw that the rain poured down in sheets. It was clear the storm had a long way to go, so they decided to stay in the cave instead of searching for a waypost on the ranger's trail.

They were still soaking wet and quickly found plenty of twigs and sticks, dry grass, and leaves that had blown into the cave over the years, using the torch to get a fire started. Taisan passed Kyus over to Genshai and said, "Mind your brother," as he disappeared into the rain, returning with several armfuls of fallen branches that he stacked up against the wall to dry.

The cave was fairly spacious and cool, and the smoke of their fire at the front was drawn out into the storm. They laid out all their clothes across the rocks until they were waiting in just their loinwraps. Then they shook out their bedrolls and blankets, removed the saddles and brushed the horses, and sorted through some food that had gotten wet in spite of their oilcloth backpacks; two loaves of bread were soggy, and some of the cheese, but an entire sack of beans was soaked so they decided to cook it that night.

Genshai had come to enjoy Taisan's campfire cooking, and even in the cave his teacher could make a delicious meal of dirty beans with charred sausage and stewed greens. It was simple and they made plenty, so they saved the rest for breakfast the following morning. Exhausted and cold, Genshai put two logs onto the fire, which steamed for a while until they began to burn. Thunder pealed from over the trees and lightning cracked open the sky for just an instant, but so long as they stayed within the cave they were protected from the rain.

He fell asleep on his bedroll under a half-sodden blanket. Tossing and turning, the dreams overtook him as the sound of the storm reminded him of those wuthering nights at Ulfghar's Ridge. The rains had come haphazardly and sideways. Angry ghosts had risen out of the ground like they were buried there, and anyone they touched was left crawling with terror, forced to confront a kind of cowardice they never knew they could possess.

The next morning his teacher was already awake when Genshai opened his eyes. He was still shirtless as he stared out of the cave, brooding deeply at the falling rain, which now fell straight down without much wind and seemed to make everything heavy. Genshai thought that Taisan was probably impatient to continue, and he also disliked the delay from their quest, even though the boy now understood the logic of waiting out the storm and was content to keep all their belongings dry as long as possible.

Kyus lay on his back on Taisan's bedroll, gripping his teething ring in one hand and babbling toward the ceiling. The sound of the rain outside the cave was constant, ringing back on every drop. Genshai put on his trousers, but he followed his teacher's example of going without his shoes and without his Aeigi jacket. They ate breakfast quickly, chewing down a bowl of cold beans and a few melona fruit from the last Season Tree they saw three days ago. The man and the boy looked out at the steady rain, silent because they both knew what was coming next.

"Your belt," Taisan said, as he looped his black belt around his waist and tied a knot just above his trousers.

Unsure of what to expect, Genshai followed his example, but instead they began with the Eight Simple Sets, familiar movements that harkened to the past – back to his upbringing in Red Tower when he practiced at dawn with Heavy Earth, their strict teacher who made all the boys of every age do push-ups, or sprints around the tower, and all sorts of other calisthenics until they were thoroughly worn out before breakfast. They trained every morning overlooking the great vista of blazing sunrises that lit up the chimneys of Auburntown just below them, the cottages of three shires, the Oathlord's fields of soy and hemp, sorghum and millet, and then the green Dellwood sprawling on for two hundred miles.

But there was no vista here. Only the cold stone wall in front of him, and the steady rain in his ears outside the mouth of the cave, and the voice of Taisan demanding, "Mountainroot, pay attention!"

By the end of the Eight Sets Genshai was breathless and Taisan looked him over critically until he said, "You're doing them wrong if you're out of breath."

"What do you mean?" Genshai demanded. He was strained more than usual from the unique way Taisan did the exercises. "I've always done it like this. You're just going too fast today."

"Am I out of breath?" Taisan asked, standing upright with his hands at his hips beside him, and Genshai had to admit the old laymonk looked perfectly composed while he himself already had beads of sweat dripping down his forehead.

"I'm sorry teacher," Genshai said with difficulty, stifling his pride to ask, "How do I do it correctly?"

"Your lungs are compressed from your posture," Taisan said as he proceeded to poke and prod his student's stance, lifting his shoulders, tilting his pelvis, raising his crown and tucking his chin, feeling completely outrageous in that position until he collapsed in a heap.

"Let's do it again," Taisan instructed, and Genshai sighed as he realized the old man wasn't going to let it go. They practiced the Simple Sets again, and then a third time after that. Whenever Taisan thought Genshai's focus was wandering he pointed to the boy's feet, or his shoulders, or even the top of his head, wanting him to be fully aware of his posture. His teacher explained that if his alignment was correct his lungs should not be compressed, and he could even carry a complete conversation without being out of breath while practicing.

They transferred the lesson into the Mountain Form. It was one of the secret forms, not taught to other monks because of several lethal maneuvers that Taisan had never even hinted at, although Genshai had kept his mind busy for months trying to examine the movements of the sequence for their hidden applications. He thought the stepping was particularly complicated, with several twists and elbow presses that did not make sense. There were kicks that sliced up at an angle with the reverse hand pulled to the waist, and then suddenly, while balancing, the leg reaped back and was raised in the air behind him, the reverse hand pointed out in front, like an eagle that dived over the mountain.

In spite of himself, Genshai panted breathlessly and Taisan pointed. "Your stance is compressed. You're revealing your actions by exhaling before you even take a step."

"I'm trying to learn the form," Genshai argued, irreverent to his teacher's efforts.

"You would learn if you paid attention to your damn breathing!" Taisan retorted with some laughter in his voice.

Still the Seat-of-the-Mountain eluded him, and any question about a stance resulted in a throw. Without fail, the old man gripped the boy's arm, stepped, and suddenly flipped him over his hip, and once again with the other side of the body, then from the corner angle. Each throw was for a different circumstance and it quickly became clear why they wore their belts since their jackets would be filthy, and the belts gave them a place to hold and grip during the throw.

"Well, come on then," Taisan said, and Genshai was expected to replicate all he had seen and felt, eventually pushing, and dumping, and slamming his teacher down from each angle – and when he was certain Genshai understood the step, Taisan said, "Then move the hand upward to grip across the target's ear, or wrap the head, and here this way," tightening around his neck until it was clear that the maneuver was lethal.

The laymonk knew every application, which prompted the boy to ask, "So how many throws are there in the form?"

"I don't know, I've never counted them all," Taisan shrugged. "Seems like there are hundreds if you really think about it."

Genshai probed inquisitively, "Is that what you learned as Zansho fighter?"

Taisan laughed as if it was an unexpected question, answering, "I suppose I did," without saying much more about it, even though Genshai burned with curiousity about this part of his teacher's mysterious background.

After that, the boy spent an hour trying to throw his teacher in freeplay. He was quick with his hands, or he launched himself to the side, but Taisan simply reacted by leveraging the boy's own momentum against him. He was brash and strong, which did nothing for him until Taisan said, "Stop trying to win," and they started to move more fluidly against each other, giving their partner passive resistance, and when the steps were correct they allowed themselves to be tossed. The boy felt more rooted, finally able to sweep across and cut the leg until the laymonk was thrown.

"Good," Taisan laughed from his place in the dirt, betraying some of his enjoyment. "Nice response to my trip attempt."

The sound of Kyus' delightful laughter bubbled to the back edge of the cave every time someone was tossed to the ground. Restless and bored, the baby scurried away from the bedrolls and Taisan grabbed him, raising him up high and then dropping him down low, as if he was exercising with the child, and Kyus stretched out his limbs, grinning, like he was riding on a smooth cloud.

Their hunger soon forced them to stop for the day, but Genshai still enjoyed a brief stretching routine alone while Taisan went to the back of the cave to meditate before they made a late lunch. He was disappointed with their foodstores, scrounging up some sausages and root vegetables, although as usual Taisan added some wild garlic and chives for a bit of flavor. They made sure to ration out the rest sparingly since the storm showed no signs of letting up for the day. At times a sunbeam brightened the forest where they could see how many whole trees had come down and how much the waters had risen in the river.

They built up the fire and relaxed on their bedrolls for a while in the late afterfade. The horses stood at the mouth of the cave and occasionally stepped out in the rain to graze, returning with wet manes and flanks. After watching them wrestle all day, Kyus demanded extra attention, and wanted to crawl back and forth, making a fuss if they became distracted by anything other than him. Taisan was more than happy to oblige, helping the baby to stand nearly by himself until his feet refused to remain flat and he tumbled over.

Genshai wondered if the old laymonk was like this with all the orphans he carried to the matron's house. He watched Taisan grin, "Good job!" or "Uh-oh, did you fall down?" anytime the baby did anything, always there to receive him into his arms. The boy dwelled on the question of his origin for some time, becoming sullen and quiet until Taisan seemed to read his thoughts and said, "I've been thinking that you're right," while the baby scrambled up to his shoulder.

"About what?" Genshai sighed.

"I think you should know where you come from," Taisan replied.

Genshai sat up in his bedroll and looked over the fire in surprise, "Really?"

"Well, it's as you said," Taisan said. "You're the laymonk now. That makes your circumstances different. Your entire job is to interact with the secular world. Besides, I knew my parents and sisters growing up, and it hasn't been an issue for me."

Genshai wasn't sure what to think of this change in attitude from his teacher. "But what about not having any attachments?"

Taisan shook his head and quoted the Scripts, "A traveling monk / may see new lands and peoples, / for him, all things change."

Genshai was puzzled, "I don't understand."

Taisan made a dismissive gesture with his hand. "Let the monks in the abbey worry about Illumination. You're the laymonk now. If you want to make attachments, you're allowed to do that."

Before Genshai had time to react, Taisan began the story. "It must be nearly sixteen years ago now that I was traveling back from a little shire called Three Oaks," describing the dense woodlands at the bottom of the province. He continued, "About half a mile outside the village I found you under an evergreen tree, that's why I named you Genshai, the old northern sign for 'a bed of spruce.' You only had a skin of milk and a swaddling cloth, and of course there was nobody in the woods, or at least nobody who wanted to be found, which made us destined for each other in either case, so I carried you home."

Taisan laughed as he remembered. "It was quite a journey. I was clear across the province when I picked you up. We were probably together for seven or eight months before I dropped you off at Joyce's house," putting the pieces together for Genshai, who laid back on his bedroll, his thoughts spinning as he recalled being set down on the wooden floor of his grandma's skinny brick townhouse.

Any memories before that could never be apprehended again, but in the core of his spirit he knew that Taisan had told him the truth.

By now the steady rain outside the cave was like a trusted friend and the gloomy light from the sky was middling gray at dawn. Genshai glanced around, vaguely wondering where his teacher could have gone since Kyus was still fast asleep on his bedroll. He was building up the embers of the fire to heat water for tea when Taisan appeared from the depths of the tunnel at the back of the cave, carrying a torch that he extinguished in the dirt.

The old man did not offer much explanation, and instead he stared out at the pouring rain. He had not worn his shoes or his tunic since they arrived to the cave and his bare feet were black with dirt. There were streaks of grime across his back and chest from when he was thrown yesterday and Genshai imagined that he was similarly filthy, but he didn't feel like going out into the cold rain to take a shower, and he certainly wasn't planning to go for a swim in the underground lake.

Without anything much to eat for breakfast they began training once again. Genshai was eager to start out, they went hard all day, and neither the weather nor the old teacher offered much reprieve. At first, Taisan decided to practice the Iron Palm now that they had the option, since they had enough liniment and a hitting bag. They found a stone ledge that was at the correct height with a flat enough surface for Genshai to set the old canvas bag down to hit, swinging his arms around again and again; and if he struck too heavily the pain bounced back through his bones until his whole hand ached.

Taisan said, "Remember to relax. As hard as you hit, you hurt yourself twice as much."

"But how can I relax if I'm supposed to hit it?" the boy asked, remembering his other teachers at home who had demanded that he stiffen all his fingers whenever he hit the bags of beans as a novice.

"The abbot says to be lighter than five ounces," Taisan said helpfully. "Conditioning is not about hitting hard. It's about receiving the same kind of impact again and again, and no more than that, so when the time comes you can hit harder than a sledgehammer."

Then, as if to prove his point, the old laymonk picked up a random stone from the ground and placed it on the boulder nearby, shifted his hips and dropped down with the flat of his palm. Genshai knew from the sound that the stone was cracked through. The two halves fell to the side and clattered to the cave floor. The boy was confused, not knowing if he had witnessed an Ascendant Power or not, and asked, "Was that the Iron Palm?"

"What do you think?" Taisan asked, clenching his fists like small square hammers. "I hardly ever strike that bag thing anymore, but if I drop my force correctly, and my alignment is correct from my heel to my palm, then I will always be able to achieve the skill."

Genshai tried to release the tension through his shoulder, elbow, and wrist as he had been shown, and attempted to drop onto the hitting bag with no effort. He repeated the movement several dozen times with both hands, rising upward and then downward, hitting the palm, the backside, and the edge until they turned red and he felt the stinging return on himself if he struck too hard.

Afterward Taisan inspected Genshai's hands, looking over his wrists and knuckles and even at his fingernails, until he commented, "You're dragging on the back strike. You had better correct that when you practice tomorrow." The boy agreed mutedly, feeling somewhat drained after the conditioning and waiting in silence as the old man tilted out some hit medicine onto a cloth and applied it liberally to all the surfaces of his student's hands, and even to his forearms and ribs where shallow bruises were blooming from yesterday's practice.

The boy's thoughts were full of applications and posture

adjustments for Mountain and Iron and Lion, until he couldn't keep them straight anymore. Each maneuver was unique to the purpose they hoped to achieve, and Genshai began to see how they were all useful for fighting, although he still did not understand the extreme focus that his teacher had on alignment across all the different methods.

Alignment! Alignment! Why does it matter so much to be aligned? Genshai thought ruefully after one of Taisan's particularly harsh criticisms while they practiced the steps of the Mountain Form.

As if reading his mind Taisan stopped the practice and said, "Do you think you've come anywhere close to the Seat-of-the-Mountain skill?"

Genshai had to admit, "No."

"Why not? Don't you know the moves of the form?" Taisan inquired.

"It's too many things to think about," Genshai complained loudly. "I can't keep alignment for everything yet."

Taisan nodded as he said, "Of course not, and when it happens it will be brief. Only Sages can achieve the Ascendant Powers when they are young. Otherwise it takes lots of practice."

"How long will that take?" Genshai implored.

"Practice the form ten thousand times," Taisan said as if it were obvious.

"Then I wish I was a Sage," Genshai wailed from Horse-Stance position.

"Trust me, you're not," Taisan rolled his eyes, and Genshai felt somewhat rebuked until the old teacher said, "Well, I've never met a Sage, so it's hard to say."

There were many legends about Sages, all the way back to the time of Sibudat. They were thought of as monks with extremely developed spirits with many, many past lives, capable of learning the Ascendant Powers with little effort. Of course the most famous was Elosai the Sage, a monk who was said to have returned from the spiritlands with the lost sword of Sibudat, the Lotusblade, the only weapon known to slay a creature of the Nether. The story seemed like a fairytale since Elosai was sent by the Sovereign on an impossible quest – to defeat the demonson Viokher who had ravaged the kingdoms, and their duel was said to have brought storms over the countryside for a whole spring, summer, and autumn until they disappeared. None knew for certain what happened to either one of them, except that the growing season was especially fruitful the next year.

"Sometimes monks are called to face evil forces," Taisan said as they settled down around the flaming embers and continued to talk in tales and fables, reminding his student of how Sibudat first carried the Lotusblade down from the Immortal Temple to liberate the known lands from the fury of the Red Ogre.

Exhausted and smelling strongly of liniment, Genshai stretched out his legs on his fleece bedroll and touched his toes. They watched Kyus crawl to the wall and use his hands to drag himself upright, looking back proudly every time. It was late in the afternoon with only the gloomy light of the day to see with. The storm clouds seemed to build for nightfall, the thunder rumbled, a cold mist penetrated the air of the cave and Genshai shuddered as he asked, "Do you think we'll encounter angry ghosts again in Westcliff?"

Taisan dropped two logs of wood on the embers as he said, "The matters of the spirits are complex," his face impassive as he considered what knowledge to give, until he blinked and said, "Every living creature large or small possesses a Great Spirit; every blade of grass and cricket in the eventide, every stalk of grain, every cicada in summer, every woman and child, they are all filled by a spirit at birth. 'We are made of light / traveling in a cycle / of different lives. Knowledge is revealed / and clouds do not drift idly / as they seem to do.'"

The boy listened to the laymonk talk. Like most of the novices he had always thought of the Enduring Mountain like a legendary hero, not even realizing he was a Zansho fighter, but ever since he witnessed him overcome the angry ghosts at Ulfghar's Ridge he had come to trust his teacher's knowledge completely. Taisan had held the Still Mind in the darkhour of that stormy night; it had brought him through the gap of time, following the shades on a painful journey across the forest. He had even entered the watchtower to recover the bewildered young Bolmak, who had been drawn into the hungry maw of the cursed room.

Taisan continued, "Spirits of the Wreath are neither good nor bad. They live in harmony with nature just as any animal would do. They can become corrupted by trauma, and can be turned toward mischief or evil deeds, but they are still spirits of the Wreath nonetheless."

"But what about ghosts?" Genshai asked, and he imagined the screams, and the snarling dire wolf, that echoed out of the shadows of the watchtower in his thoughts.

"I am not certain," Taisan shook his head and seemed to talk as if he was working out new ideas of his own. "In the hauntings I've seen before the ghost is like a shadow, frozen by grief. Or perhaps they're a remnant of what was, but is it possible that the rest has moved on and left the cursed parts behind? The abbey teaches that some lives are good, and some are bad, and that they all change a spirit's shape and color, but not that pieces will be divided from the whole."

Genshai couldn't help but to think about their last day at Ulfghar's Ridge as they searched for the bodies of the victims. They had worn strips of linen to cover their noses and mouths as they crossed the threshold of the watchtower to recover the first six victims, entering when the sun was at its highest point and the growling shadows were held at bay. More bones were found between stands of trees, twisted and knotted with bramble, their ribcages filled with vines. The men dragged each skeleton they found toward the edge of the stone road where Taisan pointed to huge score marks and some of them guessed it was the work of a wild troll, or a dire wolf in a blood fury, but Taisan insisted, "It wasn't anything like that," unable to explain more.

In the end they had decided to take the twelve corpses back to Hylmstone for proper burials by the druids of the Dual Cliffs in the shrine to the mountain god Adak Purkah. The Dweroh solemnly made their way home, dejected, twisted up with the knowledge that those shades had been chased across the frozen ridge over and over again, forced to relive their last painful moments alive for unknown decades. Even as the laymonks were leaving Hylmstone, the druids were being sent to purify the watchtower at Ulfghar's Ridge. That was several weeks ago now, and Genshai was still desperate to know if all their efforts had worked in lifting the curse.

Brimming with questions, Genshai could only ask one at a time. They talked for several hours through the early evening until Kyus eventually crawled toward Taisan and took a seat in the bedroll, cuddling into his lap and falling asleep within a quarter of an hour or so. Of course, Genshai had learned about the Wreath in the classics, but Taisan said that spirits could be found all over the world, becoming visible whenever they wished though mostly remaining hidden except for certain times of the month or during the festivals of the year like Midsummer's Eve, or the Night of Flags in autumn.

"Always assume they're trying to trick you," Taisan said. "Some are mundane and common, others are dazzling and beautiful. Whether for good or ill, a spirit always has their own agenda for revealing itself to you. They should all be treated cautiously and with respect."

"But where do they appear from?" Genshai asked slowly, trying to follow everything.

"I've heard it is like going through a curtain," Taisan answered, but the idea was confusing since he said, "The spirits have mystical powers and can disappear from one place and reappear in another place, crossing any distance, ignoring time, from behind the Veil."

"Behind the Veil?" Genshai asked, intrigued.

Taisan looked at him carefully, wanting to measure the boy's ability to understand. Finally he said, "There are two worlds. All the known lands and seas of Kuei, the world of kingdoms, empires, and free cities."

"Yes," Genshai nodded.

Taisan continued, "And through the Veil there is Shenai, the spirit country, the land of the dead, where the spirits of the Wreath wait for their time of rebirth."

"Shenai," Genshai repeated the word, and glanced around wondering if there were spirits in the cave with them at that moment, considering that they might be invisible just on the other side of the ethereal Veil.

Now it made sense when monks described fleeting visions of dryads in the apple orchard, or shades in the corner of their eye, and even the Illumidharma prancing in the air. Some monks even claimed to have visited the spirit country through meditation. They crossed the Veil with their Spirit Body, one of the Ascendant Powers of Sibudat, which allowed them to send their astral selves into the depths of Shenai and remain there as long as they were undisturbed, and certainly some of them never returned, allowing their physical bodies to wither and die.

"But there are spirit grottos hidden all across the world," Taisan said as he described secret places where the Veil was thinner and the spirits lived in harmony with both worlds: in blue coves on the seashore, or sometimes at a riverbed under a bridge, or the deepest canyon in the desert. Genshai knew there were legends of brave monks that crossed through grottos on pilgrimages in search of the true Wreath, never to return, lost in the rolling, changing lands of the spirit country – except Elosai the Sage, who was said to have used the paths of the terracotta forest to guide himself back.

"Right here in this cave," Taisan said and Genshai followed his teacher's gaze toward the darkened tunnel that led to the black waters of the subterranean lake.

"A grotto? Here?" Genshai was baffled.

The gale outside was fitful and relentless, and rain slanted in at a sharp angle. Only their blankets and the small tongues of flame in the ring of stones kept them warm. The darkness of the night seemed to settle early and all else was quiet except the soft sounds of Kyus breathing. Genshai was silent for a while as he contemplated what Taisan had said. It all seemed so inconceivable, but so had angry ghosts and dire wolves, and Genshai was coming to realize that not everything that was a legend was only a story for children.

Then Taisan got to his feet and lit the torch from the flickering fire as he said, "Come on, you may as well see for yourself," and left the horses to watch the baby snoozing on his fleece bedroll. The young laymonk followed cautiously as he paced down the tunnel, wondering what surprises the old man had planned when Taisan warned, "You must keep the Still Mind at all times. The spirits are beguiling, and the grottos are disorienting beyond anything you have ever seen. Never eat or drink anything, especially if a spirit offers it freely with a smile, or else you risk being lost entirely to their charms."

Then the torchlight suddenly broadened as they came out of the tunnel at the edge of the subterranean lake and Genshai saw the dark pool reflecting a yellow glimmer onto the high ceiling. The laymonk moved into the next cavern, which was higher than the light could reach but crowded with huge stones. The room made Genshai tremble a bit, as it was immensely dark and vast but simultaneously narrow and cramped with its massive outcroppings of rock.

"But what about the Illumidharma?" the boy asked hopefully, referring to magnificent spirits with the wisdom of many lifetimes that had chosen to give up Illumination, becoming guides for others in need.

"Always assume it's a trick of some kind," Taisan persisted. "There are a myriad of creatures that gather in the grottos, and while some are wise and helpful, most are cruel or manipulative. They're bound to create mischief, and you don't want to get trapped in their games of chance, or riddles, or even just their longwinded stories. Seconds will become days before you know it."

"But, the Illumidharma…"

Taisan interrupted, "Just remember the Still Mind. Only mindfulness will reveal the truth, and in Shenai the truth is never what it appears," as he led the boy down a narrow path, taking the left side of the fork until it came to a dead end. "Here," he said as he pointed to a darkened alcove that led into a hidden room through a narrow crack.

"You want me to go in there?" Genshai realized.

"It's no different than a night in the pits," Taisan said, which was a competition of endurance the boys did in the abbey every few months. Once they were a certain age the novices would spend whole nights and days alone in the depths of a fifteen-foot pit with no food or water. They would meditate, or practice forms, and hope to outlast their brothers in the other pits, or until their masters returned to pull them out. Genshai had never seen a spirit during those tests, but he did enjoy several summer nights alone under the stars.

"Okay," the boy exhaled nervously, wriggling through the crack until he was on the other side. As he turned around he saw the orange glow of the torch go out and he called, "Teacher?" to which there was no reply.

Then Genshai said more firmly, "Enduring Mountain?" to which, again, there was no reply.

He listened for any footsteps but discovered that the room itself had an eerie echo in which he heard his own voice called back several times. Within a few minutes he had paced around the small circumference of the room, discovering it was roughly circular with no other entrances except the single crack in the wall. He figured the room was seven feet by seven feet, and could reach up to graze the ceiling with his fingers. Once or twice on his journey, and especially now, he wished he had met the hermit of the East Ridge, the fabled Owl monk, who was said to glide through the trees like his namesake and knew the night powers of Sibudat – like darkvision – and Genshai thought that if his eyes could pierce the blackness then he would not feel so cold and alone.

The boy became angry rather than fold in to fear, muttering, "That damn laymonk! I bet he's trying to lose me in Shenai and go back and get a new apprentice," although he knew lessons always had purpose and soon he sat down in the center of the room to meditate, and thought about Sibudat's mantra, *Still as floating clouds / still as the place between thought / still as steady rain – well there's plenty of that up at the mouth of the cave!* and even in the complete blackness of the room, deep underground in the heart of the earth, a million thoughts came falling into his mind.

After all how could he be expected to achieve the Still Mind when his teacher had just revealed so much about spirits? And ghosts? And he had said so much about their sly, capricious natures! *I have to be careful now that I know that Shenai is just on the other side of the Veil,* Genshai thought about the laymonk's warnings. *I don't want to get lost forever in the spirit country.*

He was fascinated to think that the Great Spirit nested within him even now, and he wondered about how many lifetimes it had lived; and what lives were yet to be lived. Lost in his imagination, minutes or hours passed in the complete darkness. Shirtless he trembled in the cold dark air until he managed to control his breath, steadying his heart rate just as he had learned to do in the abbey. He contemplated his journeys through the northlands, and the lessons of his upbringing, searching for the Still Mind; he realized now how truly far away he had been from it all this time.

He thought about Kyus and the heat of anger swelled within him. He was furious that he had to clean diapers, and feed him, and carry him, unwilling to accept that it was part of his responsibilities now. He was furious at the man or woman that had abandoned the child on the side of the road, scornful of the Warden, and the Oathlords, and the Matriarchs, and anyone else that had allowed such a society to exist. Then he chided himself for being so selfish, except that Genshai felt justified ever since the night he came to understand the child would be circumcised.

Is that why I'm pissed? He asked himself, even though he had always known it had occurred when he was an infant since it was generally taught that monks were circumcised, but he had felt somewhat embarrassed from the moment it became clear that he did not have a foreskin, and that it had occurred without his consent. He still felt normal enough, and had no real memory of the procedure, and so decided to put it out of his mind for now.

Growing up in the abbey, he had been taught strict abstinence. The monks even had rules against self-pleasure, or male intimacy, although Genshai knew that some older boys would break their vows by bathing together, or they would descend the mountain to visit their secret lovers, or newly engaged couples, in romantic conferences that easily became the gossip of the village. In the meantime, most of the monks disapproved and tried to keep their vows of abstinence, and if it was proven that anyone had broken their oath they would be asked to leave the abbey, although it was usually only if the scandal was too great to ignore. Mostly an amorous young man with suspected lovers would be punished with extra chores and training, and limited meals, to exhaust his energy and deter him from going out at night.

Genshai had always been curious about girls, but as a novice he thought of himself as shy, or unlucky, and distracted his body and mind by training for hours, the way his teachers instructed him to do. Now that he knew it was possible for the laymonk to keep a partner, he discovered that he did want to have a relationship and while he was supposed to be meditating he could not stop wondering what it would be like to be intimate with someone. His thoughts settled on the girl he had met in Norhaal – Eryn – who scorned marriage, who wanted freedom, and now he thought that she was more beautiful than any girl he had ever seen, and wanted desperately to talk through the evening about their innermost thoughts until they had shared all there was to share.

All of these strange feelings arose in him as he searched for the Still Mind; the flames of anger and the waters of lust, passing like seasons in a year. He formed the Small Circle with his breathing. He felt that his cool skin was no different than the cool black stone all around him. His thoughts were released into the emptiness. The room was gone, and he was within a darkness that had no limit.

Beams of orange light emerged from one side. He was shocked to hear a low enchanting melody just as a tall woman came out of the pitch black as if she was striding out of his fantasies, completely topless other than a few long beaded necklaces and golden chains that looped several times around her neck. Genshai couldn't help but to gape at her ample and round breasts. She seemed to glisten with oil and had the color of burnished copper, and there was only a single cloth draped between her legs, hardly concealing anything as her soft belly rolled to the illusory flutesong from somewhere in the darkness.

"Here you are again. I knew you couldn't resist me," she said laughingly, shaking her hips, bending forward to reveal her blooming flower.

The boy swallowed and took a deep breath and asked, "Have we met before?"

She turned around and pouted, fluttering her eyes, "I'm sad you don't remember me," before she took another look and waved her hand indifferently. "Oh, you're somebody new. Well, all you monks look the same."

Her fine black hair was pulled back in a jeweled headdress above her head, and she had gauged wooden plugs in her earlobes. She smiled, once again dancing nearer to his place of meditation, and Genshai couldn't help but notice her astonishingly full breasts. Grasping his head in disbelief, he could see that parts of the vision were almost comical, as if the shape of her body, the color of her lips and eyes, were grand overstatements of the truth.

"Oh, but I like the younger ones," she proclaimed, her voice quivering. "There's a wonderful pool nearby where we can swim. I'm sure a boy such as yourself can think of all sorts of exciting things to do."

"Who are you?" Genshai asked. His hips stirred, but through the haze in his thoughts he knew there was a reason to remain seated.

She said with an exquisite breath, "I am Vikala, who wields the desired fruit," as she produced an oval-shaped berry in her soft palm. In her other hand she lifted up the bough of a tree with heavy green leaves and round clusters of pink and orange and yellow little starflowers. The fragrance filled his nose and the dazzling light through the mist seemed to glance around her hips. Vikala's eyes were half closed as she danced closer, saying, "I'm sure you're hungry," and indeed his stomach clenched with pain as he realized he had no idea how long he had been left alone in the cave. He found himself reaching for the fruit until Vikala laughed without restraint and he remembered his teacher's warnings, shoving it back into her palm.

"No! I'm not hungry."

"Well, then at least come for a swim," she tried once again to come near.

"No!" Genshai refused firmly.

Her eyebrows narrowed from the rebuke. She stepped backward and complained, "Monks are no fun at all!" and walked swiftly into beams of pink and orange light toward the branches of a distant tree shrouded in mist. The cave returned to complete blackness and the boy breathed out heavily, aware that without the warnings from his teacher, or the many lessons from the abbey on resisting temptation, he might have been persuaded to follow her away from the cave.

Genshai thought, *I need to find the Still Mind* and repeated the mantra aloud, "Still as floating clouds / still as the place between thought / still as steady rain."

His voice was emphatic within the echo of the room. The darkness filled his eyes and even though Genshai had probably been seated for hours, he hesitated to move in case he truly was beyond the Veil, afraid to wander too far in either direction.

"Are you going to be down here every night then?" came a squeaky, impatient request from nearby.

Genshai looked downward at his knee where he saw a small brown hairy figure looking at him with furious yellow eyes. His eyes adjusted to the dim glow of moss on the walls and he saw more than a dozen creatures curled in the rocks and stones, standing up from the ground like they were made from it. They were of various sizes, somewhat like bristly nighttime animals with snouts and claws.

Genshai blinked slightly, surprised. "What do you mean?"

"That's not a monk! False alarm!" came a raspy voice from within the crowd.

"It's just a little human boy," cajoled another, to which the whole crowd laughed harshly, like stones grinding together.

"I'm not a little boy," Genshai said indignantly.

"Oh now he's mad," one taunted with a harsh squeak, and they laughed again, tempting the boy to swat at them.

"I'm trying to meditate," he announced, straightening up to ignore them.

"Well, there it is," said the first creature, "A perfectly good crossing, ruined."

"Now there'll be monks meditating down here for the next hundred years," said another as they began to depart.

"Did they build a temple by the river or what?" one of them shrieked from the rear of the group as a dozen or so of the strange creatures shuffled off, almost like clumps of dirt or stones rolling downhill.

His mind reeled with questions: *What could all of these creatures be? I don't understand. Are they spirits from the Wreath? Am I in Shenai? Or Kuei?*

Then, whether it was in his eyes or in his mind, Genshai saw an orange light that approached from a distance, bobbing idly from left to right in the darkness like a specter in the air. His attention rose toward the bright lantern until he blinked and the traveler was suddenly upon him, but the light swung to the other side and there seemed to be nothing to hold it aloft.

A voice rich with texture said, "Hmm, rumors and whispers can be true. There is a monk in the crossing indeed."

The lantern lowered in a slow arc between them. It held a flickering thumb of flame inside and was made of glass, framed in coiling wrought iron that was overgrown by long vines. His eyes drew down, and he was startled to meet the gaze of a lion already upon him. Genshai was ready to leap to his feet and run away just as the lantern brightened, hanging from the tuft of a long sleek tail that arched overhead to reveal there were no walls and that he was sitting on a dark mound of earth beside three paths that crossed in an endless savannah at night.

The creature was poised and intent, staring with round gold eyes, flecked with green and rimmed in black. Its snout sloped to a broad triangular nose and a square muzzle with silvery whiskers, like a kind of spirit lion, with a thick mane of dark green leaves that fluttered in the wind, filled with hibiscus that bloomed in a train of pink and purple flowers down its back.

It held its gaze on the boy and spoke again, "The words, carried on the living wind, tell of a monk, meditating for three nights, here at the grotto. Are you he?"

Genshai kept the Still Mind, and tried to embody the placid, dispassionate expression of the abbot of Red Tower as he replied, "I am he," hardly remembering Taisan.

"Not an old man at all then," the spirit intoned laughingly, moving the lantern to get a closer look at the boy. "Not even a man yet. Just a child lost in the spirit country. Were you tricked? Did you wander here?"

"I'm not lost," Genshai replied indignantly, unable to help himself. "And I'm not a child."

"Not a very wise monk, then," the lion remarked, and Genshai felt rebuked until it relaxed its gaze, "I do not recognize you, but perhaps you are the one I hoped for, to go into the spirit country, all the way to the Aeiontree, to plead into the infinite sphere, to sit below the light of the Wreath."

"Where is that?" the boy asked, with a bit of curiosity at the edge of his voice.

"The center, where there is no center." The creature paced around him, the lantern swaying at the end of its tail. "Where the seed was planted by the Raekind, beyond Kuei, below Shenai, where questions are already answered, stories are already written, where all things are done and undone, made and unmade, at the end of all things that were ever set forth in time, and then at the beginning again."

"Well, I already have a quest," Genshai said with a note of realization. "Can you say anything about the hauntings in Westcliff?"

The spirit raised its snout to look toward an azure and starless sky; a gust of wind rustled its thick mane of green leaves and pink flowers, and eventually it suggested, "My name for your name? Your question for my question?"

With only a moment to think, Genshai nodded, "I agree."

The spirit said readily, "Then I am Andol."

"My name is Mountainroot," the boy offered his abbey name.

"Moun-tain-root," the spirit repeated the syllables carefully in its resonant voice, and Genshai felt a thrum in his ears at the sound of his name.

The boy wondered at the wisdom of giving away his name, and asked hopefully, "Are you an Illumidharma?"

"Nothing like that," the lion replied, opening its wide muzzle in a yawn. "I am one of the Pipajing, born from the Eldvalley, like my brothers and sisters, who live three by nine hundred years, all striding the ethereal Veil. So perhaps my time will come for rebirth in Kuei, but not yet." Andol brought the lantern to bear over them, putting Genshai in the center of an orange light. "Now for my question."

Genshai balked, "But I haven't asked you about Westcliff yet?"

"I heard nothing of Westcliff, you asked about the Illumidharma, and none of them are here – only Andol the Pipajing." The creature came forward until its golden eyes were just inches from the boy's face and he could smell the blooming flowers, like a fragrant hibiscus tree in late summer. Its fur was streaked with silver and gold, mulberry and black cocoa, and he could feel the dull vibrations of the lion's paw thudding under his seat with every step.

Daunted, he realized his mistake and asked, "What is your question, Andol?"

The spirit lion held his gaze for a long time. He looked deeply into the brown wells of Genshai's eyes until there was an unlocked movement, something dormant that turned over within him, and when Andol broke away the sensation was gone. He said, "I was on my way to the grotto in search of a monk," leading Genshai's gaze upward to a ceiling of clouds until he asked, "Why are you here?"

Genshai exhaled and looked around in the sudden darkness, broken from the reverie of meditation. The cave was utterly empty and cold except for the warmth of his breath. Standing upright, he paced around the black room and found that he was still very much in a cave deep under the earth. Yet he was shaken, not knowing if he had been through the Veil or not, thinking in any case the spirits were as real as people, but faded like things out of a dream.

Why am I here? Genshai wondered, unable to provide an answer.

In the darkness untold amounts of time passed. Maybe he slept and maybe he meditated, but his mind was like an undisturbed pool of water until he saw another light bobbing in the distance. Once again as he sat with legs crossed in the center of the room he heard his name, "Mountainroot," in a bold call from the laymonk's lips.

"I'm here," Genshai said, coming near the crack in the wall where the old man's face and woolly tangles of hair were brightened by the torch he held in his hand. The boy squeezed through the gap and emerged into the cavern of boulders under the jagged stone drapery of the high ceiling.

The old man looked him up and down and said, "Well, now you know some matters of the spirit, indeed."

The path went beside a row of columns and flowstones that shimmered with water, coming to the crossing of three paths. Instead of going down toward the subterranean lake, Taisan led them along a short trail that came to the precipice of another large cave. Holding the torch for him to see, Genshai was dazzled by the sudden brightness of the light reflecting off crystal walls, shards of amethyst, and piles of broken gemstones all across the cave floor. There was no path, but the monks could easily climb down to gather as much as they wanted.

"A memento?" Taisan suggested.

Genshai glanced at the glittering piles, not sure if they were real or false. He shook his head, "I don't use a meditation stone," and turned away, not wanting to take anything from the spirits.

They soon made their way back up the tunnel toward the mouth of the cave where the sun shined over the riverfront in the early afterfade. Kyus cheered happily from his place on the blankets beside the fire, and the horses whinnied and nickered upon his return, impatient to leave the cave once and for all. There was a meal waiting for him of stewed vegetables with brown tender meat that Taisan said was a pair of rabbits he had snared when the storm ended.

Genshai ate hungrily, and drank a whole kettle of greenleaf tea, as he asked between bites, "How long was I gone?" and his eyes gaped in surprise when he discovered that it had been nearly four days since he had gone into the hidden chamber.

"Four days!" he exclaimed.

"Time does not pass evenly in the spirit country," Taisan nodded, interrupting the boy when he opened his mouth, and said, "Not yet. Practice first."

Genshai agreed, and they broke apart from the firepit for a light training session with the Iron Palm bag. Taisan took up the baby for his usual sets of raises and drops, tilting Kyus from side to side to strengthen his neck, and otherwise kept him occupied while Genshai hit three sides of each hand. Striking the bag was secondary to keeping his palm relaxed. His thoughts were oddly clear, as he was still drained of all curiosities and desires and fears.

They went through the Mountain Form at a casual pace, and Genshai kept one question in his mind – *Why am I here?* – as he moved naturally in the stances that he had practiced since he had spied on the masters' secret meeting that day when he was twelve years old. Eventually that question, and every other question, dissolved into the stillness of his thoughts, and he simply moved by instinct.

He came into alignment then, awaking his Great Spirit, completely immoveable in the Seat-of-the-Mountain. No force could dislodge him, even as Taisan pushed and swept his legs. The boy stepped as he wished to step, cutting sharply, he grabbed the belt with the reverse arm and dumped the old man over his hip. Even from direct pushes, Genshai drove his opposite leg straight into the earth to become like a column of stone, which made Taisan laugh with the enjoyment of seeing his student finally get it right.

"That's the Seat-of-the-Mountain!" he exclaimed.

Afterward, in the softening light of eventide the monks went out to the river to bathe. The banks were swollen from the rainfall and the waters coursed quickly around their ankles as they washed the grime and sweat from their bodies. Genshai was quiet and preoccupied, lathering with citronella soap until he decided to use the straight razor to carefully shave his head and the soft tufts of brown hair under his nose and on his cheeks.

That evening Genshai told the laymonk everything he had encountered. He wanted answers to the appearance of Vikala, who carried the forbidden fruit.

"It was a vision of a Semori nymph," Taisan explained. "Possibly benevolent, but still mischievous. They love to seduce mortals, especially monks. Her grove is probably somewhere in the Farwood," and he explained that weak-willed men would be tempted from the path by her beauty, remaining enthralled for the rest of their lives, imprisoned at her tree in the spirit country.

Genshai confessed, "I might have gone with her. She was like nothing I had ever seen."

Taisan nodded. "I might've gone with her too," and the two of them shared a glance, knowing the temptations of Shenai might be greater than either of them could resist one day.

"But the gnomes are not very friendly at all," Genshai laughed, since he finally knew what the small bristly creatures were called. His teacher had explained they were among the Ekendra, or elementals, and that the gnomes were made from the earth and they appeared to be neither male nor female, like small dirt sprites that sought to live in the depths of the ground and have nothing to do with mortals if they could help it.

The boy was amazed to learn that Taisan had encountered many types of Ekendra over his journeys, as he said, "They come out of nature and return to nature. If you know where to look you'll always see them. Once I was in the highlands, and I had climbed to the highest peaks of Mount Durin to catch sight of the giant eagles there, but I fell, and I would have died, except a cloud appeared to catch me, and spoke to me in a woman's voice. She set me on the ground as gently as a feather and I never saw her again."

"That was lucky," Genshai said, and they laughed.

He wanted to know more, but Taisan was intrigued by the appearance of Andol from the Eldvalley as he explained, "The Pipajing are like old growth trees, or ancient whales. They are said to live a long time and to be aware of things beyond the Wreath. They are the lantern bearers, shining a light."

"But they can be reborn?"

"Oh yes," Taisan nodded. "Just like a gnome or a nymph, or any other kind of spirit in the cycle of the Wreath."

"He wanted my name," Genshai said, perturbed.

"You were trapped in his game of mischief," Taisan replied. "The Still Mind only guides you so far. You must also rely on your own cunning."

"I just told him my abbey name," Genshai said hopefully.

"It is still your name," Taisan shrugged. "Now he will always be able to find you wherever you are."

Genshai sighed inconsolably as he thought about Andol's question, *Why am I here?* not knowing if he would ever find the answer or not.

CHAPTER FIVE

Two sides of one man ride together, the war drum echoes,
choices cannot be unmade.

NEFTY A DORU

The bowstring released a hollow twang as the arrow went eagerly from his fingers, flying over the range, landing with a loud pop into the small rawhide target that was set nearly out of sight in the grass. Alone in the steppes every shot mattered, especially because their guardian Temuje always warned that every arrow they broke or lost was one less arrow to survive with.

"Don't waste anything," he had taught them sternly, as if it was his mantra, and it was obviously good advice since they had lived for years among the wild herds in the heart of the grasslands without anywhere to go back to, sleeping on a different patch of earth every night.

So Bokhili had learned to shoot perfectly to avoid mistakes. His draw and release was always smooth. His accuracy never failed. Even while riding on horseback he made shots at over two hundred feet without much difficulty so long as he wore the bone ring on his thumb. He enjoyed playing games with his cousins who threw a woven grass ball into the air for him to shoot at, able to pin an arrow through it at any height or distance.

Bokhili found that by applying all his focus into archery he could pour his anguish, his fear, his rage, into the tip of the arrow, releasing his heart into the target every time. It gave him balance and allowed him to think clearly, unlike his brother Selem, who hardly had any patience for archery practice anymore. Like all of them he was an expert shot on horseback, but Selem was more interested in fighting with his saber, or hand-to-hand. Over the years Temuje had taught them the ways of shooting and swordplay, riding and wrestling, pairing them against their older cousins and grown men until they were both more than proficient.

From a quiet place within his mind, Bokhili released numerous arrows, each one landing into the target with ease. He pinned the bowstring against the groove of his bone ring so that it held steady while he was riding, releasing his index finger and thumb at once to shoot. The others watched from around their small encampment, but as usual it was his cousin Dantai who hooted with joy, smiling exuberantly, full of unconditional support. He ran out to help recover the arrows, saying, "Those steel riders will be like confused ducks," although Bokhili's face was grim and he hardly said anything, lost in his own thoughts.

They were waiting, which was agonizing, even though it was part of their plan. Bokhili occupied himself with target practice, but Selem sat with Temuje and the other men, making sure the blade of his kilij was oiled and sharpened. They had already broken down their camp for the day, and Temuje refused to let anyone build a fire since they were so close to departure. They kept their horses saddled and tied nearby, and the men sat around on their haunches in the dirt, as much a part of the savannah as any buffalo or antelope. If anyone saw them, which nobody would since they were alone for thirty miles in any direction, they looked like ordinary herdsmen.

They had less than a dozen riders right now, but Bokhili and Selem were the only children among them, being just older than thirteen springs. They usually rode alongside the wild herds across the entire grasslands, which was said to be more than a thousand miles of wild country. Only the most loyal of their clan rode with them, the ones who had been closest to their father Usaka Kato, men who could be trusted with the knowledge the boys were still alive.

In the seven years since the Battle at Two Creeks the twins had been on the run from everyone. The chiefs of several rival clans still sought to eliminate their claim as Khanar, saying that all khagasun should be put to death; but the boys were especially hiding from the steel riders, not wanting to attract the Marshal's attention in case he came to finish what he started and slay the sons of Usaka.

In those first days after the attack it was just Temuje and Boroka who escorted the boys away from danger. They were keshik to Usaka Kato and when the battle began they swore to guard his sons, galloping away from the two creeks and then keeping up a steady trot for more than twenty miles. Temuje knew even then, just as they all gradually came to understand, that they would need to be suspicious of everyone in order to survive, and before long his paranoia became justified after they had suffered the first assassination attempt while they stayed in a family Hashaan, losing Boroka and barely escaping alive.

Temuje was the only one left, and it was through his dedication over the years that they had managed to secure the loyalty of the other men. He recruited their cousins Dantai and Baavgai who were the sons of their father's younger brother, while Huslen and a few others were part of the original keshik sworn into Usaka's service. More than once they were discovered, and if it weren't for the dutiful protection of their keshik and their old uncle Kuzhuk who kept them on the move every night, the twins would have perished within days of the attack.

As young boys it hardly mattered that they looked so much alike, since most brothers tended to look similar anyway, but as they got older it grew increasingly more obvious that they were identical twins. The story of the khagasun was known far and wide and there were still a number of people who blamed Usaka himself for the Battle at Two Creeks, saying that he cursed the Kato clan to destruction and that the Grass God Khahirazade was angry for being denied his rightful sacrifice.

"Do you know why they call you khagasun?" their uncle Kuzhuk asked them with an expectant stare. "Because your spirit was split in half at birth, and they think one of you should have been sacrificed to the Grass God."

The twins looked at each other. He had always been candid about the ancient custom of offering one twin to Khahirazade, but by now they had heard the story dozens of times. They still played the part of attentive boys, and spoke up when they were prompted to ask a question, although Selem rolled his eyes as he asked, "Then why did our father keep us together?"

Kuzhuk told the tale of their birth expertly. He had been there, waiting with Usaka while their mother Oyunn gave birth. She was the greatwife of the clan, or Usaka Kato's first wife, and when the labor began they selected a sacrificial oxen from the herd and prepared a celebratory feast. There was much excitement about a new heir to the Khanar until they discovered there were two sets of cries erupting from the tent, and instead of a naming feast, the shaman judged which child was intended for the family, and which was called to the gods. Kuzhuk waited anxiously all night to hear the shaman's decree since as Oyuun's brother and keshik he would be the one tasked with riding the khagasun at least one day away from the Hashaan, to leave alone to be swallowed up in the grass.

"She stared into the burnt ox bones for hours. She studied every crack and scorch, every bone and tooth and horn. At dawn's first light she came out and declared it was the will of the Grass God, great Khahirazade, for you both to be raised as one man on one horse, to become the left and the right hands of Kato."

It was a strange adjustment for everyone but Usaka accepted the decree, and since none except the shaman knew which child came first, nobody knew which was the true heir. As far as anyone could say they were the only twins in the entire Steppes of Thrail, which made them feel special and ashamed all at once. Both boys were raised with the knowledge that they would be Khanar together one day, and the story was widely told in all the grass families since there were several cousins who could swear by the blood of Kato that the events were true.

So without knowing which clans were friendly and which were not Kuzhuk and Temuje agreed to disappear into the cattle belt to live like herdsman until people only whispered the name Kato anymore. For years they had kept out of sight and let everyone believe they were dead. They encountered other riders very rarely but when they did the brothers were usually viewed as an oddity. Rumors spread that the sons of Usaka still lived, that they rode like one man on one horse, that they were biding their time until Qaijin the Wild Stallion came back to them from the sky.

Bokhili had always wondered, *Should one of us be dead? Should I be dead?* since he heard the word "khagasun" hushed and just out of earshot all his life, which implied that he and his brother were cursed with half a spirit.

Trying to distract himself, Bokhili checked his other supplies regardless of the fact that he had prepared everything earlier that day. His quiver held twenty-six birchwood arrows with various kinds of fletching that told him what sort of tip was at the end of each shaft; crane feathers for narrow points, duck feathers for broadpoints, and hawk feathers for the whistling arrow. After checking each one he sat quietly beside his brother and his cousins to rub wax into his bowstring until it was smooth and easy to draw.

Restless, Selem finally stood to his feet and demanded, "When will he be here?"

"Peace, boy," Kuzhuk said with a shrug. "He will come or he will not; either way we are ready."

Their uncle was quite a bit older than the other men, lean and tough, with brown skin, thick black hair, and a beard mixed with streaks of gray. He was the secondborn brother on their mother's side and when Oyunn was given as a greatwife, Kuzhuk went to the Kato clan as her sworn guard. The two of them made a home there and Kuzhuk took a second wife, but he occasionally rode between both clans to visit his first family, which was why he was not there on the day of the Battle of Two Creeks.

"But if he doesn't come then our plan has already failed," Selem replied, and Kuzhuk shrugged as if it was something they already knew, leaning back against his pack to close his eyes and doze in the late afternoon.

Temuje furrowed his scornful black eyebrows, "He may betray us to the devil and come with fifty steel riders!"

"We would see them from miles away," Baavgai said dismissively.

That much was true since Kuzhuk had chosen a small hill in the shade of the only tree for miles in every direction. Bokhili's sharp eyes saw a group of thirty antelope grazing at a fair distance, but otherwise the horizon was clear. He knew they were hidden deep in the steppes in one of the migration crossings where thousands of animals roamed, depending on the seasons of the year.

More than half of his life had been spent in the steppes. The journeys were rigorous, but riding alongside the herd he felt like he was part of them. He saw the way birds changed direction to follow the grass buffalo, anticipating their movements; and there were also herds of black-foot rhinoceros, elephants, gazelle and giraffe, deer of every type, and so many others. Most animals moved east in spring ahead of the rains and then turned south to avoid the snowpack, ranging in warmer weather all the way back to the west ridge for birthing season.

In truth, Temuje and Kuzhuk and the others were not herdsmen. They were sworn warriors that had been hiding on horseback for years, away from their families, just to protect the twins from being discovered. It was among the many reasons the brothers had decided it was time for a change. They were coming to an age when they could no longer ask their guardians to give up their lives to protect them, and they desperately wanted to return home to their camp the way it was in their memories as children.

For years they had heard of the prestige of the Kato name in tales of their wealth and their generosity, their strength and beauty, only to realize that their entire clan was now scattered across the steppes, their name turned to a whisper on the wind. Ever since

Selem could hold a kilij in his hands he had wanted vengeance, swearing, "I'll slaughter any steel rider that ever patrolled Neftya Doru," anytime they discussed their situation.

Selem was angry, but Bokhili was appalled. He wondered, *What if we are to blame?* and if their father had truly cursed the clan when he kept the khagasun together. For as long as Bokhili could remember he had carried the guilt of the massacre on his heart, knowing they had escaped astride their father's favorite horse while so many were being slaughtered. He always reassured himself, *We're alive because the Grass God told the shaman to keep us alive,* as he remembered his uncle's words, *We are one man on one saddle, the left and the right, the bow and the sword of Usaka Kato.*

Still he could not shake his feelings of responsibility. After the Battle at Two Creeks, the survivors ran to the other clans but the steel riders terrorized them for months until anyone who took in a Kato refugee seemed to be just as cursed. Over the years they were scattered like wild dogs, only accepted into the outer rings as herdsmen, or leather crafters, or servingmen. Most of the young people would never be trusted to become hatun or keshik and the women were only selected as second or third wives, never as greatwives, unable to pass on the Kato name.

"There he is!" Dantaai shouted, drawing everyone out of their thoughts. They all stood to their feet and peered south toward a rider just a mile out, wondering how exactly he had gotten so close without any of them noticing. There was only a subtle brown dust cloud rising up from a western horse, and he carried a ten-foot pole with a steel tip, a sharpened wedge that kindled in the fading light.

He was a westerner with ear-length auburn hair and ruddy skin that was bronzed from long days riding in the sun. Like most of the steel riders he wore strange metal armor like fish scales that overlapped, though it looked tarnished, with dozens of scratches and nicks and dents from years of fighting. As he approached, the westerner kept the spear tip lowered to the ground and clutched the shaft under his armpit while the men of the group spread around to greet him. They could see that when he moved his head there was a jagged scar over his left ear from an old combat injury.

Reining his horse to a stop, he said, "Peace my friends, peace my friends," with a disastrous accent.

"Garrat!" Selem said excitedly, running forward to greet their friend and protector, stopping just ahead to reach out and shake wrists, as two men would do.

Garrat released a triangular grin through his coarse beard and patted the boy's shoulder as he said; "Your grass is growing tall," using a common phrase in their language.

"We have been growing," Selem said reassuringly. It was true the two brothers seemed to change and grow at the same pace, becoming athletic and strong from their years on horseback and living only by what they tracked and foraged themselves. Yet their uncle Kuzhuk was always eager to remind them that they were still just children, not yet fifteen springs, and compared to the burly, tall, adult men beside them it was exceedingly obvious.

"Garrat," Kuzhuk said, coming forward, "The hour is close. What do you say about our plan?"

The knight scanned over the herdsmen and the group looked back, their expressions traced by the setting sun. They wore hardened leather shirts over their bare skin and wool trousers, carrying their sabers at their hips, some of them squinting in the light. Their ears were sloped and triangular, and sometimes very expressive, though mostly they were turned to capture the sounds; and the boys had identical brown faces with high, flat cheekbones and long black tresses of hair that spilled around their shoulders. Any of these men could tell the difference between them at a glance; knowing that Selem carried his saber on the left hip and Bokhili on the right, and that one was always ready with a grin and the other was quiet and serious.

Temuje always had one hand on the hilt of his saber in the presence of Garrat, whom he called the desert snake behind his back. Even though they all knew the westerner betrayed his own people to warn Usaka of the attack, and had since been exiled and hunted by the troops of Marshal Zukov, Temuje still did not trust him. A few of the others were similarly skeptical, but Garrat had come around so often over the years that it was easy for them to relax in his presence. There were times that he stayed for a day or two, and other times when he rode with them for weeks, disappearing and reappearing as he liked, although he always seemed to be able to find them no matter where Temuje took them.

Garrat spoke haltingly in their language. "The shipment from Zakariya will be in the great grass by tonight. It's a caravan of three, guarded by six steel riders…"

"That's it?" Selem interrupted.

Garrat held up a hand and said, "My friend in the oil yard told me six riders escort the shipment on the thousand-mile-trail, but when I spied on them a few nights ago I saw three drivers and eight soldiers."

"So your friend is a liar," Temuje waved a hand dismissively.

"It's not a lie," Garrat shook his head. "There are six men in armor, but they also have two marchers."

"Marchers?" Dantai had not ever heard the term before.

"Servingmen," Kuzhuk offered.

"Not exactly," Garrat replied, glancing at Bokhili.

The young boy spoke up, translating, "They are warriors that walk and fight from the ground," to which one or two of his cousins betrayed their surprise, though not Temuje, who had encountered western marchers before. In fact, after many long discussions with Garrat the brothers had learned western tactics, swordplay, and especially their language, writing out the complex characters of the king's speech in the dirt with a stick. Bokhili was the only one who could ever hope to be understood by a westerner, and Garrat said he spoke low-Arovian with even more fluency than most commoners did.

"So eleven men," Selem concluded, looking to his brother. "Sounds like it'll be easy."

Bokhili resisted saying anything. They might have fought and run to defend themselves before, but the twins had never willingly sought out conflict, which made his heart uneasy. It went against everything Kuzhuk and Temuje tried to teach them. None of them wanted to bring down the wrath of Marshal Zukov, knowing that if they were provoked the steel riders would massacre entire families in the name of protecting their shipments of oil from the Free Cities.

Yet by the time they were thirteen springs their guardians had realized the boys would never be satisfied with hiding in the cattle belt with nothing except the legacy of their great name. It was true that Bokhili wanted justice, and Selem had voiced his need for revenge so often, that they began to talk seriously about a raid even though they were not yet old enough to be called men. Selem liked to think their uncle was convinced by the virtue of their skills, but Bokhili thought the real reason was that Kuzhuk was secretly ready to go home to the meadowlands. Their life was hard, and even harder when they could not visit the different grass families for rest and care. Kuzhuk had children of his own, who he had not seen in years – their cousins, who were their loyal friends – and the twins managed to convince him to appeal to their grandfather one more time to let them hide among his people in the meadowlands.

Silence descended for a moment. The brothers exchanged a meaningful stare, communicating with their ears turned down. The men stood around awkwardly as if trying to determine who their leader was, eyeing Temuje, Garrat, Kuzhuk, until young Selem stepped forward and said, "Let's ride for the plains crossing," which mobilized them to leap on their horses, coming around the tree, down the side of the hill, and galloping south across the grasslands when the sun was on the horizon like a half closed eye.

The twin brothers rode one single horse, Selem holding the reins and Bokhili on the back with a birchwood bow in his hands. For the last seven years they had ridden their father's stallion, a steppe horse with a tan color and a long white mane that was taller and faster, and tamed from the wild herd by Usaka Kato himself. Sometimes a mount was named in honor of a slain rider, becoming a ghost horse, and usually they were released back into the wild to run and live freely, yet without fail Usaka always returned to their camp. It was certainly a comfort to the twins when they were just little boys, as if calling for the ghost horse was like calling to the spirit of their father.

The boys traded places quite often, riding in a larger saddle that could fit them both, and combined they were the weight of one man with heavy gear, although as they grew older it became more and more obvious that they were sitting too close together. Of course their uncle Kuzhuk didn't want them to appear anymore peculiar than they already did, so a few years ago he arranged for Usaka to sire as many as twenty foals with the hope that they would yield two good colts for the boys to claim one day.

It was a great honor to be descended from a ghost horse, and they made several visits to the ringfamilies of different clans where the Kato people had been displaced. It was a good arrangement for them since the owner of the mare gained the use of the foal so long as the horse remained loyal to the Kato family for the day when they were called back to their Khanar, and their were plenty of people that didn't believe that was ever going to happen.

They rode south for less than two hours to the place they had picked where caravans often stopped for a rest. There was a creek where merchants often watered their horses and pitched camp, building fires that could be seen like orange jewels in the black night. After setting out from Zakariya the caravan was probably seven or eight days into its journey on the thousand-mile-trail, with still a half-month to go before they would make it all the way to the Snake River in the Canyons of Quay, and Bokhili had no idea how much farther it was after that to Shijing, the last city of Arovia. They were virtually in the middle of nowhere, with Neftya Doru as the only defining landmark, itself not much more than a dirt wagon track.

Following Temuje's example, they slowed to a complete stop more than three miles away in a bluff of waving grasses. The sound of horses in the steppes was not so unusual but Temuje was cautious anyway. He whispered single-word directions; but their plans had been discussed and rehearsed so many times that they had no need for a long explanation. The group split, leaving Selem, Temuje, Baavgai, and Garrat to advance on foot while the others rode in a wide circle until they were flanking the camp. It wasn't a complicated plan. They would pin the steel riders with arrows from the creek and force them to run right into the curved blades waiting in the road.

Bokhili dismounted the ghost horse easily on the south side of the encampment. He withdrew two arrows from his quiver, moving as silently as a cat until they came to the edge of the shallow creek and crouched in the grass. He pretended they were on a hunting excursion, creeping onto an unsuspecting herd of antelope with his uncle and his cousins Dantai and Huslen, all armed with birchwood bows. They stayed hidden for several long minutes and Bokhili knew his brother and the others must have been holding their position for nearly half an hour, waiting for his signal to attack.

Waiting for what? he asked himself. Most of the steel riders were asleep and the fire had died down to the last pieces of burning wood. He saw two men who seemed to be awake, passing a gourd of wine back and forth as they chatted quietly until one of them stood up to walk to the river and urinate next to a tree.

Once they were separated Bokhili lifted his bow and released his first shot in a high volley. It was a whistling arrow, made of carved animal bone with several horizontal grooves that allowed air to slide through until it was shrieking like a hawk. Both sentries glanced around in sudden surprise but Bokhili's second arrow and Dantai's first landed like deadly stings in the back of the man at the river. Just as they planned, the remaining sentry called out to the steel riders who emerged confusedly from their tents in all manner of undress with swords drawn.

"It's the damn twillies!" someone declared in the king's speech.

"Where are they?"

Bokhili drew out two broadpoints from his quiver and led his group in releasing two more volleys that rained down over the camp, ripping through it. Bodies collapsed to the ground amid shouts of pain and the steel riders hardly had a moment to think before four men appeared out of the darkness to attack from behind, their blades slashing mercilessly, ringing out with every deflection until one man unleashed a harrowing death wail when his belly was cut across by Temuje's saber.

On the south side Bokhili ran shouting with his uncle and cousins to join the fight. Just as they had hoped, the rain of arrows had diminished the westerners to half their men and it was a simple matter of outnumbering them. The last man faced off against Selem and Garrat, while Baavgai circled like an opportunistic leopard with a hungry sneer as they managed to turn him around, cutting on either side as he collapsed. Anyone left alive was soon dead from their wounds and the sounds of battle faded into the night until all that was left were their quick conversations.

"We did it, khagasun!" Selem said in hushed exuberance, using the word like a term of affection that meant more between them than 'brother.' He wiped the blood from his sword on the clothes of a dead man while Bokhili recovered the broadpoints that were salvageable, even though he couldn't find the whistling arrow anywhere. At first he tried to hold his breath when he yanked the shafts out of the bodies, pretending it was the same as hunting wild game; but it wasn't the same, and he knew that he had killed at least two of them.

The men congratulated each other and even Kuzhuk seemed elated by the small skirmish, so Bokhili kept his feelings to himself. Instead he went to recover the horses since they wanted to be heading south as soon as possible. Kuzhuk counted the barrels of refined oil and tallied up several trade items while the others searched the pockets and pouches and found square pennies, a few silver and gold coins, and little else of value, before they dragged the bodies a mile north into the tall grasses.

Daybreak was only five hours away, and Bokhili slept uneasily, his thoughts preoccupied with what they had done.

CHAPTER SIX

*The Battle for Heaven, a play, "Would that I received your
love evermore, or just your praise into my heart, like a father
to a son, for all the mighty tasks you have asked me to do in
your name – and for the Mother of the World."*

THE SHEPHERD'S HOME

They set out early, departing from the cave in the forehour
of dawn. The light was middling gray and the air was cool
as they went down the hill of the riverside to rejoin the
ranger trail. Genshai tried to look back, but within a few minutes
the foliage swallowed the cave entrance and it was gone. Even
though he was absolutely certain the experiences were real, already
there were long gaps in his memory, and now sitting at the
crossroads seemed like a dream. Only the most emotional moments
were in sharp clarity, or the things that left him with questions. The
mysterious appearance of the Pipajing was made even more difficult
by the fact that he could only remember the pleasant tones of
Andol's bold voice, but scarcely anything of what was said between
them, except the question that lingered in his mind, 'why are you
here?'

The horses were eager for the journey, both of them reacting
to the need to make up time on the road. Taisan carried Kyus

strapped tightly against his chest and urged them into a steady canter that took them on the northward trail for another day with only a few breaks. The weather was warm and humid under the leafy bowers of the forest and when they broke into the rolling countryside in the late afterfade the wind was suddenly cool and there were scant, wispy clouds over the mountains to the north.

"We're sixty miles seaward," Taisan called out as they went down a little-used bridlepath through the long grass in the lowlands of the Auburn Range. They rode past the eventide; the sun descending until all they had left to see by was a pink ribbon of light on the west horizon. As they unpacked their bedrolls, Genshai looked east toward the center of the range and imagined that he could see Red Tower standing upright from the peaks in the gathering darkness.

The two laymonks spoke very little after a long day of heavy riding, and they stretched while Kyus crawled restlessly in the grass, going as fast as he could. They shared baked oats and nuts, a raw carrot and some radishes, and pieces of pemmican from their saddle rations. They drank cool river water from their skin, giving the last of the milk to the baby, and before long they reclined on the grass in the mild night to look up at the brilliant sky. Without a fire, the stars were bright and plentiful; their constant white and yellow lights winking every so often by movement that might have been bats in the sky or – he realized – spirits in the Veil.

"There's no moon," Genshai commented as he held Kyus in his lap and allowed the boy to scramble all over him.

"It rises late," Taisan pointed to the east, where there was only a bare sliver of light at the rim. "It's a new moon. The clerics call that a Hidden Bloom."

"Does that mean it's Livendor now?" Genshai asked, since the weather of the day had felt like it was the beginning of summer.

"Indeed," Taisan nodded as he pointed to the five stars of prominence that broadened over the sky. "That's the constellation in the zodiac called the Five Rivets of the Shield of Shao Daan."

"Well, who is Shao Daan?" Genshai asked, since he didn't know the legends of the Raegods at all.

"Just one of the heroes of the Lost Age," Taisan shrugged, until he saw that Genshai was interested and wanted to know more. He thought deeply for a moment, the three of them staring up at the immeasurable stars as he said, "There was once a girl thousands of years ago that charted the stars at the lighthouse of Seers Point. She was the one to discover the tales of the Raegods and all their children written in the sky, eventually setting them down in the Book of the World," as he described when the zodiac of the Eurysus Calendar was said to have been developed two eras ago, at the beginning of recorded time.

"The story goes that Shao Daan was the son of the god of justice," Taisan continued.

"Shao Daan was the son of a god?" Genshai asked disbelievingly.

"So they say," Taisan shrugged. "In the Lost Age, the Golden Mother sent her champion Livvenahara down from the heavenly island to sire a child that would stand for the Laws of Heaven. Of course, he was born with a rigid sense of right and wrong; gifted with the strength of five hundred men, but his appetite was so enormous that it took an alliance of five kings to keep up enough food for him. He was sworn to cleanse the riverlands for settlement, holding sword and shield, fighting off devils and ghosts by himself."

Genshai sat with the baby, both confused and exhilarated.

"Now the village defenders wear the patch of Shao Daan, since his shield was the shield that protected all people," Taisan concluded.

They let the matter fade into silence under the stars. The boy had never heard this much from any monk about the Raegods before, not realizing until now how much lore there was that predated the monks of the Aegin Tradition. He wasn't sure what to believe, but he knew the disciples of Sibudat were products of that time when warlords and seers were tearing the world apart with conquest. He now understood why their ancient teacher of peace and wisdom was said to have carried the Lotusblade, which he used only to protect the innocent.

Genshai lay back with Kyus settling to sleep under his arm and stared up at the blue night streaked with white stars. He was soon lulled to sleep by the soft regular breaths of the baby, dreaming of spirits and godly warriors, and then subsequently he was awake just as the glimmers of dawn teased his eyelids. Clutching the child, he sat forward on the fleece bedroll. The grass around him was damp with dew and their horses were grazing widely apart in the pasture.

In a rare instance he had woken earlier than his teacher, who seemed to be in a deep slumber with his eyes tight, lying on his side under his quilt. Genshai asked himself, *Isn't a vision of Shenai just like a dream?* And wondered if that was what the abbot at home had meant by crossing the First Gate when he taught them to meditate into the spiritlands.

Genshai went to gather the horses and returned to find his teacher awake and alert. Before anything else could be done they practiced the Simple Sets and several other calisthenics, breathing in rhythm, staring boldly into the face of the rising sun, which was a reddening blaze until it became a gleaming yellow disc that he could hardly glance at while they practiced. Taisan took frequent breaks from the routines to catch the scrambling baby. He lifted Kyus in both arms and dropped him low until the child was waving his arms and screeching with laughter.

Soon they were riding on the bridlepath until they joined a wagon road from the crest of a hill. By midmorning they had already gone fifteen miles when they pulled beside a small bridge that crossed a brook adjacent to the road to water the horses and take a light meal of rations. He hardly noticed his hunger, feeling strangely complacent as they gave the baby the last of their dried fruit to suck on and Kyus drank greedily from the waterskin, whining for milk even through there was none.

The hills were filled with green clover and flocks of sheep roamed everywhere as they journeyed westward. On the right the ridges went jaggedly upward to the tree line of the mountains, and on the left were wide pastures that were swept by the winds from the sea. Holding the child in the sling against his chest, Taisan urged them into a fast trot across several miles and by now Genshai was accustomed enough to riding that he no longer bounced onto his rear as much, having discovered that he could relax his waist and hips in anticipation of Meora's movements until he felt completely at ease.

The rocky crags of the Auburn Range joined the shore and the salt marshes were like black shallows that stretched out to what was known as the Larenn Sea. The vastness of the water was overwhelming; it was unlike anything he had ever seen. Genshai tasted salt in the wind and watched long white lines of surf break and roll in the distance, hearing the call of gulls overhead. Genshai pointed excitedly at the broad white sails on the sea, and said, "Look at the boats!" as the fishermen caught the wind to return home for the night.

The main road led down to where the village was built in a rounded bay with a port of ships as wide as the town itself. The whole place seemed to spread upward from there, and the Oathlord's hall was obviously the timber lodge on the highest ground while most of the other buildings were two-story wooden houses and stone cottages with black tiled roofs, or shabby hovels by the seafront.

There weren't many travelers on the road but there were a few folks that looked on them curiously, not accustomed to strangers in Westcliff. The old laymonk had a way of appearing approachable and soon he struck up a friendly exchange with a shepherd that came down the road holding his crook with a trained hound at his heels. Nobody seemed to recognize them so far, though Genshai was certain that folks would eventually know that they were monks by the look of them.

"How long has it been since you've traveled here?" Genshai asked.

"A long time," Taisan admitted. "I haven't had occasion to come so far west. The people here probably haven't seen a monk in ten years."

"Is this whole place cursed?" Genshai asked, looking around.

"I don't think it works like that," Taisan shook his head. "It's usually a building, or a person, that bears a curse."

They quickly found the shrine in the square overlooking the docks. It was a wide building with a stone foundation that was finished with timber columns and eaves that gave the roof a gradual peak. "The Three Sisters," Taisan pointed to three granite statues, impressively sculpted and standing in a line at the front of the shrine, and the boy recognized the symbols of Maitreija, a maiden holding flowers and sheaves of grain. The middle statue was Alloraiah, goddess of the hearth and family, with her cauldron; and the last was Yuemaiah, goddess of the flock with her shepherd's crook. They all had lovely, weathered expressions, and the stone was faded as if the statues had been there for many years.

Just as they were looking around, perhaps twenty clerics emerged from the doors of the shrine, many of them wearing shawls of different colors to cover their hair in the wind. They spread into smaller groups and soon disappeared into the village streets to walk home after their daily observances. Genshai couldn't help but to glance away with shyness when the women gaped at the monks on horseback beside the statues. The last people closed the doors and one of them produced a large brass key to lock up the shrine for the night. She was an older lady with a stately bearing, wearing the holy vestments of a Matriarch around her shoulders, accompanied by two younger girls that wore blue and green cambric school uniforms.

The laymonks dismounted and Taisan said, "Mind your brother," as he unloaded Kyus into the boy's arms before he took up his staff and walked toward the three women with one hand open and upraised.

Genshai clutched the baby to his shoulder and took the reins of both horses to a hitching rail that overlooked the fish markets. There were a number of boats that came slowly to port. The dockworkers signaled with their hands and tossed ropes across the gaps to ease the ships into each pier. When the planks were down fishermen hauled entire baskets into the marketplace. Kyus looked quickly from left to right, fascinated by birds flying and the glare of light off the black waters until Meora brought her head close by and the baby grabbed clumps of her brown mane in his tiny fist, shrieking with joy.

Within a few minutes the old laymonk returned with the small group and said, "This is the Matriarch of the shrine, Agatha Wynne, the Lady of Westcliff and her two daughters," and Genshai remembered her husband was just appointed by the Warden to oversee Westcliff, and she had been sent to reopen the shrine.

"Milady," Genshai bowed politely as he gripped the babbling baby in his arms.

"You're the only ones the Warden sent?" Lady Wynne demanded stiffly.

"Yes, but we are the monks of Red Tower," Taisan said reassuringly.

Agatha glanced at the infant in the boy's arms and hardly seemed to suppress her annoyance as she said, "I suppose I'm glad you've finally come. Our letter made it to the Warden more than two months ago and the hauntings are only getting worse. We've been waiting, but now six more people are cursed," to which the laymonks exchanged glances with each other.

"Where is the site of the haunting?" Taisan asked.

The Matriarch narrowed her eyes, as if she was rebuking them. "This entire village is haunted," and the girls beside them stiffened uncomfortably at their mother's stern displeasure.

Taisan nodded patiently, "Of course," and then he explained they had been traveling for the better part of two weeks to make it from the Hall of the North to the saltcoasts. Through some stilted conversation the Lady Wynne crossed her arms and made it clear she thought the Warden should have responded sooner and sent more men, without babies in their arms. The old monk's golden face paled somewhat and he seemed unsure of what else to say.

"But mother, it must be in our favor that they're arriving in the first quarter of Livendor," one of the girls said hopefully. She appeared to be around the age of nineteen being taller and more rounded than her sister, and all three women had skin the color of teak and long fine black hair partially covered by a shawl, but nonetheless blowing around their faces in the wind. In spite of himself, Genshai began to feel curious about their names, and the touch of their hands within his, until he took a silent breath and reminded himself of why they were there.

"We will need to read the auspices tomorrow," the Matriarch replied without wanting to commit to any kind of judgment, but she did arch an eyebrow in Taisan's direction. "Although, you might be right, Alina. The hero Shao Daan fought back spirits, ghosts, and devils, and here are two monks ready to help."

"Shao Daan wasn't a monk," the younger girl contradicted.

"That's enough Ysma, don't speak out of turn," Lady Wynne admonished her daughter, who seemed to be about sixteen and was quite a bit skinnier but not as tall as her sister, holding a book and a bundle of parchment sleeves, which made her look very studious.

"Lady Wynne," Taisan glanced at the sun's descent, which was about forty-five degrees above the horizon. "My student and I have been riding all day but I do think we need to begin as soon as possible."

"Of course," she nodded her head, pleased with the old man's remark.

The group went on the village road that overlooked the fish markets where the stalls would be open first thing tomorrow morning. Now at eventide there were more than two-dozen vessels moored at the docks but Genshai could see several others that stayed out on the sea, anchored overnight. The road turned along the hillside and went around until they were at the highest point of the village where the Oathlord's timber lodge was built in the old style of the northlands.

The place was on a wide parcel of land in front of a massive forest on the leeward side of the hill. Of course nothing would match the size of the Warden's lodge in Norhaal, but the family still enjoyed high rafters and fine wooden furnishings ahead of a broad fireplace built of rough stones stacked to fit each other. They settled around a smooth oaken table and soon two servants came from the kitchen to offer refreshments of wellwater and pitchers of light tablebier; they brought a platter of brined vegetables, salty sheep's cheese, and fillets of sturgeon that had just been smoked on pinewood that morning, served with a cold white sauce of capers and minced pickles and smeared on warm flatbread just out of the oven.

Holding Kyus on his left knee, Genshai used his other arm to help himself to the food, hardly noticing while the two girls glanced at each other with slight smiles the way sisters do when they each find something amusing. Kyus whimpered hungrily, until the servants brought milk and softened root vegetables for Genshai to feed him with, and he managed to deliver a spoon to the child's mouth in between his own bites. In the meantime, Taisan listened attentively to Lady Wynne, who frequently crossed her arms and took in sharp breaths like she was readying herself for something. His hazelbrown eyes were soft and welcoming, but with his gray fluffy hair and travel-worn Aeigi jacket he hardly looked like someone who could fight off angry ghosts at midnight.

Agatha hardened her face and said, "They appear every night the Lotus is in Bloom and whomever they encounter by their touch is stricken with madness."

"Your letter said there were six shades," Taisan said.

Lady Wynne looked away, "I don't know for certain. That's what the witch says."

"The witch?" Taisan asked curiously.

"A woman that came here last winter and took up residence in the tavern in exchange for charms and fortunetelling," Lady Wynne said irritably. "She claims there are six, but of course there's no way to be sure."

The baby cried out sharply and Genshai looked up sheepishly, "Well, I guess he doesn't like pickles," and the ladies of the Wynne family all exchanged glances, the girls wondering if their mother would lose her patience, since every little thing lately seemed to set her on edge.

"When did they first appear?" Taisan asked.

"I can't say," Agatha released an exasperated sigh and rubbed her temples as she explained, "We only came here a year ago. My husband, Euiger, and the Warden are first cousins you know, on his mother's side." She continued with biting sarcasm, "There were ill tidings from Westcliff, so in his glorious wisdom Headel decided to send us here to restore the shrine of the Three Sisters," explaining that her husband's maternal grandfather was lord of Westcliff, and without a male heir the lands had fallen into their hands when the old man had died.

"At first we liked it here," Ysma interrupted, her eyes darting to her mother who said nothing, pursing her lips. "Dad used to say that he spent every summer here as a boy, sailing with his grandpa."

"That was before the hauntings," Alina said grimly.

Between them all they told the story. In the weeks after their arrival they learned the folktales of angry ghosts that rose at midnight during the full moon, and some people even claimed to have seen them on the roads like gossamer fabric that shined in the moonlight and spread a cold fear into their hearts. None of the family had believed in the curse. Alina and her mother had faith in the gods, Euiger was a brawny and fearless knight, and Ysma was simply too studious and smart to be caught believing in superstitions and fairytales.

Agatha shook her head, "We thought these women were just uneducated, ever since the shrine was abandoned decades ago," as if that explained why they believed in gossip and rumors. Then, during the next full moon the tides rising on the salt marshes seemed to come with a wailing on the wind that Lady Wynne said was so hollow she thought it was the breeze from the sea, but at some point it had become like a shrill bell that was louder in their ears than even the voice of someone in the room next to them. The shades began to rise out of the foothills in frenzied rushes toward the sea. They flashed through the streets, and chased people into their homes with impunity.

People were shocked when the first guardsmen to draw a sword against them began to descend into speeches of madness and fits of violence over the next few days. It made no sense, but soon the Oathlord himself saw a ghost in the street. There was no denying their existence after that, and every month they claimed more victims until now there had been several deaths, and there were twelve people locked in the jail cellar inflicted with madness, "Though we won't be able to keep any more if this continues," Agatha sighed, pressing her fingers firmly into her temples as if she was exhausted.

Taisan asked, "Lady, where is your husband?"

The family exchanged uncomfortable glances and one of the servants loudly clattered some plateware together as she cleared the table.

"My husband was the fourth man to be cursed," Agatha said, blinking her eyes quickly while her daughters each looked downward to conceal their expressions. Almost as if she were angry with the monks, she demanded, "So what can you do about all of this?"

"There are no guarantees," Taisan said carefully. "The matters of the spirits are questions for us all, but there are some steps we can take."

"Such as what?"

"First we need to find the source of the haunting," Taisan said. "Genshai and I will go out tonight in search of the ghosts."

"But tonight isn't a full moon," said Ysma with a curious expression.

"Nights of the Hidden Bloom, like tonight, are also known to be favorable for spirits," the old laymonk said, using the cleric's term to refer to the thumbnail moon. "We may be able to communicate with them."

"What good would that do?" Agatha demanded, not knowing the difference between ghosts and spirits. "We don't want to enrage them further."

Taisan replied knowingly, "My Lady, they are not enraged. They are in torment."

After that, there was not much else to say. The Lady Wynne did not offer them lodging and neither did Taisan ask for it, but at her request the servants did give them a flagon of milk and new diaper cloths for the baby. Genshai felt like the two daughters were on the fringes of the main hall the whole time, although whenever he looked around they weren't there, and soon the monks were sent outside at eventide to ride their horses down the road around the hillside toward the village.

The town was not very large, though there were three taverns at least in the market square and one additional inn down by the boardwalk. Each of them had lamps in the windows and smoke rising out the chimneys, being partially busy with guests since every sailor in port seemed to be looking for a night of comfort ashore, and there were a few merchants in town looking to haggle at the fish markets, or meet with the shepherds about wagonloads of fleece.

"Which one?" Genshai asked, tentatively curious about each tavern.

"The one with the fortuneteller," Taisan remarked as if he had given it some thought.

Soon they dismounted and tied their horses to the hitching rail at the livery in town, and Taisan crossed the road to ask folks that smoked their pipes and drank their mugs of beer on the front porch of the tavern if there was a woman reading cards inside. Genshai began to get annoyed with Kyus, who whined and kicked impatiently in the sling as if he were eager to crawl around with the dogs that ran through the alleys. It wasn't until they went down the boardwalk that they found what they were looking for, a tavern called the Siren's Song directly overlooking the harbor where the ships bobbed in the dark waters.

They stepped through the doors where the room was dimly lit with oil lanterns and a fire blazed in the hearth. Several rough looking sailors glanced at them before turning away uninterestedly to resume drinking while two men caroused laughingly at the bar with the innkeeper as he poured tankards of ale from the faucets of four huge barrels tilted on their sides. Then suddenly an ample curly haired woman rose up from her seat with her breasts hanging out of her dress as she led a sea-weathered man by his finger across the room.

Genshai's eyes widened at the sight of several women sitting around the hearth wearing tight corsets, revealing bodices, or long robes and nothing else. They wore black kohl on their eyelids and red pigment on their lips, and their faces brightened as they talked with men, taking their rough hands into their soft palms. Taisan scanned the room, unconcerned with the scene of the brothel, and took a step toward the bar when suddenly a girl swept forward in a flowing skirt with a bare midriff and grabbed Genshai by the firm muscle of his arm, saying, "Well, you're fresh off the boat aren't you?" she said looking him up and down.

Genshai revealed somewhat shakily, "We're the laymonks of Red Tower."

"Oh, a monk boy," she exclaimed, putting her hands on her hips, "Does that mean you're a virgin?" looking back at the girls who were all ready with laughter.

Genshai looked bashful, not knowing what to do until his teacher grumbled, "Alright, leave him alone."

"Whatever you say, old man," she shrugged indifferently, turning around with a whirl of her skirt to rejoin the others.

Kyus cried abruptly, tired and hungry after a long day of travel. The entire tavern fell silent as Genshai produced the child from his sling and held him awkwardly in his arms as he attempted to comfort him, which only made him cry harder. "Get that baby out of here," the innkeeper demanded, embarrassing the boy which made the women cry along with laughter until Taisan took the baby right into his arms and rocked him back and forth, quieting him down instantly.

Holding the child, Taisan asked, "We're looking for the fortuneteller. Is she here?"

Some of the women glanced at each other pointedly, sitting in plush chairs beside the fireplace. One of them sat forward, she was lean and as pale as cream and ash, like the people of the Empire of Kenan, and she grinned with bright red lips, saying in an eastern dialect, "She knew you would come."

"Where is she?" Taisan asked easily.

"Tonight, Mistress Tauva is reading the stars," the pale woman pointed to a closed door in the corner that seemed to lead out toward the beachfront.

As they moved, Genshai couldn't help but glance back for another look at the girl that first approached him. She was certainly older, he guessed in her mid-twenties, memorizing her short ear-length black hair and slender frame, knowing the slant of her smile, holding the gaze of her calm lidded eyes until the door was closed behind him. Then they were beside the boardwalk leading to the seashore at night with only the stars to see by and the sound of the waves crashing.

"Well, Taisan, I should have known it would be you," said a woman's voice from the shadows where she was puffing a pipe of pure sweetleaf and nursing a frothy tankard of porter on the table beside her.

"When I heard your name, I hardly believed it," Taisan confessed, holding his staff with one hand and the baby in the crook of his other elbow.

Mistress Tauva sat forward to strike a tindertwig against the table and lit an oil lantern to break the darkness. Bands of smoke drifted around her head and shoulders, trailing up from the embers in her pipe. Her eyes were traced in black kohl and her long brown and gray hair draped around her shoulders. She sat back and crossed her legs, wearing a fringed skirt and old leather boots. There was a small booklet on the table with a nearby quill and inkwell, although it seemed to Genshai that she had been sitting silently and alone for a long while.

"I thought you were dead after that Midsummer Eve," Taisan said, vaguely broaching the subject. "I tried to search for you."

"Not dead. Just gone a long time," Tauva answered evenly. Her eyes glinted like flint in the lamplight, and her lips were pursed and alert which made her face look sleek in the shadows of the boardwalk.

Taisan nodded somberly, "I was sorry we lost you."

"Not as sorry as me," Tauva replied shortly as she crossed her arms, looking at him expectantly. Her wrists clinked with beaded bracelets and charms inscribed with the godmarks and there were three or four talismans around her neck. Not only that but she also had a line of holy symbols tattooed down the ridge of her forearm, accompanied by a bold crux that was partially obscured by her sleeve, the sign of the Mother of the World and the key of life.

"So, you're reading fortunes now?" Taisan observed the thick deck of oracle cards that sat comfortably on a deep blue silk sash. He moved to take a seat in the empty chair across the table and settled the baby onto his lap, keeping the cards just out of his reach.

"That and other things. A woman has to live somehow," Tauva shrugged as she took a short swallow of beer and then puffed twice on the glass pipe until the ember brightened, exhaling a heady plume of smoke all around them. "The girls here need a healer. You know, someone who can treat womanly concerns."

"Then are you a ghost finder now also?" Taisan inquired curiously.

"It's easy enough to find them," she said matter-of-factly. "They appear outside the village on the first rising of the Lotus in Bloom."

"And then where do they go?"

"Everywhere," Tauva said. "They scream through the streets for three nights. Anyone they encounter is afflicted with a devastating fear, and if they touch you it will cause a raving madness."

"Like how?" Taisan wanted to know.

"The first man was a defender. He tried to draw a sword against one, but of course they're just apparitions," Tauva said in a low tone.

"What happened to him?" Genshai asked, despite himself.

Tauva glanced at the boy and said with the harshness of smoke in her voice. "In those next few days he seemed normal enough, but his wife came to me for a reading and said he was speaking nonsense, jumping at movements, or whispers, that weren't there. He was not himself anymore. He stopped arriving for guard duty, and he was seen walking after people, baring his teeth, even barking like a dog. One day he harassed a young girl so much in the street that she ran home crying and her father beat him up, saying he was sick in the head."

"His wife?" Taisan asked worriedly.

Tauva's eyes tightened, the only sign that she might be affected by the story, as she said, "By the end of the week he had strangled her, and then he cut his own wrists with a rusty nail."

"By the gods!" Taisan appeared shocked. "Have there been other attacks?"

"Oh yes," Tauva nodded. She told them of a young sailor who had no strange thoughts at all until he set sail and within a night had hung himself from the mast of the ship; and most recently a townswoman who tried to slice her daughter's throat after supper but was stopped by her oldest son. The town Alderman had given standing orders that the guards were to hold each person touched by the ghastly finger in the jail cellar to prevent them from harming anyone else.

"Of course, they don't want my help until they need it," Tauva said resentfully, "But the madness is clearly a transferred memory."

"Transferred memory?" Genshai asked.

"Bits and pieces most likely," Taisan suggested.

"Perhaps," Tauva said dismissively, "But the unrest in Westcliff is different than other hauntings I've seen."

Taisan nodded until he said, "I will need to tell you about Ulfghar's Ridge then," bouncing the baby naturally on his knee.

The fortuneteller's eyebrows lifted curiously, "I have always heard rumors there was some kind of wolf attack years ago," as if she already knew the story.

"What about the Oathlord?" Taisan asked. "Euiger?"

"He was the fourth man to be touched by the ghost woman,"

Tauva explained. "By morning he started on an angry speech to the Alderman and while he was still coherent his wife convinced him to be taken into custody."

"And now?"

"None of his words make any sense," she shook her head, "And he's been chained down to keep him from cracking his own skull against the wall."

"Do you know where the ghosts come from?" Genshai asked.

The woman's sharp gray eyes looked at the boy. She appraised him up and down before she said, "I thought you'd never ask."

———

By the darkhour after midnight, Mistress Tauva had taken them on a rough wagon trail through the foothills of the Auburn Range until they were ten miles from the village. She had asked one of the brothel girls with a baby of her own to keep an eye on Kyus, and for a few copper bits she graciously agreed. Earlier that evening they had stabled their horses in the local livery where Meora and Snowcap could refresh themselves, and on the long walk Tauva acquainted them with the folktales she had learned in the few months since she had arrived to Westcliff.

"All the old people say there used to be hundreds of sheep out here," she told them, pointing to only two hovels where the shepherds still released their flocks on the slopes, since everyone claimed the foothills were haunted and had moved into the south pastures.

"But what happened?" Genshai asked eagerly as they went down the uneven dirt road.

"People rarely speak of it for fear of the curse," Mistress Tauva answered grimly as she held the torch over her head. She talked easily and had a regular stride, much like the laymonks who were accustomed to walking long distances. They listened intently as she said, "But in time I learned of the shepherd who used to live at the end of this road and went mad during the full moon and murdered his entire family three-score years ago."

She explained there were only a few elders left alive that had any memory of it, but every child in Westcliff knew the story. Even when nobody wanted to say anything, she managed to gather bits and pieces, eventually learning of the abandoned shepherd's home while giving palm readings for the old fishwives, who warned her not to go there since there were low-spirits that caused mischief to travelers, and gave nightmares, and people had seen the blue silhouette of a girl on the road.

After nearly three generations all that was left of that night were rumors and secondhand accounts. Some wool traders and weavers said he was the son of a man that had survived the Battle of Gládmere, and had possessed a touch of cruelty ever since, but the shepherd was a friendly enough young man with a lovely family; yet one old grandmother said he always reminded her of a wolf hiding in fleece. Nobody really knew what happened, but that night the sounds of a girl shrieking in the hills were so clear that it summoned three defenders to the end of the road where they assumed that outlaws had set upon the house, drawing their swords and entering the door, never to emerge again.

"I talked to the widow of one of the men who found the bodies," Tauva glanced back at them with a stern expression. "She said the next day the shepherd's flock was loose all over the mountainside, so his troop of defenders kicked open the door, but he refused to speak of it. Only that the floorboards were soaked in blood. She said her husband was filled with so much misery that he hung himself, nearly ten years later."

"Are there any records in the Alderman's archives?" Taisan asked.

"The records are sealed by a magistrate's order," Tauva said contemptuously, "Besides, they won't let me in anyway. I'm a witch, you know."

Preoccupied, Genshai's voice emerged, "Did they take him into custody?"

"The shepherd disappeared," Tauva replied. "Some people say

he ran away on all fours howling like a wolf, south toward the Farwood."

Genshai's mind reeled from the shocking details of the story, having never heard anything like it before. He was disturbed that the shepherd escaped and never faced justice for the murder of his family, yet his instincts told him that not all things were as they seemed, and folktales too easily became truth when there were no other answers.

Holding the sagebrush torch aloft the fortuneteller said, "That's where they come from," as she gestured to a line of broken fence that led to the crude shape of a house tucked into many layers of darkness. Already the young monk felt a gathering fear that prickled his neck and he sought out the Still Mind to remain calm, reciting the words to himself, *Be as still as a floating cloud!*

"Are they in there now?" Genshai asked shakily.

"Most likely," Taisan nodded, furrowing his gray eyebrows. "But you never know what other mischief makers are around, so we must be careful."

"It is the night of the Hidden Bloom, after all," Tauva nodded.

The young boy remembered that the Veil was thinner on nights of the new moon, and his thoughts turned to stories of flashing sprites, or Semori nymphs, that enticed errant travelers off the road. Genshai suddenly realized that they were the only ones around for miles, and he began to feel more and more uneasy with every glance up at the old shepherd's home.

They stood at the crest of the road as Taisan considered things until he eventually said, "We need to know what's there and now is the best time to find out."

"Should we all go?" Genshai asked, looking back and forth between them.

"Forget it! I'm not going," Mistress Tauva shook her head. "I already know what happens when you deal with spirits. I'll be here when you get back."

Taisan gave a short nod of approval and then turned his eyes onto the young laymonk as he asked, "Are you ready?"

Genshai exhaled and replied, "I'm ready."

They left their packs in the road but kept their staves in hand. Their eyes adjusted to the darkness as the light of Mistress Tauva's torch faded behind them. The old man led the way, and with every step the two monks kept the words of the Still Mind on their lips, settling into the cadence of five syllables, "Still as steady rain," again and again, until Genshai felt the tranquility of meditation arise in his thoughts.

The wooden hovel was in ruins. One side looked like it had collapsed years ago. The walls were black and rotted, and the grasses and hedges had grown over them until the house hardly looked like it was there. The splintered door hung in the front entryway. It swung on a single hinge and beckoned them into the silent and granular darkness.

Genshai moved to take a step but Taisan placed a hand on his shoulder, his face alert as he whispered, "We are not alone," and the boy followed his gaze upward, toward the roof of the house where they saw a hulking shape perched at the peak that glared down at them with fierce red eyes.

From around the backside they heard a booming laughter and soon the dark figure on the roof turned away and Taisan said, "They know we're here."

"Who?" Genshai asked.

"The Guaiono," Taisan said seriously, "Weird devils."

"Guaiono?" Genshai repeated more to himself, and he knew from the stories he had read in the abbey that there were all kinds of these devils; they were low-spirits that were more like hulking monsters and cruel apparitions.

Taisan said, "Sometimes cursed ground seems like home to a Guaiono and they leave the spirit country on nights of the Hidden Bloom and then never go back."

A crow called from somewhere nearby and there was a haze of clouds that covered the stars until the night was oppressively dark. Taisan led the boy around the corner of the house, past the wooden sheep pens, coming into the eerie firelight that flickered in slow motion, like a crystal cracking into shards. Genshai's eyes quivered and his vision blurred. His heart raced and he was suddenly gripped by a dreamlike confusion.

"We are the monks of Red Tower," the old teacher declared in a clear voice, which helped bring the scene into focus for the boy.

A broad greataxe leaned on a pile of firewood, made of a rough wedge of ore with a gnarled oak handle easily the length of a man. Small shapes darted around in the darkness until they were surrounded by a horde of dim, blinking yellow eyes, and at the edge of the firelight they saw the shirtless body of a huge man sitting against the fencepost, his voice mocking them, "Uh-oh, here come the monks of Red Tower?" accompanied by a chorus of scornful laughter from all around them.

"We have come to answer the call of Westcliff," Genshai said shakily.

Suddenly he felt a massive weight leap onto his shoulders, much to the amusement of the audience hidden in the shadows. Long and sinuous arms wrapped around his neck and sharp claws dug painfully into his ribs. Genshai let out a shout as he grabbed desperately for anything within reach until he snatched the creature's head and flung it over him in a tumble of black feathers. The creature crawled on his knuckles like an ape, with greasy black fur and dingy feathers on his shoulders, scowling at them as he leapt up with a gust of air from his enormous wings.

"Kalla hates monks!" the voice boomed from the edge of the crystal firelight. "Especially little boys playing pretend," to which they ducked as the winged monkey dived out of the sky once again to shriek at them.

There was a raucous laughter from all around as a horde of small monsters no taller than their hips came crawling from the shadows and slammed into their knees as they ran past in either direction, nearly knocking them over.

"Goblins," Taisan realized.

Genshai felt grubby hands at his waist and belt and looked down to see several grotesque faces hissing at him, scrambling back into the darkness just as he kicked them away like they were rats. They had sickly yellow eyes, and some of them bristled with coarse hair and had tusks like boars, or were mottled red and green, and had tails like dogs. They seemed like hungry scavengers that snapped their jaws at each other for the first bite, running all around them until Genshai snatched up his staff and waved it frantically to keep them at bay.

"Stay back!" he shouted.

Getting to his feet, the giant grabbed the hefty greataxe like it was nothing and came forward until he was in full view of the fire. They were astonished at the hulking monster that stood twelve feet tall without a head on his shoulders, menacing with a wide toothy maw that spread at his navel, he stared intently with blood red eyes where his nipples should be. His breath was like a revolting fog, and Genshai dropped to one knee as pangs of terror washed over him. The creature was like nothing he had ever seen. Every glance toward the grotesque mouth made him quake with fear until he held his eyes closed with one hand, shuddering, unable to form a single word.

"Iron monks are usually so tough and chewy, but at least this boy looks like he has some meat on his bones," the headless giant observed, speaking every thunderous word from out of the teeth of his massive belly, his neck stump blackened and scarred like the burnt wick of a candle.

Taisan was shaken but he managed to say, "Xinga! What reason do you have to be here? There are no weddings to disrupt. There are no grooms to behead and no brides to kidnap," as he recalled the old stories about this particular monster, when Xinga the soldier was spurned by his lover and executed by his enemy on his wedding night, his spirit becoming a vengeful Guaiono that haunted adulterous lovers that lied and cheated for each other.

With an effortless swing of the axe the headless giant rumbled, "This land appeals to me more than others! There is a murder stain, and plenty of human flesh right here for me to feast upon! Why would I go anywhere else?"

The winged monkey dropped into the firelight and shouted,

"Let's take them back to the breach and eat them there!"

"No, fool!" the giant snarled from its toothy belly, "Do you want to share with the others?" and Genshai quailed with fear as he took in Kalla's greedy expression, drooling like a lecherous old man, as if the beast could not imagine sharing a single morsel with anyone else.

"Mountainroot," Taisan gripped his shoulder with one hand to remind him of their mantra. "Be as still as floating clouds."

The boy nodded gravely. He muttered the words in a rhythmic cycle until the Still Mind returned to him. Through the fog of fear and disbelief Genshai came back to his feet and lifted his gaze to the distended gnashing belly. The headless giant seemed to think it was funny and laughed without restraint as disgusting hot waves of his breath rolled over them. Swirling with nausea, the boy leaned on his staff and tried to find the clarity that he had once achieved in the caves of the Farwood.

"Begone!" Taisan steeled his mind. "You don't belong here!"

The two devils glanced at each other and burst into a horrible laughter, as if his words had no meaning over them. Then without warning Taisan lunged forward and smacked the winged monkey on the forehead with his staff, much to Kalla's surprise, he whipped the iron tip into the creature's face, across the cheeks, against the temples, into the eyes, as he declared, "Begone! Begone! Begone!" with every hard hit until the shrieking monkey retreated to the edge of the firelight and leapt up into the air to spread his wings.

I don't understand – how can he fight spirits? Genshai wondered as his teacher moved without any hesitation.

The giant stood massively over the old laymonk and swung the long axe in one hand but he moved too slowly to get anywhere near Taisan, who skillfully thrust the tip of the staff into the monster's red eye to blind him, jamming his nipple harshly until Xinga howled in pain. Then, like he was wielding a club, Taisan gripped the staff around the middle and beat the headless giant on the legs and waist with the heavy heel until he chased the beast away from the firelight.

Rising out of a daze, Genshai looked at the slow moving crystal shards that flickered in every shade of orange and red imaginable, tinged with yellow and breaking into the air like floating gems. The crowd of little monsters seemed to writhe forward and tightened the circle around them, gnashing their teeth and claws. Instinctively the boy went forward to kick out the fire and scattered the blazing logs until the ground gleamed with coals and so much heavy gray smoke enveloped the area that they could no longer see.

Then, as if caught on a new wind, the haze cleared away and they found they were alone. The starlight returned and the bare curve of the thumbnail moon was high over them. Any trace of the fire vanished and there was no sign of the Guaiono spirits anywhere behind the shepherd's home, yet when Genshai peered into the darkness he felt like he could see small figures running away, ducking around the corner of the house, or diving into the overgrown hedges, their dim yellow eyes blinking away as if they were never there.

"Damned devils!" Taisan snapped. "These lands have been cursed for a long time. I should've known they would have moved in here eventually."

"Have they been the cause of the hauntings?" Genshai wondered, confused, still paranoid that the monsters would reappear.

"No, of course not," Taisan replied shortly. "They're opportunists, and ghosts don't bother with them the same way they bother with us."

Genshai was shaken by the strange visions. In all their journeys so far such unnatural monsters like the Guaiono had never confronted them, although he knew there were hundreds of stories of their existence. They were weird, malevolent devils, and he shuddered as he thought, *They're more like nightmares than spirits!*

"Where did they go?" he asked.

"Back to Shenai," Taisan answered. "That was good thinking with the fire. I'll have to remember that trick."

"You fought them," Genshai was surprised.

"We were in the Veil, straddling the two worlds," Taisan nodded as he brought up his staff to show his student the small gray iron cap that was riveted firmly to the tip. Genshai had indeed noticed it before but it never occurred to him that it was important until the old laymonk said, "Spirits dislike hard iron, but it can only make a difference in our world," which enabled his staff to have some function against them as long as he wasn't past the Veil.

"They were terrible," Genshai held his head for a moment, which was still swirling with anxiety.

"Oh yes," Taisan nodded. "The Guaiono prey on your fears."

Genshai was dumbfounded as he came to realize that without the Still Mind he would have collapsed into terror, and Kalla might have lifted him through the Veil, all the way to the breach where he imagined there were countless other people imprisoned by their own fear.

"Come on," Taisan went quickly around the corner past the front door that swung slowly on a single hinge and beckoned them into the void of the old shepherd's home. They heard a whispering speech that pushed them and drew them at once into the doorframe. "Don't look," Taisan warned but it was too late since Genshai's eyes were filled by the surreal darkness and he might have stepped across that threshold if it weren't for the sound of Taisan's familiar voice shouting, "Come on!" as he yanked him away.

Quite suddenly Genshai awoke to the torchlight at the crest of the road where Mistress Tauva said, "What happened? You were barely gone for ten minutes," just as the two monks hurriedly grabbed up their packs and the old laymonk led them at a quickened pace for nearly a mile until she asked breathlessly, "Did you see any spirits?"

"That and more," Taisan acknowledged, slowing down the pace until the two of them were walking beside each other. He explained what happened, and said more than once, "I will have to meditate on this," his voice obviously disturbed.

"It seems like we'll need to come back tomorrow to place wards," Tauva said, and they began to make plans.

Genshai felt the heaviness of his pack as he walked in a bleak exhaustion. He held his staff in a loose grip and was falling asleep even as he put one foot in front of the other, barely noticing when they came into the narrow cobbled lanes of the village. He yawned tiredly and went where Tauva directed him, not knowing where he was, as he laid down in a restless slumber, fearful of the headless giant that laughed ruthlessly and the darkness of the Veil that blotted out the stars.

It was just after dawn when Genshai heard a vague shout from the street outside and the creaking of floorboards above him. He woke up with his legs hanging off a short bench in a spare crawlspace under the stairwell. When he emerged the boy found the common area of the Siren's Song was virtually empty except for a few women that sat in the light of the open shutters, all wearing loose robes, wool cardigans, and blankets around their shoulders as they sipped on steaming mugs of tea.

They giggled together as one of them said, "Oh I know, he's so handsome. I love when he's in port," while another sighed with a dreamy look on her face. He thought the women looked different in the cool morning, with their hair untidy and their faces clammy and clean. At night they were sensual partners that promised hours of heat and fire, but in the rising light they looked like women of the ocean, disheveled, made out of air and water and sand.

The tavern smelled like stale beer, pipe smoke, and ashes. Genshai went to the kettle of hot water on a trivet in the bed of coals and poured himself a mug of black tea, conscious that the women were watching him. He was suddenly aware of how he must have looked, a scrawny kid wearing an oversized tunic tied in front by a black belt, not at all obvious that he was meant to be a well-trained warrior. Genshai looked around uncertainly, not knowing where his pack of supplies, much less his staff, had been placed, not to mention where his companions had gone.

"Your teacher left with Mistress Tauva over an hour ago,"

came a slightly familiar voice. The boy turned around to see the same woman that had approached him last night in the tavern, averting his eyes quickly when he noticed that the silk robe she wore had folded open slightly and he was able to see directly toward the slope of her small breast.

"Thank you," he said somewhat stiffly. "Did they take Kyus with them?"

"Kyus?" she asked.

"The baby?"

She shrugged and pointed, "He's here. The girl has him in the nursery down the hall."

Genshai looked in that direction. It was the same corridor down which he saw pairs of people disappearing the previous evening. He swallowed nervously and wondered what sort of things had happened there while they were gone last night before he realized he was gawking and straightened up.

She tilted her head and said, "What's your name then?" scanning him lazily.

"Genshai," he responded feebly.

"Well then, Genshai, my name is Irisol," she replied with a slow blink of her eyes.

"Irisol," he repeated, not knowing what else to say.

"Stop confusing the boy, Iris," one of the women called from the table in the light of the window, accompanied by a few mirthful grins, and, "Come eat before it's all gone."

With a subtle smile on her lips, Irisol withdrew back to where the women ate a light meal of smoked whitefish and creamy cheese on flatbread, topped with scallions, alongside a pitcher of blonde tablebier for anyone who wanted it. He could hear them giggling and one of them asked, "Why are you bothering with him? Monks never have any money," as she sat the table, crossed her legs, and held her head upright.

Feeling obligated, Genshai decided to go down the hall to check on Kyus, since after all he was an abbey child now. There was a short corridor that turned left down a much longer hallway with doors on either side. The entire place smelled of perfume and incense. The walls were bare except for the unlit oil lamps and there were nine or ten doors that swung open into darkened rooms where the bedcovers were tousled over.

Coming to the last room in the hall he listened at the door for the sounds of a baby, although he couldn't hear much except a voice that said, "By the gods, you're so hungry this morning!"

Without thinking Genshai opened the door and revealed a young woman that sat shirtless with Kyus latched to her nipple, concealing her other breast. She sat in a rocking chair under the light of the south window, her dark hair cascading around her left shoulder. He froze in place, knowing that he had intruded, although she hardly seemed disturbed at all by his arrival as she said, "Oh hello, is this your brother? It must have been awhile since he was fed, but he definitely remembers how," as the baby clutched the flesh of her breast.

"Yes, thank you," Genshai stammered, "We found him about a fortnight ago, so I'm not sure if he was…" he paused at the words, "…or not."

The young woman seemed completely unconcerned, rocking the chair with the baby in her arms. She appeared to be in her mid-twenties and for the first time Genshai noticed the cradle nearby with two babies on their backs and a small bed along one side of the room where two little children were still drowsy in the early morning. He wondered if this woman was their mother, until he realized that any of the sex workers in the Siren's Song could've had a child that needed caring for.

She adjusted her position in the chair and her other breast hung unoccupied and open until he quickly said, "Okay, thank you," and left the room as fast as possible, feeling flushed and bewildered. Genshai walked to the common area and within moments he was outside on the boardwalk, wondering how long Taisan would have them staying in the Siren's Song, once again out of his element as he thought that he had never expected to have friendships with girls at all, let alone prostitutes.

As he walked along the dark sands of the rolling seashore he couldn't help but to visualize Irisol, her small chest and waist, and the shape of her eyes as they stared at him, not really knowing how far he was allowed to let his mind wander. *Where do I even start?* Genshai asked himself; very quickly realizing that Irisol probably had no interest in a virgin monk boy anyway, burning with undue embarrassment from the shame of his own thoughts.

That morning he noticed he was becoming more accustomed to the taste of salt on his lips, and to the pending wind from the sea. At the end of the boardwalk he saw more than a dozen ships with great white and red and yellow sails on the horizon. The whitecaps rolled over again and again. It was like nothing he had ever seen, vast and limitless beyond sight. The movements were irregular, breaking one right after another, happening in long streaks down the seashore until he could no longer predict anything. The waves were hypnotizing and he found himself slipping into the Still Mind as he practiced the Eight Simple Sets by himself at the end of the boardwalk.

Each movement fell out of his arms and legs like they had been done already a thousand times and he came to see how the secret of body alignment was there all along, aware now of the rising in his Great Spirit. He lifted his legs for the basic kicking sets, and the three Lion Forms, and of course the Mountain Form, before he eventually returned to the boardwalk at the end of the hour, walking back across the soft flat beach. The sand went down into his shoes and when he ended up back at the Siren's Song he sat in Tauva's chair and shook out each one. He crossed his legs and stared at the west horizon, his mind calm and neutral after a particularly vigorous practice alone.

"There you are," Taisan said as he came around the corner of the tavern and took a seat across from the boy. He looked out at the water sloshing against the pier until he asked, "How did you sleep?"

"Alright," Genshai shrugged, but the memories of the shepherd's house came unbidden into his mind, which made him glad to have spent the morning alone by the sea to meditate.

Taisan replied carefully, "We'll need to go back there today."

"I know," the boy replied.

There was a preoccupied silence between them. The old laymonk considered his next words carefully, "The lands of Shenai and Kuei are very different, but they are two parts of one whole."

Genshai nodded, not wanting to interrupt.

"Shenai is a land of passion and obsessions," Taisan cautioned. "It is a land of enthusiasm, but also a land of rage and lust and appetite."

"Everything is so heightened," Genshai nodded.

"Exactly," Taisan encouraged. "And strong emotions while you're in the Veil are just what would get you lost in the spirit country. If you lose control you will never be able to escape, and the longer you stay on the other side the more difficult it becomes to keep the Still Mind."

"The other side?" Genshai questioned.

"Yes," Taisan glanced at him, "The Veil is between both worlds, so we can all exist there. But the spirit country is wild and limitless, and everything is heightened, like you said, beyond what we would normally see and hear and feel. It is very easy to become confused, or even to go completely mad, if you stay on the other side of the Veil for too long."

They talked through the morning, and Genshai learned that Guaiono spirits stayed close to the breach, a crack in the spirit country to the Nether. They were weird devils with unpredictable appetites that often enjoyed challenging monks, and even clerics, to games of wit and strength to get them to refute their beliefs. The old man said, "When a monk can be made to follow them, or collapses in fear at the sight of them, then the Guaiono becomes emboldened. If you remain balanced in your thoughts then they have no power over you. They might even become more afraid of you then you are of them."

"But they were awful!" Genshai declared. "I never knew a spirit could be like that."

"There are worse things than that," Taisan replied evenly.

"But, you have the iron cap on your staff," Genshai commented, as if that answered everything.

"That wouldn't help against a demon from the abyss," Taisan shook his head, "They have greater powers than any low-spirit, and cannot be turned away by iron alone."

"A demon?" Genshai asked.

Taisan faced the wharf, his gray brows furrowed until he said gruffly, "Come on, Tauva's probably waiting for us by now," and left the chair to pace down the boardwalk until they were at the front of the tavern on the cobbled road. Genshai followed along, pleased that Taisan had at least answered a few of his questions although now his mind raced with the stories he knew about demons, like the Epic of Elosai the Sage, or the tale of Sibudat and the Red Ogre.

Taisan led them on a single-lane road back toward the main square ahead of the fish markets where the statues of the Three Sisters looked to the southeast. A number of young girls were gathered around the front steps; some of them wore the blue and green school uniforms while most of them wore whatever dresses and shawls they had since their fathers were just fishermen and their mothers were weavers. There were perhaps two-dozen girls of all ages and it seemed that Lady Wynne's oldest daughter, Alina, was calling the assembly to order.

Genshai searched for Ysma, who was closer to his age, but instead caught sight of Mistress Tauva waving, "Over here," where she waited near the far end of the square beside a small cart hitched to a mule.

"Did you get everything?" Taisan asked as he approached, glancing into the cart that was loaded with several boxes of supplies, a large wooden trunk, their oilcloth backpacks and warrior staves. Genshai immediately took up his weapon and twirled it twice in his hands. It was just a simple eight-foot hickory stick, straight and smooth, but it felt comfortable to have with him, although now he thought he would have to get one of those iron caps.

"Mostly everything," Tauva replied. "I had to search all over for the alchemist that works for the shrine now. He wasn't keen on parting with the incense ropes, but I managed to compel him," she said with a narrow smile, flashing a small dagger on the belt at her waist.

Taisan asked, "Did you find any peachwood for the wards?"

"Not exactly," Tauva said. "There are no peach trees anywhere for hundreds of miles, but I found this," she produced an elegant peachwood bow and a quiver of arrows fletched with white feathers. Its limbs were made from many layers of polished wood that had streaks of yellow and orange and pale green through the grains, elegantly curved into the center where the left hand would grip to notch an arrow.

"Well, now here's an antique," Taisan marveled, drawing the bowstring back and noticing that it had a good tension and could probably still be used for hunting. "Where did you find this?"

"The guardpost actually," Tauva said. "Unlike the alchemist, I think the new Lawkeeper actually likes me, so that made things considerably easier."

"That always helps," Taisan nodded with a grin until he noticed that Genshai gave him a confused look and he explained, "In some towns on festival days a defender will dress in the costume of Shao Daan and march in the streets with the holy peachbow."

"Low-spirits hate peachwood, boy," Tauva said as she urged the mule forward, "Because Shao Daan chased out evil during the Lost Age with a bow that was given to him by Andriani, the goddess of the peach grove of the heavenly island."

"What about the Season Tree?" Genshai suggested, though he knew it was forbidden by monks to cut down or burn its wood.

"Those trees grow roots in both worlds and have no effect at all," Tauva dismissed, as if she knew this fact very well.

The three of them walked at a steady pace. The sun shined brightly while the cart rattled on the uneven road and Genshai listened as they discussed what they knew of the story of the mad shepherd, and what happened last night. Among all the supplies they brought with them he saw fresh cut boughs of juniper and holly, and more than a dozen sagebrush torches. There were also long coils of incense rope made of hemp paper woven with sandalwood and cedar, or camphor and rose that made the entire cart smell fragrant and spicy.

A chest of old talismans also rattled in the cart. They seemed to be holy symbols of the Raegods and Genshai noticed they were chipped, or cracked, or the paint had faded on the wooden ones, and he couldn't help but ask, "What happened to these?" as he gestured toward a broken scepter carved with the bust of an eagle, a dingy and faded silver chalice, and several other items in similar disrepair.

While the fortuneteller led the mule ahead of them, Taisan said in a low voice, "Mistress Tauva was once a cleric of the Raegods."

"She was?" Genshai said a little too loudly.

The old laymonk revealed, "I knew Tauva more than twenty years ago, when she was the High Matriarch of the Ladies of the Patient Field."

"What does that mean?" Genshai asked.

"It means she was the boss." Taisan cleared his throat and said, "At one time she was the seer for the Warden of Norhaal, known throughout the entire northlands as an eminent healer and midwife."

"What happened?" Genshai asked.

Taisan sighed, "She got lost in the spiritlands."

"She did?" Genshai proclaimed.

"You can both knock it off," Tauva called from around the mule. "I know you're talking about me."

They kept silent for a long while, which was just as well since Taisan thought back to all those years ago when people were going missing during the new moon, trudging in a half-sleep through the forest all the way to the black bear caves, one of the most well known grottos in the southwest of the province. Brimming with confidence Tauva had been ready to parley with the spirits, convinced that she could compel them to cease their mischief as she crossed into the ethereal Veil, never to return.

Now, somehow she's come back, Taisan thought, *And I'd really like to know how,* since she appeared not to have aged at all, and she had given up the life of a cleric to travel alone, becoming labeled as a witch, which was often considered an insult for women that practiced healing, or read the will of the gods, outside the shrines. It was a loaded word since there was once an inquisition, centuries ago, when witches were burned at the stake for practicing the Forbidden Lore of blood rituals and human sacrifice.

Before midday they arrived to the shepherd's home, bringing the cart close to where the front door hung on a single hinge. The entire left side of the house was overgrown with hemlocks and in the daylight Genshai could actually see that a portion of the roof had collapsed inward. The chimney tilted precariously and it looked like it would only need one or two good windstorms to knock it over. Of course in the midmorning light there was no trace of any weird devils, or small monstrous goblins, yet they did not dismiss the chance that they were lurking unseen just on the other side of the Veil.

Genshai discovered there was quite an involved process in purifying the land, which began by twisting the boughs of holly and juniper into wreaths tied with twine and driving them with stakes into the corners and along the property line. He knew the Guaiono disliked the holy sign of the Wreath, and Taisan said as long as the boughs were fresh and green they would be like wards around the house.

"It's not enough," Taisan said, "But it's a start."

Then Tauva returned from the cart with nine wardposts, which were about her height and made from cedar. They were stained yellow and carved with the eighteen godmarks of the zodiac, painted a dull red and fashioned into stakes that looked like they had been hammered at the top a number of times. She gazed upward at the sun, and even squinted at the jagged slopes of the mountain range, until she decided where the central point would be within the property and set down the first post. Then she took equal strides out and gave instructions to the laymonks until they had pounded the wardposts down at each cardinal point around the house.

They soon brought out the long incense ropes, which were twisted together to form a loop at one end, and hung them from hooks at the top of each post. The nine lengths waved slightly in the wind like braided tails and then they walked around to each entrance and nailed them into the doorframes. "Don't go inside," Taisan warned, and even in the daylight, peering into the house was like peering into the ferocious throat of a wolf, that faded into darkness down the length of the hallway. At times there was movement in the corner of his eyes, or he turned his ears to the sound of voices, only to find there was nobody there except his own teacher and Mistress Tauva.

"I feel like we're being watched," Genshai said as he looked back at the shepherd's house when they returned to the center wardpost.

"Of course we are," Taisan replied. "This is their home after all."

"Who?" Genshai asked foolishly.

"The ghosts," Tauva arched her eyebrow as if it were obvious.

"Here," Taisan passed the peachbow and the quiver of arrows into the boy's hands. "The youngest person always plays the part of Shao Daan."

"What do I do?" Genshai asked as he held the bow with his left hand and looked down at the smooth curve of the limbs.

Taisan explained, "When I light the wardposts you just shoot as far and high as you can in every direction."

"I've never shot a bow," Genshai admitted.

"It's pretty simple," Tauva said tersely. "Just draw the string and let go."

"Let me show you." Taisan took back the bow in his hand and quickly notched an arrow as he said, "Best not to have you shooting at me by accident out there."

After a cursory lesson, Taisan lit a sagebrush torch and went out to the east wardpost to light the incense. Genshai managed to notch and draw the bow to its full length just to release the string poorly and have it collapse in his hands, snapping the wooden arrow in half. Mistress Tauva sighed deeply as if she was unimpressed. "Keep your left arm firm when you let go, and keep your right elbow in line with the arrow at all times," until he released a shot that went high and far.

They continued until all the wardposts were lit and Genshai had fired a volley in every direction. Each arrow went higher and farther than the last, and it was assumed that they were the first boundary a Guaiono devil would need to cross if they wanted to return to the shepherd's home. The central post in the property was the last to be lit and the fragrance of the incense ropes was spicy and mildly intoxicating, filling the house with the pungent smoke as the embers smoldered slowly through the hemp paper.

Taking up the scepter of the eagle in her hands, Mistress Tauva began a long chant to the Raegods to bless the land. "Meditate," Taisan instructed the boy and soon he was seated in the pasture in search of the Still Mind as he listened to Tauva calling the names of the gods under the midday sun.

Restless and unsure, Genshai opened his eyes. He saw a boy that stood alone in the field, not much younger than him, his head twisted like a toy doll. He was pale and faded in the sunlight as he looked forlornly toward the house where wispy faces peered around the rubble of the collapsed wall, shimmering like they were tricks of the light.

Genshai blinked and they were gone, but he knew for certain they were there.

CHAPTER SEVEN

*From the Epic of Elosai the Sage, "They battled for three
seasons. Elosai rode on a cloud, chasing gray smoke. Storms of
rain and fire fell over the lands of Kuei every time their
weapons met."*

THE CURSE OF WESTCLIFF

Several days of summer went by. Clouds gathered over the sea, sailors came and went in port, and it wasn't long before everyone knew the monks had arrived to lift the curse of Westcliff. Taisan quickly managed to befriend the local shopkeepers, fishwives, and especially the Alderman, and now a few of the dockworkers waved to him every morning as he passed.

Lately Taisan had been disappearing before sunrise, which left Genshai to look after Kyus, who was in the care of the wet nurse, giving the boy plenty of time to eat breakfast with the ladies of the brothel, especially Irisol. They all began to get familiar with him and he started to know their names, bashful and shy whenever they teased him, much to their delight. They often sat in the sunlight in the corner, setting the table with slices of sourdough sprinkled with coarse salt, cold potatoes mixed with scallions and cream, hardboiled eggs and pickles, dry cheese and thin strips of cured mutton.

There was Ollah, a round and plump lady with her curly hair tucked under a headwrap in the morning, who jeered, "Are you even paying for a room?" and Gwyneth who was in her early forties waved her hand, "Isn't he just the new busboy that sleeps under the stairs?" and Kysenia, the white girl from the eastlands, leaned over to whisper to Irisol, "I heard that monks are circumcised. Is that true?" to which he blushed hotly and they all laughed uproariously at his expense, until someone said, "Don't worry, she likes it. That's how all the men are in the east."

Irisol managed to interrupt their teasing and guide the conversation as she said, "The rumor is that you're here to chase out the ghosts."

"So far I think we're trying to help them," he replied a bit uncertainly.

"Help them?" Ollah scoffed as she buttered some toast.

Genshai shrugged. "I guess so."

"You're too young to know anything about ghosts," Gwyneth remarked offhandedly, catching sight of the confidence that shrank from his eyes as she poured tea for herself. "Well, look at you! You're just a boy!"

"I've fought ghosts before," Genshai declared, "And I've seen all kinds of spirits, like the Guaiono," pretending to be brave when really those memories had been the subject of several of his nightmares.

After breakfast, while most of the women went to bathe, Irisol usually smoked a pipe of tobacco on the front boardwalk. She asked him questions, until Genshai told her that he had grown up in the abbey and had just come of age to take the Oath last winter, and he learnd that Irisol was twenty-one and had spent all of her life in Westcliff. The tables were turned when it became clear that Genshai had traveled to Norhaal, not to mention that he was significantly more educated than most men who barely knew how to write their own names. He knew symbols of High Arovian that she had never seen, and he could quote the Scripts as easily as if he held the book in front of him.

"Didn't you go to the shrine school?" Genshai asked.

"There was no shrine here when I grew up," she retorted quickly.

"You could go now," Genshai suggested helpfully, even though she was older than any of the girls in school.

"Lady Wynne doesn't approve of our work," Irisol dismissed the idea with a wave of her hand. "Besides, that doesn't mean I don't receive brideprice inquiries. Some of them are fairly significant offers."

"Really?"

"Oh, yes of course!" Irisol said easily. "Sometimes it's a man's greatest fantasy to marry a girl like me so that no one else can have her. It's flattering, but I'm not interested, even though all the others say I should take a good offer while I can, since I'm not getting any younger."

Genshai couldn't help but to feel a strange jealousy, and those first few nights were painful. Even though they had no pretenses with each other beyond friendship, the boy was obviously still attracted to this slender, earthly woman, and knowing that she sold her intimacy to different men every other night made him feel absurdly possessive. Irisol flirted with a number of weathered and handsome sailors, just as all the other girls did, before they each disappeared down the hall. She seemed to enjoy it; keeping up with more than a dozen boyfriends on long sea voyages who all knew the lovely Irisol would be waiting for them at the Siren's Song when they returned to port.

After dusk, he always felt out of place when the room filled up with men for the evening, and the bartender was glowering at him from across the room. Irisol ignored Genshai completely, carousing loudly with her friends; they drank rounds of ale and shots of highland whiskey and filled the common hall with laughter and harsh smoke while the bard played songs until after midnight. It was confusing, since he realized, *I'm the laymonk and she's a sex worker, how can we be involved anyway?*

Genshai distracted himself from his unreasonable jealousy by walking under the light of the partial moon, all the way across the beach where the tides rolled over, flattening and drenching the sand. If he looked to the south the coastline was like a curving edge and there was no limit to the darkness under the starlight. When he felt particularly foolish and annoyed, he practiced the Mountain Form, or the three Lion Forms, kicking up the sand with his bare feet and looking back to see the signs of his frustration erased by the sea.

Sometimes Mistress Tauva gave private readings in the lamplight in exchange for silver coins. She traced a man's heavy palm, or intently flipped an oracle card as if it held a piece of meaning from the universe. Other nights she played tiles with a crowd of sailors from the different trawlers, drinking tankards of ale and keeping them happy with dirty jokes that made them cringe with laughter. Taisan usually spent most evenings talking to folks on the street corner and paid no heed to the activities of the brothel around him.

Long after the tavern had settled down and everyone had gone to bed, the old laymonk and the fortuneteller started to conclude the evenings by sharing a pipe of sweetleaf between them. For several nights Genshai had passed them in the empty common area as he returned from his lonely walks on the seashore. Sometimes he waited until well after midnight when he was too exhausted to think about all the footfalls coming up and down the stairs above his cot. He would immediately collapse into a dreamless sleep, being unable, or unwilling, to hear anything.

"You're going to need to talk to that boy," Tauva said when she saw his gloomy charcoal expression on his way to bed. "He's out of sorts, and he needs to be ready when the Lotus is in Bloom."

Taisan puffed lightly from the pipe. "He's young. It's natural for him to be out of sorts about a thing like this."

"He's also been sheltered his entire life," Tauva pointed out, a trail of smoke rising up from the glass pipe on the table. "You should at least explain some things to him."

He furrowed his gray brow and gave a tight nod of his head, acknowledging that she was right, lost in thought.

<hr>

The following morning Taisan woke Genshai in the forehour of dawn. It was earlier than he was accustomed to and the entire common area was black and empty, with only the sounds of their footsteps creaking across the floorboards. Taisan had already steeped a pot of black tea on the embers of the hearth, and after the boy visited the washroom they left without any breakfast, walking away from the boardwalk, past the harbor, over the cobbled roads of the village.

Genshai wished he had been able to stay back as he thought about how the women would whisk around him in their different states of undress, and how they fussed over him, teased him, badgered him to eat, and made sure he was taking care of himself, like they were his cousins and aunts. But the old laymonk had his own plans for the morning and led him past the wharf and around to the other side of town.

On the north hilltop the black saltmarsh was more noticeable, expanding at a great distance to the south where rivulets of brackish rolled through the dunes. When the tides were out during the spring and summer, shepherds released their flocks on the shores to graze which gave the meat a distinctive, salty flavor. From that vantage point Genshai saw some fishermen so far away their sails looked like low hanging clouds before they disappeared into the colorful horizon.

"This way," Taisan said, drawing the boy's attention back to their errand. He led Genshai to a square timber building with bars in the windows and a wooden door reinforced with heavy iron bands. On the wall the Shield of Shao Daan was cracked and worn, faded blue and white, and as soon as he entered Genshai realized they were in the local guardpost. Three of the town's defenders sat at the table in front of them, glancing at the old laymonk as if they had come to expect him.

"Back again, Taisan," one of the men called out.

"Has anything changed?" he asked.

"Only if you consider screaming by night and crying by day," one of the other men replied sourly.

The first guard frowned, sitting a bit lower in his seat than the others. "Not much has changed since you were here yesterday," he replied, smoothing a hand over his long beard. "Is this your apprentice, then?"

"I'm Genshai," he introduced himself, to which the man said nothing. In fact his only response was to scan him up and down as he rose from his seat with a ring of keys in his hands.

Taisan said graciously, "This is the new Lawkeeper, Hebrahm."

"I suppose you want to see him then?" Hebrahm grunted, hardly even taking a second look at Genshai. The commander was shorter than both monks, his coarse black hair streaked white around his ears, and he had a thick, curly beard that flowed down from his face with a line of decorative wooden beads in Dweroh fashion.

"Are you from Hylmstone then?" Genshai blurted out.

The Lawkeeper glared at him, "I'm from right here in this village," as he unlocked a door that was riveted with iron bands, leading them to a narrow hallway that joined with a stone stairwell and descended into the jail cellar. The air was dank and cool as they went down into the corridor with six locked doors on either side. The commander went through without difficulty, but the monks had to duck their heads slightly and there was no light other than what spilled down the stairwell from above.

Taisan struck a tindertwig against a huge tallow candle that was mounted on the far side, which provided an orange glow around the last few doors. Immediately there were the sounds of chains clinking and scraping, then spare mutterings, or a brief cry of terror that was suppressed into quiet tears. Through the small window of bars in the doors Genshai saw shadowy figures bound in shackles, or completely restrained with sailcloth jackets and leather belts.

"They're tied up!" Genshai declared.

"It's better this way," the old defender said grimly. "They try to kill themselves otherwise."

"But they're suffering…"

"Be silent, Genshai," Taisan shushed uncharacteristically, which promptly made the boy realize the seriousness of what they were doing.

"Is that my son?" came a torn, wretched voice from one of the cells. Genshai peered into the window and was immediately startled back by two manic and red tinged eyes that appeared out of the darkness. The prisoner's hands were manacled from behind yet there was clearly old blood, black and dried, near a seeping wound on his forehead. His hair was greasy and tangled around his ears and neck, and he was coated in grime and obvious filth.

"Guilford, my poor son. Guilford," he muttered, crying anguished tears, "My poor son."

"This is Lord Euiger Wynne," Taisan said solemnly.

Genshai couldn't help himself as he peered inside where Euiger released a mournful howl, shaking the chains behind his back. "This night, this night, this night will never end," he cried as he collapsed into a heap. "Everything is so dark. Please let me go. I won't say anything to anyone. I won't. I won't. I promise," until he choked on his own words.

"What is he talking about?" Genshai asked his old teacher, who shook his head and pressed a finger to his mouth to indicate they should be silent.

"Release me," the man shuddered desperately, his head on the ground and his arms chained behind him. "Curse you, may the gods curse you."

Suddenly there were shouts from the other cells, turning Genshai around in fear. Several prisoners shrieked and threw themselves against the walls while one man in the corner barked hoarsely like a dog. The narrow stone corridor resounded with their hysteria, and in the dim candlelight there were shadows of movement behind each door. Prisoners paced in circles or pulled with all their strength at their chains, and even those that were bound to their beds convulsed uncontrollably.

"Just kill me!" a woman screamed. "No more! No more!"

Wynne appeared once again at the small window of bars,

shrieking, "Don't touch her! Please! No! Leave her alone!" before he collapsed to his knees; his brown eyes wet and shimmering, mouth gaping, as if he was witnessing the most savage, traumatic thing anyone could imagine.

"Please, I can't do this anymore," the Oathlord cried until he was so frustrated that he ran at the door with a growl, "Let me out!" until the chains snapped him back painfully. He hunched under the low ceiling and sobbed, "Please, no more," followed by a harsh chorus of shouts from all around them.

"We had better leave before one of them tries to hurt themselves," commander Hebrahm said, visibly disturbed as he climbed the stairs with Genshai right behind him. "Sometimes they hit their heads against the walls, or try to choke themselves with the chains."

"Do they ever calm down?"

"Never," Hebrahm looked back with a churlish expression. "One of them will get started and then the others can't help themselves. They're like rabid dogs in cages, except dogs are put out of their misery."

At the top of the stone steps they noticed that Taisan had not followed them, and Genshai called, "Teacher?" with a crack in his voice.

The Lawkeeper said, "Sometimes he stays down there for an hour or more," before he quickly departed.

Genshai looked cautiously around the corner until he saw Taisan extinguish the candle at the other end. The old laymonk's face was inscrutable as he came out of the darkness and the boy realized that he had been meant to hold the Still Mind, quickly reciting the mantra even though he knew that he had already failed the test, being chilled to the bone by all those signs of madness.

Gasping for fresh air, Genshai burst through the door of the guardpost into the cobbled street overlooking the shrine of the Three Sisters, comforted by the brightening sky, the taste of salt on the wind, the whitecaps breaking in the distance. Unperturbed, the old laymonk exchanged a few words with the defenders in the office and soon emerged from the door just as the vestments of the holy cloth came over the small rise of the hill.

Taisan waited patiently as the Matriarch approached with her two daughters, Alina the eldest with apprehensive, fluttering eyes, and also Ysma, who seemed to scan everything prudently. At the sight of the monks wearing their Aeigi jackets, Lady Wynne clenched her jaw and said contemptuously, "I would've thought you'd be spending your time with whores and witches."

"Assistance in our travels can come from all folks, my lady," Taisan said politely.

She snapped back, "Well, I don't see why you need to come here every day?"

Taisan replied knowingly, "The forehour of dawn is when the madness is the most quiet. It's easier to learn what their message is. The people here are victims, but they may still have answers to give," he said, taking some satisfaction as Lady Wynne's face opened with new understanding. Genshai also had not realized that his teacher was disappearing so early in the morning to sit with the cursed prisoners, but it was not unusual for him to let the boy figure things out as they happened.

Agatha quickly recovered, demanding, "Have you not already driven the spirits away with the help of the witch?" referencing the wardposts that were still staked in the ground at the site of the haunting.

Actually a few times now the monks had withdrawn their horses from the livery and ridden to the end of the long road in the foothills to give Meora and Snowcap some occasional exercise. They walked around the boundaries and checked for signs the wreaths had been disturbed, and which ones were starting to become brown and discolored. Genshai felt comforted when he saw the fixtures they had made, ritual boundaries positioned between them and whatever evil would come next, though he knew it was only a matter of time before they failed.

"Spirits are fickle things," Taisan answered readily. "Something happened in that house years ago, and now we have to wait until the next full moon to try and commune with the angry ghosts."

"And what good will that do?" Lady Wynne snapped, finding it all so difficult to believe in spite of her husband's madness.

"I'm not sure," Taisan began, almost as if he were speaking to himself. "When ghosts appear again and again it means they have unfinished business. Usually they've been tortured or murdered, and that trauma is so significant that they can never fully rest, unless…"

"Unless what?" she demanded.

"Unless funeral rites can be performed again," Taisan replied coolly. "By the clerics of the Raegods."

"Funeral rites?" Lady Wynne's eyebrows narrowed, her mouth drew tight.

"Then the ghosts might give up their anger at the full moon," Taisan nodded. "They might be appeased."

"How would we do that?" Ysma asked.

"The bodies," Genshai realized, looking at his teacher.

"Yes," Taisan nodded. "We need to find their bodies and properly honor them."

"Impossible," Agatha scoffed. "That was three-score years ago. Nobody knows what happened to them, and besides the story of the shepherd is just an old tale."

"There's truth in all old tales," Taisan replied. "I believe the village archives might have the answers."

"The archives?" she scoffed. "It's impossible to find anything in there. I would be surprised if you could even take two steps into that room."

"I can show them," Ysma spoke up quickly, looking between them. "I've been to the archives before to drop off the new birthcharts."

Agatha's expression softened somewhat as she thought about it, until she said, "Yes. Ysma, you should go with them. Alina can help me with your father."

"I can do that," Alina replied. "I mean I want to see him."

"Maybe we can finally begin to put this nightmare behind us," Agatha nodded.

She moved toward the door when Taisan issued his own request, "Does this mean you'll perform the rites?"

Lady Wynne raised her head and looked down at them as she agreed, "If there are indeed bodies to be buried, then the sisters of the shrine will give the rites," before she turned to disappear inside the guardpost. Her oldest daughter Alina exchanged a meaningful glance with her younger sister and followed their mother inside, readying herself for the difficult task of taking care of lord Wynne in his cell.

Taisan seemed not to see the two young people waiting beside him as he considered all that had just happened. He looked over the salt marshes at midmorning. The day was warm with sunlight coming through the clouds overhead. Flocks of seagulls could be seen over the entire beachfront rising and falling on currents in the air, floating in the shallows, waddling in the harbor as they scavenged for food.

Finally Taisan came out of his thoughts with some verses from the Scripts, "Knowledge is revealed, / and clouds do not drift idly / as they seem to do."

"Are we going to the archives then?" Ysma asked somewhat curiously.

"Indeed we are," Taisan nodded resolutely. "Lead the way."

They walked for a short time before Genshai couldn't help but blurt out, "The madness is so much worse than I thought."

"What did you think it would be like?" Taisan asked, noticing that Ysma turned one side of her head back to hear what they said.

"I guess I thought it was more like melancholy," Genshai replied.

"This time the madness is deeper," Taisan said, shaking his head. "It is a disruption of identity. I believe Lord Wynne is still in there somewhere, but something else is in front of his mind and that's what we see and hear now."

"Why do the ghosts do it? I don't understand."

Taisan sighed, "I don't know. Perhaps to communicate, but what?"

Before long Ysma led them to the village clerk's office across the square from the shrine. There were two old women at the front desk that seemed to know the Oathlord's daughter, letting them all through without any fuss even though they shared a few nervous expressions as she went by. Taisan made his way back to a large study where he paid a visit to the old Alderman Crainog, who had been elected multiple times over the years and was the most trusted man in the village.

In the meantime Ysma led Genshai toward another door that she pressed open and walked through as if she had done it many times. It was impossible to see how large the room actually was past the rows of wooden bookshelves coated in dust and cobwebs that stretched all the way back to the darkened corner. Each shelf was filled with thick hardcover tomes, or leather-bound ledgers, and stacks of scrolls, without any indication of what they were. In fact, numerous aisles between the shelves were nearly impassable from the piles of books thrown into the room in no particular order.

"These are the archives?" Genshai looked crestfallen at the dark, dusty room, which was nothing like the neat and orderly library at the abbey.

"Nearly eight hundred years of records, maybe more," Ysma replied, reaching for an oil lantern that hung on a hook nearby.

Old man Crainog appeared in the door, bent over a cane, wearing a long white beard and a single monocle on a cord around his neck as he pointed a finger and said, "Be sure to file those papers in the second stack," and spent several minutes lecturing Genshai on where he should toss the annual fishing permits, market licenses, and other similar things until Ysma couldn't help but to stifle a laugh behind his back.

Eventually the two old men left the young people alone to work and Genshai sighed despondently, "This is going to take forever."

"Well, at least it's a place to start," Ysma shrugged.

The next day Taisan decided he was going to the Season Tree by the main road outside the village for a few hours. "You should go back to the archives and meet Ysma again," he said, even though Genshai complained there was nothing to be found there, and they would just be wasting their time, and just putting the Alderman's library in order for him.

Since their arrival, however, the old teacher had received a number of questions from people about the classics. Prompted by the hauntings, it was clear that thoughts of death and what came after were weighing heavily on folks' minds, and the Aegin Tradition offered a promise that all suffering had meaning. Some sailors wanted to know whether evil deeds could be absolved, and their wives wished for a future of comfort and wealth, so Taisan knew that the only way to answer all their questions was to hold a discourse at the Season Tree.

"I'll be back in the afterfade," Taisan said when they arrived to the clerk's office and spied Ysma coming down the road. He looked like he was about to depart until he turned back and said with a note of humor in his voice, "Don't get distracted," as if he knew something the boy did not.

"I won't!" Genshai assured him, even though he slightly resented the advice since he felt that after yesterday's introduction to the archives he and Ysma were becoming friends.

"Well, just be respectful to the young lady and get your work done," Taisan told him pointedly before he turned down the road and nodded politely to Ysma as they passed.

She advanced quickly to Genshai with a restrained smile on her face.

"Good morning," he began, questioning her, "What is it?"

Barely able to contain herself, Ysma blurted, "I have an idea where we should start today, since I think it's apparent the Alderman doesn't care if we find anything as long as the archives get organized."

"Is it that obvious?" Genshai rolled his eyes.

She continued as she led him through the village clerk's office and opened the door of the archives, "I think we should start with the property records. Maybe we can find a deed for the house."

It seemed like a good idea until he stepped inside the door and he remembered how impossible the whole task would be. At first, they couldn't go anywhere without tromping all over a pile of books, and before long they were sorting through them. They made stacks of what seemed like market revenue receipts, organized them by date and eventually uncovered all kinds of village council transcripts that went back for several decades. Ysma sat on her knees as she looked over each book and her long fine mahogany hair draped over her shoulder onto their pages.

There was an old catalog system carried on from whoever first began the library centuries before, but the Alderman had made it difficult for them by lapsing in his work and nothing from the last fifty years or more was even listed. Ysma was very focused as she explained that each entry had a bookmark in the front cover of descending characters that corresponded to a catalog card, a mix of High Arovian symbols, with an interesting stamp that indicated the category of the item.

"Are these old Dwern characters?" Genshai finally asked.

"Of course, look at this," Ysma said as she lifted up the town charter from a nearby stack of permits and licenses. It was clearly written in Dwern, and he read that it granted privileges of self-governorship to the Oathlord in exchange for his fealty, and the taxes from the fish markets, issued by the Warden eight hundred years ago. Ysma told him that there were a number of families in the village that could trace their heritage back to the Dweroh tribes that once came there from the Hylmrodes.

By midday the two young people had gotten most of the aisle cleared when their stomachs growled and they stopped for lunch. Genshai left his staff in the archive and they walked down to the wharf to browse the fish markets. The gulls called overhead, drifting like white and blue shades against the sun shining off the waters of the sea. There were a dozen stalls where the fishwives sold their husbands' catch from the day before, haggling for wagonloads to be taken out to the smoke huts in the countryside.

He saw whole cod and haddock that were nearly as long as his arm, each with distinctive dorsal fins, otherwise they looked much the same, with white bellies, streaks of green, and opalescent scales. Then they came across entire sturgeons and the boy gasped at the size of them, about the length of a man with gray and silver scales that shimmered in the sunlight.

Ysma explained that the salt marshes were incised by a number of creeks that rose and fell with the tides and it was there that the sturgeon went upstream to spawn every other year. She said, "It's like a nursery. There's an agreement not to catch from the shallows since the fishermen don't want to destroy the population because the sturgeon reproduce so infrequently."

In the meantime the deep sea was plentiful with all sorts of other fish. Some trawlers went out just beyond sight of shore for several days to catch heavy nets of tuna that were cut into delightful pink fillets and sold by the pound; or black sea bass, with round scales that overlapped each other like shiny coats of mail. There were even crates of wriggling beach crabs, which reminded Genshai of giant bugs, despite the savory smell rising out of the simmering cauldron that made his stomach churn with hunger.

"Let's get that," Ysma's russet brown eyes flashed.

"I don't have any money," Genshai admitted, slightly embarrassed.

She glanced at him and said boldly; "Don't worry," as she produced a small pouch of coins from within the folds of her dress.

After she paid two silver dragons, taking back a few bits of change, they each had a steaming bowl of soup. Genshai was thrilled by the subtle flavors of the mushroom and ginger broth, the shellfish and tuna served with bean sprouts, snowpeas, and a handful of dried seaweed crumbled on top. The white broth reminded him of the clean temple food he had grown up with, though as soon as he took a bite of succulent white scallop the similarities ended there and he couldn't help but announce, "Hmm, this is really good!" to which Ysma giggled happily.

They sat on the edge of the wharf and watched the boats moored along the piers, and Genshai hardly spoke, unsure of what to say even though there were a dozen questions that came into his mind. The slow movements of the sailors and the singular wagons that came in and out of the market made the village seem very calm and dreamy in spite of the new summer season. He had noticed the only people that came to the Siren's Song were the same men that came ashore every fortnight, and everyone knew everyone in the village until they were all accustomed to never seeing any strangers.

"Until you and Taisan came along, my family and I were the newest people in these parts," Ysma observed.

"But did everyone gossip about you as much as they do about us?" Genshai asked sarcastically.

"Probably twice as much," she replied, holding her chin out proudly until they both laughed.

They talked lightly and Genshai found himself enjoying Ysma's company more and more. She was smart, and had a unique interest in the boats, pointing to the masts and sails and using all the nautical terms. He liked her enthusiastic smile, not wanting to interrupt her while she talked animatedly about the harbor. Her skin was clear like polished amber, and she wore a light short-sleeved blue dress with soft-soled shoes, and yellow and orange sashes around her waist that indicated her status as a student in the Shrine of the Three Sisters.

Eventually they headed back to the archives, refreshed after lunch, joking about how they could have eaten twice as much and they should just go back for seconds. Genshai was suddenly aware of Ysma's height, up to his chin, and her presence as she moved beside him. He wanted to glance over at her, or at least to lock eyes with her at some point, just to find out if they shared any kind of connection, and he wondered if she had received any marriage inquires, until Taisan's words came rising out of his thoughts, "Don't get distracted," and he tried to shake everything away.

They returned to the dark and dusty room for another round of searching. At first it seemed impossible, but in fact the pile of logbooks from the village council meetings were suddenly very compelling when Ysma found one that described a heated debate between the Alderman and the Lawkeeper of the defenders, dated from the autumn of 972 EC, nearly forty-seven years ago.

"Here's something," Ysma muttered as she flipped the pages rapidly, until she revealed, "They wanted to burn the house down!" and it seemed the Lawkeeper of the guards at the time, Sir Daelyn, demanded in an emergency council meeting that they ought to burn the shepherd's home down with warfire. The Alderman, and the Matriarch of the shrine, acquiesced, and supposedly the meeting ended since that was the conclusion of the transcript.

"What is this?" Genshai pointed to the next page that was stamped with a rather large square sigil with identical loops and bands on either side of a circle in the center.

"That's the Magistrate's Seal," Ysma said, "The rest of the transcripts were probably never included in the book as part of a judge's order."

Indeed they could see several pages were missing from the binding, and while there were dozens of other logbooks for all the successive years, none of them seemed to have any other details that were relevant to the shepherd's home. They searched for a while longer before they heard a shrill bell ringing from the shrine, which indicated it was the last hour before eventide.

The village clerks had gone home already and the young people locked the door with the key the Alderman had entrusted to Ysma, who was an honest enough girl in his opinion. Glancing at each other briefly they waited a few moments longer in the market square under the blazing pink sky, knowing they each had to go their separate ways. Her silken mahogany hair flowed around her shoulders in the wind and she looked at him expectantly, as if he was meant to say something.

"I have to go practice," Genshai finally said even though he didn't want to.

"Do you want to come with me to the kiln?" she asked suddenly.

"The kiln?"

"Yeah, some of my pots are getting fired tonight," Ysma said, which intrigued him. He took up his staff and went with her, going across the potter's row where several women sat on wide terraces outside their homes and kicked the flywheel, using wet hands to mold black clay. They introduced themselves, though he hardly remembered their names because they all turned to the young girl, clucking after her until she quickly agreed to go out to the saltflats with them to harvest mud.

"Anything that will get me out of going to school with my mother," Ysma said in a low tone so that only Genshai could hear as she led him to where the kiln was like a jagged spine down the hillside.

"It's a dragon kiln!" she exclaimed as they descended the slope on a worn path beside the earthen walls. He was pleased to learn that the kiln was covered on all sides by red brick from the quarry at Auburntown, and there was a rectangular chimney at the highest point on the hill. The passage at the mouth was only big enough for a single person to pass through, but they still managed to help the elderly women carry heavy pieces of pottery into the inner chambers and place them on stone shelves.

Ysma took a few extra minutes and removed her outer garments, trying to avoid getting the holy cloth dirty. She folded up her blue dress and yellow sashes and set them in a wicker backet at the bottom of the steps as if she had set them there many times in the past. Wearing just her loinwraps and a light linen top, Ysma moved ahead to help the older ladies haul down crates of pottery from the top of the hill and Genshai just followed her example, working together as they began to move larger pieces into the kiln.

"Over here," Ysma pointed to a corner where he placed a rather large round globe with a narrow mouth and a flat bottom.

A bit flustered, he tried to avoid staring at her body as he asked, "What is this?"

"It's a fermentation crock," Ysma said proudly, "I made that one."

"It's huge," he said, since it was about the size of his torso.

"We throw it in two parts and then blend them together," she explained, and pointed to more than two-dozen pieces of pottery that were waiting to be fired in the inner chambers of the kiln. Aside from crocks there were pitchers, cisterns, and tableware, and all sorts of other things of various sizes, although Genshai thought they could probably fit three times as many items if they needed too. The mouth of the dragon had a huge firebox that faced the seaside where they received a good regular updraft from across the beach to feed the flames.

"They light it every other week," Ysma said as the older women took turns loading the firebox with kindling. They were all eager to contribute, and fussed with each other about how to begin, double-checking that the pottery was placed correctly in the kiln so the heat would sweep upward to the chimney. Genshai began to see how many of them were descendants from the Dweroh since they had dark brown complexions and were shorter in height with round ears and noses, and larger hands and feet.

There was a cord of wood at the top of the hill and Genshai volunteered to haul armfuls down to the front of the kiln. He removed his Aeigi tunic and began to split firewood, taking the opportunity to practice the stances of the Mountain Form. Swinging the maul with every squat, he began all motions from his hips until there was more than enough fuel for the whole night. The two young people worked side by side in the golden eventide. They stole glances at each other while the other person had their back turned, intrigued by the firm ripples in their abdomens, the sight of tense calve muscles, their chests coated in sweat from the exercise.

The kindling was soon lit by a tindertwig and the old women stood back while Ysma made a tall pyramid of wood, and by the time the sun was angled more than twenty-five degrees to the west she had built a blazing fire. The women agreed to take turns through the night, and two of them stayed behind to feed the mouth of the dragon while the others ambled back up the hill toward their homes. Ysma came to sit beside him. She took off her sandals and pressed her bare feet near his in the sand. They looked toward the flat seashore where the sky was enflamed like the skin of a peach and the sun was the fruit ready to sink down on the branch.

"Thank you for showing me how this works," he said. "I've never seen a dragon kiln before."

"They used to have three other kilns," Ysma said, pointing down the hillside even though there was bramble and tall dune grasses that obscured the view.

"Well, child, everything was busier before," one of the old ladies said from nearby, obviously eavesdropping on the two young people. "Nobody wants anything made in Westcliff anymore."

"Because of the hauntings?" Genshai asked.

"Everyone says it's cursed," she complained. "The milk turns sour; the cabbage wilts, wine turns to vinegar, and water turns to piss."

The second woman added, "My brother is worried this year the fleece won't sell, and they still have bales in the barn from last year."

"All because of the mad shepherd," the first lady announced.

"Who was he?" Genshai asked.

The two women looked at each other uncomfortably, as if their minds touched on stories that were better left forgotten. The young monk estimated they would have been girls when the murders occurred, living their entire lives in the shadow of the curse without ever knowing what Westcliff was once before. They didn't even remember the shepherd's name, or really any of the names of anyone involved, but they knew where the house was and nobody went anywhere near it if they could avoid it.

"He was just crazy," she said, tending to the fire.

Genshai asked, "But what would make a man go mad so suddenly?"

"Ghosts," Ysma said as if it were obvious, standing up to make her point, her voice strained, "Ghosts made my father go mad," before she suddenly walked off into the darkness.

Everyone was surprised and one woman said, "Now look what you did! That girl was going to harvest clay with us tomorrow."

Genshai ran after Ysma, shouting, "Wait!" but she was already gone. At first he became worried that she was walking alone in the streets and thought, *What if she encounters a Guaiono?* not even considering other more practical dangers for a young girl until he saw her silhouette in the light of the gibbous moon as she went up the hill to her father's lodge and he realized Ysma knew the way better than him.

Unsure of what to do, the boy turned back to the market square and paced through the gathering darkness to the boardwalk. It was still early since a line of orange light could be seen from the west horizon and there were numerous lanterns in the windows of the cottages on potter's row where families prayed to the Three Sisters for their blessings in hearth, harvest, and flock before suppertime.

His mind raced as he thought about how Euiger Wynne had encountered a shade one spring evening under the full moon. Now it seemed obvious that there were all kinds of low-spirits, or apparitions of the dead, that could corrupt a man's thoughts. Genshai considered that if the shepherd had also stumbled across some kind of mischief maker in the road so many years ago, it might have sparked the entire chain of events that had led to these ghosts wailing in the moonlight, making good people go mad.

It wasn't long before Genshai returned to the Siren's Song in the hour after sunset. There were some people quietly having drinks, and just a few of the brothel women were around, occupying themselves on a slow night. He saw Mistress Tauva and Taisan completely engaged in a game of tiles as he passed by them on his way to bed unseen, as if he was an invisible spirit himself.

Ysma did not appear in the archives for the next two days, and

Genshai was somewhat at a loss without her. He was in a gloomy mood, and sorted some books and filed some papers for a few hours each day, but eventually left to find a quiet stretch of beach to practice his forms. By the third day he resolved to go find her and apologize for any misunderstanding when she showed up at the archives, perfectly cheerful, ready to continue the search.

"I was worried you wouldn't come back," Genshai admitted. "I didn't mean to..."

"We went digging for clay," Ysma interrupted, as if that was all that needed to be said to explain her absence, and he chose not to say anything further. Instead he showed her what little progress he had made and she quipped, "Well, it seems to me like you should be glad I'm here, since you're obviously not going to find those sealed records all by yourself," and they both laughed.

So for the next ten days the two young people searched the archives for anything relevant to the year 972 EC, forty-seven years ago. The old Alderman continued to be unhelpful, and the only judge in the village was a young scholar that had just been appointed by lord Wynne at the end of last year, and he had no idea where anything was. There were entire shelves of legal books, civil court cases, and even voter records from town assemblies, and Genshai thought that each book was just as dry and dusty on the inside as they were on the outside.

It was no coincidence that he had been skipping breakfast, snatching up some slices of bread and a handful of fruit on his way out the door, since he was eager to meet with Ysma every morning. He just wanted to stand near her, or laugh with her about the way things were written, or read silently for hours in each other's company. The ladies of the brothel even teased him sometimes, and Ollah shook his shoulders and said, "Oh, your first girlfriend, how cute!" which made everyone laugh even though he had no idea if Ysma felt the same way about him. They all knew from village gossip that the older sister, Alina, was nineteen and had received several brideprice inquiries, but now all the suitors had withdrawn their offers amid rumors that the family was cursed, and as far as anyone could tell Ysma had received no inquiries, which made him feel more comfortable becoming friends with her.

She was like a natural sleuth as she scanned the shelves, arriving one day with a new idea as she said, "The shrine might not have been making birthcharts, but I'll bet the village treasury at least kept some accurate tax records," as she looked at a shelf of account books, which were compiled by the Alderman and notarized by the clerk every year. She went down rows and rows of numbers, the tallies of gold and silver strings, all counted to the last square Lirro from as far back as 950 EC, and further if she really wanted to keep going.

"Look, it shows the revenue from the autumn wool markets," she said as she pointed her finger toward the written figures.

"Does it show which shepherds paid their taxes?" Genshai asked.

She flipped the page and nodded, smiling a little, "Their names are here, how much they sold, what they earned and what they paid," as she went through the list and attempted to read the handwriting of the village clerk from those days. They soon found the name of Jakkob who kept a flock of a hundred twenty lambs and ewes at the Clover Pasture at the end of the road. He paid his taxes for several years, although after 972 EC his name mysteriously disappeared from the lists.

"We found him!" Genshai said excitedly.

"Not just yet," Ysma shook her head. "That's just a name. We need to find the sealed records."

Nevertheless once they knew the name of the mad shepherd it was only a matter of time before they were searching the birthcharts. There was a span of years when the shrine had lapsed in its duties, but if they went back far enough there were entire folders that contained marriage licenses, brideprice contracts, and deathnotes, all signed by an Alderman or magistrate and then notarized by a clerk of the archive. The letters and borders were raised to the touch, and each page had the sign of three rings pressed in blue ink at the corner of the page.

"What does this mean?" Genshai asked.

Ysma looked up from a sleeve of papers and squinted her eyes at the symbol, "Those are the rings of the Three Sisters. That means a cleric officiated the ceremony."

"For all of these?" he asked.

"A cleric is needed for birth, marriage, and death," Ysma said as if it was obvious, although she wrinkled her forehead in thought, "We usually write the birthchart and officiate the naming ceremony a fortnight after the baby is born, but it seems like there's a gap of twelve or fifteen years here from when the shrine was closed."

"Birthcharts," Genshai repeated, a bit sullenly. More and more he realized that people took the position of the stars and seasons, the clouds, the sun and moon, quite seriously, making him wonder about his own birthchart and the mystery of his own origin. He wondered why the monks didn't teach the Book of the World, or any of the myths of the Raegods, since they seemed to be such essential parts of the lay people's culture, and yet there were also endless stories within the Aegin Tradition alone and Genshai wasn't sure which was more necessary to know.

They worked well together. At first each of them was silent in the mornings, but eventually the sound of their laughter filled the dusty archives when Genshai cracked a joke about the Alderman who he called 'the old goat,' or when Ysma pointed out something funny about how mismatched the catalog cards were to the shelves in the first several rows. They uncovered a desk that soon became buried again with all the books and scrolls they intended to review, reading for hours in the glow the lamp. Ysma was careful to look at everything, not wanting to read the pages too quickly, while Genshai just skimmed for key characters in the rows – ghosts, wolves, shepherds – figuring if nothing was mentioned it wasn't relevant.

In that time they managed to find Jakkob's birthchart, his father's deathnote, the deed to the house, and the marriage license between the shepherd and his wife, Hallah, who was a creamer and a dairyman's daughter from Auburntown. They had a customary brideprice contract, although Jakkob did promise to pay twelve gold Aurants to her widowed mother for ten years after the date of their betrothal. They lived in the house his father built at Clover Pasture, selling wool and cheese in the markets, and from what Genshai gathered they had two children, although their birthcharts still eluded them.

"They're not here," Genshai groaned in frustration. There were still six shades to account for, and there was no sign of their deaths in any of the folders in spite of nearly a fortnight of searching.

"It's like they just stopped existing one day," Ysma shook her head.

They glanced at each other in the light of the lamp, clearly not wanting to waste another hour in the crowded, untidy, dusty library, and Genshai suggested, "Let's take a break," to which she was ready to agree. Their long lunches had become a regular thing to look forward to every day, and Ysma gladly paid for his meals in the harbor even though some afternoons Genshai did manage to bring a few coins from his teacher to pay for their food.

"Come on, you have to try this!" Ysma said with characteristic enthusiasm as she steered him down the boardwalk. They stepped around the offal strewn over the walkway since nearly every kind of fish made its way to the four wooden chopping tables, each of them soaked in blood and water, fat and brine. The cleavers came down with thunderous chops, and scraped the fish heads into a pot of a hundred severed heads, and even some of the innards went into smaller jars with the roe of a pregnant fish, which were like piles of tiny soft rubies that would eventually be pressed into the most delicious pastes and sauces. A number of large crocks were layered with freshly sliced fillets and packed with salt and Ysma told him they would be buried in the countryside for up to a year. Later, somebody would add portions of cooked brown rice, or heavy millet, mixed with crushed garlic, grated ginger, and chili peppers, before they were sealed again with ceramic lids for another year or longer.

She brought them to where a man was hauling wet baskets onto the docks, and a woman said cheerfully, "Back again, Ysma," from the prow of their small boat, wearing a bandanna to keep her dark hair behind her ears, a basic loinwrap and a scanty top that exposed her stomach and slim shoulders.

"Don't you ever get tired of them?" a young man laughed nearby. He was glistening and nearly naked except for his loinwrap and Genshai was suddenly very flustered by their beauty, since they were lean, hardened, and deeply bronzed from long days under the sun. He learned that they were gatherers; their little boat would drift in the shoals while they searched for mussels in the muck, or some days they sailed down the shoreline to a small bay where they collected oysters when the tide was out.

"Can I just show Genshai?" Ysma pleaded as if she hardly noticed their nakedness at all.

The man smiled, "Anything for the Lady of Westcliff."

He stepped easily onto the dock and stood shorter than Genshai, bending over to pull an oyster from a bucket of brackish water. The shells were irregularly shaped and dull blue and green, with many ridges and textures, like small treasures curated by the sea. Producing a short straight knife, the man jammed it directly between the shells and twisted slightly to pop it open. The blade curved around to sever the muscles from the top and bottom until he revealed the oyster to Ysma who slurped it down and tossed the shell into the waves with a delighted grin. In seconds there was another oyster shucked and ready, the bulb of silvery flesh swimming in a pool of brine.

"Try it," Ysma insisted, and she laughed when Genshai tried to slurp it down and let the juices run all over his chin.

He was shocked as he chewed the soft, salty morsel, guessing that it was the flavor of the sea itself. He ate another oyster out of the fisherman's palms, and by the third he figured out the proper slurp technique. Everyone teased him for making a mess, and after a round of laughter Ysma thanked them and left a silver dragon for the half a dozen oysters they had eaten as they walked away.

Still hungry, they found where a few sisters set out buckets of pink flatfish and fried them on the streetside in butter in a small cast iron, selling them for a penny apiece. They even cleaned the sand out of cockles and let them sit in salt water until they were ordered, flashing them for less than two minutes in the pan before mixing the open shells in a savory red sauce, served with a hearty scoop of fermented vegetables and crushed celery seed, which prickled his nose from the unexpected spiciness.

They relaxed into a friendly banter, and Ysma asked the monk boy, "Is the food this good at the brothel?"

"It's pretty good!" he replied until he caught sight of her expectant expression and said quickly with the bowl in his hands, "But definitely not as good as this."

"That's right," she raised her head haughtily and said, "There's nothing in there that you can't get out here."

"I can't say I disagree," Genshai said, raising his eyebrows as he wondered, *Is she saying what I think she's saying?*

Ysma continued with a knowing expression, "My mother told me that the clerics of Seers Point are actually taught to be exceptional lovers."

"Really?" Genshai was surprised.

She gave him a funny look as if it was a joke and they soon burst out laughing from the unusual tension between them.

"Well, there are the Ladies of the Orchid," Ysma said, telling him about the courtesans devoted to Cemensa, the goddess of love and beauty. "Once a girl is Chosen for her they learn all sorts of skills that make them desirable partners. Of course there's poetry and music, storytelling, dancing, and maybe one of the Schools of Lore if they're suited for it. You can imagine how popular their shrines are in old-Arovia."

Genshai nodded along, unsure exactly what she meant or how to respond.

They walked around the village streets for a while, staring out at the triangular sails bobbing on the horizon. Ysma told him, "When we came to Westcliff, my dad said his grandpa gave him sailing lessons when he spent summers here was a boy. They used to go on trips so far out to sea that he could barely see the shore," she glanced at Genshai and said, "Next summer he was going to take us sailing, south all the way to Pelidor so we could see the colossal statues."

Genshai wondered if it had been so many months since Euiger was cursed that Ysma wanted to think of him as gone abroad in his sailboat, putting his imprisonment out of her mind. Yet, it was clear the village clerks, the group of potters, and a handful of sailors, all gawked at her, or acted like she might spread the curse to them. She suddenly asked him, "Did you know they've been calling him the mad knight?"

"I didn't," Genshai concealed, even though he had heard the term bandied around quite a bit by the sailors in the tavern at night.

"Everyone thinks my dad is some kind of criminal but he's not!" Ysma cried out, her chin quivering as she took a deep breath.

"I'm sorry," Genshai tried to say encouragingly. "He's obviously a victim in all of this."

She glanced up but it was like she didn't see him, her mind racing as she said with a note of realization, "We should be looking for the condemned criminals!"

Genshai looked at her, "What do you mean?"

"There would be fewer of them," she said, wiping her eyes. "And they wouldn't have cleric stamps if they didn't receive the final rites."

"Why would they not receive the rites?" Genshai asked, confusedly.

"I don't know," she answered, but quickly said, "Clerics only refuse to do the rites for severe criminals."

"Then they would not have been properly honored," Genshai realized.

"Exactly," Ysma gestured with her hands.

They looked back up the hill as the shadows deepened in the streets of the village, and Genshai said, "Lets go," and they both moved through the market, until Ysma eventually took him down an alley in a shortcut toward the Alderman's archives. They entered the set of doors until they were in the back room once again where they struck a tindertwig and lit two lanterns, resuming their search for the next few hours.

They used her idea to trace down the official deathnotes for anyone convicted of severe crimes, which were all filed inconspicuously on a shelf of defender's reports. There were more than a hundred parchments that described all sorts of violence by rapists, murderers, pirates; all sentenced to death, the corners of the pages stamped with yellow shields indicating that a defender had carried out the task. Then, her hands grazed a leather envelope closed by a Magistrate's Seal that she pried open to reveal six official certificates of death dated on 972 EC, forty-seven years ago.

Genshai said excitedly, "Now we found him!"

Silently, Ysma leafed through a handful of pages although she nodded, which seemed to mean she had to agree it was promising.

It was difficult to know what to look at first now that so many clues were within their grasp. Each deathnote was indeed missing the blue rings of the Three Sisters and were stamped with the yellow shields instead. They also found two birthcharts for the children, Guilford and Merry, shamefully tucked away as if they had never existed. There were also the sealed council transcripts; including the Lawkeeper's vague and poorly written reports about coming upon the house and retrieving the bodies. The crime was promptly blamed on Jakkob the shepherd, who had escaped, and Sir Daelyn never took down any statements from his men on what they discovered within the house.

Yet, within the envelope they came across a small vellum notebook titled, "The Sworn Testament of Shigyn, Defender of the Shores of Westcliff," which was dated 975 EC, three years after the death certificates were notarized. So far it was the only written account of what happened, and reading over his shoulder Ysma gasped at the first words, *Everyone wants to forget what happened, but I'll never forget…*

Those pages were chilling, and very quickly Genshai realized that it was the exact thing they needed. He wanted Taisan and Tauva to look at it as soon as possible, gathering up a folder of all the items they had collected over the last two weeks just as the bell rang for the final hour of light before eventide. They emerged while the sky was ablaze with the setting sun, turning the clouds pink, shining off the dark undulating sea. Folks passed quickly through the square as they headed home for the day, looking at the young people with suspicion, or with a slight dread etched into their faces.

"Look," Ysma sighed. "They're at it again."

Genshai followed her eyes to the statues of the Three Sisters where their adult counterparts were in a heated discussion. They approached, hearing Mistress Tauva snap toward the Lady Wynne, "Well perhaps the shrine has not helped these people as much as it should have."

"I doubt there is much you could have done differently," Agatha argued, gesturing back to the house of the gods. "This place was boarded up and falling down when we came here."

Tauva's eyes narrowed like flint, "But you still won't provide healing to the sex workers."

"We offer free healing on Sabat day as we are bid to do by the Sovereign," Agatha countered, "But by all means continue with your witch-healing. I've heard you treat the whores for diseases and unwanted pregnancies."

"Peace sisters," Taisan held up both hands, "A friend calls to you, / stand ready to lend him aid, / an arch of support."

Tauva turned her glare onto him as she said, "Don't even start with me."

Taisan's eyes widened as if he knew the danger he was in, like a rabbit stuck between an adder and a hawk. The laymonk stepped back to greet the two young people as they approached and Genshai barely gave him a moment as he said, "Look," and pulled out the six deathnotes, followed by the deed to the house, pages of council transcripts, and the children's birthcharts, until he had constructed a story for them to hear.

Ysma added proudly, "And they weren't buried in the

Westcliff memorial ground," which drew the Matriarch and the fortuneteller into the discussion.

"Where were they buried?" Tauva asked impatiently.

"It's on the certificate," Ysma pointed to a column of script on the deathnote.

Taisan looked closer at a few of the pages in his hands and finally said, "Somewhere called Barrowgrove."

The sharp voice of the Lady of Westcliff rang out, "The Barrowgrove is southeast of here by more than an hour."

"We'll need to pay their graves a visit," Taisan replied.

"There are no gravestones," Agatha explained, "For hundreds of years the Barrowgroves have been the burial site for criminals convicted of severe crimes to which death is the only sentence."

The two young people exchanged glances, as if they knew something the adults did not until Genshai announced, "We also found this," and produced the vellum journal, the Sworn Testament of Shigyn.

Impressed, Taisan said, "Good work you two," as he took the journal from Genshai's hands.

"We should try to leave early tomorrow morning," Tauva said while glancing over the deathnotes.

Lady Wynne raised her chin, eyeing the fortuneteller disdainfully. "I trust that you will have all the assistance you need from the witch," then turned to command her daughter, "Ysma, it's getting late. Time to go home."

"But, mother, I want to help find the…"

"You are not going to the Barrowgrove," Agatha snapped. "It is an unholy land."

Tauva said condescendingly, "Well, as Matriarch of the shrine you wouldn't want to be asked to do anything about unholy land, would you?"

Rebuffed, and with a complicated expression on her face, Lady Wynne turned around and began striding away from the three statues. Ysma followed, not saying anything even though she looked back helplessly half a dozen times. They were soon gone and Taisan turned a hard expression toward Mistress Tauva until she said, "What? She called me a witch."

"She always calls you a witch," Taisan replied unsympathetically. "There's no point in aggravating her. We still need her help."

Tauva released an exasperated sigh as she turned around on the cobbled road, going past the markets, down onto the boardwalk toward the Siren's Song.

That evening Taisan and Genshai completed their usual training with the Iron Palm bag, hitting again and again in three hand positions before practicing the elusive Mountain Form. Genshai had yet to achieve the Ascendant Power, but every time they trained the boy felt that he was getting closer to a new understanding of the Seat-of-the-Mountain. Still the mysteries of Westcliff invaded their thoughts and Taisan ended their practice early to rejoin Mistress Tauva at her table outside the Siren's Song to read through all the documents.

Obviously, the most compelling piece of evidence was the firsthand testimony of the young defender named Shigyn who told his story to the cleric Karina, stamped with three conjoining rings. It was dated three years after the event and was taken down in secret by a notary of the village clerk's office, containing their signatures – in the cleric's neat and measured hand, while Shigyn's was a messy flourish.

None of them knew who Shigyn was or what happened to him, but they knew that Karina went on to marry the next Oathlord, Haegra Wynne, who was Euiger's grandfather, and was sent there by the old Warden. Genshai realized, *Karina is Ysma's great-grandma, and when she died the shrine must have closed!*

He waited patiently until the end of suppertime when each of them had read through the journal. The brothel was quiet on a weeknight, and several women eavesdropped at the open windows, but to anyone looking out they mostly seemed to be reading from an old book and didn't begin any kind of meaningful conversation

until long after nightfall when the stars of Livenahara came out –
the Five Rivets in the Shield of Shao Daan – directly in the middle
of the sky.

"Tomorrow is the first night of the Lotus in Bloom," Mistress
Tauva said as she observed the gibbous moon rising.

"I saw most of the trawlers pull out today," Taisan replied,
dropping the testimony on the table.

"Sure," Tauva nodded, "None of the sailors want to be here
when the ghosts come."

"Everyone is afraid of the madness," Genshai said, deep in
thought.

"I don't think it is a madness," Taisan replied, "I think it's a
message."

The others looked at him until Tauva asked, "A message from
whom?"

"From the ghosts," Taisan said. "And it's only now, after so
many kinds of dishonor, that they have risen up to convey it."

"A message of what?" Tauva wondered.

"The story of what happened to them," Taisan explained,
"Like you said, it's a transferred memory. But they are only splinters
of what they were. A shade is frozen in the moment of their torment
and the only way they know how to communicate is to spread that
torment to others."

"What if it wasn't the mad shepherd at all?" Genshai offered.

"Well then who?" Tauva wanted to know.

"Something worse," Genshai began. "What if it was somebody
he met on the road? Or something from across the Veil that drove
him mad?"

"I think you might be right," Taisan agreed readily.

"Why are you so certain?" Tauva asked, pointing to the
collection of evidence. "These papers say that everyone believed
Jakkob killed his family."

"Shigyn and Karina didn't believe that," Taisan disputed.
"Why else would they swear in this testimony in secret? Besides, it
also says that the bodies were ripped apart, just like they were at

Ulfghar's Ridge, and no man has the strength to do that, and I know it wasn't a dire wolf that attacked that watchtower."

"Then what was it?" Tauva asked, crossing her arms to reveal the Mother's crux tattooed on her forearm.

"A Guaiono?" Genshai suggested.

"I don't think so," Taisan shook his head. "The Guaiono cross the Veil when the moon is hidden. First, they must break your will and then they'd rather enslave you forever then eat you. Only when they're tired of making threats and playing tricks will they actually consider hurting anyone, terrifying though they are."

"A demon," Tauva realized, raising her eyes intently, like sharp gray flint.

"Indeed," Taisan agreed, as if he had been thinking it for a long time.

"Isn't that uncommon?" Genshai asked.

"There hasn't been a demon in the lands of Kuei since the time of Elosai the Sage, three hundred years ago," Taisan replied. "At least none that we know of."

"The signs are certainly there," Tauva nodded as she looked back through the pages of the guardsmen's testimony. She said, "I have to admit I never thought of that. Since my imprisonment I am much more suspicious of spirits, and I might've believed a Guaiono would cause a man to go mad just for its own entertainment."

"Make no mistake," Taisan said gravely, "These people were killed for the entertainment," and the young laymonk wondered what his teacher really knew, since Taisan was the only one to achieve the Still Mind back at Ulfghar's Ride, and while talking with the madmen in the jail cellar.

"This changes things," Tauva said, pursing her lips as she usually did when she was concentrating. "I will need to gather supplies for tomorrow's trip…" she trailed off, beginning to make a mental list.

"We still don't know where they're buried," Genshai said. "How will we find them with no headstones?"

"I have an idea for that," Taisan replied, as if he wasn't concerned.

A brisk wind from the sea swept over the boardwalk in cool gusts, prickling their bare skin. Genshai was suddenly very tired when he saw that the wide and slightly incomplete moon had risen to the zenith of the sky. Yawning, he moved toward the door, as Taisan said pointedly, "Be ready before dawn," to which Genshai nodded before he crossed the empty common area and passed through a storeroom and collapsed onto the cot under the stairwell.

He slept fitfully. He saw a hungry wolf that prowled in the foothills, stalking the shepherd's son when he emerged to check the pens.

––––––––

The sworn testament of Shigyn the defender was grisly and troubling to read, yet Taisan wanted to be prepared for what he would face. Going over the story again, he tried to put himself in two places at once, wondering how it felt to gather in secret to make this statement and also what it was like to be among those men that stood at the threshold of the shepherd's home, unsure of what they'd find inside.

Shigyn was twenty-two, and among five other guardsmen that had all gathered at the Clover Pasture that day in the late autumn. Their commander Sir Daelyn was an old knight that had served in the Sovereign's Army during the Decade of Two Kings and was a survivor of the Battle of Gládmere at the end of the civil war. The young cleric Karina also accompanied them from the shrine, and like all of them she was not prepared for what they would find.

"I remember it was completely still," Shigyn had said, "Even the wind from the sea had stopped blowing as Sir Daelyn went up to check the door. It was barricaded on the other side; so Josiah and I tried to shove it open until the bottom hinge snapped and the door swung like it was breathing out thousands of tiny black flies, buzzing in our ears, stinging like barbs on our faces and necks until we were all shaking our cloaks at them; but in the end we had no choice but to go through," and Taisan knew exactly the sight of that swinging door and the whispering speech that had curled into their ears.

"The room was dark and the air was foul. Actually, it stunk so bad that Brandt ran back to throw up in the ditch. It felt like the shadows were pressing down on us from every corner, and the light of my lantern was dim, like my wick was running dry, but I know it couldn't be. Broken furniture was thrown all over the floor. There was no easy way through, and I nearly jumped out of my skin when the Lawkeeper said, 'Clear this out!' and we had to move a broken table, an empty barrel, a few wooden chairs which were snapped in half, or looked like they had been chewed on, like how a dog chews on a stick."

"Then what happened?" the Lady Karina asked.

"Somehow I tripped," the guardsman continued, his testimony written in the neat handwriting of the scribe. "I regretted it right away. It was awful, I put my hand in something wet and then I saw her next to me on the floor, ripped open – like a doll with all the stuffing taken out," describing the shepherd's daughter; her ribs snapped open, most of her inner organs ripped apart as if a wild animal had ravenously eaten them.

The scribe had made note of the time in the log, writing the numerals horizontally where a new set of rows began, and Taisan realized they had taken a break before transcribing the next part of the statement.

"We found Hallah. She was dead. Nailed to the mantle of the hearth through her wrist, and the smell of shit was everywhere until we realized she was covered in it. Our three missing men were there too. Their swords were bent in half, and they were mutilated, even ripped apart, their legs and arms piled up like sticks; one of them, his head was turned all the way around. The floorboards were soaked in blood, and old Daelyn said it was like nothing he had ever seen, and he was there at the Battle of Gládmere, in the butchering woods."

The transcript stopped and there was another mark for the

time that indicated when they had started again nearly an hour later. Taisan could only imagine that Shigyn was distraught, or angry, pacing around until the cleric Karina could set his mind at ease to resume. When they began again Shigyn said, "The defenders stood in the road arguing. Everybody was talking all at once, and Josiah said, 'I'm not going back in there,' and somebody else said, 'Let's burn it down' and Karina, you had agreed, so the Lawkeeper volunteered to go back in and drop a torch.

"But the house refused to burn. The torch sputtered out, and the kindling smoldered like it was too wet. Even the hearth refused to take a flame. We spent two hours trying to light a fire until it was too dark to see and Josiah threw down his tools and said, 'This place is cursed!' and walked away with a few of the others. We left it for the night, but I guess that Sir Daelyn called an emergency council meeting because the next day he told us they had decided the bodies should be removed and the house burnt down with warfire."

Karina began to speak. "That's when the Matriarch brought more clerics from the shrine and we all gathered at the house."

"Not that there were any volunteers," Shigyn said. "I probably wouldn't have gone back inside if I didn't see Daelyn set down his sword and shield, and I knew he would do it alone if he had too. Eventually a few of us followed him, wearing masks and gloves, trying to find all the pieces, since there were five bodies in the house. We wrapped them in canvas sheets, but it wasn't until we were nearly done that you found the boy in the field."

"Yes," Karina replied. "I found him getting pecked by crows in the pasture. He suffered a broken neck and severe lacerations."

Shigyn said, "Well, we might have missed him if you hadn't seen him. He was just a little boy, not yet ten, so we put him in the bag with his sister. That's when we learned that the Matriarch had decided not to risk bringing the curse back to the village, so she ordered the Lawkeeper to take them all the way out to the Barrowgrove for burial. After we separated, I remember the bags were shaking so much in the cart they looked like they were alive, tied up with ropes as if they would escape.

"When we got there Sir Daelyn threw a stone into the Barrowgrove and we dug a pit at the place where it landed," Shigyn said. "We dumped them in together, and without a prayer or anything we hurried up to bury them since everyone wanted to get back home before eventide. Nobody said anything, but I know what we were all thinking, like, what we just saw was more brutal than war or slaughter; how could one man do all of that?

"I cried for a long time," Shigyn admitted. "Even though the others punched the back of my head, and told me to shut my eyes. They even pushed me down and left me to walk back to town by myself. I wanted to die, but I didn't want to add to the pain that everyone felt. I waited until nearly dawn to come home, and I took a bath as soon as I could, and then I burned my soiled boots, and all my other clothes, and I slept for more than a day. I didn't find out until three days later that Brandt had gone for a swim that same night and drowned himself."

There was another time stamp as they paused, but by then Shigyn's testimony was nearly done. He claimed that Sir Daelyn blamed it on Jakkob the shepherd, and the magistrate sealed all the records so that nobody could learn what the council had deliberated during the crisis. It was easier to vilify a man that had disappeared than to admit it was dire wolf, or something worse, that could still be on the loose somewhere in the lowlands. Regardless, before long folks as far as Norhaal knew there was a curse on Westcliff and the old Warden anointed Haegra Wynne to take over the lodge, which put the rumors to rest for a time.

As Taisan considered the story, a seed of curiosity had grown in his thoughts all night; why had Shigyn decided to give his testimony in secret three years after the day of the incident, yet his words written on the last page of the book said it all: "Everyone wants to blame it on the mad shepherd and forget. But I can never forget."

CHAPTER EIGHT

*THREE NIGHTS IN LIVENDOR, MIDDLE OF THE
MONTH, 1019 EC*

*The full moon rises like a lotus in bloom, a clay pot breaks
into pieces; the past returns.*

MADNESS

Restless in the forehour of dawn, Genshai gathered up his pack and walked out to the beachfront. The dreams of flickering, mournful shades faded. The wind came in gusts from the sea, spraying the sand into the air at the height of the dunes. The tide was high, filling his eyes with the creeping waves that vanished into white surf until he was unable to see anything in the distance, as if the water and the darkness were one.

Genshai practiced every form he knew. He warmed up with the Eight Simple Sets, followed by the three Lion Forms, and then he reminded himself of the basic hitting sequences – the Eight Kicks, the Eight Elbows and the Eight Palms – and a few others he hadn't practiced in months, before he finished with the Mountain Form; every movement guided by his hips, falling away naturally. With a kind of mental clarity he stepped and twisted and sat in Horse-Stance, then he simultaneously kicked and punched and sat in Horse-Stance on the opposite side, then he cut and reaped with his leg, sitting in Horse again, and so on, breathing easily, the meridians aligned, the warmth of his Great Spirit rising within him.

Taisan had warned him that he would need to prepare the Still

Mind and soon Genshai found a log to sit against and began to meditate beside the crashing waves. The sky brightened to make the sea a cerulean blue with bare clouds overhead, which reminded him of their mantra, and how on their journey his teacher had talked about the Small Circle breathing. Genshai took easy natural breaths and drew his awareness down through the Navel Gate, up the spine and around the back of the head to form a loop of his essence.

He was reminded of the lines from the classics, when Sibudat had said, 'Greet the rising sun, / and all things, with openness / nourished by balance. Awaken yourself / by shedding identity / and releasing form. All myriad things / carry immortality / within their spirits!' and Genshai could barely comprehend what it meant to shed his identity, but he did begin to understand that all people, and animals, and even the devils he had met were all alike in the one way that mattered, which was that they possessed the same thing he possessed, something as endless and indeterminable as the sea itself.

If only it was as simple for me as it is for those waves, Genshai thought about releasing form, relaxing the Still Mind all at once as he sighed, *I don't even know what I'm doing here as it is,* almost more unsettled than before as he hiked back to the boardwalk. He had gone down the beach until he was just out of sight but was still only a few minutes away from the Siren's Song where he sat down to rinse his sandy feet with a bucket of brackish water and put on his soft leather shoes. It was only a few minutes before dawn and Genshai took up his staff and backpack and went around the corner.

Everyone had agreed to meet at the livery and Genshai walked at a quick pace on the cobbled road until he reached the square around the shrine. The town was foggy and silent except for the crying gulls and the tossing waves. Taisan was already there with the stableman getting their horses saddled and Meora bucked her head impatiently at the sight of Genshai's approach. He traced the white swirl between her eyes and she nudged forward insistently until he was rustling her mane with his hand.

Genshai looked around at the number of horses getting saddled and saw Tauva beside a man sitting on a stool wearing a tattered and faded blue woolen tunic with a hood. They appeared to be talking intently and his wild gestures revealed the clattering chains and the manacles on his wrists, as he said, "Blank paper, under the floor, I can't find it by myself," until his jaw tensed and he hunched down and began to hit the edge of the iron cuffs against the side of his head.

"Stop that," Tauva yanked on the chain between his hands, and Genshai saw clearly that it was Oathlord Wynne from the jail cellar.

"You freed the lord?" Genshai asked his teacher.

"He's hardly free," Taisan remarked.

"You brought him out of his cell?" Genshai asked more directly.

Taisan grimaced as he looked across the square to where a train of clerics approached from around the statues of the Three Sisters, and said, "Here comes the Lady of Westcliff."

The Matriarch came ahead of a dozen women and girls, and a cart pulled by a mare that came to a stop. Genshai expected the Lady of Westcliff to demand, 'What's the meaning of this?' at the sight of her husband but instead she instructed the stableman to saddle her horse, and then called out to her daughter, "Alina, ride with your father; Ysma take over the mare and cart," before she named five other women to accompany them on the road and meet them at the Barrowgroves.

"Be certain to hold your flags high, ladies," Agatha said and they all produced long aspen poles with yellow and green banners bearing the blue rings of the goddess sisters, fluttering rapidly in the gusts from the sea. They looked prepared for a hike with waterskins and hard soled leather boots, and they wore the usual cambric dresses for a humid summer day. He couldn't help but notice Ysma also wore the holy cloth even though she was still a student, fitting in with the other women like she belonged among them. He caught her eyes once, but she quickly averted them down to the task at hand, and Genshai decided it was just as well that they didn't become distracted, although he felt that she seemed anxious and confused by the sight of her father.

Within minutes they were ready and the stableman assisted Lady Wynne onto the horse, and then Alina with her father. Mistress Tauva declined and mounted the horse herself, wearing comfortable riding pants and high boots. Taisan mounted Snowcap, nodding toward Genshai who stepped readily into the stirrup and urged Meora ahead of everyone. He led them southeast on the main road toward the Season Tree outside of the village, followed by Alina holding her father in front on the saddle as he twisted his head to look around.

"I'm pleased you decided to join us," Taisan said to the Matriarch.

"You made quite a compelling case this morning," Lady Wynne replied, a bit chagrined.

"Any amount of help is appreciated," Mistress Tauva said coolly as she was riding past.

The Matriarch straightened up in the saddle and looked quite formal with the blue and silver vestments around her shoulders. Her hair was tied neatly behind her head, and though it looked to be just as fine as her daughters' it was fading into shades of gray. While the horses sauntered down the road and the cart trundled at a slight distance behind them, Lady Wynne hardly broke her composure at all when she asked the laymonk, "Do you really think my husband can help?"

Taisan nodded, "I believe Lord Wynne still has a part to play in all this."

She shivered involuntarily in spite of the warmth of the rising sun and said, "Tonight the Lotus is in Bloom," as if it were a foreboding subject.

"Yes," Taisan nodded grimly. "They'll appear unless we find their burial place."

Agatha shook her head. "I don't know if this town can withstand another loss."

"You have my word that I will not let anyone be harmed," Taisan said without hesitation. She seemed to take heart in that and urged her mare forward until she was riding beside Alina where her husband rested his head on her shoulder and looked weakly toward his wife, only being able to speak in strange whispers that meant nothing to either of them.

Taisan rode in silence for the rest of the morning and readied his thoughts for what might come. The horses moved quickly ahead of the clerics that held the banners over their heads as they hiked, waving long tassels and flags that rippled in the wind and were meant to attract the Raegods and draw their eyes onto them. The cart and mare was further behind all of them, and the monk's two long hickory staves could be seen leaning on the corner with several other stakes and poles.

Eventually they came to a fork where Lord Wynne lifted a quavering finger toward the westward road and a stand of trees in the distance, muttering, "Now. Now. There."

"Yes," Lady Wynne agreed. "Those are the Barrowgroves. I remember when we first came here last year Euiger showed me all the limits of our new lands."

The Oathlord stirred in the saddle so much that Alina said, "Mother!" just as her father snatched the reins from her hands and kicked the horse so aggressively that it launched down the road ahead of everyone.

"Shit!" Tauva cursed.

Without thinking Genshai snapped his heels in the stirrups and Meora knew instantly to follow, leaving behind a cloud of dust.

"It's this way!" Euiger shouted back and Alina clutched her father's waist as he raced around the unfamiliar turns.

Genshai was able to make up the distance when the road straightened into the tall pine trees and they each came alongside each other. Holding his reins, he gripped the saddle with both legs for fear of losing his seat as he reached across the gap. Unable to grab the horse the boy did the only thing he could think to do and snapped a punch into Euiger's face, making his body go limp in the saddle.

"Hold on!" Genshai shouted, snatching up the reins and drawing back until both horses came to a halt in the road.

They must have been riding for several minutes, and found themselves alone in a shaded part of the road between several stands of evergreen trees.

"Are you okay?" he asked.

"I don't know," Alina shuddered, clearly shaken from the frenzied gallop. "He grabbed the reins from me." Her father's head rolled back onto her shoulder and he sat limply on the saddle as if he had no strength.

"He must be in a hurry," Genshai replied as he looked around.

The others soon approached and Lady Wynne came into the lead with a worried expression, calling out, "Alina?"

"We're okay," she answered back, holding her father around the waist while trying to steer the horse. "He wasn't trying to hurt me."

Agatha glanced around as if to remind herself of where they were. "He's brought us to the opposite side of the Barrowgrove, but there is an old trailhead over this way," she said as she led them past the pines toward a place that overlooked several broad and knotted oak trees; their deep green leaves whispering in the wind, their hollows gaping, as if the trees mourned for all the souls trapped there.

They dismounted and Genshai went immediately to Alina's mare and said, "Let me help you." The man slid from the saddle and Genshai held him under the arms, tightly against his chest until he glanced over and saw Euiger wide-awake with bloodshot eyes, smirking at him.

Suddenly the Oathlord snarled and jumped to bury his teeth into the boy's neck as the two tumbled into the grass. Genshai kicked him off, flipping Euiger onto his back and knocking the wind out of him. He crawled to his knees and gasped, "I promise, I'll be good," as if he were a different person, until he staggered down the slope, muttering strange words, "We must prepare for her return. Prepare, prepare for her vengeance, as it is foretold."

"Let him go," Taisan said as they all watched him loping between the trees, growling, and raising a howl like a wolf.

The line of six marching clerics soon arrived to the grove ahead of the cart. They breathed heavily and lowered their banners after hiking nearly four hours through the humid morning, taking long draughts of the sacred water they carried at their hips. Ysma was panting and there were damp circles of sweat under her arms, although she was doing a fair bit better than the other ladies that had just marched for ten miles holding the banners upright for the gods to see.

Lady Wynne strode toward the sisters of her shrine to commend them on the march. "Well done ladies, now let's begin by setting the flags to consecrate the grounds."

The Matriarch produced a scroll case from one of her saddlebags and unrolled several drawings of the Westcliff region until she found the map she wanted, pointing to the Barrowgroves. From the road, the copse of oak trees was nearly thirty acres across. It was not exactly a recognizable shape but she sent each cleric to the edges and corners where she determined the flags should be placed and later when the clerics returned they confirmed that the banners seemed to enclose the entire grove.

In the meantime Ysma and Alina unloaded several crates and chests from the back of the cart, tossing two shovels into Genshai's hands.

"What are these for?" Ysma pointed to a set of wicker boxes with lids, under which they could hear the cooing of birds and the fluttering of wings.

"Catch and release," Tauva said sharply as she took them under her arm, wielding an unlit torch in her other hand as she went into the forest.

Ysma's brows narrowed with uncertainty, but she continued to prepare ten bronze braziers of cedar wood and distributed them with her sister to the other women. They were all relatively silent as they worked, but Genshai managed to exchange a few solemn glances with Ysma. Even though he wanted to talk about Shigyn's testimony, and ask how she was feeling about her father, Genshai thought better of it. Instead he tied several wreaths of holly and juniper with twine. He watched as the clerics spread through the grove of trees, and stepping carefully like unearthly shadows behind thick clouds of smoke. They prayed in whispers to the Three Sisters, and to the Golden Mother, and the Mover of Stars, and all the Raegods, and went to the farthest edges of the Barrowgrove to consecrate the lands.

"Genshai," he heard Taisan call, and the boy gathered up the wreaths and the shovels and ran in to the woods.

The old laymonk stood against his staff under the broad bower of an oak tree, perhaps a little more than seven hundred feet from the horses. Mistress Tauva was nearby with a sharp intent in her eyes, holding the talisman of protection in her hand; a small iron shield on a chain of other charms and symbols. They could hear the sound of Lady Wynne's voice giving commands to the clerics in the distance, though it was difficult to make out the words. The maddened lord searched the roots of trees, distracted by the fluttering of leaves, chasing shadows under the sun.

"I think he's getting close," Taisan said quietly to his student beside him.

"Everything looks so different now," Euiger muttered. The chains rattled at his wrists as he staggered between the trees staring upward at the coiling branches, peering into the spaces between them. Then, as if he recognized where he was, he dropped to his hands and knees to inspect the soft earth, and then laid down between three wide oak trees to stare up at the leafy canopy that lifted outward, taking his eyes with it into the sky, as he released a deep breath, finally content.

"That's it," Taisan said with conviction.

He took up a shovel and headed toward the place. Without much persuasion Euiger moved off into the nearby trees while they began the process of digging a hole. The boy knew better than to question his teacher's reasoning and instead he went into the difficult task of widening the pit and thrusting out the soft earth with the shovel. The aromatic cedar smoke filled the grove while the laymonks pounded down the spade with their feet and removed the soil and gradually all the clerics came to watch.

Mistress Tauva stood on high alert as her eyes scanned the forest. She set out several large tallow candles at the roots of the three oak trees and lit them with a tindertwig. They were like many hazy thumbs of flame. She occasionally saw Oathlord Wynne as he paced back and forth through the trees, anxiously looking toward the pit for any sign that he had picked the right spot.

After a while the boy scraped through several inches of hard packed earth as he said quietly, "We're already four feet deep, maybe it's not here?"

Taisan shook his head. "No. It would have to be quite deep to prevent scavengers from getting to them."

They kept digging and broke into harder soil, tossing it higher along the edge to avoid having it tumble inward. They had removed their tunics long ago and were covered in dirt and sweat. Like everyone, they were hungry since nobody had considered bringing anything for lunch, but the laymonks kept working through midday, digging deeper and wider. Then, just as Taisan tilted water into his mouth the boy's shovel pierced through the dirt and uncovered a dirty brown canvas, and he said, "I found something."

"Yes!" Taisan exclaimed as he grabbed up his shovel to uncover more of the canvas.

Together they widened the hole on either side, and some of the clerics wondered aloud how many had been buried until Tauva replied, "Shigyn said there were five bags in his testimony," just as Genshai managed to find the corner of one, yanking it up and using the shovel to dislodge it from the others. By the time they had found the other end of the bag the sidewalls of the pit had started to cascade down and soon they were shoveling again to widen the gravesite.

The next time they were ready Genshai volunteered to stand

in the pit and hoist the bags upward toward Taisan and the others. It took several long minutes, and the solemnity of what they were doing did not escape him; each bag had lain undisturbed for decades, and as their bones rattled in his ears he had to summon the Still Mind to finish the task. Afterward, he clasped his teacher's arm to come over the edge of the pit and saw the five canvas bags laid in a row, each of them tied with heavy rope as if they would escape.

The clerics all crowded around, quietly calling on Maitreija and Yuemaiah and Alloraiah of the Three Sisters; and then the Queen of Heaven – Andriani the Mover of Stars, the maid of the peach grove – and especially Aurelai the Golden Mother who was believed to have created the world from her egg.

Tauva came forward with the two wicker baskets in her hands. Kneeling beside the bags, she carefully opened the lid of one basket and reached within to produce a stark white dove that looked almost gray in the shadows of her hand. Holding the bird tightly she raised it over her head and walked within the ring of worshipping clerics as she proclaimed, "By the will of the gods we welcome these shades from the earth and release them back to the sky!"

Suddenly she produced a short dagger from her belt and cut the dove's throat, severing its head entirely. There was a shocked murmur among the clerics until Lady Wynne shushed them and said, "Quiet," allowing the fortuneteller to resume the strange ritual. Mistress Tauva held the dove's head in one closed fist and gripped the body in the other hand until every bag had been sprayed with the sacrificial blood. She dropped both pieces into the depths of the grave as if they were no longer important and reached for the second wicker basket to produce another dove, its white feathers smeared with the red from her hands.

"Fly free!" Mistress Tauva released the dove into the air, fluttering upward through the branches until it was out of sight.

"Praise the Three Sisters!" Ysma said instinctively, raising her arms, "Praise the gods!"

"Praise!" the other clerics repeated, lifting their voices through the Barrowgroves, holding their hands high, "Praise! Praise!"

Panting heavily, the women all drew back at once from their worship and lowered their arms, turning away from the scene. Full of emotion, some of them took long walks to summon the power of their faith for the strength to do what still needed to be done. Once the ritual was complete there was still the matter of returning the body bags to the shrine for proper burial rites. They had brought sailcloth litters so that two women could take up the poles at either end and carry a bag down the road as long as they walked at the same pace, each one with a wreath set in the middle.

The women talked sparingly as they worked, until one of the older clerics said snidely, "I'd like to get that lazy husband of mine out here to do some this dirty work."

"Women do all the dirty work," another woman chimed in.

"Isn't that the truth," someone agreed, "They might reel it in, but we have to chop it up, don't we girls?"

Taisan could hardly blame them since they were doing the hardest part of the job. Lady Wynne had said that the clerics would need to carry the bodies back to the shrine for the final rituals, yet even with all eight of them there was still one litter that needed to be carried. Of course his student Genshai volunteered, which was characteristic of the boy, and he promptly passed over the reins of his horse and went back to take up the heaviest litter. The weight was lifted from behind when Mistress Tauva rolled up her sleeves to join the train of clerics; and not a single one of them objected to her presence, and when they sang the holy songs in the name of the Raegods, Tauva's strong voice joined them for every chant.

Carrying the litter in front, Lady Wynne began with the names of the Three Sisters from oldest to youngest and they all repeated the syllables like an ongoing echo until every one of them had said it after the person ahead of them, "Maia – Maia – Maitreija / Allo – Allo – Alloraiah / Yuea – Yuea – Yuemaia."

They called the name of the Golden Mother in the same way, Aurelai the creator of the world.

Then they honored the Queen of Heaven, Andriani the Mover of Stars, and Amaritabhe, the silver god of wisdom.

There were so many gods, and when they began to call upon the others Genshai complained, "Why is this one so heavy?" as he adjusted the poles in his hands.

"They buried the boy and the girl together," Tauva replied with a grim set of features, her muscles taut as they marched.

Finally they arrived outside the village where folks watched suspiciously from the steps of their homes. Taisan even saw some fearful fishwives shuttering their windows and boarding up their doors as they passed. Hebrahm the Lawkeeper and three other guardsmen came to meet them and soon the street cleared ahead until it was completely devoid of people as they marched into the square around the shrine.

The clerics set the body bags down at random around the three statues, ready to relax their arms and legs. Panting, his young student put his hands on his head and walked in circles while the clerics shared the last of the water from the skins at their hips. Several women emerged from the shrine after waiting all day for their return. Almost at once there was a rush of people from the wharf and a crowd appeared all around them, containing a number of sailors, defenders, and even the old Alderman Crainog among them.

"I knew I'd find you here," said a surly man with gray scruff on his cheeks. He grabbed one of the clerics by the cloth of her neck and dragged her back. "You're cursing yourself, you foolish woman."

She kicked him hard in the shin and smacked his head, knocking him down, "Now who's the fool?" to which a handful of people laughed.

"Lady Wynne," the Alderman called from the crowd, waving his cane. "How can you be aligned with this witch? Doesn't she live in the brothel and treat whores for their diseases?"

The noblewoman held her head upright and said, "No woman receives a disease unless it's from a man, and I suspect we've treated a fair amount of your own ill-gotten ailments on healing day," to which there was a joint sound of laughter and jeers. "Now, I am the Matriarch of this shrine and the Lady of Westcliff and I must insist that we begin the rites as soon possible. Lawkeeper, please dig six graves in the cemetery to be ready by tomorrow morning…"

Someone in the crowd objected, "That's holy ground!" to which there were shouts of, "The ancestors will be cursed!" and, "You'll doom us all."

People shoved against each other like the powerful sea and suddenly Oathlord Wynne was thrown to the ground, disappearing from view. The old Alderman shouted, "Drive the curse out of him," and half a dozen people ruthlessly stomped on his arms and legs until Genshai ran in and pushed them apart, dragging Euiger away until he was able to stand by himself; his dark hair disheveled, long strands whirling around his face as he looked fearfully at the crowd.

Taisan found it necessary to swing his staff to keep the people back, shouting, "Defenders confirm your oaths! Are you the shields of Shao Daan or not?" which forced Hebrahm and the other guardsmen to form a brave circle against the villagers that pressed in around them. The clerics gathered up the poles of each litter as quickly as they could and took the body bags directly into the shrine so that they could begin funeral rites. Lady Wynne and her daughters disappeared in a commotion of blue-clad women; their dresses flowing in the wind until the doors shut firmly behind them.

The Lawkeeper and nine other guards retreated back from the statues until they were protecting the steps to the shrine. The crowd roared unhappily. People threw rotted onions and potatoes, and someone said that they had brought the curse down on the village while another man shouted, "We should get our harpoons next time."

"Get those shields up!" Hebrahm commanded even though the crowd was thinning out of the square, and he soon decided, "We'll stay here in case they come back."

"They'll be back," Tauva said shortly, observing the western slant of the sun. "It'll be nighttime soon. The madness comes with the moon."

"What about him?" Genshai indicated to Euiger, who paced and whimpered, his chains clinking at his wrists.

Hebrahm glanced quickly at his own men, wondering whom among them he could trust until he called out, "Konlyn. Markova," and two young guardsmen came forward with their banded shields in one hand, armed with swords at their belts. They were panting, a sheen of sweat visible on their foreheads, but they had clear eyes that looked toward their honorable Lawkeeper, waiting for his commands, which were, "Get him to the jail and report back."

"Moonrise is an hour after dark," Tauva said to them all like it was a warning. "The Lotus is in Bloom tonight."

<hr>

They didn't return to the Siren's Song until dusk, when the orb of the sun sat on the line of the horizon at sea. By the time they had visited the livery to put up their horses for the night and then headed all the way to the brothel they were dragging their feet with exhaustion. Along the way Tauva managed to find a few friends in the street, telling them, "Make sure you're home before dark, and burn cedar in the fireplace," since she knew that the shades would be there soon.

Taisan wondered, *Have our measures worked? Will the ghosts be satisfied?* Even though he felt very confident that they had recovered the correct bodies, but there was no way to know for certain. They made their way to a table where the three of them collapsed into chairs. They were dejected and dirty and tired and still had yet to see what the full moon would bring, and from where they sat they could hear a baby crying, like a plaintive animal repeating itself.

Everyone was curious about what happened at the Barrowgroves. The bartender came around twice to check on them, and even shook the boy's shoulder roughly as he said, "A young fellow like you ought to have the energy for a stout at least," to which Genshai released a withering glare and the man promptly left them alone. The women of the brothel eavesdropped on every word, and after a serving girl delivered a pot of black tea, bowls of hearty clam chowder, and fresh butter biscuits, they all swarmed over her for any information she overheard them say.

Really, most folks already knew everything they needed to know from the rumors that had gotten around. The old stories were on everyone's mind, but people gossiped about how the laymonks, and even Lady Wynne, had been coerced by the witch's blood magic to bring the cursed bodies back to the village. Or that the mad knight looked as if he was ready to bite through someone's neck, and one of the men with a mug at the bar said, "More likely the summer moon'll be drawing the wolves out of the Farwood tonight."

"I can't believe they think we would try to bring the curse down on them," Genshai remarked just as a group of sailors went by the windows, hollering slurs at them as they passed.

Tauva replied sarcastically, "They think evil will desecrate their holy places, which shows how little faith they have in the clerics of their own shrine."

"But the Matriarch is doing the rites," Genshai acknowledged.

Tauva nodded and said, "You have a point, I hadn't expected that."

"Then why are all these people so angry?" he asked.

"They're afraid," Taisan answered.

"Fear is an irrational response," Tauva grumbled unhappily. "Those ghosts were victims. They were hurt beyond anything we can imagine. It wasn't their fault."

"They might be victims, but they are still causing harm," Taisan replied thoughtfully. "They're stuck in the place they were in when they were hurt, but their grief has caused more grief; their suffering has caused more suffering, so the people misplace their anger toward them and not toward the true culprit."

"The true culprit," Genshai said quietly, his brows furrowed, deep in thought.

"There were only six bodies in that grave," Tauva commented to Taisan. "We still don't know what happened to the shepherd."

The laymonk nodded. "Yes, that would be the last piece of the puzzle."

While they talked the various women emerged into the common room as if they were drawn there. Some wanted company in anticipation of the night, while others just wanted to look out the window at the crowds gathering at the wharf. The wet nurse came out holding young Kyus as he cried incessantly, piercing everyone's ears until Taisan stood to his feet, took the child into his hands, and rocked the baby until his crying was reduced to a soft whimper, as he consoled, "It's okay, it's okay, little guy. I'm here. I'm here. I'm sorry you're so upset tonight, it'll be okay."

The winds howled across the salt flats, rattling the shutters. They could hear the subtle crashing of waves in the distance and for several minutes they all huddled as if they were enduring a storm. They kept their faith in the iron talismans that Mistress Tauva had nailed in every windowsill, forged in the shape of godmarks, but nonetheless she went around and told them to keep their lanterns lit all night and even arranged for the cook to set out a basket of offerings on the boardwalk.

A ship's bell began to ring from out of the silence of the wharf. Not in the orderly way the sailors usually did to indicate that they were moored, or to call out the time of day, or that there was fog in front, but frantically clanging as if it was an emergency. Through the shutters they could see dozens of fists upraised in the crowd at the docks. Taisan glanced down at Kyus and held his expression tightly as he passed him back to the wet nurse, even though the baby reached out with little hands, yearning for him.

"I think we had better get back to the shrine," Taisan said urgently.

Genshai leapt to his feet, as if their brief rest and meager portions of food had refreshed him. He passed his teacher the iron tipped staff and they went outside, treading on the cobblestones with the fortuneteller right behind them. The night air was chilly at the level of the docks and there were a number of men with lit torches that shouted, "They've brought the curse down upon us!" and other similar things, although it was the old Alderman who spun them a story of wolves and witches, as he said, "Our shrine is cursed! Those monks are in conference with the mad knight and his wife, and tonight they're summoning ghosts to haunt us all!"

Without saying anything, Taisan quickened his pace up the slope of the road to where the three statues were ahead of them in the square. Coming to the front steps there were only four guards standing around, and he asked, "Where is Hebrahm?"

"He went inside," one of the men answered as he passed a flask of whiskey over to his companion and said roughly, "Don't mind us, just getting in a some liquid bravery."

"I'm going to need it if we're fighting ghosts tonight," the other man commented sourly.

"I don't think it's ghosts you need to be worried about," Genshai pointed to the light of torches that cut back the darkness in the street and they heard the clamor and shouts that echoed through the night as a crowd of hundred people spilled into the square. The defenders leapt up, grabbed their banded shields from nearby, and formed a small half circle around the steps of the shrine. They all wore the quilted defender's tunic with leather spaulders and bracers, and the shield of Shao Daan embroidered in white on their heart, carrying swords at their hips.

"Stay back!" Taisan declared forcefully. "Don't come any closer," which seemed to halt the crowd at the place where the three statues stood facing southeast.

The doors of the shrine opened and then slammed closed. Within moments Hebrahm and three other men returned to the steps where they added their bodies to the defense. Almost immediately there was a clatter of rocks on the cobblestones and the guards instinctively thrust up their shields as the commander declared, "They're throwing stones!" and Genshai turned away, crouching and covering his face while the guards held shields in front of Taisan and Tauva.

"They won't stop," Taisan explained in a hurry. "The madness is spreading."

Another volley of rocks showered down over them and

Hebrahm snapped to his men, "Keep those shields up!"

"Let us pass! Let us pass!" came a set of shouts from above the noisy crowd. It was the two young guardsmen shoving their way through with a line of six others behind them. Folks pressed on all sides but the defenders were able to back each other and push out with their shields until the crowd had no choice but to spread apart for them as they joined the defense of the shrine.

"Let them come," the Lawkeeper said eagerly as the young officers clambered into their half circle.

"He escaped," the one named Konlyn said breathlessly. "The mad knight escaped!"

"What?" the old laymonk said, horrified as he looked out at the torches flickering like spikes across the square.

"There's more to worry about than one crazy man," Hebrahm decided as he began to issue orders. "Post up with shields against those rocks! Don't let anyone around the other side. If they are gripped by madness they might burn it down, even if their own wives and daughters are inside, but do not draw swords on these people!"

"No swords?" Markvoa asked. "They have weapons of their own out there?"

"No swords," Hebrahm insisted.

"He's right," Mistress Tauva said, "Or else people will be talking of a bloodbath in Westcliff for the next fifty years," and in spite of being known as a witch, she received several nods of understanding from them.

"Watch out!" Genshai shouted as a sudden hail of rocks battered against the shields, and everyone crouched down with their hands over their heads.

Taisan saw Mistress Tauva react just a little late, taking a rough-edged stone directly to the side of her ear before her hands could be lifted in time. She slumped to her side and Taisan leapt to cover her as another set of rocks rained down on them, protecting the fortuneteller with his body as the stones landed on his back.

Several confused sounds came from across the square. Three or four men advanced with torches and there were shouts of, "Burn the witches!" and the mob of people moved closer and closer to the shieldwall. There were even a few men menacingly carrying hatchets and cleavers, nets and javelins, as if they were waiting for the real violence to begin.

"Teacher?" Genshai said, as if to ask what they should do now.

Kneeling down, Taisan looked at the woman on the ground, the wound at the side of her head bleeding profusely past her ear and neck and he said, "Tauva needs to be treated, as soon as possible."

"We need to find Euiger," Genshai contradicted, thinking the mad knight might harm someone.

Taisan shook his head, "No. She'll die if we don't do something," gathering up her limp body in his arms as he said, "Follow me!" and ran back toward the shrine, dodging around the corner until they were in an alley where Taisan remembered Tauva had revealed that she knew where the side door was since she occasionally traded with the alchemist of the healing chapel without the Matriarch's knowledge.

"Here they are!" someone shouted, to which four burly sailors appeared at the far corner of the building armed with cleavers and knives.

They approached just as Taisan pounded on the side door, and began to set Tauva down as gently as he could on the cobblestones. Genshai came out to meet them with the staff ready in his hands. He showed no fear at all. Shouting like animals, the sailors attacked his student just as Genshai snapped the tip of his staff into the first man's face as a diversion and then swung his weapon in a fast circle to keep the others at a distance. Taisan looked on with pride as his young student easily defended against four older, and arguably more experienced, fighters.

Every time they came forward Genshai leveraged the heavy heel of the staff around like an eight-foot club, striking knees, hips, necks, until they were all so bruised and wounded that they had to stop to reconsider their approach. They looked crazed, their eyes wide and bloodshot, their jaws gaping hungrily, and he would have joined his student to fight them off if he had not been suddenly attacked from behind by a lanky man with a greasy ponytail that held a boning knife. Taisan reacted by blocking his midsection with the staff, bringing his hands together to beat the knifeman over the shoulders three times before he switched on the last hit to blast the iron tip through his ankle, forcing him to collapse.

Panting and invigorated, Genshai clutched his staff and looked around at the men that filled the road, groaning in pain. He knew that one man likely had a cracked collarbone and another was unconscious from a blow to the side of the head that had sent him down hard. Compelled to look, the boy pressed his fingers into the sailor's throat in search of a heartbeat, finally content that the man still lived just as Taisan called, "Help me with her."

They hoisted Tauva up just as the door opened and Alina appeared. Ysma stood adjacent to her sister within the stairwell that led down to a recessed chapel of the shrine where there were ten beds on either side of a long room. As she hung in their arms the fortuneteller's wound was obvious to see and the two girls immediately brought her into the chapel where they could clean her head and wrap it with a compress of medicines. The sounds of prayer could be heard inside and there was an intense smell of juniper and cedar.

"How much longer until the rites are complete?" Taisan asked.

The two girls looked at each other and said, "We're still finishing the first body," to which both monks dropped their mouths open in disbelief.

It seemed that Lady Wynne had determined the bones would need to be laid out on blessed linens and each victim should be given the highest honors if they were to truly appease the ghosts. Wearing cloth gloves, the women had the grisly job of removing the bones one at a time, taking every precaution to avoid dropping anything, which was an omen of bad luck to whomever was so clumsy. It took longer and was quite redundant, but Agatha now believed they were called on by the Raegods to bless the bodies and to honor the ancestors and to end the curse of Westcliff.

Incense burned through the sanctuary hall. The braziers were lit with cedar on which they threw wreaths of green juniper that filled the room with gray smoke. Each body would eventually be wrapped in the burial cloth made of many woven colors, with little sheets of hemp paper folded against their bones; stamped with yellow squares, or blue dots and red bands. They were types of ghost money that their souls would bring to their ancestor's halls in the afterlife. As many as they gave to the dead, the clerics were obliged to burn an equal number for the Raegods, the ashy tatters rising up with the fragrant smoke to the peaked ceiling of the shrine.

"At that rate it'll take all night!" Genshai moaned.

Taisan warned them, "Barricade your doors," as they returned to the street level where Ysma glanced at the men lying all around the alley.

"Now what?" Genshai asked.

Taisan nodded. "Now let's find Lord Wynne."

There was a sudden piercing shriek from the east of the village. It was a hollow, unearthly sound, and they both looked at each other, knowing exactly what it meant.

"Is the moon rising? I can't see," Genshai looked out toward the sky, yet with all the houses and the height of the cliffs there was no way to see the moon.

"They're coming so I assume it hardly matters," Taisan said.

"But why?" Genshai asked, "They're being honored as we speak."

Taisan realized, "It's not enough," remembering vividly the strange and perverse tortures he had read about in Shigyn's sworn testimony. Then he had a thought that might've been a gamble, and he said, "I know where we need to go."

His student nodded trustingly, "Okay."

Taisan looked at the noisy mob in the square and said, "We will need to fight our way through."

Genshai's eyes were like shimmering obsidian in the nighttime and he said, "I'm ready," with admirable conviction.

The boy can fight better than any of these men, Taisan realized, focusing instead on getting himself ready. He was quite a bit older now than he was in the days that he fought in Zansho tournaments, so many years ago. He took steady measured breaths and summoned the Still Mind as they rejoined the shieldwall. Nearly two-dozen defenders held the line against the surging crowd as Hebrahm shouted, "Back away! Back away, now!" while his men shoved their banded shields into the villager's knees and roared like bears.

"Burn the witches!" someone shouted, hurling a torch toward the front door.

Hebrahm snapped, "Go put out that fire!" to which a young man exited the line to quickly stamp out the torch.

"Do you still order us not to use our swords?" Markova demanded as someone beat against his shield with a club until he thrust up with the top edge, mercilessly breaking the man's jaw.

"No swords!" the Lawkeeper commanded, speaking directly to the old laymonk. "As soon as we draw swords it'll be a massacre."

"Then Westcliff will truly be cursed," the laymonk agreed.

"But we can't hold them all night," Hebrahm replied.

Taisan nodded, "My apprentice and I will go out. No swords."

The Lawkeeper looked at the two monks in surprise and then set his face with determination. "Not before we make a path for you! Guards, get ready to make a lane!" he shouted to all the defenders on the shieldwall. Each of them edged forward, back-to-back, until they pushed the mob apart and gave the monks just enough room to run headlong into the center of the crowd. The defenders returned back to their shieldwall and the monks were left exposed to the anger of the crowd.

Without warning, someone came charging with a harpoon. Genshai immediately dodged out of the way but Taisan merely sidestepped and blasted the attacker's shins with a merciless blow of the staff. Then, in both hands, he waved his weapon haphazardly at anyone that came within range. It was effective, especially after one man was struck in the ear and another took a brutal hit that made his hand go numb and drop his weapon, and Taisan guessed he had broken his arm.

The crowd backed away, which allowed a man with two hatchets and another with two cleavers to come forward.

Genshai panted, "What kind of curse is this?" just as the butcher came out swinging and the boy was forced to parry and retreat with long steps.

Taisan moved to intercept the hatchet man. His staff was like an extension of himself and he kept his opponent at a distance, whipping the iron tip around to the knee, and then he reversed direction to hit squarely in the neck from the side. It was a brutal strike that dropped his enemy to the ground, and when the old laymonk caught sight of his legs seizing and his eyes fluttering he was not sure if the man would live or not.

Putting it out of his mind, Taisan watched as his young student parried back the two cleavers. With at least seven feet between them, the boy realized how much room he had to step, and he thrust the rugged tip ruthlessly three times like a spear into the butcher's chest, before he swung widely in a cutting arc that was impossible to see in the darkness.

The man collapsed, screaming, "My leg! My leg!"

Suddenly Hebrahm's strong voice came from behind, "Charge!" and the defenders surged forward, butting, checking, and pummeling with their shields, doing whatever they could to break up the crowd without drawing their swords. Folks backed away rather than receive a broken jaw or a bloody nose, and soon the monks managed to force their way through to the other side.

"Come on!" Taisan urged, and they went running into the streets at night.

"I think I broke that man's leg!" the boy exclaimed.

"It was either you or him," Taisan replied shortly.

The bright moon rose over them and the monks raced through the streets until they were stopped by the sight of three apparitions

– defenders in quilted tunics with their swords drawn. Marching shoulder to shoulder, they were translucent, silver and blue in the moonlight, their movements piercingly loud like nails dragging over slate. Taisan saw their wounds, their bent necks and ripped faces, their skeleton arms and legs that had been snapped and gnawed upon. They flickered out of sight and reappeared down in the square as if they were crashing through a panel of glass, sending people running in terror.

"Look," Genshai pointed his staff down the road where two more awful shades approached. They saw the young shepherd's son, his head twisted around, while his sister released a high shrill cry and the monks were forced to see her squelching innards tumbling out of her belly. The young girl hardly cared, dragging her guts under her feet; her wails piercing their ears as she passed by them and entered the rest of the village.

Taisan saw the disgust and confusion spreading on his student's face, and shouted against the wind, "Mountainroot! You must keep the Still Mind!" to which the boy nodded and tightened his jaw.

People went in a mad spread through the village. The apparitions flashed into the cobbled lanes, and anyone that was touched by the ghastly finger was frozen in fear as it cut deeply into their thoughts, collapsing them into incomprehensible suffering. As he turned back to the east road Taisan saw the last shade standing in the most weary and aggrieved posture; the shepherd's wife, flayed everywhere, sternum cracked open, holding her bloody heart in her hands, her eyes crazed by all that she had witnessed, creeping forward out of Oathlord Wynne in the street.

"Euiger!" Genshai called, but the mad knight ran away, disappearing into the darkness of the foothills. The ghost of the shepherd's wife ignored them, and began to drift down the road, screaming in utter horror, not from the pain of her own wounds but from the hideous tortures she had witnessed. A ship's bell rang frantically in the distance for several minutes and there was someone clanging pots and pans together. They could hear the subtle roar of men brawling and then the shriek of angry ghosts as they took their victims in the streets, passing over their death throes to anyone they touched.

The monks turned and left the noises of the village behind, going at a quick pace under the trees by the road until they were completely enveloped in silence except for the sounds of their own feet. They each breathed easily and made the journey as swiftly as two running deer. By now they were certain they knew where to go, coming over the crest of the road where the full moon hung low over the abandoned house and they could see the twinkling stars high above.

"Look," Genshai whispered, pointing to the silhouette that disappeared into the shadows of the house.

"He's going inside," Taisan realized.

The two laymonks went closer, stepping carefully through thick bramble at the side of the road as they came upon the door that possessed the hungry darkness of a wolf's throat, always drawing them inward even as the frame widened outward. Holding his composure, Taisan readied his staff and he told Genshai, "Wait here," and strode without any hesitation into that inky blackness, as if he was parting a curtain that fell back in place after he went through.

At once there was the sound of frantic sobbing and gasping breaths from the hearth. Coming into the main room, Taisan saw by the moonlight that fell through the ruins of the roof where the mad knight held up a heavy stone to hammer down a crooked nail through the palm of his left hand, screaming as he drove it through like a wicked stake into the mantle. The stone clattered to the ground and Wynne slumped with his left hand suspended in the air.

"Euiger?" Taisan said as he came through the coarse darkness.

Blood streamed down his arm and Euiger gazed at the ruins, his eyes shimmering as he pleaded in slow gasps, "Please stop. Please stop hurting us."

"Who is hurting you?" Taisan asked, his Still Mind holding firmly at the sight of the man's self-mutilation.

"My beautiful daughter," the mad knight wailed as he looked away. He reached to something that was not there and touched the rusted nails on the mantle. "Jakkob, don't leave me. I beg you, don't let me die alone," waiting for a voice that only he could hear.

Taisan bent down to comfort Euiger who suddenly snapped his face forward and launched himself out, held back only by the nail he had driven through his hand. "Do you think I'm not here too? Bastard monk!" Wynne snarled like a wolf.

"Begone demon." Taisan held forth his staff, standing fully aligned.

The mad knight yanked mercilessly, ignoring the pain as he tried to rip his palm from the nail, screaming, "I will eat your heart! I will crush your bones in my teeth! I will ravage your body! I will feast on your spirit until there is nothing left but ashes!"

"Begone demon!" Taisan said once again, hitting an Iron Palm on Wynne's forehead to strike him down against the hearth.

Immediately Euiger's demeanor changed, becoming once again terrified, he cried, "Jakkob, what's happening? What do we do?" as new layers of shadow crept from the corners of the house; clouds covered the moonlight, and they became lost in the void of memory and time where trauma hides.

Taisan held the staff upright with both hands as he steadied his breath, striding the line of clarity. The six shades were there, called from the village to the house as if they were actors that moved through the motions of that dreadful night, which began with the sounds of an invisible beast snapping its jaws. Distorted through time, discordant and earsplitting, there was no mistaking the beastly growls just as the furniture was destroyed and great marks appeared gouged in the floorboards.

Euiger seemed to lay his eyes upon a great evil and released a terrified scream. The shepherd's wife sat over him like a gauze shroud, forced to bear witness as an unseen force eviscerated her daughter, breaking her open to be eaten like prey. Then the defenders charged when they ought to have waited. Their swords bent in half against its hide and their banded shields splintered in its hands. In a cacophony of sounds they were crushed and battered and thrown in a whirlwind around the room followed by an awful cackling laughter as the shepherd's wife was forced to watch the beast crack their bones in its jaw like they were twigs.

As might have been expected, when all other delights were gone and all other amusements were spent, the beast turned to the shepherd's wife. Together she and Euiger released cries that were like streaks of sound pounding into Taisan's ears, her body flayed, her heart removed, until her eyes were lifeless and she was utterly destroyed. The apparitions in the room faded until Wynne was all that was left after the ghosts had played their part.

"Why?" Wynne demanded, crying upward.

"Who?" Taisan demanded. "Who did this?"

"Aaah – aaah – aaah," Wynne coughed, choking out the sounds, "Aaaz – laaak – aaah," he repeated once again as if they were difficult to produce, "Aaaz – laaak – aaah. Aaaz – laaak – aaah."

"Aazlaka," Taisan repeated the name, and summoned the harrowing vision of a monster that filled the height of the room, standing on ram legs, it reared the vicious head of a wolf, black horns protruding from its brow. The beast was covered in greasy, bloodstained fur and swung a long bristly tail, unashamed of his nakedness. His eyes glared like dirty yellow lamps lit with a red flame, and he stomped forward baring teeth the size of swords and snapping his black claws.

"Fool! Say my name again! Call me out," the beast demanded, his voice distorted. Taisan was stricken with fear at the sight of his nightmares brought to life here in a vision through the gap of time. The stench of feces and carnage prickled in his nose as if he were there and the old monk could not help but to shrink back as the beast seemed to rise higher, striding forward, until Genshai unexpectedly leapt in from where he had been watching everything just inside the doorframe.

"Begone Aazlaka!" the boy thrust his Iron Palm into the belly of the beast like he was tearing through a paper lantern. The demon lumbered back and Genshai waved his hickory staff, splitting the image apart. The shadows retreated like frightened snakes. The silence returned, the clouds cleared, and the moonlight dropped in wide beams over the gaping roof, filling the entire room so that they could see each other as clearly as if it were daytime.

The boy helped his teacher to his feet and asked, "Are you okay?"

"How? I don't understand," Taisan replied as he held his hands over his eyes, breathing heavily.

Together they managed to pry out the nail from Euiger's palm, and helped the weakened and barely conscious man across the room and over the threshold of the door. They made their way to the road, going slowly with his arms around their necks. Taisan took deep haggard breaths, searching for the Still Mind once again, wanting to put away the flashes of all that he had witnessed, the chaotic delights of the demon, and the many years of trauma Aazlaka had caused to these people.

There were still unanswered questions. *What happened to the shepherd?* Taisan wondered, *And where did Genshai learn to do that?* although for now he just wanted to take comfort in the bright moonlight.

Soon they all managed to walk without any help. Euiger Wynne was in a daze, rubbing his eyes and looking around as if he was just waking up from a long difficult sleep, but Taisan saw that Genshai trudged down the road with his eyelids half closed. The poor boy had been awake since the forehour of dawn and now at their slow pace Genshai probably wouldn't be back to his cot until sunrise, although Taisan thought, *By the look of him, that boy might just fall asleep while he's walking down the road.*

"Mountainroot," Taisan said, wrenching the boy awake. He pointed back to the full moon beaming over the foothills where they saw six little shards of light rise up from the shepherd's house, going so high they went out like sputtering candles.

"Where do they go?" Genshai asked.

Taisan said, "I've heard they go to live on the far side of the moon," knowing that those little flames were all that was left of their souls.

Genshai nodded, tired but satisfied, and soon they continued their long walk under the Lotus in Bloom.

The sun rose over the Auburn Range and the eastern light was soft through the cobbled streets of the village. The long shadows were cool and blue. Gulls cried on the wind accompanied by the sound of water sloshing against the hulls of ships moored in the harbor and folks slept late through the morning. Puffy clouds gathered in the west, white and purple over the vast undulating waters of the Larenn Sea where several sails were painted in sunbeams that descended on the horizon in the distance.

After a long eventful night, Genshai and Taisan didn't return to the Siren's Song until just after dawn. At some point the older laymonk decided to keep Euiger Wynne with him, who instantly fell asleep as soon as he lay on the mattress while Taisan nodded in and out on his bedroll, disturbed by yellow eyes that flashed out of the darkness. After a while he gave up on sleep and sat with his legs crossed to meditate, reciting the Still Mind in this thoughts, *Still as floating clouds, / still as the place between thought, / still as steady rain,* as he drew his breath down through his Navel Gate and up the spine, around the back of the skull, creating the Small Circle, exhaling quietly.

Genshai slept for barely three hours before he was awake. Like his teacher he was unable to set aside the disquieting scenes they had witnessed together, and the boy felt conflicted about hurting people. After a while he got up and found Taisan in the common room drinking a pot of black tea as he sat silently and stared at the light glinting off the iron godmarks in the windowsills. Most people in the brothel slept through the morning, and when Euiger Wynne also emerged from the stairwell they went out to discover that the whole town was slumbering like that.

Nearly everyone had little to no memory of what happened the previous night. It was as if they were waking up from an unusual dream with mysterious wounds, cuts, and even broken bones that needed treatment at the healing chapel. People moved slowly down the street, or on the deck of a ship, drowsy in those first hours after sunrise. Some folks had complete lapses, not remembering the attacks they made on the laymonks or the defenders, or that they had tried to burn down the shrine with their own wives and daughters and sisters inside.

Euiger wore the manacles around his wrists and squinted in the sunlight at the shingled roofs of the village as he said, "This is all so familiar to me."

They decided to head to the healing chapel to see how far along the rites were progressing, and Genshai was eager to catch up with Ysma, while Taisan wanted to visit Mistress Tauva and see how she was doing. The square was empty except for some rubbish left behind, yet there were still four defenders posted at the front steps and the door of the shrine remained barricaded from inside. With a weary expression one man waved the monks to the side of the shrine where another guard stood by the door to the healing chapel.

Both Alina and Ysma bustled down the length of the room as they visited every bed where people lay with wounds of all kinds. A dozen others sat on crates and barrels and held cold compresses against their broken jaws, split noses, or concussions that all could have easily been from the edge of a defender's shield, or the heel of a monk's staff. Blushing furiously, Genshai felt awkward when he recognized one or two of them that he had injured, wondering if they would always suffer from the wounds he inflicted.

"Now, Mistress, please don't move around," Alina was objecting as they approached. "You have a severe concussion," her voice faltered as if she were at the end of her patience.

"I'll be fine," Tauva grimaced as she sat forward and tried to get to her feet.

"Just quit moving and rest," Taisan said sternly.

Then, as if sitting upright made her dizzy, Tauva held her head in one hand and covered her eyes, announcing, "Alright, alright, I surrender, for now."

"I know the feeling," Genshai commiserated. "Do you want some hit medicine for the bruising?"

"No!" she bluntly refused, "I can't stand that stuff! The smell alone will make me throw up."

Taisan gave her a brief summary of what had happened last night, and eventually he said, "The bodies will be buried in full honor today, but I believe the ghosts are already appeased."

"What does it all mean?" Tauva asked, glancing at the boy curiously.

"It was a message," Taisan started to explain, before shaking his head, "No, I need to meditate on it for a while."

"I want you tell me everything," she insisted in spite of the pain in her head.

Quite suddenly they heard several voices rising from the street outside and Ysma went to the door to see what it was. As if nothing could stop them, the women of the brothel came marching down the stairs in a flurry of colorful linen dresses, silk scarves, woven cardigans and woolen shawls, crowding into the healing chapel. They filled the space between a dozen beds, wearing kohl on their eyes and red wax on their lips, their hair styled as if they were welcoming guests into the tavern.

"Mistress Tauva, we heard you were hurt last night," Irisol said worriedly amid all the women chattering sympathetically to the injured men they knew.

"I'm alright," Tauva answered with forced vigor.

"We wanted to help," Ollah said and pointed up to a cart parked at the door with a cauldron of steaming fish stew made at the Siren's Song earlier that morning. At first Alina objected but it became clear the ladies of the brothel were just going to do whatever they thought was best and before long they portioned out hearty bowls of seafood to the sailors, eventually fussing over the young girls so much that they were forced to take a break and eat.

Up until that point Lord Wynne had been sitting in the corner, inconspicuous among the other patients. He turned his head to every little thing with the awe of a curious child, keeping quiet, content with being ignored. He was dirty and unkempt, his hands covered in grime and blood, his eye and cheek bruised. When his daughters sat down to eat, he watched them confusedly, as if trying to place them back into his memories. They stared at each other, but Euiger was as tame as a household dog waiting at their feet.

Genshai went into the sanctuary hall where he saw the clerics tiredly holding up their vigil, hoarsely chanting the names of the Raegods until the last sacred candle burned down and the last money page went up in smoke. With the observances ongoing, the clerics rotated between chants until they were all fed, taking short breaks through the morning before they resumed their duties, as if they had no need for true rest. The Matriarch never stopped. She held up her palms to call on the Three Sisters and blessed the six burial shrouds, her arms and face gleaming with sweat from the exertion in the firelight.

The boy was impressed. "These women are tireless, don't they ever sleep?"

"They're all mothers at least," Tauva said as she pointed out several fishwives, dyers and weavers, the midwife and her daughter, and half a dozen others that were used to waking up in the forehour of dawn and working through the darkhour of the night. Genshai glanced over at Ysma until she noticed he was watching and he quickly averted his eyes. They were soon beside each other in the chapel in a stiff, shy silence, not unlike all the other times they had enjoyed together before.

"You should really be lying still with the compress on your head," Ysma said.

The fortuneteller grimaced, and she said bluntly, "You should really quit worrying about me, girl, because if I'm right that man over there needs his leg set and treated or he'll die of infection," as she gestured to one of the sailors that had attacked Genshai last night. His bone was clearly misaligned but not broken through, and the alchemist had put him into a patchy slumber with meadowsleep, which did nothing to stop him from crying out, or twitching with pain.

Ysma glanced over nervously and said, "I've never done that before," and her face was a mixture of confusion and readiness.

The fortuneteller released an irritable sigh as she replied, "I'll show you," and gathered her strength to sit forward to get a better view of the wound.

Going pale, Genshai rushed out of the healing chapel just to avoid becoming sick to his stomach from the painful sounds of a man having his bones set. He was impressed with Ysma's ability to stay focused in spite of all the challenges, knowing that she hardly ever expected to become a healer. He stared for several minutes at the masts of two-dozen ships bobbing in the harbor until Taisan emerged into the side street with Euiger.

The chains still rattled between his wrists as they went across the square. "This is Westcliff," the Oathlord realized. "And that's where I live," he pointed with his bandaged hand across the village, to the height of the hill where the timber lodge could be seen.

Euiger's memory was scattered with the images of all that had happened, like the fragments of a broken pot. He followed Genshai and Taisan when they went to visit the guardpost and found Hebrahm the Lawkeeper and several other men as they dozed in cots, or played a quiet game of tiles, or otherwise nursed their wounds from the previous night. None of them had anything much worse than bruised ribs or broken noses, although one or two had received stitches from Alina that morning, and they were careful not to gossip about her beauty with her father standing there.

They stayed around the guardpost for the rest of the day. Eventually Hebrahm came along with a ring of keys and released Lord Wynne from the manacles, and after someone commented that they hadn't heard anything out of the jail cellar in a several hours the Lawkeeper went down to see all the prisoners asleep in their cells like hounds exhausted after a day of running. Euiger was silent, but then so was everyone else until a few of the men all agreed to go out to the cemetery and get started on digging six graves to complete the funerals.

Shovels in hand they took a path through the fifty acres behind the Oathlord's lodge around the leeward side of the hill, going into a shady cemetery with dozens of rows of gravestones, obelisks, and mausoleums. There were several posts inscribed with the godmarks along the pathways and the rows were well maintained, although Genshai knew that people usually swept the graves during the Night of Flags, or on Ancestor Day, honoring their parents, and grandparents, and so on.

He couldn't help but think; *Monks don't have families to remember them,* because the death of a monk was said to be insignificant, unless they were the subjects of legends like the great Sibudat, or Elosai the Sage. Otherwise they went to unmarked graves and were remembered only by those brothers and friends that knew them by their abbey names when they were alive. Monks were taught to embrace change – and death – in pursuit of Illumination, just to join a handful that were said to have risen like stars away from the earth.

The holes were dug quickly since they had half a dozen shovels but more than three times that many men who had nothing else to do. Soon a boy ran up to shout, "They're coming," and they looked out to see a parade of clerics that raised their flags with the three rings and carried six bodies neatly wrapped in new burial shrouds out to the cemetery, marching past crowds of curious villagers.

The clerics went the entire way up the hill, behind the lodge, into the memorial woods. People lined up in the street to watch, and some folks followed at a distance since for some reason it seemed like the most important thing to happen in the village in years. They soon laid the wrapped bodies to rest in their individual graves and threw down early blooms of marigolds as final offerings before the soil was poured back over and tamped down. The clerics chanted the final rites just as the Matriarch sprinkled the holy ashes in a line around the graves, walking around them once more with her arms upraised before her task was complete.

By the end of the afterfade they came back down the hill like a bedraggled sisterhood, followed by the guards with shovels over their shoulders.

Markova said, "Well then, can we say that's the end of that?" and the defenders all relaxed enough to exchange a few words, like, "I tell you what, I'm ready for a whiskey," alongside a few nods of agreement, and a woman in the holy cloth answered, "How about a pint of ale and a pipe of sweetleaf?" to a round of laughter that faded as they walked away.

In the shade of the memorial woods Euiger called, "Agatha," his voice finally familiar to her again. Blinded by tears, he approached uncertainly until she opened her arms and welcomed him into her soft embrace, shivering in spite of the summer air. His body and mind had been taken against his will, maimed and threatened, and now Agatha allowed herself to believe it was true her husband had finally returned. Their two daughters came in for a family embrace and he cried, "My girls, I'm so sorry."

"None of that," Agatha said, her face awash. "Let's all go home," even though they continued to stand there together until nearly everyone except the monks had departed.

Straightening up to his full height, Euiger spoke for himself for the first time in a long while as he decided, "There's something I need to do first."

They went down to the guardpost and at his request Hebrahm sent a young runner out to spread the word that the maddened prisoners were being released. Only the old Alderman Crainog and one or two others questioned the wisdom of letting them go, but Taisan took them aside for a quiet discussion and eventually persuaded them to respect the Oathlord's command. A small crowd appeared as each victim emerged from the door at eventide, hiding their eyes from the orange rays of the setting sun. Most of them were sallow and withdrawn, and they had trouble reciting their own names to Alina, who wanted to make a record of their survival.

Husbands and wives were reunited after so many days apart, anxiously waiting and waiting. Forlorn children were received back into the arms of their parents. They wept with fear and joy all at once, not knowing what torments they had suffered, but gripped them tightly around the shoulders to lead them home. Unsure what the night would bring, they were eager to follow any advice they could get from the monks, or the clerics, and even the fortuneteller as she emerged from the healing chapel.

"Don't forget to keep your lanterns lit," Tauva reminded folks until the windows of every cottage released yellow squares and arches of light into the streets. The full moon rose from the east and seemed to hang for a long time over the village, and it was a test of their faith when the sea wind wailed over the salt marshes, breathing a sigh of relief when it diminished to nothing. If there were any spectral sounds in the alleys the vigilant old wives banged on their pots and pans for several minutes, which was sure to frighten off whatever shade or invisible trickster might be there.

That night, almost everyone slept soundly for the first time in Westcliff in over forty years. There was an unsaid change in the town, as if a great burden they had been hauling was relinquished back into the sea. People still blamed the mad shepherd, not knowing anything about demons, and Taisan was hesitant to change the story for fear of spreading worse rumors about the place then already existed.

It's better for everyone to believe the curse was lifted, he realized, yet Taisan felt distressed, knowing that deep in his thoughts were the true scenes of what had happened in the shepherd's house all those years ago. Exhausted beyond anything he had ever felt, he was still afraid to sleep, fearful of the nightmares that would come every time he closed his eyes. Taisan knew that with the Still Mind he would be able to process these invasive images, but it would take several weeks, or even months of meditation to really incorporate them into his daily thoughts without being unsettled by them.

Yet, like everyone, his student slept for hours, not even disturbed in the slightest by the crying wind. Taisan was quite proud of how Genshai had carried himself through the trials of Westcliff and already plenty of stories had begun to spread about the laymonk's apprentice and his prowess with the staff, and of how the boy held fast and strong against the curse of the house. It was clear now that Genshai was well on his way to mastering the Seat-of-the-Mountain and the Still Mind, which meant he would soon crave deeper physical and spiritual challenges.

Taisan had always harbored a secret love for the boy. He had chosen Genshai as his successor, since that was the way of things in Red Tower, but it was the old abbot that had given the boy his abbey name, Mountainroot. One day his student would be sent abroad on his own, destined for far more than Taisan could even begin to imagine, but for now he was content to have the boy with him on this journey.

The next day there was exuberance in the air. It was a relief that nobody heard or saw the angry ghosts. For once nobody was stricken with madness. For once nobody had given in to suicidal thoughts. It was the Sabat day, which provided everyone another excuse to sleep late and avoid any real work, although as usual there were fishwives in the market, and ship bells rang out all morning as sailboats came and went from their piers.

As soon as the nursemaid emerged with the baby in her arms, the laymonk couldn't wait to get his hands on him. Delighted, Kyus snuggled into the old man's arms and rested his head on his shoulder, babbling, declaring his intent never to be separated again. Genshai joined them for a sunny day on the beach, and it was like returning to a routine. They caught up on everything they could think of — every calisthenic, every martial arts form, and every fighting drill until their hips and legs were sore from the exercise. Afterward they spent an hour stretching and breathing while the waves crashed without rhythm and the gulls rode the wind, singing all day long.

When they returned people ran excitedly down the boardwalk, saying, "Have you heard? There's going to be a festival," and soon the rumor spread that Oathlord Wynne and his wife the Matriarch had declared a new annual celebration on the last night of the full moon before midsummer in honor of all the victims of the curse.

"Can I go?" Genshai asked with a hopeful expression, wanting to see Ysma since he felt their time in Westcliff would be coming to an end.

Taisan shrugged, "If you want to."

The old laymonk had rarely ever said anything about Genshai's nighttime excursions down the beach, or his late evenings with the Oathlord's daughter at the dragon kiln, except to remind him to be awake by dawn every day. Taisan was lost in thought as they walked; he trusted the boy, but he was still unsure of what his responsibilities were as Genshai's guardian and teacher.

When they returned, all the women of the brothel were rushing around the common area in various states of undress. They shouted their demands to the maidservants for soap and hot water, clean towels and clothes and scented oil, and half a dozen other things to refresh their rooms for guests. Irisol stopped in front of him. She wore her somewhat immodest silk robe and raised a skeptical eyebrow as she asked, "You're not going out like that tonight, are you?"

He glanced down at his monk clothes, a bit chagrined, "What do you mean?"

"Let her help you, boy," Tauva cackled from nearby, "You'll make a far better impression."

Suddenly she summoned three or four other women to stand around him. They poked the acne off his face, scratched his head, and smelled his breath, until they had decided what needed to be done. Irisol dragged him down the hallway to a private washroom where she told him to strip and bathe, holding his dirty, sweat stained Aeigi jacket away from her like it was a disgusting creature. Wearing just his loinwraps, he sat down in front of one of the maidservants to have the downy fluff shaved off his face, until Irisol said, "I like his hair the way it is," and they left it to bristle around his ears.

At the end they smeared a black clay and seaweed scrub all over his face and neck and shoulders until he felt like he was coated in mud, and when Taisan stuck his head in the room he stifled a laugh until he went back up front and told Tauva, "He looks like he's emerging out of a swamp!"

It wasn't as if Genshai had trouble with washing, but now he enjoyed the lavender scented soap and pouring steaming hot water over his shoulders and legs in a proper bathtub. Afterwards, he discovered that Irisol had left him a set of woolen slacks and a sleeveless blue linen shirt that would be perfectly comfortable in the balmy summer night. Genshai emerged through all the perfume and sweetleaf smoke to be greeted by the decadent smell from the kitchen where the cook had made a special dish, simmering salted lamb shoulder in a cauldron for several hours with garlic, onions, and sprigs of laurel and rosemary until it was so tender the meat shredded off the bone. It was served hot on a bed of white beans and parsley, topped with stewed tomatoes that reddened the whole dish in his hands.

As the boy ate, Taisan bounced the baby on his knee and said unexpectedly, "You and I better have a talk about sex."

"Do we have to?" Genshai grimaced, "Mistress Tauva told me all about safe sex, and she's a physician. Besides, we've been living in a brothel for weeks. I think I've figured it out."

Taisan could hardly argue with that, but he said anyway, "If you seek to be an iron warrior there's more to consider than how it works," which intrigued the boy's curiosity. He knew that usually when the novices took the Oath at fifteen the scholars gave a brief lecture on the meridians, the bodily emissions, and reproduction – but today it was Taisan, who had honestly never thought it would come up before now.

"Your vital essence is used simply by existing," he began. "You know the sea at your Navel Gate?"

"I guess so," Genshai replied, touching the knot of his black belt.

Without much explanation the laymonk continued, "You can receive some vital essence from the world, from food and water and air, or even from other people, but that sea at your Navel Gate is your original source and as you age it gets smaller everyday. Sex and self-pleasure can deplete your essence, but no more than a day of hard labor would do. It's actually all the hitting and pounding of the Iron Style that steals your essence, until all that's left is a little pond."

This made sense to Genshai, and he had heard as much before in the abbey. It explained why the monks took a vow of celibacy and practiced complex breathing exercises to redirect their sexual passion upward into their body meridians, learning over time to repress their thoughts of temptation. It was a long held belief that the monks would never recover from the rigorous training if they didn't remain celibate, but of course the hit medicine and body oils were what mainly assisted with healing from the subtle damage of the Iron Style conditioning methods.

"Form the Small Circle," Taisan instructed his student, and continued to explain that by breathing down into the Navel Gate, the sea of essence would be refined and used to achieve impossible skills. This part of the meditations was something that Genshai was newly aware of, and nobody but Taisan had ever described how to align his meridians in such detail before.

"But you have a partner, right?" Genshai asked, since it was clear that Taisan was in a discrete relationship with Dannol, which must have included romance of some kind, making the boy very confused about the right course of action.

"I'm not telling you not to do it," Taisan replied. "Just to know the exchange you make every time you do."

Genshai nodded, feeling a bit subdued from the conversation.

"There are other ways to preserve the sea at the Navel Gate," Taisan said.

"How?" Genshai asked.

"Some things I've already taught you," the old man made a few broad motions and pantomimed pieces of the eight sets. "Just remember the Small Circle breathing, and keep your bronze bell raised up…" before he waved dismissively, "You'll be fine. You're just a kid. You'll have energy for a thousand years, besides, right now you need to be more careful with your hands."

"My hands?" he looked down at his broad, thickened palms.

"I've told you before. Your hands are like weapons!" Taisan exclaimed as if it was obvious. "Your grip will bruise someone if you aren't paying attention. Haven't you ever noticed how the abbot never touches anyone?" which was true, the abbot Horn of Ram characteristically kept his hands at his sides, reputedly leaving black and blue marks for weeks on a regular person with just his fingertips.

"But that's because he knows the Poison Touch!" Genshai answered as if this advice shouldn't apply to him.

Taisan said, "Just be careful. Make your touch lighter than five ounces," which was always good advice.

"For the Mother's sake, you monks sure do have a lot of rules against a good time," Tauva proclaimed, coming over from where she had been listening to their entire conversation, dropping a pitcher of light tablebier between them.

"Should you really be drinking beer with a concussion?" Taisan asked.

"See what I mean," she sat down and produced a pipe already packed with green flakes of sweetleaf and drew a tindertwig from her purple headband, which concealed her recent injury. "Go enjoy yourself, Genshai, just be sure to receive consent, and stay mindful of the young lady's virtue."

The boy glanced at his teacher and saw Taisan scowl at Mistress Tauva who lit her pipe as she said, "Now let's play tiles. I owe you for that beating you gave me yesterday," as she puffed the mouthpiece and released a plume of smoke that spread like a net above them.

Genshai withdrew Kyus from the old laymonk's hands and delivered him to the wet nurse since nobody wanted to see a baby in a brothel after dusk, and the girl that watched the children was paid very well. When he returned the place was suddenly packed with men looking for a mug of beer and a woman to wrap their arms around. Smoke gathered thickly within the walls and the ladies of the Siren's Song caroused together at the hearth, laughing with old friends in a blissful euphoria as if it was the first night of respite any of them had enjoyed in months.

Soon he emerged onto the busy boardwalk under a cloudy moonlit sky and just managed to avoid a line of rowdy young sailors that ran into the joyous night. There were dozens of people around. Young couples took romantic walks to the seashore, and in the harbor the bargemen, sailors, and shipwrights were gathered around a barrel of spiced porter at the dockside where they sang songs and filled the night with the sounds of their drums and fiddles and flutes. Most of the windows in the winding cobbled streets were lit with lanterns, and for the first time in years people walked home on a warm summer night without the grip of fear in their hearts.

He heard a familiar call, "Genshai!" and turned to see Ysma at the edge of the main square. She grinned and waved for him to come meet her and he thought Ysma looked as if she was standing in the Veil itself, framed in flickering shadows, her amber face brightened by the lamplight. Her long fine hair waved around her shoulders and she wore a light summer dress that was tied with a sash. Folks were on all sides of them, walking in happy pairs and threesomes, or huge parades that kept time with pots and pans.

"Come on," Ysma grabbed his hand, which felt tiny in his grip.

They came upon more than seventy people gathered blissfully in the square around the statues of the Three Sisters. Partially Hebra, partially Dweroh, they were all heights, but thickly built, their complexions like brown soil and black clay, their hair long and wavy, and their beards curling over their necks and collars. At times he could detect the subtle accent of the highlands, rolling consonants that gave them a lilting musical quality.

Parked ahead of the shrine was a wagon with four casks upright on the back end where folks filled their mugs from the flowing faucets and stood shoulder to shoulder, talking and drinking in celebration. She told him that her father had decided that a night of festivities was what they needed to keep the angry ghosts at bay, and at eventide Euiger had brought out and tapped four casks from the cellar of the lodge.

"One of them is a pear cider steeped with cinnamon bark that I want you to try," Ysma said excitedly as she led him to the back of the wagon and snatched up two small wooden cups that she filled with a frothy clear liquid that smelled of spice and tasted sweet like pears and honey.

"There's my mother and father," Ysma whispered, ducking to hide on the side of the farthest statue. They glanced around the corner and saw Lady Wynne talking to a few of the old fishwives that expressed interest in having their daughters ordained in the shrine. Certainly nobody suspected them of being witches anymore, and in fact Lady Wynne spoke quite highly of Mistress Tauva, saying that she possessed a special knowledge from outside the shrines, but that she was still faithful to the Raegods in her own way.

Alina talked nearby with a young man who might have been a suitor when the people all cheered and toasted to the Oathlord, and Lawkeeper Hebrahm, and to the other heroes of the night until they had drained half their cups.

"How is he?" Genshai asked about her father.

Ysma's nose crinkled with discontent as she said, "He's okay. He can't remember much. Like our birthdays, or when they got married, or how long we've lived here. His memories are like fragments now with big pieces missing."

"I'm sorry," Genshai shook his head, unable to think of anything from the classics that was more appropriate.

They continued to talk for a long while, and several more times the two young people snuck up to the back of the wagon. After the pear cider there was the common tablebier that was served in all the local taverns, golden and grainy with a slight bitterness. Then they tried a heavy roast stout that was aged in a whiskey barrel from the Namaya Highlands; it was as black as pitch oil with a warm brown froth, and at first Genshai disliked the bitter harshness until Ysma exclaimed, "But it tastes just like dark chocolate!"

They walked away with cups full of abbey ale. Ysma said that her father had brought the barrel all the way across the province from their farmhold, saving it for the most special of celebrations. Genshai was very familiar with the smooth, bready flavor, sweetened by apple cider, since he had helped brew the beer during his upbringing, just as he had pressed the cheese and harvested the herbs and gathered the apples since he was a little boy.

They went across the terraces that overlooked the dunes, and down the steps past the mouth of the dragon kiln. Long after they had finished their cups they walked on the flat seashore right as the tide was arriving. Ysma went ahead of him on the shimmering black sands under the white flower that bloomed in the sky, her hair twisting in the wind like brown ribbons as she peered into the crashing sea. For many years afterward, on all his journeys and in all his memories, Genshai returned to that night with fondness, when they shared first kisses and first touches.

They walked farther than they had ever walked, finding an estuary, perfectly radiant in the moonlight. Wanting to swim, Ysma removed her clothes without any hesitation. They dipped between the river and the sea, wading in the shallows, coming around each other like elusive fish. Her hands gripped his skin as she said, "You're beautiful."

"You're so beautiful," he replied sheepishly, unsure what else to say.

They explored without restraint. Yet, they were still just young people enjoying an unripe intimacy, not yet ready for anything more. They laughed together when Ysma revealed that she had asked the women of the Siren's Song about him, and they had given her advice on how to talk, and walk, to get him to do whatever she wanted, and he blushed until she said, "You really are too easy to tease, you know. You take everything so literally."

They didn't return to the dragon kiln until long after the darkhour of midnight, walking in the empty streets until they came to the end of potter's row and wrapped their arms around each other's waists. The taste of salt lingered on his lips from when she said goodbye, and he watched her go up the hill in the moonlight.

CHAPTER NINE

From the Oral Stories of the Wild Stallion, his greatwife said,
"Go, Qaijin. Feel the love of the cool moon in the sky, but
remember your oath of marriage. Ride back to me, Qaijin!
Qaijin, ride back to me!"

MUHTESEM

After the night of the raid, Temuje was eager to put as much distance between them and Neftya Doru as possible, but neither Garrat nor uncle Kuzhuk seemed overly concerned. The westerner suspected it would be days, possibly weeks, before anyone realized the shipment was off schedule. "They might never even find the bodies," Garrat said, considering how far back they had hidden the corpses from the road. "In a month the scavengers will have dragged them off, and as long as none of our keshik say anything nobody will be any wiser."

Temuje disagreed. "The devil will know what we did before summer is gone," since he felt that the story of a missing shipment would get around and Marshal Zukov would have no choice but to send someone to investigate.

While Bokhili was distracted by these issues Selem was exuberant about the spoils of their victory. He went around with Kuzhuk and tallied everything, peering excitedly into jars and sacks. The first wagon was loaded with all sorts of goods; pots of wine and black vinegar, dried apricots, emmer and rice, pistachios and almonds, whole cloves, cassia bark, red saffron, and half a dozen other spices, not to mention a wooden lockbox with steel bands riveted across the surface. It was a small box that jangled with coins when Selem shook it in his brother's face, but they had not found a key anywhere among the corpses.

In the other wagons there were ten barrels of burning water and four barrels of bulk tar, some of which smelled like rotten eggs. There were also pots of lamp oil, white wax and grease, and several other items that would be useful to their people, otherwise they intended to sell most of the barrels in the port city of Tesuradad, which was well known for shipping goods all over the world by the channels of the Kalish Ocean. Their uncle Kuzhuk was confident that even if no merchants bought the shipment, they could at least sell it at a lower value to any of the smugglers that roamed the coastline.

Aside from the three horses that pulled the wagons they now had six extra mounts complete with western riding saddles with longer stirrups, and once they were underway Temuje made the brothers ride each horse. It was fairly common for Thrailans to rotate between two or three horses during long journeys, yet Temuje was more interested in familiarizing the boys with different mounts, their sizes and speeds, their temperaments, their saddles, until they were able to ride any horse comfortably. In the meantime Usaka the ghost horse left them, galloping into the great grass to rejoin the wild herd, although they knew he would return when they needed him again.

The boys raced each other across the steppes like speeding arrows. They held their saddles tight with their legs, their long black hair waved like manes. Back and forth they went, riding and playing all day with the inexhaustible energy of children until even the horses were worn out. Afterwards, Selem liked to test Temuje and Kuzhuk's patience, going so far ahead that they were out of sight with nothing around for miles but the wind thrashing against the switchgrass and the sky layered in puffy white clouds that mounted higher and higher.

"You know all uncle wants us to do is stay hidden forever," Selem grumbled, his ears stiff and turned back. "What is the point of hearing all about the Kato name if we can't do anything? I want to be Khanar of the clan like we were meant to be! Besides, I'm sick of herding, and have you noticed that Baavgai's feet stink like dung whenever he takes his boots off?"

"He always says we need to wait until we're men," Bokhili said, his voice calm in spite of his brother's outrage.

"What does that even mean?" Selem shouted, his ears alert and high. "Fifteen springs? I feel like I'm a man now."

"You're not even fully grown up yet," Bokhili rolled his eyes.

"I can wrestle as well as any of them," Selem boasted. "I'm definitely better than Baavgai."

"He stomps you in the dirt every other day," Bokhili said as he stared at his brother with steady brown eyes until Selem met his gaze and couldn't help but to laugh.

When the caravans came into view they ambled back in that direction, and Selem said with a sly smile, "You know, after this Moon Festival I'm going to have a lover."

"How do you hope to achieve that?" Bokhili was surprised.

"When we get to the Hashaan, I'm going to ask Togeni to be my evening flower," Selem answered readily about a girl they knew in the Kovol clan. "I think she likes me."

Selem was extremely curious about girls and often revealed that he wanted to become Khanar like their father just so that he could marry five or six times. Yet their uncle never let them forget they were considered one Khanar and they were meant to make all marriage pacts together one day, bearing a wide family. He seemed to think that any children that came from their wives would be thought of as sired by one man, and perhaps it would make the question of an heir less complicated.

Bokhili groaned, "That means I'll have to wear the mask all night."

Selem smirked knowingly, "Don't pretend that you aren't going to sneak off like you usually do."

It was true; Bokhili took whatever chance he could to be alone, since his cousins always surrounded him, his watchful uncle, and especially his brother. Even while they were riding, herding, and tracking, Bokhili still never felt true solitude as long as the keshik were there. Going for a walk by himself in the savannah was dangerous, and whenever they visited one of the grass families there was always the nagging fear that someone would notice them as twins and he would be kidnapped if he went out alone.

After several weeks of riding, they passed from the great grass to the meadowlands – from Böyuk Ot to Muhtesem – where fields of poppies bloomed orange, yellow, and scarlet like the sun. Clusters of white clover, threadleaf, and all sorts of other wildflowers grew freely on either side of the trail, and Bokhili knew that some flowers were edible and harvested by the shamans as medicine while others were extremely poisonous. They went carefully, mindful of rattlesnakes, or viper's nests, hidden in the meadows.

These were their mother's fields, and Bokhili could not help but to think of the last time they were there with Kuzhuk five years ago, when their grandfather, Aminjon Kovol, had banished them from the Hashaaan. His people feared the curse of the khagasun, and despite his love for their mother, his daughter that was lost in the massacre at Two Creeks, their grandfather could not take the twins into his protection. In fact, he had no choice but to denounce his son and his family to appease the fears of the rest of the clan, since they had no desire to draw the wrath of the westerners into the meadowlands. Yet, at the onset of the migration season, the twins had still managed to convince Kuzhuk to appeal to his father to allow them to pass through his fields to Tesuradad, thinking that now that they were old enough he would respect their claim to vengeance.

Eventually they arrived to the Kovol clan, which seemed to rise up on the horizon like a mirage. The encampments of their people were called Hashaan, which meant 'widening circles' and in the distance they appeared like a ripple in a pond. The ringfamilies were usually serving people, cooks, and herdsmen while the inner circles were filled with crafters, traders, horselords, and even closer were the honored warriors and sworn guardians, and finally there was the Khanar's tent in the middle, surrounded on all sides by his wives and children and all his grandchildren.

The Thrailan people made their homes with round yurts paneled by heavy animal skins, which were easy to dismantle. They had used the tents for generations to move in the migratory patterns of the bison, antelope, zebra, and wildebeests, like the wind spreading seeds over the steppes, but sometimes the Khanars made permanent homes for themselves in the center of their territory, gathering four or five hundred people into a small village. They dug out the floors to grant them more space, and filled their tents with the luxuries of the east and the west. Their grandfather had even made a kiln to fire mud bricks, which allowed him to build small rooms where they butchered animals and tanned leather, or heated a forge to temper iron, which was an exceedingly rare mineral in the grasslands.

Permanent structures meant they had a place to defend and they were easy to find, but there were still plenty of grass families that lived as they had always lived, with small encampments ready to move at a moment's notice. Horses dotted the horizon as far as they could see, walking together, running wild, but always near the Hashaan. After all it was their custom to allow the horses to graze freely. They were never tied down, never offered hay to fatten them nor warm stalls in which to wait out the winters. This accounted for their heartiness, since there were certain times of the year the steppes easily reached below freezing temperatures.

Yet, the sons of Usaka never let their horses free anymore. It had been one of the primary lessons that Temuje learned after the massacre. The horses of the Kato had been grazing all over the creekside and anyone who tried to escape or fight had difficulty retrieving them, which caused a big portion of their clan to be butchered in the first wave of the attack. Since then Temuje had insisted that their small band of men always tie down their horses, except for Usaka the ghost horse who always roamed as he wished.

Smoke rose up from numerous campfires and just before they

arrived to the outer ring the two brothers played a handgame which determined who would wear the mask, asking their cousin to decide how many fingers to display, which Bokhili won by chance. Long ago Kuzhuk had tossed them a fringed shawl and the dark gray veil that girls wore when they became hatun warriors and he had said that they were still short enough that one of them could pass as a sister in training. Everything but their eyes were concealed, and their uncle didn't care at all if they complained about wearing a girl's dress so long as it meant they were safe while they visited the Hashaan.

"I'll wear it now, but you have to promise to switch with me later," Selem insisted.

"What does it matter to you?" Baavgai wanted to know, his horse ambling next to them.

"I have plans for tonight," Selem said roguishly as he arranged his disguise.

"The spirits of trickery have descended on that one," Dantai grinned.

They arrived to a hut in the outer ring where there were several simmering cauldrons of rice and small grains, hot ceramic slabs where flatbreads baked for only a few minutes, and nearby were long spits of peppers that roasted over coals. Under the shade of the tent was a butchering table lined with pheasants, a long necked swan, twenty or thirty rabbits, and the offal of a roe deer. Their noses hardly prickled at the rank smell of wild game, yet the meat simmering in oil was tantalizing, coated with red and yellow spices, or sweet black sauce, with succulent peppers and onions, until their mouths watered.

"Smells good, Arucci!" Selem called out loudly in spite of his disguise.

"You always say that cousin," Arruci flashed a proud smile as he stirred two cast iron skillets. He came around to greet them as they dismounted on the edge of the Hashaan where the air was smoky from so many campfires. People went between yurts, and the rolling sounds of their language could be heard everywhere, completed by the nickering and stomping of horses, men cheering, and the ringing of a hammer on an anvil in the distance.

"Father, I wondered if the winds would bring you today!" Arucci grinned, his ears turned in either direction. When they stood beside each other their cousin's resemblance to his father Kuzhuk was obvious; they had the same lean face, the same height, although Arucci's hair and beard was thick and black.

He wore a wool shirt and sash like a serving man, who would be tasked with stocking wood for the fires, butchering the wild game, or preparing platters of food for the Moon Festival that evening. Arucci was nineteen springs now, born in the Kato clan to his father's second wife, and during the massacre at Two Creeks, Arucci managed to recover a horse and escape. He was only twelve at the time, and galloped away when the army descended on the camp, leaving everything behind.

Since then he was raised with Kuzhuk's greatwife, Ibakha, who scorned him, and put him to work washing clothes at dawn, cooking in the afternoons, and scrubbing pots and pans in the evenings. There were a number of Kato people with similar stories scattered in the ringfamilies of the Kovol clan. They were considered suitable as second partners, or good serving people, but they were never given the honor of being close to the Khanar for fear of the curse. It was the way of things, and ever since Kuzhuk had taken up his oath to protect the twins his father had denounced him, and had sent Ibakha to the edge of the clan. She was now expected to arrange the cooking and cleaning for the inner rings, and also advocate for her own sons as they tried to make a name for themselves as horselords or keshik.

"No! No!" Ibakha appeared from around the tent, ears flattened back, shouting, "Out with you!" as she chased everyone back to their horses and wagons.

"Ibakha," Kuzhuk came forward with a generous smile. "It is only your loyal..."

"Desert snake," she hissed at him. "You arrive just in time to disrupt all my plans. Now Batir will never be allowed to swear the oath to become keshik."

Kuzhuk was surprised, "Batir? Becoming a keshik? Who has been training him?"

"Dadjon," Ibakha crossed her arms, referring to her second husband. "They ride together often."

Kuzhuk nodded, his expression muted although the small group could see his shoulders stiffen as if he was irritated. They all knew that Dadjon was his older brother and had taken up his responsibilities to Kuzhuk's children from Ibakha ever since he began to ride with the twins. It was no surprise that Batir wanted to be keshik, which was an honorable pursuit for any young man, yet he had to gain respect as if he was born on the outer edge of the ring.

"Did you know this snake would come?" Ibakha demanded of Arucci, whose ears turned down in shame.

"No," he stammered, "I mean, I wasn't sure."

"I won't take your trouble here," Ibakha pointed to the herdsmen and the three wagons of stolen goods, and the two boys, knowing completely who they were. She scowled, "Don't return to my hut until you are alone, or not at all."

Kuzhuk backed away from the heat of her ire. Arucci looked on helplessly as she snapped, "Now pluck those birds! Quickly! And keep all the feathers," forcing him back to work while the rest of them gathered at the edge of the camp to discuss their plans. Already they knew they needed to conceal the wagons and Huslen, Dantai, and Baavgai were tasked with circling to the far side of the Hashaan where they could park among all the others. They planned to discretely trade the extra horses, having many friends among the Kovol clan, most of them honoring their relation to Kuzhuk.

Garrat came around as the wagons began to move. He had a way of being silent and unseen, staying as far on the edge of the camp as he could during their discussion with Ibakha. Even so, with such auburn features Garrat was very recognizable to most of their people as the westerner that had warned the Kato clan of the attack, becoming a traitor to the Sovereign's Army, but as a result he was unwelcome anywhere so long as Marshal Zukov's steel riders were searching for him.

"I had better migrate," Garrat said in their language, making them laugh at the improper use of the word. He grinned slightly through his grizzled beard, looking older and wearier than they had seen in a long while. He handed his spear to Bokhili as he mounted his saddle, stepping his foot in the long stirrups.

"Where will you go?" Bokhili asked, passing the spear back to him.

Pulling up on the reins of the eager horse, Garrat said, "I'll listen for any word of our deeds. If Zukov plans to investigate he'll send scouts first. If needed, I will give my spy false knowledge and lead them to the wrong place."

Temuje grunted, "Spiders are only useful when they catch flies."

"Indeed," Garrat agreed, but then switched to low-Arovian as he asked Bokhili and Selem, "How soon do you want to raid again?"

The two brothers looked at each other and Selem answered in the king's speech, "As soon as possible."

"Well, they have caravans that depart Zakariya every week," Garrat replied quietly. "But that would be too frequent not to be noticed."

"We don't want to be noticed yet," Bokhili agreed. "Let us finish with Khanar Kovol here, then we will ride west for three weeks to meet the ibexes coming into the plains. We can plan again when the seasons have changed."

Garrat nodded, then waved farewell to Kuzhuk and Temuje who each had a look of confusion on their faces. It was clear they didn't like when the brothers used the king's speech but they couldn't argue that it was helpful to have a contact like Garrat who knew the ways of the western devils. Over the years he had helped them on numerous occasions, always arriving just ahead of patrols of steel riders to warn them in time to escape, even when they were lost in the wilderness of the steppes Garrat always seemed to find them.

Without a second look at the knight, Selem said eagerly, "If we go now we'll catch the last hour of the games before the sun sets," wanting to see the usual archery, wrestling, and riding contests that happened during the Moon Festivals.

"We're just getting supplies," Temuje chastised them gruffly, since as usual he was eager to leave by daybreak.

Selem lifted the veil from his face and argued, "Wouldn't you want us to see the best of the Kovol clan? So we can learn?"

Temuje's ears were stiff, and he glowered at them until their uncle Kuzhuk said, "I want to see my son compete," which decided it for them.

They crossed several rows of yurts until they were in the crafters ring. Mostly there were leatherworkers and tanners, although there were some weavers and carvers who would barter for food, horses, or clothes. They knew it wasn't a true market, like the fabled streets of Tesuradad, but they still enjoyed looking into the tents to browse the carved bone jewelry, the woven wool shawls, and so many other things.

Selem plucked up a beaded necklace with red and gold feathers and a carved wooden talisman, peering at it through the strip in the veil and asking his brother, "What do you think of this?"

"For you?"

"For Togeni," Selem said as if it were something he had thought about.

"Keep moving," Temuje barked and pulled the boys along, hardly noticing what they were doing.

They looked like a brother and a sister to anyone that saw them, since Selem wore the garments of a girl. Only women who became sworn warriors wore the veil and a woven grass rope around their waists. They were called hatun, and it wasn't unusual for them to have swords and daggers concealed under their shawls. Sworn to modesty in the ancient tradition of the War Women of Qaijin, they were only permitted to expose their bodies and faces to other women, but never in the public of the Hashaan.

There were a number of riders and herdsmen, mothers and their children, all gathered in the center for the games. A handful of hatun women walked together with purpose, getting through a crowd and making a path for their uncle to follow. Cheers erupted around them as sixteen men wearing thick leather vests wrestled, tripped, and flipped each other onto the soft earth. It was a fairly common display during festival time at any Hashaan and usually the wrestlers all fought in groups, gradually becoming eliminated until the last two competitors had everyone's attention.

"Look, there's Batir," Selem pointed at Kuzhuk's first son, who was nearly twenty years old, leaning heavily into his opponent just ahead of where their grandfather sat in esteem over the whole clan. Batir was lean and tall, and mercilessly yanked his opponent left and right, and stuck out his leg and tossed him over his hip without any trouble. Ibakha stood with her second husband Dadjon in the crowd, hoping the Khanar would look on them favorably and give Batir a chance to swear the oath.

Kuzhuk hardened his face, "Come on," and took them around until they could no longer see the games through the crowd. By then the riding and archery contests were already done and everyone enjoyed an hour of spirited wrestling before the celebrations of the Moon Festival began. There was no denying the excitement in the air; folks were drinking sour emmer ales and dandelion grass wine, although the ceremonial beverage was kumiss, fermented mare's milk, so light that they could hardly get drunk from it.

They came to the head of the crowd where a number of keshik guardians gathered in front of the Khanar. They were men armed with sabers at their hips, wearing heavy leather vests or gray wool caftans. Bronzed and bearded, they smelled like fragrant oil, all laughing and cheering alongside each other. One or two of them noticed Kuzhuk's approach and recognized him as the second son of the Khanar, and someone whispered into the old man's broad triangular ear, drawing his attention away from the games.

"Batir won!" Selem said, high pitched in excitement from beneath the veil.

It was true, Kuzhuk's son was the last one standing, taking deep breaths as he waited for any kind of acknowledgement from the Khanar. In return, his grandfather abruptly stood up from his wooden carved chair and left without a word, entering his tent with a single glance toward Kuzhuk who followed until they were out of the sun. Even as the crowd cheered and many warriors came around to congratulate Batir, the young man's face was clenched tightly in an expression they had seen their uncle make a number of times.

"Many greetings upon you, my son," the Khanar said gravely as one hand gripped the central pole of his tent. Their grandfather Aminjon Kovol had been leader of his clan for nearly fifty years and had carefully spread his grass family across the meadowlands. He looked like Kuzhuk, with a narrow nose and sharp black eyes, but his skin was sallow and his beard thin and white, and he wore a turban on his balding head.

Kuzhuk came forward and touched his fingertips against the elder man's shoulders in a gesture of respect, "Many greetings father, are you peaceful and well?"

"There is peace in our meadow, so I am well," Aminjon nodded, until he looked sharply at the twins and said, "There is peace until the devil hears the story of how Kato has returned." The boys glanced at each other until their grandfather snapped, "Take off that mask," and Selem removed the fabric from his face, his hair a tangled mess, his ears alert in either direction.

"Many greetings, Khanar," Bokhili saluted with both palms open and Selem quickly followed his example.

"That's enough of that, now come here," Aminjon waved a hand and the two boys ran to embrace their grandfather, breaking the tension in the room somewhat. They were careful not to be too rough since they knew the man had fallen from his horse years ago and was as frail as a dry stalk of grass. Aminjon had spent the better part of his life ensuring the legacy of the Kovol clan, amassing the luxuries he now enjoyed in his late seventies. His tent was recessed into the ground by four feet which made the room feel high and cool, filled with many benches covered in furs, blankets and pillows.

The boys brought a wooden chair from the edge of the hut and their grandfather released a groan as he sat down on the cushion. Once he was comfortable he peered at them shrewdly as if none of them knew what he knew, "Do you think my birds and spiders would not tell me about three wagons of oil in my camp?"

Kuzhuk said quickly, "We only hoped to spare you the trouble, father…"

The old man raised up his weathered palm, effectively silencing his son, "Answer for yourselves now. Don't let this man here claim it was his choice to attack the steel riders and bring their goods here."

Selem replied hotly, "Grandfather, it is past time that we take our revenge."

"These actions make you into criminals with the devil from the west," the old man replied. "Do you think putting us all at risk is worthy of your revenge?"

"We wanted to see if it could be done," Selem argued, his ears forward. "We wanted to show you that we're ready."

"Ready for what?"

"To be Khanar," Selem stomped his foot.

Their grandfather released an unintentional laugh, the way an experienced man can't help but to laugh at the innocence of children. Their uncle sometimes did the same thing and Bokhili knew this would irritate his brother, stepping forward to interrupt as he said evenly, "We are not criminals if we plan to spread the wealth to our people," at which nearly everyone looked at him.

"Say what you mean." Aminjon furrowed his brows.

"Grandfather, we would never ask you to take any risks that would harm your clan," Bokhili said. "We just ask for a few sworn keshik to help us smuggle oil through Muhtesem to Tesuradad."

He shook his head, "And what do you offer for this request?"

The brothers looked at each other as if they were communicating without speaking and Bokhili said, "Everything."

"Now, hold…" Kuzhuk spoke up but was quickly interrupted.

"Everything?" Aminjon demanded, ears alert.

Selem shrugged, "What do we need it for? We are just riders in the herd after all."

The old man began to understand their meaning. He would

be the beneficiary of all their trade with the merchants of Tesuradad. They planned to share the wealth so that both the Kovol and the Kato clans grew strong and prosperous, and so long as only a few keshik were involved the people would be left blameless. The sons of Usaka had no need for barrels of crude oil, or chests of the devil's silver; just the glory that came from battle. They wanted the name of Kato to be whispered about as renegades to the steel riders, to undermine the hold of fear that Marshal Zukov had over them, to raise the spirit of their family far and wide.

"Temuje," Bokhili called to their loyal keshik and he approached from near the tent flap carrying a burlap satchel, unveiling the wooden lockbox. He produced a hammer and chisel, and with three quick hits he broke the latch and allowed the lockbox to tilt open, spilling out several dozen gold and silver coins at the old man's feet, along with many slips of paper stamped with the official bank seals of Zakariya.

The old man's eyes widened and Bokhili said, "There are riches like this crossing the steppes every day."

They all knew it was true. For more than a hundred years there had been wagons making the journey back and forth. In those days only the outcasts and criminals raided Neftya Doru, which brought dishonor to their clans and eventually the wrath of the Sovereign's Army. Bokhili understood that if they became a significant threat the scalpings might begin again, just like it was after the massacre when anyone with the Kato name was hunted down. He didn't want to be guilty of that again, since he had always felt that it was because of him that his family had become cursed.

Yet none of them could think of a way out of their exile. None of them could conceive of any other way to free their people and restore honor to their name. In any case, by the old clan laws Bokhili knew they were justified to want war. Marshal Zukov and the steel riders had committed a crime against his clan. They would do it again if they wanted too, and they needed to be stopped.

The Khanar sighed, "It seems your mind is decided."

"It is," Selem said vigorously.

"It is," Bokhili agreed, his ears turned left and right.

Aminjon finally said, "We can only give you Kato people from the outer ring."

The brothers glanced at each other and nodded in agreement. They soon tidied up the loose currency and flying-cash until they were hidden away, resting easily with their secrets. They poured out several cups of kumiss to enjoy and the flavor was like hot almond cream, thin and sour. Their grandfather prepared a clay pipe from a nearby tray with a blend of dried tobacco, poppies, and hemp flower and they shared it until the smoke had gathered into bands and loops in the air.

The two men talked for a while, their irritable shells softened by the herbs and drink as Kuzhuk said, "Father, may I plead with you?"

The old Khanar's eyes were half lidded and he gestured as if to say, 'proceed.'

Kuzhuk bowed his head and said, "Make my son Batir keshik for the clan. He was born here. He is Kovol by blood, son of my first wife Ibakha, who is daughter of Manara Kovol from the herds. She is a good a woman. They don't deserve to be punished for my mistakes."

Aminjon shook his head dazedly. "What mistakes? Your oath to protect two innocent boys, my own grandsons?"

The two brothers glanced at each other; Selem was bleary from the smoke but Bokhili remained clear and focused since he chose not to participate. They each knew the story since Kuzhuk always told the truth – their grandfather was also khagasun. When Aminjon was born the other infant was sent away into the meadowlands where it was abandoned. None knew what happened to those babies. Some believed the Grass God, Khahirazade, plucked them up on his journeys across the steppes, while others said that devils took them back to the underworld and ate them, placated until the next sacrifice.

Just to see a twin was a disturbance, and by now enough people had suggested that to be born khagasun was a Kovol quality, and from what Aminjon could see it was true the half-spirits did come from his bloodline, although until now they were never left alive. Their grandfather had always wondered if he should have died and his brother should have lived, eventually realizing the burden of that decision rested with the shaman, just as it did with the sons of Usaka when they were kept together to be raised as one man.

Nevertheless, after the massacre everyone was fearful of the twins and the curse of Kato, especially when the steel riders were running down their people, scalping them for a bounty, murdering them for sport. At first Aminjon refused to blame Usaka or the twins when the devils from the west were obviously guilty, yet when Kuzhuk left his greatwife and family to ride with the twins and keep them safe the Khanar had no choice but to condemn his second son, sending Ibakha to the outer ring and turning his grandsons into serving men. So long as the Kovol people believed they were safe from the curse, their grandfather rejected them in front of the Hashaan.

As children these subtleties were not so apparent to them, and until the twins reached a certain age they did not fully understand their uncle's sacrifice. Now that they were on the edge of manhood they could see that Kuzhuk was forced to accept that his family was dishonored by his actions. With a pang of guilt Bokhili knew dozens of people were affected just by their existence. Obviously Temuje, who swore to Usaka to be their guard and caretaker, and all their loyal cousins, and of course all the survivors of the massacre with their name. He often wondered how much better off they would all be if he had died as an infant, the way he felt he was meant too.

Yet Aminjon was clearly struck with grief. Not only had he denounced his own son but he had also lost his oldest daughter Oyunn, and whenever he looked at the twins he could see the many expressions of her bright face. It had torn him apart when they never recovered her corpse or properly laid her to rest, and he had invasive thoughts of the kind of torture she must have suffered at the end of her life. Those images plagued him until it seemed an easy thing to give his consent to a campaign of vengeance when that was all he had wanted for the last seven years.

Suddenly the tent flap was pulled back and Dadjon entered. His thick beard was streaked with gray and he stood bulky and tall, with coils of black hair visible on his chest. His ears sprang up rigidly at the sight of his younger brother Kuzhuk and he scowled at the twins sitting across the room. Selem hurriedly tried to put his veil back on, but Dadjon said, "Let us not pretend you're a girl, nephew," crossing his arms over his chest and looking down his nose at his own father, as he demanded, "What is the meaning of this? Do you treat with khagasun now?"

The old man snapped, "I am Khanar here, and I will treat with whoever I see fit."

"We are only visiting for the Moon Festival," Kuzhuk tried to reassure his older brother, his ears lowered. "We are leaving at first light."

Dadjon pointed a finger at him, "If anything you do threatens us we will have more than words."

"The only threats to us are the devils from the west," Selem spoke up.

"The words of children don't carry much weight with me," Dadjon said with the same stern expression as his father and brother. The twins promptly fell silent, wanting to see what their grandfather would do, listening when Dadjon revealed, "I came to plead with you about Batir."

Both Kuzhuk and Aminjon looked up as they realized the man's purpose had honor. It was understandable why he was upset to see them sitting with the sons of Usaka instead of a young warrior from their own clan, descended from their own bloodline. Anyone that watched the games that afternoon could easily agree that Batir was the victor. The young man was not a herdsman, he was a fighter, and they all knew his grandfather had hardened his heart to him because of Kuzhuk.

"Do not punish Batir for the actions of this man," Dadjon's voice was resolute. "I have taken his mother as my second wife and all her children are my children. I have followed the clan laws in this regard," he glanced pointedly at Kuzhuk, "and I have trained Batir myself in riding, wrestling, and archery, the three skills of all keshik and hatun warriors. You know him to be an honorable…"

Aminjon raised an old weathered palm and nodded his head, "I agree, Batir will be keshik," to which everyone breathed a sigh of relief, including Temuje who had been silent the entire time. Then the old man turned one ear to the twins and said, "But I have enough keshik, and so do you Dadjon. So I have decided that Batir will swear to the sons of Usaka," to which Kuzhuk's ears went up stiffly, and Dadjon clenched his fists, but the old man continued, "If they swear to honor their oath to him and protect this family."

It was true the bargain went both ways. When a man became keshik they swore to protect the clan and the Khanar from all danger, the Khanar in turn welcomed their families into the ring as if they were bound by blood. It was a system of honor that ensured trust between them that went back to the ancient days when the Khanar decided what direction they should go in the steppes. They were cousins, sons, and brothers, but occasionally new warriors arrived from across the grasslands if they heard a Khanar was true to his oath, building up the forces of the clan.

Selem stepped forward without hesitation, "We will accept him as keshik if he swears the oath to Kato," saying his own name in spite of all its ignominy.

Dadjon glared at Kuzhuk who offered a tight shrug that meant he could not disagree and the older brother threw up his hands in frustration as he withdrew from the tent, "Be careful, or you will bring the curse of the khagasun down on us all."

"Ah," their grandfather waved a hand dismissively and returned to the conversation with Kuzhuk about arranging for Batir to join them.

Soon the sun was gone and the boys' ears twisted toward the sounds of revelry from outside. Without exchanging any words the twins crept away from the side of the conversation as soon as Temuje went across the room to light an oil lamp, slipping out when his back was turned. They disappeared immediately into the crowd of people, like any other two children running through the night.

"Take this," Selem said, tossing the veil over to his brother as they came to a stop in the bridlepath between rings. They quickly exchanged clothes and Bokhili donned the mask, the shawl, and the woven grass belt until he looked convincingly like a girl training to become hatun.

"Did you see how Dadjon reacted?" Bokhili asked.

"He's always like that," Selem said, one ear turned up and one pointed out.

"Yes, but we should not anger him," Bokhili sighed, knowing that their uncle disliked them because they were a reminder of his dead sister, and the curse that hovered over their family.

He imagined that in the days before their birth, Kuzhuk and Ibakha and Dadjon were quite happy with their arrangement. Those kinds of relationships were common in the grass families. Sometimes a woman would marry a man and his brother so that in the event her primary partner died her children would be in his care. Other times a man had several wives, and those women often had second or third husbands of their own until there were bridges between all circles of the clan. Even Temuje was married to his brother's wife, and sometimes she met with her own partner of choice on specific nights.

There were often marriages between distant clans when the herds came together in new prairies for the summer and winter festivals of the Grass God. Those couples might only meet once or twice a year, and it was a time that usually coincided with young relationships and new pregnancies, the trading of greatwives, and many fruitful alliances between Khanars.

Bokhili continued, "What if we bring the curse down on us again?"

"Don't think like that, khagasun," Selem frowned, his ears sloped back. "There's no curse except the curse of the steel riders."

"Yes, but…"

"Enough," Selem said. "Why else would we still be together if the shaman didn't know we were meant to do this?"

It was an interesting idea, but there was no way to know for certain since their clan's shaman had been missing since the day of the Battle of Two Creeks. She was likely dead along with so many others, but there were still a dozen cousins that could swear truthfully that she had commanded Usaka Kato to keep the khagasun together, which may or may not have been his downfall but nobody could argue that it was not Marshal Zukov – the devil from the west – that had held the sword.

Selem shook Bokhili by the shoulders, "Stop thinking, brother!" drawing him out of his gloomy mind. "I don't care about that right now. I want to find Togeni. Are you going to help me or not?"

Now that he wasn't wearing the veil it was easy to see Selem's natural grin and finally Bokhili relented, "I'll help you."

"Praise the gods," Selem said, throwing his hands up.

Drums beat out the rhythm of old songs, and the chanting of singers rose up from the center of the camp. There was food everywhere; women handed out skewers of horsemeat and cups of rice, or even steamed sesame buns covered with honey, and cups of dandelion wine. By then any boys and girls less than fifteen summers were sent to bed in the children's huts to be watched over by their old crones and grandfathers, but the two brothers were disguised as warriors in training and the people hardly took a second look at them as they explored the fringes of the crowd.

They found a place to approach the center where dancers stepped in unison around a bonfire; their silhouettes writhed and twisted like spectral forms, the voices of singers lifted into the night sky with the pounding of drums. The shaman of the clan presided over the ceremonies. They sat at the head of the crowd and wore a carved wooden mask to conceal their identity, accompanied by seven girls with grass wreaths on their heads, wearing sheer silk garments.

They worshipped the full moon rising in the east, calling his name, "Ayzata! Beautiful and bright! Ayzata! Like a flower in the night!" as they told the tale from a thousand generations ago of when Qaijin the Wild Stallion embraced the God of the Moon at midsummer, when the yellow star came so close it nearly touched the edge before Qaijin was said to have pulled away. Silence descended on the crowd; the dancers ceased to move, a single drummer was reduced to banging out two short beats and a third that was allowed to echo and die. They were about to begin the fire trance, which Bokhili had always wanted to attend.

"Come on," Selem called and Bokhili saw that his brother had found a group of boys and girls their own age with Togeni among them, glancing in their direction.

"What are you even going to say to her?" Bokhili wanted to know.

Selem shrugged. "I'll say I'm Arucci's cousin from another Hashaan, or something. If she were worried about the Kato curse she wouldn't look at me like she wants me to come talk to her."

Bokhili was doubtful but his expression was hidden beneath the veil.

"Come on," Selem whined, "I just want my first evening flower."

Bokhili heard a second drum join the rhythm of the first. He glanced at his brother and said, "I don't think you need me for that," and within seconds they were each running in opposite directions, desperate to be alone. In his disguise Bokhili went toward the crowd encircled around the enormous bonfire where they burned huge bundles of dried switchgrass and hemp, with sacrifices of fresh wildflowers. Some people smoked clay pipes and the air was tinged with the thin vapor of burning tar, the essence of the poppy, which introduced them into the trance.

The shaman strode forward wearing the mask carved with the face of the moon, painted white with blue loops around the eyes. The voice of a woman emerged, strong and vibrant as she called, "This is the eve when Qaijin meets Ayzata!" She wore a tall headdress of many hawk feathers and long skeins of horsehair that spilled around her shoulders. A brightly colored cloak hung down to her knees tied with many little bells that rang out with every step. She was like an apparition herself, or a spirit from the other world and soon she raised her hands, chanting, "Ride back to us, Qaijin! Qaijin, ride back to us!"

A third drum added to the cascading sounds. The dancers paired together until they were coupled man with man and woman with woman, just as it was said to have happened in the story. The fire trance was underway as they moved in double pairs, stepping widely, dancing in front of each other, pressing their hips together like pieces that fit for the briefest instance. Already they were covered in a sheen of sweat and oil, yet now their bodies were tantalizing to watch as they deliberately removed each other's silk coverings.

The Moon God was said to have been full of passion. He rose over the Wild Stallion every night in earnest for his touch, yet Qaijin was sworn to his first wife, Yelena, who was also a War Woman of their people. Their attraction was so full that she eventually allowed him to cross the sky to meet the moon, but not without reminding him of his oath to her. Yet after that ancient midsummer, all those that wanted Qaijin to be with them, Yelena, or Ayzata, or even his own father Khahirazade, could not tame the Wild Stallion. He pulled away. He rejected his purpose, riding to the west; he became the yellow star that raced across the anterior of the sky. Ayzata was brokenhearted and turned his bright face away from the earth, which was said to have created the phases of the moon.

The shaman called across the grasslands, "Ride back to us, Qaijin!"

The singers answered, "Qaijin, ride back to us!" The drums beat heavily in a rhythm, joined by the blowing of ram horns, all coming together again and again like the flickering of the flames. By the end every dancer was standing in a circle, men and women beside each other, stark naked, their hard brown bodies shimmering, brightened by fire.

The crowd broke apart, couples and groups staggering away.

They went into each other's tents and shared their marriage bonds. Outsiders were especially welcome and it was an opportunity for everyone to enjoy their second or third partners that came from a distance. Bokhili went away that night aroused, his thoughts and worries suppressed, unsure if he had entered a trance.

There were many campfires that dotted the darkness, and he heard the sounds of laughter and excitement as he crossed the bridlepaths, in a daze of love and rejection, under the amorous moon.

CHAPTER TEN

*THE FOURTH DAY OF ALLORA, THE NINTH
MONTH OF 1019 EC*

*From the Scripts of Sibudat, "Matrons earn lumier / for the
life of every child / their good hands send home."*

THE MATRON'S COTTAGE

Like a blazing column in the midday sun, Red Tower Abbey stood at the precipice of the auburn peak in the distance. They were now within hours of home and Genshai stared upward as if he were seeing it for the first time, feeling a thrum of excitement within him. He had not expected to be so eager, yet whenever they came closer, day-by-day in sight of it, he felt like he was on a pilgrimage home. Rather than feeling homesick throughout his journey, Genshai had mostly just missed his friends like big Tennan who was a student in the Iron Style, and Astel and Beryl who were training to become scholars, and little Jakk who had yet to take the Oath, and now Genshai was excited to tell them everything about his adventures.

They had stayed for a while around Westcliff, enjoying the cheerful seaport now that the curse was lifted. Word spread across the west quarter of the northlands that something had changed and by midsummer the town was busier with wool merchants and fishmongers than it had been in forty years. Genshai and Ysma fell into the routines of a summer romance. They swam in the ocean, and they ate the endless supply of seafood in the harbor, and in the eventide when they parted ways they whispered about their inner desires, inspired by all they had done together.

He knew that rather than accept any marriage inquiries, Ysma had resolved to study at Seers Point like her mother had done, and after many family discussions they decided take a much needed voyage in Lord Wynne's sailboat down the coastline to the tip of the peninsula, where she would attend school. The weather promised to be fair for the rest of summer, and they figured it would be faster than taking the long journey by land. Genshai met Ysma on the boardwalk for a stilted goodbye while the crew prepared to depart, loading the boat with supplies scattered over the pier. He was saddened to say farewell, which they had always known would happen, but he felt pleased to see her so excited for the future.

After that the monks embarked for home by joining a caravan headed east on the quarry crossing, a road that went alongside the Auburn Range for three weeks as the tower rose gradually higher on the summit of the mountain ahead of them. Flocks of sheep dotted the foothills, and the wagoner had plans to sell to the weavers in Auburntown, so he stopped at every shepherd's hovel on the way and loaded their three wagons with the last bales of raw wool until the next shearing day after autumn.

They were a family of travelers, a man and his wife with two young girls around the age of ten and an older boy of fourteen who made himself very useful from sunup to sundown. They all seemed quite capable of steering their mules and making camp every night, but Genshai was especially grateful because the girls made good nannies for Kyus, who had grown plump and tall while they were in Westcliff until he seemed to weigh twenty-five pounds. He wriggled impatiently in the sling while they rode on horseback, whining all the time, or crying all night until the experienced mother held out her hands and took Kyus into her arms and smothered him to sleep with her bosom.

Frustrated after several weeks of childcare, Genshai felt that he was caught in an unrelenting cycle. If the baby cried he desperately offered milk, or the teething ring, or he checked if Kyus needed his diaper to be changed; or Genshai plucked him up and walked around trying to soothe him, repeating again and again until something worked. Even though there were times when Kyus was charming, and by now Genshai was terribly fond of him, as long as they had to care for a baby it was hard to train, or meditate, or do anything that he thought he should be doing.

"He's so annoying," Genshai complained to Taisan one day while Kyus cried during their morning practice.

Taisan shrugged uncaringly, "That's the way they are. They need constant attention," and held out a finger, "Just remember to be lighter than five ounces," not wanting Genshai to forget that his touch could hurt the child.

"Well, I'll be glad to see grandma Joyce," Genshai said, even though his heart melted every time he looked down at the baby's eyes, which were like big golden acorns.

As they traveled Genshai couldn't help but to look into the trees that overlapped and blended into the Dellwood, wondering, *Is there a spirit grotto? Or maybe an elemental that lives in there,* and decided that from now on he would have to treat the forests, rivers, and caves, with the utmost caution and respect. *Especially if there are spirits just on the other side of the Veil,* he thought.

All around Auburntown there were fields of barley, wheat, and soy, and the occasional hopyard, all of which were busy with hands going down the rows, getting ready for harvest. They passed Oathlord Braydon's castle on a dirt track from the granary, waving to the miller's sons as they went by, and soon they were at the edge of the village and Genshai beamed with joy. Nearly every building was made from the famous red stone; especially the greathouses that were as ancient as the tower itself, the crimson guildhalls, and the Shrine of the Three Sisters, which had high vaulted ceilings and peaked arches, coiled stonework, and sculptures that were the color of cardinals, and sweet cherries, and faded vermillion. The streets bustled at midday with folks heading back and forth, and the boy felt exceedingly familiar with the village since he had been raised at the height of the mountain that overlooked it every day.

Staring down the cobbled roads to the marketplace, Genshai instinctively lifted his eyes to the tower at the peak of the mount, which was far greater than he could even fit into view.

"Hey, Taisan!" someone called, and before long it seemed that everybody knew they had returned. The old laymonk was a fixture around Auburntown; sometimes he was there for several weeks, and other times he was gone for months, turning up just when he was needed. Most folks nodded their heads in respect, just as they did for any monk, since they knew that Red Tower attracted pilgrims three times a year, and nearly all the shopkeepers were approved suppliers of the abbey and could sell their goods to visitors at a higher price.

When they arrived to the market square and Taisan decided it was time to part ways, Kyus began to cry when the family trundled off down the road, and then during the whole time that Taisan was gone stabling their horses at the livery. The boy paced around the street with the wailing baby in his arms as he said, "I'm sorry, I know, I know, I'm sorry," wondering why they didn't just go to the marketplace where he knew that Madam Joyce lived in a skinny brick townhouse tucked between two shops just off the square. He still had fond memories of that place where he knew the old matron kept many knickknacks on her shelves, and he had slept in a narrow room of bunks with his brothers as a little boy.

When Taisan returned he said, "Let me try," and took Kyus into his arms, which was like falling into the softest cloud, quieting the child almost instantly. By now it was obvious the old man liked babies, and over the years his teacher had become very familiar with caring for them and reacting to their needs, having infinite patience. Taisan changed the baby's mood completely. He swung him in his arms as he walked, and he let Kyus clutch his tangled gray hair in his little fists, showering his forehead with kisses amid the baby's happy squeals.

Instead of going to the old matron's house, Taisan led Genshai along the outer edge of the village, eventually turning south toward the Redshire. The boy recognized the area because the abbot Horn of Ram enjoyed coming down from the mountain several times a year with a long procession of monks and novices to give demonstrations of the Iron Style, touring the village and the surrounding shires.

"Where are we going?" Genshai asked.

"I was thinking that we'd visit Winneral and Albard," the old laymonk finally explained. "There are some repairs at the abbey that he can help us with."

The boy shrugged, hardly giving it any thought since he had known the young couple for almost two years, ever since they moved to Auburntown and began to come up the five-mile trail on Sabat days. It seemed like Albard could fix anything, from the crumbling stone steps outside the temple to the leaky roof above the brothers' dormitory. He was often seen striding across the terraces with a bag of tools, following Red Leaf and a few others to where he was needed on any number of repairs that had been accumulating over the years.

In the meantime Winneral volunteered by baking two-dozen loaves of wheat bread with a kind of nonchalance that made chef White Flower step aside and let her run the kitchen her own way. Once she accidentally brought them a meatpie, and immediately apologized when one of them said, "It smells so good, don't tempt me," and another exclaimed, "I wish I could eat it!" since many of them had given up meat to join the abbey.

After that she made decadent pastries filled with caramelized sweet onions, beets and carrots, or spinach and mushroom and parsnip, all loaded with soft, creamy goat cheese from the abbey; and at harvest time she made incredible apple pies with slices of melona fruit, fresh wildberries, and crumbles of baked oats and walnuts all over the top, which every monk appreciated since they weren't accustomed to desserts.

The boy was hungry just thinking about it. He knew the apple harvest was not far away and the monks would need every set of arms to carry bushels to the cellar to be pressed into cider. Winter was coming and there would be no need to travel, so Genshai was eager to resume his training with master Small Lion who was the keeper of the Seventh Form, and also Listening Wind, the master of weapons, who could teach all Ten Staff Methods. Not only that but he was curious about visiting the East Ridge where the Owl Monk was said to live alone in a cave, disappearing into the shadows, practicing the Poison Hand, and the other Night Powers of Sibudat.

The laymonks moved one after the other down the road. Taisan looked ahead, holding the iron tip of his staff upright, followed by Genshai as he braced the baby in the sling, and carried his staff in the other hand. They came to where the Season Tree grew beside the road. The leaves were deep green with broad lobes that sloped to a point, clustered around white starflowers that smelled faintly of citronella. Genshai couldn't help but wonder what spirits were around, or if they were being followed by something just on the other side of the Veil.

He stopped by impulse to gather the ripened melona until he realized how close he was to home and instead bit through the green skin, chewing a mouthful of the white fruit, which was sweet like a pear in late summer. The road split into winding lanes where brick cottages seemed to pop up through the trees, and they followed one of them south a long ways to the edge of the shire where the Oathlord's barley fields began. Along the roadside to the left was a wooded plot that rose up to the height of a grassy knoll in the backyard of the property where Genshai saw the red stone well that he and several other monks had helped Albard dig last autumn, which was no small feat for a young builder.

In fact, all the neighbors in Redshire remembered when that last plot was only an abandoned hovel overgrown with brambles. Now there was a little cottage in the shade of several oak trees that overlooked long furrows to the south. It was a well-made home of interlocking stones with a broad thatched roof around the chimney, all made with red bricks from the quarry and straight planks of cedar timber that Albard had hewn and milled himself. Portions of the walls were plastered and white, and it seemed to be something that he would get around to finishing eventually.

Just as they had hoped, Albard was home in the late afterfade. He was cutting the grass alongside the house with a scythe and waved a hand to greet them as they approached the front path. It was the last day of the week before Sabat and usually the stonecutters went home early, ready for a day of rest, although from what anyone could see Albard was tireless. He spent any extra afternoon finishing one of many projects around the cottage and sometimes the guild allowed him to take on smaller repair jobs for extra coin even though he still had not technically earned his Guild Seal.

After all, Albard had been on a jobsite since he was old enough to hold a hammer. His father was head mason at Sawyer castle, and Albard had learned nearly every skill in the trade from the other guildsmen that worked with him on the walls. He was twenty-two now, but the rumors were that he had given up guild membership under his father so that he could move to the Auburntown even though it meant he had to start all over again as an apprentice, since most guildleaders favored their own sons for membership.

"Good tidings, Albard," the old laymonk waved.

"I was wondering if we'd see you before winter," Albard said as he reached out to shake wrists with them both. He had shaggy brown hair around his ears and a bushy brown beard, and Genshai thought his broad shoulders and bulky arms looked just as formidable as any iron monk of Red Tower.

"We're here now," Taisan said congenially. "Are you ready?"

Albard's eyes widened just as there was a soft cry from within the sling and Genshai asked pleasantly, "Oh, are you waking up now?" glancing down at the baby. The steady pace of travel always put Kyus into a light sleep, and without fail the baby woke up again once they had stopped moving. Kicking his feet, he was suddenly heavier, and from the foul smell Genshai recognized that he would need to be changed and cleaned now that he was awake from his nap.

"Ready as ever, I suppose," Albard answered carefully.

He led them under the curved doorframe into a wide rectangular room with a hearth along the wall and the kitchen with a small oven on the far side. As usual there was a cauldron simmering over glowing embers and the shutters were wide-open to let in sheets of midday light. The monks leaned their staves beside the door, passing through the cottage to the backyard where Winneral was returning from the chicken coop with a basket of eggs that needed washing.

"Well, I thought for sure you'd come home maimed, or with a broken arm," Winneral said sarcastically to the boy.

"I did alright for myself." Genshai stood a bit more upright.

"What brings you all the way out here to the edge of town?" Winneral asked, glancing with interest at the soft rounded shape in the sling. She was short and had small features, with a narrow chin and bright hazelgreen eyes, keeping a tight wry smile. Like most northerners she had a tawny complexion, though men like Albard who worked outside were tanned like golden wheat, or like brown barley that stood ready for harvest in the field.

"We're on our way to see Madam Joyce," Taisan said, before he turned to Albard, "But I wanted to stop here and ask you about rebuilding the second washroom in the brothers' dormitory."

"It is in pretty bad shape," Albard said, "I took a look at it while you were gone."

Taisan continued, "We should try to start on it before the first snows, don't you think?"

"Now wait just a minute," Winneral held up a hand to interrupt them before she turned to young Genshai and asked, "Tell me, who is this?"

"This is Kyus," the boy grinned, hardly able to contain the squirming baby, and it was as if he sprang out of the sling into her hands. Winneral held him with his legs dangling, looking into his round face, his cheeks dimpled with a wide toothless smile, his brown shock of hair swept upward. Kyus was not a small baby either and he writhed in her hands, looking back and forth at everything.

She laughed impulsively when he clutched her collar and laid his head against her neck, groping for her chest until she bounced him in her arms, singing out, "Well, who's a handsome boy?" Kyus seemed slightly confused but he couldn't help but to erupt with laughter as she carried him around.

Taisan said, "By the weight of him I think he's just under a year old."

Being a young woman of twenty, Winneral had no experience at all with newborns, or children, and could hardly guess how old a baby was much less know what to do with one. She never had younger siblings and never spent much time in the nurseries at the shrine since she had always worked with her mother and father in the kitchens of Sawyer castle.

Taisan told the story of how they found him crawling in the shrubbery on the road outside Norhaal, and said, "Poor Genshai thought it was a boar! He nearly jumped out of his britches!" to which they all laughed, even the boy who knew that his teacher would never let it go, but thankful that Taisan had left out the part where he had been relieving himself in the ditch.

Before long the two men were talking business by the back door while Winneral offered to hold the baby. Genshai said, "I think he needs to be changed," and sure enough Kyus had a full diaper that needed to be washed. They didn't have any kind of changing table but Winneral watched as the young laymonk set the baby in the grass to remove the soiled cloth, as if he had done it many times.

Kyus grinned cheek to cheek as Genshai wiped his bottom, saying, "Did you poop? Did you poop? Now don't worry I'll get it all cleaned up for you," before he withdrew a clean linen diaper from a leather pouch fastened to his backpack. In seconds he had the cloth wrapped around the baby's hips, setting him upright, but immediately Kyus crawled away furiously, prompting the boy to retrieve him and place him right in Winneral's arms.

He's growing up, Winneral thought about her young friend.

They had only been gone since late winter, but already Genshai seemed more mature. Maybe it was that he looked older to her now. He was hardened and lean from his long journey, and carried himself as straight as an upright post, and he even looked to have grown two inches since he left earlier that year. There was light stubble on his cheeks and his dark walnut hair was short around his ears. She knew Genshai had taken on a strange role, but Winneral thought it suited him since she could never have imagined that he would stay cooped up in the abbey for the rest of his life when he was so clearly meant for adventure.

As if to demand her attention Kyus thumped his tiny fists against her chest and brought Winneral out of her thoughts and back to the moment in her backyard. The baby yearned and reached and kicked within her arms, making Winneral wonder how much of the movements of motherhood were really instinctual, *Do I have to be able to get pregnant to be a mother? How do I even know if I'm holding him right?* as she tried to switch arms, and then different positions, finding that she didn't have the strength to hold him for very long.

"Is he restless?" Genshai asked, reaching for the child. "I've been doing some squats with him, like this." He held the baby under the arms and encouraged Kyus to pump his legs in what could be called a squat. His feet were mostly flat, occasionally tensing to grip the ground, and soon Kyus stood with a proud grin as he kept one hand clutched onto Genshai's finger and the other on his pant leg, as the boy said, "See, he can almost stand by himself."

"Come here, Kyus," Winneral reached out both hands, looking down at him expectantly. "Come here, baby."

And with that Kyus took one step and then another, letting go of Genshai's finger and toddling eight more steps before he collapsed into Winneral's arms.

"Did you see that? He walked!" Genshai exclaimed, amidst their cheers of delight.

"He'll be doing the Iron Style in no time," Taisan smirked.

They tried again, but Kyus was eager to get onto the ground after that, crawling without any trouble through the soft green grass. Winneral moved unconsciously with him. She wanted to catch him and humor him and guide him, plucking him up whenever he roamed too close to the chicken coop, or the woodpile, or toward any other random dangers.

She found Kyus eagerly waiting for her gaze, and it pricked her heart with sadness. Even as he babbled joyfully, waving his arms with delight, she could not help but to think, *What sort of world is this? Here is a boy that nobody wants, when it's all I've longed for, but I cannot have.* Kyus no longer squirmed in her arms, but laid his head on her shoulder, murmuring and cooing his contentment and Winneral felt her spirit stir. It was a palpable force that began to rise from her navel. It was inexplicable, yet at the same time it was just what she wanted to know about herself. She glanced over at Taisan who chatted casually with her husband, suddenly aware of why the monks had visited that day.

The afterfade was a blur. Winneral played with Kyus for a long while, forgetting all about her chores, neglecting to make supper for the evening. Looking up at the sky she could tell it was late afternoon and within two hours the light would be gone. They all knew the laymonks would be moving on soon, although by then only Genshai was unaware of the reason they had visited. She realized they were waiting for her, and it was time to make a decision when Taisan finally stood up and said, "Well, we had better get going to see Joyce before dark," as they moved through the house to collect their staves and backpacks by the door.

Winneral shot her husband a glance and he was ready to make eye contact, nodding his agreement. She admired his rugged, hairy features, and longed to see him be a father. After all they had been through and left behind, for the last three years it seemed they would never have a family, but while she clutched the baby in her arms she saw a way for her to become a mother, even if it wasn't the most conventional.

Without knowing exactly what to say, she asked, "Couldn't he stay with us?"

Taisan paused for a moment and looked at them discerningly.

"Certainly, but do you mean that you'd become a matron for the abbey?"

Her husband shrugged as if he respected her decision either way. Winneral looked down at Kyus in her arms. The baby was tired after playing so enthusiastically and he snuggled into the crook of her elbow and laid a hand over her left breast. She noticed that carrying him was becoming easier and without a second thought she said, "Yes, of course," as if she felt that by speaking it aloud there would be no way for her to withdraw her agreement.

"Alright then," Taisan nodded, his face revealing a satisfied grin as he told them, "They are abbey children, so you'll just need to care for them until they're five years old, or at least capable of starting school."

"How many do we need to take?" Albard asked.

Taisan shrugged, "However many you can handle."

"One is enough for now," Winneral said as she held the baby closer, not wanting to think about that inevitable day as she asked, "What next?"

"We'll be back soon with supplies and funds," Taisan said. "He will need an examination by the clerics at the shrine, but otherwise he'll be in your care until he's older."

Genshai knew that when Taisan said 'examination' he meant 'circumcision,' which the boy did not want to dwell on, changing the subject with some excitement, "I didn't know you wanted to be parents!"

The couple glanced at each other and Winneral tried to say casually, "Of course, we've always wanted to have a family," without saying much more about it even as her thoughts raced back and forth in her memories.

The group talked for a few minutes longer but the old man was eager to get on the road before dark. He went over to the baby in Winneral's lap and planted a whiskery kiss on his head, turning away from the child as he had done many times in his life before. Genshai came up with a wistful expression as he said, "Well, alright then, goodbye baby," letting Kyus grip his forefinger in his little hands one last time.

It was clear Genshai wasn't ready to leave but Taisan plucked up his staff beside the door and was departing down the front path as he called out, "Let's go," and the boy trailed after him into the late sunset.

That evening was filled with unexpected joy as they each got to know their new son, holding him in their arms, or setting him on their laps as he gazed around curiously. At first Albard bustled through the house and gathered up anything that might be dangerous for a crawling baby, sweeping the flagged floors, tidying up the firewood, and finally setting down a bundle of thick wool blankets in front of the hearth where Kyus could crawl while they were watching him.

Winneral prepared a cold meatpie from the larder for supper, indicating with a suggestive tone, "If I had a bigger oven I could bake more at once. I might even be able to quit the Oathlord's kitchen once and for all," since she was eager to find any opportunity not to work there because she disliked the chef, who was an irritable drunk, and it was a long trek out to the castle just to work as a prep cook.

"Well, it ought to be alright," Albard said, "But there are a lot of other things to do around here."

Winneral smirked, "Yes, but I'd still like a bigger oven."

They watched as Kyus pulled himself up on the hearth, filling the cottage with his buoyant laughter, and Albard commented, "Well, he's a happy little guy, isn't he?"

"Go get your flute," Winneral suggested and Albard hesitated until she urged him again. He returned with a carved wooden pipe he had purchased on a whim in the market when they first arrived to Auburntown and they were still renting a flat in the village. Albard found it among a few spare things in a crate on the back of a merchant wagon and bought it for six copper bits. Every few nights her husband sat on the back stoop to play and Winneral was surprised that he possessed this hidden talent, being amazed that he could even blow out one note until he began to recover the memories of playing a dozen different flutesongs from his childhood.

After just one or two false starts Albard played a long slow melody broken by low rolling tones. Kyus looked around, intrigued by the music until he realized it was coming from the new bearded man sitting in the chair by the hearth. Then Albard played an uplifting song with high plucky tones that seemed to climb up over each other, falling down to the bottom before beginning again, which Kyus enjoyed immensely.

They talked throughout the evening and Winneral knew her husband's mind was already turning with plans to build a crib, and a changing table, and whatever else they needed. They realized the old laymonk had said Kyus might be the first of many, though there was no way of knowing when they would come, so they discussed building bunks in the front corner, and Albard insisted, "One day, we'll have a proper washroom," since they each dreaded the trek to the outhouse this coming winter. They didn't care about the cost, allowing the ideas to settle in their minds as they contemplated what their home would be like one day.

The baby dozed off, swaddled on her chest in the fading glow of the hearth. *I can't believe this is happening,* Winneral thought to herself as they prepared a bundle of quilts on the bed between them for the baby. Her husband was soundly asleep within minutes, yet Winneral had frenzied thoughts, reliving the flashes of pain and blood, imagining it wasn't real; that Kyus was not her child, or worse that he would be gone when she woke up and she would only have the memory of him, like how it had been after her first miscarriage.

She was grateful when Kyus cried in the deepest part of the night and she was there to pluck him up, walking softly out to the chair by the hearth where she let him whimper in her arms until he was dozing once again. Her feelings were complicated. She knew she would never be able to bear a child, and Winneral didn't want to think about the losses they had suffered, or the cruel rumors they had left behind.

She enjoyed the life they were building in Auburntown. Two years ago they had arrived with just their packs and a small pouch of gold Aurants. They rented a flat and quickly found jobs, and Albard made friends with the local Alderman who knew of a few places to buy, or if they were really desperate, a vassalhouse that was available, which they wanted to avoid since it would make Albard a fieldworker indentured to the Oathlord.

That's when Albard found the burned-out old hovel on a plot of land overgrown with trees at the farthest edge of the Redshire. To her it looked like a set of crumbling walls without a roof, but he walked her through each room and described the potential, saying, "It's perfect," more than ten times before she agreed they could buy it. They struck a deal with the Alderman, who told them the seven acres was once used as a livery for oxen that plowed the south fields until a fire burned it down more than two-dozen years before.

By the end of the first summer they had cleared the briars and thorns so that Albard could uncover the original foundation. He did all the work himself, tirelessly from dawn to dusk. He came back from the quarry to spend a few hours building up the walls with freshly hewn red stone, and then raising timber rafters with the help of one or two guildsmen and several monks. He laid granite flagstone floors and eventually thatched the roof with straw, dry reeds, and pine tar until they were sleeping within the walls during the cool autumn nights and Albard could set to work finishing the double-layered brick hearth just in time for winter.

There was still some idle gossip about them in Auburntown but Winneral was content with that since it was natural for folks to be curious. Besides, Albard was steadily gaining a reputation as a builder and it wasn't long before they were welcomed to the neighborhood, especially after the abbot seemed to favor them. People joked that Winneral had charmed him with apple pies. One of their neighbors had even said that the abbot must have known them from another life, but it was no secret that they had been volunteering at the temple some evenings, and every Sabat day, since they first arrived.

Winneral thought, *More likely all this started because he hated hauling buckets back and forth,* referring to Albard and the well in the shire, which was a quarter of a mile away. All last winter, her husband had insisted, "Why should I walk all that way for the rest of my life, just for ten gallons? I'd rather dig a well now and save myself the trouble," which seemed like an impossible task to her, but as soon as the ground was mostly thawed at the end of the second month of the year he began the long process of excavating the soil and mortaring a stone shaft.

It took eleven days, and several of the neighbors were convinced he couldn't complete the task. They thought he'd have to call in the guild leaders and hire a team of masons for help, but instead Albard worked day and night removing buckets of soil, cutting away roots and rocks, using a smooth oaken measuring rod to check the width of the well shaft. He asked a few monks like Red Leaf and Oakheart and even young Genshai and his friends to sit nearby and remove the dirt, and to watch the hole in the event that the shaft collapsed on top of him.

He mortared in good red stone and like most wells in the area it was more than fifteen feet deep. Now he enjoyed a short two-minute walk out to the knoll in the yard instead of a hike down the road to wait in line for the entire shire to get their water. Winneral knew it was the way Albard thought about things: "Working for tomorrow," as he called it. Needless to say the guildleaders were impressed. They had even visited their cottage under the pretense of seeing how he was settling in just to catch a glimpse of his craftsmanship and to offer him actual masonry jobs, ensuring him they would grant him a Guild Seal after he had paid his dues.

Not even a week later, in the third month of the year, during the Night of Lanterns, the abbot came down from the mountain to tour the village in a wagon, and asked, "Where can the monks find water in the shire?" until a neighbor said, "Albard has a well," and suddenly a hundred people were gathered in the road outside their property as the old abbot, followed by a line of monks, came to ask if they could draw water from the well.

Albard was more than happy to host the abbot of Red Tower and soon the people gathered into the back acres of their cottage to sit in the grass or against the trunks of trees. The youngest monks began with acrobatics, wheeling and flipping, climbing on each other's shoulders, tumbling down like feathers, as if they were playing a game. Then several of them demonstrated the Iron Body, breaking wooden staves over their shoulders, splitting bricks with their knifehand, blasting their fists through slabs of stone.

Folks were astonished when a brave young monk no older than seventeen stepped forward to balance three bricks on his head and allowed one of his young friends to swing a sledgehammer overtop, cracking the bricks straight through. He displayed his Iron Head for all to see without even a scratch on it, running off to the side while the next monk kicked through a pine board that was three inches thick. Afterwards the boys all joked around, shoving each other into line as they waited for the herbalist to brush them with the pungent hit medicine

People whispered about the second abbot, Body of Steel, who had a surly expression as he called monks forth to demonstrate. He was impressive with his bare chest strapped in dense muscle, always displaying the impossible feat of breaking several clubs across his ribs, or even against his neck, which was dangerous since the shards of wood could easily cut his throat. Folks thought he was the most feared monk of Red Tower but everyone agreed that the young and shining master Small Lion was the most skillful with his forms, and the monk Listening Wind twirled and whipped the staff so aggressively that everyone backed away.

Winneral had come to realize that the abbot was older than he looked as he sat with her on the bench by the back door and watched his students. He kept his hands clasped in front and she could see his thick wrists and palms, having learned from Taisan that the abbot was hardened by stone and could accidentally injure someone with just a finger if he wasn't careful. They had each come to know each other's mannerisms very well over the last year, and she felt that he treated her like a beloved granddaughter without knowing exactly why.

The laymonk stood nearby, and he pointed and said, "My student, Mountainroot," about the boy who had stepped forward to bow respectfully to Horn of Ram. This was before his journeys, when he had just sworn the Oath; and she had decided she liked his new abbey name but she still planned to call him Genshai since he was appointed to become the next laymonk after all. Winneral watched the boy set his dark eyes against the slab, blasting his fist through with purpose, a loud applause bursting out from the crowd as the pieces clattered against the other shards.

The abbot approached and Winneral was surprised when Horn of Ram moved from the bench without her noticing. None could hear what the master said to the young student, but Mountainroot ran around to the front of the house and quickly returned with a piece of rough-hewn red rock that came directly from the quarry. The crowd's interest was piqued, anxious to see what would happen as the Horn of Ram settled his hips and knees, controlling his breath. In a decisive strike, with no unnecessary movement, a crack shot through where the abbot landed his palm over the raw stone. Pieces crashed to the ground and people cheered as if there was no question why the monks of Red Tower were so legendary.

When the abbot returned to his seat, Taisan said, "You're showing off again," to which the old man's eyes glimmered and Winneral realized that perhaps the Horn of Ram wasn't always so detached after all.

Actually, she reflected, that was the week the laymonks had departed for the Namaya Highlands, and Taisan and Genshai were gone for eight months. It hardly prevented the abbot from visiting the shires twice more over the summer, and they never had any objection to hosting in their yard. Albard even built a set of wooden benches so the old mothers and young girls had places to sit instead of on their dresses in the grass. It gave him a certain reputation and soon people began to pass Albard their alms in the absence of the laymonk, since most monks graciously refused to take money into their hands.

Even the village Alderman began to attend the gatherings in their yard, along with the guildleaders, and even a few knights of the Oathlord. The monks displayed their skills, coming in breathlessly to draw cups of cool water before they leapt back out as soon as the Body of Steel called on them. Following the demonstrations, Albard built a big bonfire with dry brush, allowing the monks to mingle with the townspeople all through the eventide.

At first Winneral was surprised that they would usually tap a cask of strong abbey ale, and maybe another of golden cider blended with blackberries and wildflower honey. Most monks were generally sober but she learned they were sometimes permitted to consume what they made themselves at special gatherings. They were abstinent in other things as well, taking strict vows of celibacy, remaining vegetarian, and even refusing to handle money or precious items to the point that some of them had never touched a single coin in their entire lives.

These things might have been virtues in the Aegin Tradition, but as they stood around the bonfire some errant young men brought out flasks of highland whiskey, and while the monks only wet their lips they laughed just as drunkenly as the folks that took full swallows. They consciously avoided all pipes of tobacco and sweetleaf, and mostly restrained themselves to one or two mugs of beer; but that didn't stop them from showing curiosity about other things. After all, the girls of the village gawked at the muscular warrior men, and there was plenty of gossip about which lady was having an affair with which monk. Sometimes the teenage boys and girls even disappeared for an evening in the farmlands and Winneral felt that Horn of Ram regarded these celebrations as natural for young people to do.

The old abbot intrigued her. He was in his eighties and had apparently earned the respect of all these muscular young warriors, yet he didn't look nearly as imposing, being only just as tall as she was. It was confusing when he talked about internal alignment, or the Still Mind; and Winneral became completely lost when he referred to his students by their abbey name and later they introduced themselves to her with their worldly name. Some of them were even men who had been raised by Madam Joyce and had left the abbey in pursuit of their own family, but still believed in the teachings of the Aegin Tradition.

They all sat in various postures on the ground or on stools where they could listen comfortably. The abbot gazed over them with his eyes half closed. He stood upright and moved with a fluid grace that was unlike any of the elderly people she had ever met before. His voice was like a rolling wind as he quoted the wisdom of the ancient teacher, "We tread in moments / and countless threads of life merge / and then unravel," pausing between lines to offer his own interpretation, "Change defines life. Your spirit must embrace each thing, and then release each thing, again and again. Live in the moment, but set free the image of the moment, or you will only live in the illusion of your own mind."

Horn of Ram allowed silence to exist for a long time, and when he next spoke, Winneral thought he was looking directly at her. "Sibudat says, 'Be ready for change, / nothing endures beyond time / and all forms will end. Shed your attachments, / release your worldly tethers, / set free love and hate. Cast aside the past, / the future is not yet here, / live in the moment."

He concluded, "All changes are short. Your journey will continue in this life no matter what," and then after a brief pause the abbot raised a finger and said, "Don't forget to smile," to which all their faces brightened.

Drifting through her memories, Winneral heard the sound of the abbot's voice in her head as she cradled the sleeping baby all through the forehour of dawn. She thought about how she had just volunteered to receive orphans from the road, rear them up, and give them away to become students of Red Tower, maybe even to take the Oath one day. She wondered, *What am I getting myself into?* looking down at Kyus as he made small snuffling noises.

By now she had a suspicion that her husband had planned all of this, maybe even as far back as their very first visit, or even before they had ever left Sawyertown when he had suggested, "What about Auburntown?" and she resolved to have a conversation with him tomorrow, wondering what in his mind prevented him from divulging to her his idea to become a matron's home.

Perhaps Albard thought Taisan would not ever come, and he was unwilling to give her hope for a son, or a family, they might never have.

She imagined that one morning Albard had visited Red Tower instead of going to the stoneyard. He must have listened to the abbot's discourse in the temple and afterward he would have met with him and asked about the matron tradition. She didn't know whether or not it would fill the wound that was left open since before they moved to Auburntown, but she could hardly blame Albard for trying, as she thought, *At least I'll be able to watch this one grow up.*

EPILOGUE

THE FOURTH DAY OF ALLORA, BEGINNING OF AUTUMN, 1019 EC

The Book of the World, "The Golden Mother shaped the egg of the world, and waited a thousand days to invite the Raegods down from the heavenly island to begin building it to their desires."

THE TOMB OF MYOCHUS

From within a fitful, unnatural sleep, he heard the sound of his father's voice calling his hidden name, "Aud!" through a dream of a flag that fluttered in the sunlight and twisted like a long silver ribbon. The call repeated itself; "Aud!" again and again like it was an urgent message, drawing him out of his slumber. He opened his eyes to the darkness and choked on the stale air of the sarcophagus, his entire body twitching and quivering after he had lain on his side for so long.

Spare memories of his final days came crashing into his thoughts – rain pounded down from low angry clouds, a concert of hellhounds shrieked over the nearest valley; the assassins of the Shroud closed on him in the forest.

But even though he had slept for years, Karwyn drifted back into a formless slumber that lasted for several more hours. When he finally stirred again he had only the slightest strength to whisper, "Release me," which allowed the huge coverstone to slide off and crash onto the floor, shattering to pieces like glass. It took considerable effort for him to sit upright and he discovered that his fingers had less than half their function, and that his muscles were soft and numb. His legs collapsed underneath him as he stepped out of the sarcophagus and he crawled on his knees to the lowest of six wide steps where he groaned as he sank down onto his rear, his sounds echoing through the long hall, disturbing a deathly silence.

Karwyn's eyes adjusted into silver discs that glimmered like mirrors, or the eyes of a cat. The darkness was not as oppressive as it had been in the sarcophagus, and from where he sat he could make out the smooth slopes of the high ceiling and three rows of coffins all the way to the back of the main room. They were limestone boxes carved along each side in elaborate tracery and marked with the blessings of the Raegods to grant their spirits safe passage in the afterlife.

He felt confused. *Just like an old, old man past his time*, Karwyn thought bitterly, but every so often he brushed the dust from his vast memories just as he did from the sleeves of the tattered gray robes he wore on his shoulders. His body ached from disuse. His stomach grumbled and his throat was parched, but somehow Karwyn knew that there would be nothing there for him inside the depths of the tomb. The old wizard sat unmoving for hours at the bottom of the steps and gradually he came awake again after a long meandering dream about his mother; having visions of her smooth black skin, and her generous smile whenever he would cast sprays of light and color into the courtyard at the Home of the Silver Chalice, the shrine where they lived when he was a boy.

Memories returned in flashes – crossing through time – many faces rising up in his mind, although without context they faded away as quickly as they appeared. Some of them he knew very well – recalling their names – like Zentha the Painted Woman; and the innocent young monk Elosai, who presumed to seek out the Lotusblade and hold it against the demonson who had wrought havoc in the kingdom for years, *But that was so long ago. I can't even say what happened, or how it ended,* Karwyn thought with disappointment as he held his brow with his thumb and finger.

He came to know the contents of the crypt, sending his silver vision forward to explore without moving. It was a massive stone vault, and the walls were carved with hash marks and dots that told the story of the warlord Myochus and his sons, ancient kings from the Lost Age more than two thousand years ago. There were storerooms that once held gold, precious gems and jewelry, pots of wine and baskets of food, and four generations of the royal family rested there. At the far end were pits of bones where the house servants, concubines, and sworn warriors and even their horses were slain and laid beside each other to attend to their masters in the afterlife.

What a waste of precious time on earth, Karwyn thought; yet in the era of King Myochus they believed that all their chosen servants had the divine honor to reside with them in their royal halls in the country of the dead. There were still similar traditions in many cultures across the world, but now instead of ritual sacrifices the clerics of Seers Point burned offerings of incense and scented ropes and holy papers, and prayed for the spirits of the dead to find their guide that would reunite them with their ancestors.

Growing up in the shrine of wisdom by the shoreline, he had once loved to study the stories of the Lost Age. As a boy he had kept a stack of histories by his bedside, gripped by the tales of kings marrying queens, monks quarreling with warlords, and endless politics. He was particularly intrigued by the mythologies of the Raegods and their children, since it felt like he was learning about his own father, and his brothers and sisters, and the choices they made thousands of years ago that shaped the world.

When he finally embarked from the Home of the Silver Chalice, his aging mother gave him a rare handwritten copy of the Book of the World, which told the story of how the Golden Mother created the world from her egg and allowed the Raegods to populate it with their favorite things. His memory was so fragmented that he could hardly say now what all those stories were even about, having lost the holy book somewhere on his journeys many years ago.

Who am I, really? Karwyn strained to remember, but he felt so rundown that he could hardly move, sitting in a dull state of exhaustion, as if he had just walked fifty miles through the riverlands.

The dreams came unbidden, like a torrent over him. He saw torches held high, the vineyards hazy with fumes. Armies of holy knights marched in front of him, the Paladins of the Dawn who scoured the countryside for the followers of the Jade Eye; burning out their temples, breaking down their sacrificial alters in a great purge until they were satisfied. Entire families were accused of witchcraft and dragged from their homes to be sentenced to burn on a pyre of unholy books, relics, and idols of the Fallen One.

Did I do all of this? Karwyn asked himself, disturbed by the sight of the inquisition, but of course there were other nightmares in the depths of his mind.

He shuddered when the horned demonson Viokher emerged from a shroud of smoke, wielding a burning brand – he bowed to the High Priestess of the Jade Eye and awaited her command. Beside them was Dedras, a common thief with the vile and implacable book chained to his wrist by an iron cuff. Withering away, he was enslaved to the Mal Goetia's evil powers so that it could leech his life from him, or until he sank to the bottom of the ocean by the weight of it.

Karwyn awoke with a start, slumped at the steps and uncomfortable. He fumbled for his staff in the darkness, a twisted olive branch as tall as him with a knot in the center polished by his grip, holding it upright and dragging himself to his feet. He groaned shamelessly as his knees tightened like knots and the rest of his body was numb from sitting for so long, unintentionally using the spellvoice until the entire tomb was rumbling with the echoes of his pain.

The ancient wizard climbed the wide steps toward the grand square doorway, his eyes glinting like silver coins as he gazed at the massive slab of granite that no single man could ever hope to move alone. "Now how do I get out of here?" he wondered aloud, his throat hoarse and dry. His hands traced the holy godmarks inscribed on the doorframe, consecrated by a priestess to ward any thief who broke the seal of the tomb. Of course the place had been looted centuries ago when those old kingdoms collapsed during the second era, which meant the huge stone was filled with cracks, held together by his invisible magehand.

Making a fist, pulling, twisting, flattening his palm, Karwyn's voice became distorted with power as he said, "Fall down," which allowed the stones to collapse, scattering all over the entryway. He shaded his eyes as he entered the light of midday, suddenly bathed in the glimmering colors of leylines that coursed in currents just above him, pulsing intermittently in emerald rays, or descending like pearly bubbles – idle waves of cobalt, flashes of scarlet like a forge – or striped brown and yellow sandstone.

They were thrilling to behold, and now Karwyen remembered as a young man he had resolved to follow the mysterious streaming colors that only his secondsight could see in the sky above his head. After a long walk through the lower valleys of the Danic Rivers he eventually came high enough to study the leylines, even trying to touch them. The abandoned tomb was a surprise to discover, and back then he thought it would make a good place for a sanctum, returning there many times over the years.

The slopes were verdant green and he stood at the edge of the escarpment where the lands descended steeply, stretching as far as his eyes could see in every direction. The watercourses carved the surrounding valleys in nine branches and eventually washed into the sea seventy miles away. A single hawk shrieked, wheeling over the green hills, and some trees grew along the shallower slopes while wispy clouds drifted over the pale blue sky.

Even at that height Karwyn had to wait until the hour of eventide before the currents shifted low enough for him to reach with his fingertips. At first they curved gradually, as if displaced by the setting sun, until five streams of color surrounded him. By instinct, Karwyn raised his hands to pull on each leyline like he was unraveling thread from a spool. The raw powers twisted around him in loops, tightening down like knots until suddenly his eyes flared with silver beams of light.

Then he allowed it to happen. The frayed threads connected to his bare flesh, sparking at the touch. Karwyn gasped in shock and his body took in everything at once without consideration for what he could hold, hastily absorbing the raw forces. Within minutes Karwyn's thirst was quenched, his stomach was full, the strength returned to his body, and he was emboldened with the familiar power to shape the world that only the Mageborn could possess. Karwyn was like an empty jar, and when he was filled past the brim he shouted, "That's enough," forcing the threads to retract before his body became suffused, and overwhelmed, with the elemental powers.

A hazy vapor rose off his shoulders as he collapsed to his knees, reaching for the staff for support. Breathing heavily, the old wizard was exhausted and invigorated all at once. The silver glow of his eyes faded and Karwyn stood near the entryway of the tomb in the gathering darkness, looking up at the immeasurable stars that appeared to shine brightly after his long slumber. From their placements and the thumbnail of the moon he guessed it was the third or fourth day of Allora, named for Alloraiah, one of the Three Sisters that people everywhere worshipped – daughter of Amaritabhe the Wise, which he realized, *She is my sister I have never met, and probably never will.*

There were still significant gaps in his memory. He was missing the events of entire centuries, although he was now aware that eighty-six years had passed since the Battle of Gládmere and that fateful night he went to sleep in the tomb. Certain images were fresh in his mind – visions of his last hours, as if they had just happened – his friend Endell Norr gripped the hilt of his sword and said in earnest, "Go, we'll hold them off," as soldiers clashed with the Red Knights at the Arch of Anatheia on the kingsway, nearly at the gates of the capital, and there was not a single person who didn't imagine what evils they would commit once they broke through the last lines of defense.

The House of Halidor had ruled peacefully for a little over a hundred and thirty years, but that day Karwyn was truly worried that they were at the end of their line. The Red Knights were ruthless, wearing black striped hoods and baring sharpened teeth, fighting like they were starving tigers. They had used the Gládmere to flank opposite sides of the city until the men were butchering each other for hours, littering the trees with thousands of dead soldiers. Karwyn had never seen such devastation, even after a decade of bloodshed when nearly a million infantrymen, clerics, and knights had already given their lives.

Karwyn paced urgently through the gilded Hall of Mirrors in the royal palace as the countryside blazed with warfire and the sounds of battle could be heard from the ramparts of the Acropolis. The leylines on the earth bristled with more energy than he had ever seen, and red lightning struck in the distance. The sky bloomed with fire. Hellwinds whipped around them. He could sense amidst all the carnage of the battle that somewhere the Red Seer was channeling the worst sort of spell, although without the Mal Goetia Grimoire chained to her hand he had no idea how it was possible.

He leapt from the walls and a gray hawk rose up through the storm beating its wings. At that height the bodies of the slain were just brown husks, their eyes open and blank, scattered over each other like spent walnut shells. Karwyn flew to the center of it all, where he heard the hellhounds yipping and shrieking through the forest. The sky was the color of blood and the moon was a jade sickle just above the Acropolis, and when he came to the nexus of the spell he returned to his true form.

The mage pulled the rare energies toward him until a crackling sphere descended into his arms. He seized with power. His blood burned from within. Even if he had wanted to, Karwyn could never contain the charge, raising his voice like thunder through the winds; he fell to his knees and released everything into the sky. He thought, *Can this be how I finally die?* as several explosions of red lightning hit the earth across the valley of Gládmere, resounding after each other for several miles.

By instinct a gray hawk rose up and flew south on stormy currents, arriving to the old sanctum hidden in the valley of tombs. Karwyn came in haggard and afraid, he threw back an arm to assemble the coverstone as he muttered, "Let me close my eyes for a while," and climbed into the empty coffin named for the lost king's grandson whose bones had never come to rest there. He muttered the incantation of somnolence as he lay down, summoning a deep restorative sleep.

It was strange that although the events of the battle had happened in his recent memories, many years had passed since Karwyn had actually held the red lightning in his hands. There was so much he yearned to know, wondering, *What happened after the Battle at Gládmere? Did Endell survive?* He realized that there must now be a thousand things to catch up on, people he needed to find – places of power that must be secured, enchantments to reinforce – if he could only remember where to go and what to do.

Within the sarcophagus Karwyn found a worn cloth satchel where he had laid his head to sleep. He set out each item to remind himself of what they were. Nothing he possessed was conventional for a traveler, since he had no need for things like tindertwigs, or a bedroll to sleep on, or even food and water. There were several other more unusual items, like a dingy silver plate, three black candles, a long piece of whalebone carved with symbols, and finally a hunk of smoky quartz about the size of his palm that gleamed in the starlight. He also had two journals, which contained hundreds of entries that were reminders of his many travels, observations of leylines and their crossings, incantations and gestures of magic, illustrated sigils and wards, all written in a code, or a confusing shorthand.

In his true form he was a wizened man, with a waist-long beard and wild tangles of gray hair that flashed with threads of gold and silver. His skin was the color of black umber, although his scars had a purple hue, and he was very small and slight framed. When he removed the tattered gray rags from his shoulders the fabrics mended themselves into a modest robe in his hands, and he wore a talisman of hard iron around his neck at all times that protected him from the charms of spirits.

His body gleamed with arcane sigils and coiling script – neon blue and leafgreen, red as a cardinal, yellow as the sun, shimmering when they were fully charged. He even had the eight-sided mageshield tattooed on his back, which protected him from most things that were magical, or mundane; although the other marks were simpler spells that he liked to use quite often, like the magehand inscribed in his right wrist and the werelight in his left.

Once all his objects were pulled from his satchel and restored by his touch, Karwyn was not sure what to do. *Should I cast a spell, or begin a ritual?* He asked himself, uncertain what arcane words to pronounce, or gestures to trace in the air, considering what little he could remember.

I need to know more about the world, Karwyn realized, reaching instinctively for the grubby silver plate among his possessions. The rim was engraved with symbols, and while he peered into the surface he used the spellvoice, which echoed across the valley as he said, "Show me Red Tower."

The haze in the surface cleared and relayed a scene more than a thousand miles away. The wizard was relieved to see the abbey still standing on the mountaintop with the village nestled comfortably into the foothills. Karwyn had always admired the iron warriors, believing they were the most formidable, even if they were the most rigid, of all the Aegin monks; but already the tower had been rebuilt once in his lifetime, and he felt it was now more crucial than ever for his plans for when he was near the end and would no longer be needed to answer the call of the gods.

His invisible eye roamed across the mountainside where two laymonks, a man and a boy, made their way up the five-mile road. They looked weary coming home in the darkhour of midnight, yet they set a steady pace all the way to the summit where the tower loomed over them like a giant shadow against the stars. Few things had changed, and as usual the fire was ablaze in the pavilion of the Eternal Hearth. Karwyn became convinced that all was well there; and he memorized the boy's broad features, his dark brown hair and black eyes, gathering a name into his thoughts until he spoke aloud, "Mountainroot?" as if acquainting himself with the phrase.

Unfortunately the scenes dimmed to a haze. "That's it?" Karwyn grumbled as he exhaled on the plate, shining it with his sleeve, as if he was trying to coax the image back. *I must truly be an old man now, I can barely summon a scrying spell,* he thought bitterly, yet in retrospect it seemed that the charge he had absorbed from the leylines was quite small. He assumed that it would take some time for him to recover his full capacity, preferring not to think of how he had stopped the Nether Gate, of how he had held red lightning in his hands – and of how he might be wounded forever.

He was desperate to know what became of his friend Endell Norr. *Did he die at the Battle of Gládmere? Or did he ever go home to Red Tower like he had wanted?* From what he could remember Endell was the youngest son of his father the Warden of the north and had been committed to the abbey as a boy. Endell had even taken the Oath, but when the civil war began he surprised everyone by arriving to the battlefield in dirty monk garments to reunite with his brothers and fight for his family name.

And there is still the Order of the Shroud to be concerned about, he recalled, aggravated since he now realized the cult of the Jade Eye had actually survived for hundreds of years without his knowledge. They had changed into a secret cabal of assassins and spies that wore shrouds over their faces and continued their rituals of blood magic and human sacrifice to the Fallen One. It was obvious now that they had infiltrated the Acropolis and undermined the Sovereign from within, and after his long absence Karwyn worried their spies would be everywhere, invested in everything.

With the patience of the long-lived he stayed there for hours in the darkness as he considered what to do. He knew it was the powerful voice of his father that had called into his thoughts, drawing him out of his somnolence by the use of his hidden name. Centuries ago, as a young man Karwyn was easily convinced to act in the travails of the world, hungry for knowledge and power; but now he wanted more than just one word from his father, who had only ever called his name whenever he needed him for a task. Karwyn stifled the feelings of resentment that arose in his heart. He knew he had been created to serve the gods, to act by the wisdom of Amaritabhe, in exchange for long life and the powers of leymagic.

"Aud!" came the voice of his father to his ears, and the sight of Amaritabhe hovered in the air, coiled and ready, with a menacing intent in his eyes, which were wild, smoky, and green.

As much as he might like to, the mage could not ignore the sound of his own name, or the pull on the tether that drew his body toward his destination. In just a single word, his father conveyed all that he needed to know – *Go to the Bay of Whales. Find the daughter of the Queen of Heaven. Teach her what you can* – giving him the image of a skinny fourteen-year-old girl with bronze skin and straight black hair. Her face was sleek and pointed, ready to spread into a cheeky grin as she danced on the street with her troupe to illusory music, unaware that she had a purpose that she was made to fulfill.

"Anaya," Karwyn said her name, and allowed his voice to join the wind that whirled through the valley.

In time the visions subsided. Karwyn looked back over the five pillars of the tomb of Myochus and his sons. It was truly a place for kings. The front was easily four times taller than the average man, built at the height of the valley after a long narrow trail that inclined gradually along the slopes. They had known to build their resting place on that site, but so far Karwyn never discovered why or how, and he had realized long ago some mysteries might never be answered.

I will need more than scrying to keep up on things, he thought as he picked up the chunk of smoky quartz that had charged in the hidden moon all night. It was a raw shard that fit perfectly in the palm of his hand, black at the base and gray at the tip. The old mage stood up, and made a point of looking around the columns at the tomb entrance like it was a game of hide and seek, as he called out, "My friend, are you there?" and held the quartz in front of him to cast a dull light across the brush at the edge of the path, asking again, "Are you there? Don't be afraid. I know it's been a long time, but I'm here now."

There was an excited yowl from over his shoulder and Karwyn turned around but saw nothing; then his quartz light scanned over a creature that leapt into view, appearing directly out of the fabric of the Veil. Her big triangular ears swiveled around expressively, and she had soft luxurious fur with rings of graphite and magenta around her tail, front paws like a climber and hind feet like a cat. She moved easily between the dual worlds, disappearing and reappearing from the range of his quartz light, a trick of the shadows, releasing an aura of pink and purple shapes with every movement.

She was different than he remembered, and Karwyn asked, "Are you the one?" until she yowled unhappily and leapt into the air as if she was standing on something invisible, and stared at him with shimmering turquoise eyes.

"Well you've grown up since I've been gone, I hardly recognize you," Karwyn replied, quickly recalling her name, "Leua, beautiful and wise Leua. Will you help me again, like you did before?"

She relaxed as he extended his hand to greet her. She was a Querere, a creature unlike any other. They were said to be a kind of sphinx from Shenai that could become invisible and pass through walls, possessing a secondsight that allowed them to perceive many things, being quite useful as knowledge seekers that descended from the heavenly island on errands for the gods.

Leua circled around his feet, basking in the glow of the quartz, brushing with her tail, purring pleasantly until Karwyn couldn't help but to reach down and scratched between her ears as he said, "You are quite a helpful creature, do you know that? Would you like to go out and learn some things for me?"

ACKNOWLEDGMENTS

First and foremost, I would like to express my sincere gratitude to Ayla, my wife, for her eternal patience as I have developed this fantasy series over the last several years. There are a hundred things I could point to in the book that came from her, so I've come to consider Ayla as my development editor. It is a very fulfilling partnership, and I have to admit this novel would never have come into existence if she had not patiently sat through a dozen retellings of every chapter before it was honed into the book it is now. She asked me difficult questions about the characters, and I was forced to answer, "How do they feel?" "What are they thinking?" which every author ought to answer to justify why their people do the things they do.

She made the story better, but Ayla was not alone. I'm very grateful to my copy editor and beta-reading group, who were able to point me in the right direction in several chapters, and advise me on what segments to keep and what to postpone for the next novel. I am thankful for the countless conversations I've had with my sister Allie, and my good friend Joe, about the development of this book. Their input, along with many others, has been invaluable. With their help the story advanced to the next level, and it received the "Kill your darlings" treatment that I had learned in college fiction writing workshops. The novel was chopped from 180,000 words to 115,000 words, which actually became much more manageable to work with, and more like what I like to consume as a reader of fantasy.

Of course, this novel would not exist if it weren't for the people that came before me who are no longer here. This book is dedicated to my grandmother Joyce, who encouraged my interest in reading and writing, and my grandfather Guy, who was always an arch of support when I needed it. My grandmother was obsessed with the difference between 'to' and 'too,' or, 'then' and 'than,' and my grandfather would read my scifi stories and say, 'I didn't like the captain, he wouldn't act like that,' and tell me how a man in command of a starship should really act. They gave me a unique place to grow as a writer, a place I think any artist needs to nurture their talent, a place where they can be vulnerable without judgment.

I must also acknowledge my father-in-law, Roger. Over a decade of friendship, he had seen several drafts of my writing, and as a voracious reader of everything, including fantasy; he gave well-considered advice on the plot. Roger loved anything gritty and hard, and he wanted the villain to be front and center, to start the reader on a wild ride. I think he liked my idealism in the story of the monks, but not my meandering prose, since he always said to me, "You have to get to the drama! The conflict! The action! As soon as possible, let's go!"

These three have crossed to the other side of the Veil, but not before they taught me about our family, their lives, and what great burdens they had always carried. I'm proud to be tied to these people, and to so many others, who have given me their time, and grace, to make me into the man I am.

M.A.B. WYMAN

Malkam is an aspiring author living in Three Oaks, MI, brewing beer by day and writing novels by night. Born and raised in Kalamazoo, Malkam is proud to be a child of deaf adults (CODA), and a graduate of Western Michigan University with a Bachelor in Fine Arts. He is a dedicated student of martial arts and has studied Taiji and Kung Fu for more than twenty years. Malkam is an avid reader of literature and poetry, and has been participating in storytelling and performance art with Indigan Storyteller Workshops since 2013.

Mountainroot is the first book in the *Saga of the Laymonk*, a series of adventures within the Known Lands of Kuei.

www.ingramcontent.com/pod-product-compliance
Lightning Source LLC
Chambersburg PA
CBHW030133310726
48970CB00005B/1425